A Palace in the Popples Part 1

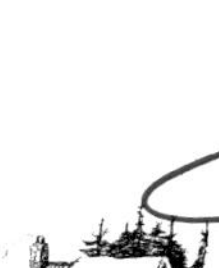

Order Information:
Banksiana Publishing Co.
611 22 3/4 Street
Chetek, WI 54728
Phone 715-924-4668
mertcowley.com

A Palace in the Popples Part 1

**Written and Compiled
by Mert Cowley**

Banksiana Publishing Co. / Chetek, WI

Copyright © 2005 by Mert Cowley/Banksiana Publishing Co.

All rights reserved. Except for use in a review, the reproduction
or utilization of any of this work in any form or by
electronic, mechanical, or other means, now known or hereafter
invented, including xerography, photo copying, and recording,
and in any information storage and retrieval system
is forbidden without the expressed written permission
of the publisher.

All correspondence and inquiries
should be directed to:
Mert Cowley
Banksiana Publishing Company
611 22-3/4 Street
Chetek, WI 54728

Manufactured in the United States of America

Library of Congress Control Number   2004090026

ISBN 0-9627867-8-0

FIRST EDITION
10   9   8   7   6   5   4   3   2   1

Printed 2005

Dedication

I wish to dedicate *A Palace in the Popples* to the fallen hunters and the survivors of the hunting tragedy which occurred in Sawyer County Wisconsin, November 21, 2004.

What took place that day in the deer woods of northern Wisconsin inflicted a lifetime of heartache and pain not only to those who knew and loved the fallen hunters and survivors, but to countless thousands of us who share the pain and the grief with them.

As word of the tragedy spread throughout the North country that day, those of us who had been out hunting came to the realization that we knew the fallen hunters and the survivors even though few of us had met them and we suffered with them. They were fellow deer hunters.

We weren't with them that day, but November 21, 2004 taught all of us something that should never be forgotten: how unpredictable our lives are, what a delicate balance our lives are in, and how, in a moments time they can change.

We lost a fine group of deer hunters that day. The hunt will never be the same.

THE FALLEN HUNTERS

We've put ourselves in your place
    a hundred times or more,
And thought, "That could have taken place
    outside our cabin door."
"Would things have ended differently
    if we'd been there with you?"
Then had to face reality
    when there's nothing we can do.

But in our hearts and on our minds
    the "fallen ones" will stay,
In camp with us each season,
    as we start each hunting day.
These words we've hung, above the door
    so others know we care
To say before we leave our camp
    "THE FALLEN HUNTERS" prayer.

* * * * * * * * * * * * *

"Be with 'THE FALLEN HUNTERS,' LORD
as you have always been,
We pray LORD such a tragedy,
does not occur again."

Mert

Author's Note

"The best laid plans of mice and men will oft-times go astray." Can I ever relate to this one.

Over the years I have developed a theory that every person will, no matter how they may try to avoid it, create at least one "MONSTER" during the course of their lifetime. Not only am I living proof of this, I am exceptionally good at it.

This book is a prime example. It was not my intention when I started this latest "monster" of mine to end up with two books but somehow I did. As the saying goes, "stuff happens."

Over the course of two years and 2700 hours later, what began as an effort on my part to preserve a part of our hunting, fishing, and trapping heritage spiraled into something beyond control. It went from something quite routine to something quite out of the ordinary.

I had gone to great lengths to acquire the finest photographs I could find and develop a story line that could encompass 150 years of outdoor activities and tie them all together. As painstaking as it was, I believe that I accomplished that. However, my problems lurked on the horizon.

When I took all that I had written and assembled to have it laid out in book form, it didn't take long for the printer to discover that I was faced with a slight problem. I had too much material.

On four separate occasions I weeded, I thinned, and I tossed some 250 pages of finished material. Finally I reached the point where there was nothing else I could remove. It was down to the bare bones.

I was left with a choice to make: print what I had as one book or print what I had in two parts.

The sheer size and weight of the end product, the cost of printing the "monster," and the price I would need to ask for a book in order to come out made it an easy choice for me to make.

So instead of having one book that would require two men and a small boy to tote around, there will now be two books which will be far more manageable to handle.

Mert

Foreward

Old photographs of deer hunting stir the imagination, for they provide a look back in time for those of us who will never experience such a hunt. The photographs depict a time when life went by at a slower pace, when relatively few chose to deer hunt, and when competition was at a minimum. There were vast tracts of untouched wilderness to hunt where bucks grew to maturity, and there were more than enough of them to satisfy the pioneer spirit that dwells in all of us.

—*Mert Cowley, <u>Dawn of the Deer Camp</u> (2001)*

In his **<u>Sand County Almanac</u>** (1949), Aldo Leopold tells us the best way to preserve our great hunting heritage entails reenacting hunts of yesteryear, recreating the pioneer spirit within us – allowing young boys to go "Daniel-Booneing in the willow thicket below the tracks." Mert Cowley has been "Daniel-Booneing" in the deer woods for most of his life. That is what the Jackpine Poet from the Pearly Swamp Camp does best! And now after a prodigious amount of deep-digging research, photo collecting and creative writing he brings us his magnum opus: **<u>A Palace in the Popples</u>**.

Mert Cowley loves old photographs, illustrations, oil paintings and miscellaneous memorabilia on deer hunting, trapping, fishing and logging and so do I. In fact both the Jackpine Poet and Hemlockbark frequently compete with one another in E-Bay auctions for purchasing priceless deer- hunting memorabilia of the past to enhance our manuscripts and preserve our great deer- hunting heritage. The Jackpine Poet with his latest tome of historic fiction emerges as a tireless soldier in the perpetuation of our great deer hunting culture.

Historic fiction revolving around the theme of deer and deer hunting remains a unique genre of American literature with roots deep in our past. We think of course of James Fenimore Cooper's historical novels **<u>The Pioneers</u>** (1823) and **<u>The Deerslayer</u>** (1841) which introduce Americans to the legendary deer stalker Natty Bumppo and the chronic deer problem – the paradox of managing a public resource on private property.

When you eat the venison you become the deer Natty Bumppo tells us in **<u>The Deerslayer</u>**. Who will ever forget his homeopathic view of eating deer meat?

"I crave no cloth better than the skin of a deer, nor any meat richer than his flesh. Well may you call it strong! Strong it is, and strong it makes him who eats it!

"They call me Deerslayer. I'll own; and perhaps I deserve the name, in the way of understanding the creature's habits, as well as for the certainty in the aim; but they can't accuse me of killing an animal when there is no occasion for the meat or the skin. I may be a slayer, it's true, but I'm no slaughterer . . . I never pulled a trigger on buck or doe, unless when food or clothes was wanting."

Frank Forester's snazzy Shakespearian novel **<u>The Deer Stalkers</u>** (1843) also comes to mind when we think of deer hunting and historical fiction. The action of the novel resides in and around the 19th century backwoods Dutchman's Tavern in the Warwick woodlands of Orange County, New York, where old Frank Forester, that dean of modern sporting ethics, delivers some of the most horrendous poetic orations on deer hunting ever entertained in the history of Western civilization:

*But hark to that sound
stealing faint through the wood!
Heart hammers, breath thickens,
swift rushes the blood!
It swells from the thicket
more loud and more near
'Tis the hound giving tongue!
he is driving the deer.
My rifle is leveled – swift tramplings are heard –
A rustle of leaves – then with flight like a bird,
His antlers thrown back,
and his body in motion
with quick rise and fall
like a surge of the ocean –
His eyeballs wide rolling in frenzied affright –
Out bursts the magnificent creature to sight.
A low cry I utter; he stops – bends his head,
His nostrils distended,
limbs quaking with dread;
My rifle cracks sharp –
he springs wildly on high,
Then pitches down headlong,
to quiver and die.*

Frank Forester's deer hunts usually ended sitting in the glow of the campfire, eating venison steak and indulging in a "brimming bumper or two of port." One can still hear the toasts of his club of good fellows:

*A Club of good fellows we meet once a year,
When the leaves of the forest are withered and sear;
By the motto that shines
on each glass it is shown
We drink in our cups the deserving alone.
A bumper, a bumper, ourselves right true men,
We'll fill it and drink it again and again!*

Oh! Yes – the romance and adventure of historic, deer-hunting fiction. With a quantum leap in chronology we next encounter Frank Waters' ***The Man Who Killed the Deer*** (1942), the classic story of Martiniano, the man caught in the conflict between Native American rituals of the deer hunt and the alien 20th century white man's deer hunting legislation. This poetically and politically charged novel highlights the Taos Pueblo struggle for Blue Lake. In fact the novel became instrumental in the legal resolution of that battle in the Pueblo's favor when President Nixon signed the official Act of Congress restoring the sacred Blue Lake to the Taos Pueblo on December 15, 1970.

This novel of Native American mysticism and deer hunting rites and rituals has remained in print for more than 64 years. During the Psychedelic Sixties this cult classic went through 14 editions and reached sales as a mass market paperback in excess of several million copies. In this novel the deer ultimately becomes a symbol for conscience – not only in an individual, but in a tribe, a community, a federal government and a cosmos. The spirit of the deer becomes the conscience for maintaining a proper spiritual relationship with the land. This timeless and extraordinary book written with great poetic elegance provides us with a deer hunting ethic we need to follow and honor:

"Nothing is simple and alone. We are not separate and alone. Man, the breathing mountains, the living stones, each blade of grass, the clouds, the rain, each star, the beasts, the birds, and the invisible spirits of the air, we are all one, indivisible – nothing that any of us does but affects us all. In the old days we all remember, we did not go out on the hunt lightly. We said to the deer we were going to kill, we know your life is as precious as ours; we know we are all one life and the same mother earth beneath the same plains of the sky. But we also know that one life must sometimes give way to another so the one great life of all may continue unbroken. So we ask your permission, we obtain your consent of this killing."

The next classic example of deer-hunting fiction we encounter in Zane Grey's romantic western ***The Deer Stalker*** published in 1949. This novel based on an earlier magazine serialization of it in ***The Country Gentleman*** in 1925, focuses on the grim paradox of the Kaibab deer problem: protecting deer in a National Forest by eliminating deer hunting and "eradicating" such natural predators as wolves and cougars, which eventually led to deer overabundance and death by starvation due to a limited food supply. In the novel the main protagonist Thad Eburne, a buckskin-clad Forest Ranger riding the range on horseback with a Winchester Model 1895 in hand, tries to protect a herd of 50,000 deer that are doomed to die of starvation on Buckskin Mountain in northern Arizona.

The book describes the government's miserable failure at trapping and transplanting deer, including an abortive attempt to drive ten thousand deer down the Grand Canyon and across the Colorado River, which was led by author Zane Grey himself. Grey used the deer irruption situation to illustrate the baneful effects of man's meddling with the basic laws of nature in the absence of sound, scientific underpinning. Paramount Pictures, interestingly enough, tried to produce a film based on the story of the greatest deer drive ever attempted in American history, but failed because of the studio's difficulty in obtaining film footage of the event. This historic and stupendous deer drive – known as the "Great Kaibab Deer Drive" – and Grey's genuine portrait of the deer stalker have become part of American culture.

While other contemporary authors use the deer-hunting context to create mystery, murder and adventure stories, one thinks for example of Mark T. Sullivan's The Purification Ceremony (1997), a trophy-deer, horror story in the snowbound isolation of British Columbia, Mert Cowley presents the reader with a very unique variation of historic fiction by mixing fiction with non-fiction, interspersing magazine articles from the early American sporting literature into the brew, while at the same time creating poetry and humor and compiling a marvelous photographic collage of the whole affair.

In ***A Palace in the Popples*** we find the story of the hunting, fishing and trapping activities of four generations of the fictitious McCracken family: Silas, Charlie, Henry and Hank. The book which covers the period between the 1820s and the early 1940s, takes the reader on hunting and trapping adventures into the Western mountains, moose hunting in the wilds of Canada and back to the rivers, lakes and forest regions of Northeastern Wisconsin in search of muskies, bear and quality white-tailed bucks.

With its hundreds of fascinating pictures the book stands as a masterful, photographic extravaganza of the history of the deer hunt and outdoor adventures.

"Deer hunting," Dick Kaner once with WJMC Radio of Rice Lake, WI reminds us, "when distilled to its essence, is memories . . . of impossible shots and incredulous misses . . . of dreams and of nightmares . . . of camp and of camp life . . . and of ghostly brown bucks. It's fogged scopes, misfires and frozen actions. Its snow and rain, bone chilling cold, teeth chattering and frozen fingers and feet. In the slashing, the swamps, and the jack pines, with rifle, bow and muzzle loader, Mert Cowley has been there. This teacher and poet have been on stand to watch the dawn break. He knows the feelings and expectations, the success and the disappointment. Deer hunting. Mert Cowley has been there. Thank goodness he was."

And to this fine characterization of my friend Mert Cowley – legendary deer stalker, teacher and poet – I say "Amen!"

Dr. Rob Wegner, Ph.D.
White-Tailed Deer Historian
Former Editor & Co-Owner of
Deer & Deer Hunting Magazine
Deer Valley
August, 2005

A Palace in the Popples

Preface

I take a great deal of pride in the fact that I'm known as being a man of my word. For this reason, I feel I should explain my change of heart for doing another book after I said I was done writing. (I'm also known for my ability to make a short story quite long as you will soon see.)

In the foreword of my last book, *Beyond the Shadows of the Pine* I explained why I was going to be put my writing on hold for a while. Due to some recent health problems, I felt that I needed to devote my time in other directions in hopes of accomplishing a few things that I had not yet done, namely downing a respectful buck and building a hot rod coupe like one I'd had my heart set on since I was a kid.

The Buck

I took care of my first priority less than a month after the book came out when I dropped a decent buck on the last evening of the Wisconsin bow hunt prior to rifle season.

That evening found me seated in a ground blind overlooking a large and very active scrape. I had been on stand since mid-afternoon and had remained motionless for nearly two hours without seeing a thing. The popple trees surrounding my blind were beginning to cast the last of their shadows and I had resigned myself to the fact that darkness would soon spell the end to my hunt.

A dry swamp lay to the north of my blind but was hidden from my view by a small rise some thirty-five yards straight ahead of my blind. Several times during the course of the afternoon my mind had wandered off to a rifle hunt four years earlier that had involved this same swamp.

(That particular season I had placed my ladder stand on the rise, facing to the South with my back towards the swamp. That was also the season I realized on opening day that my back was to a major deer trail. Several deer managed to pass by me during the course of the day without so much as a shot being fired.

I managed to hear one of the deer approach from behind long before I ever saw it. I had turned slowly to the right and sure enough, there came a large doe headed straight up the rise towards my stand. As I turned, she caught my movement, slammed on the brakes, and stared straight up in the tree at me. She raised her right leg, stomped once, then twice, whirled, and took off headed north. That's when I saw him. His body was huge, his rack wide and heavy, and it jutted well out beyond his ears. The ten or twelve points he carried were dark-stained with ivory-like tips that were noticeably short in proportion to the width of the rack. I figured his rack had a spread in the neighborhood of 24 inches.

When the doe wheeled and took off, she stretched flat-out and headed for parts unknown. The buck quickly realized that the best thing for him to do was to depart ASAP so he in turn wheeled and took off right behind her. About a hundred yards out, she made a brief appearance between a couple of popples, providing the only opening I would have for a shot. I rested the crosshairs right there, reasoning that the buck would soon appear and present me with a shot. He never did. He swung to the right where she'd gone left and they both disappeared over the hill. I never will forget the sight of that buck.)

Suddenly, a slight movement caught my eye as I stared towards the top of the rise. I focused in the direction of the movement, and there it was again. The movement gradually began to take the shape of set of antlers swinging from side to side. The rack was wide, short tined and heavy. I froze as the large-bodied buck came into full view and stopped less than 25 yards straight ahead of me.

At first, the buck appeared quite nonchalant; focusing his interest on the nearby scrape. Suddenly he lifted his head, turned so that he quartered me, and proceeded to stare directly in the direction of me and my blind. My only thought during this time was, "I'm not even going to get a shot." He continued to stare at me for the better part of a minute, and I fully expected him to bolt any second and take off for heavier cover.

Instead, evidently content that all was well, he lowered his head and concentrated on freshening up his scrape. That gave me the chance I needed to make my move. I raised my bow, placed the sight right behind his right front shoulder, and let fly.

He never flinched as he took off stretched flat out, headed east towards a nearby logging trail. Normally, I would wait half an hour before taking a blood trail but with only a few minutes of daylight left, I took off in the same direction that the buck had taken hoping to find some sign of a hit.

I found the spot where he had taken off and marked it with my jacket. I looked ahead and spotted some more freshly turned leaves. That gave me a line of travel so I marked that spot with my handkerchief. Then I began to look for blood.

By that time, it was beginning to get dark enough to require the need for the small flashlight I always carry in the woods with me. I crisscrossed the path he'd taken looking for blood as hard and fast as I could as darkness quickly approached. However, not a single drop of blood would glisten for me in the beam of the flashlight.

By that time I'd reached the old logging trail, and I paused for a moment in total frustration, haunted by the same old questions that had confronted me several times before. Was history repeating itself? Had I missed another one? Had I just managed to muff another great chance again? Why couldn't I luck out just one time?

I was about to mark the spot where I was standing so I

could resume my search in the morning when something, inches away from my boot, glistened in the light of my flashlight. I dropped down to my knee, touched the spot with my finger, and rubbed the substance between my fingers. It was blood! I had hit the buck!

Excited by the good news, I started up the logging trail, and there was blood again, lots of it this time. Up ahead where the buck had landed on his next bound was the same thing, blood all over the place. I'd not only hit him; I'd hit him good!

Rather than continue on the trail and take a chance of jumping the buck out of his bed, I marked the spot where I quit trailing and headed back to my van parked down on the road. When I reached my van, a call on my cell phone brought my hunting partner Bill Rhiger, his trailer, and a million-candle power flashlight to assist us in tracking.

Fortunately, we were not in for a long night of tracking. The buck had traveled less than a hundred yards from where I'd quit tracking and had collapsed in a pile. When we walked up to him, I leaned over and touched his eye with the tip of an arrow just to be safe. There was no reaction whatsoever. Death had come within a few seconds after I'd hit him.

He was a gray-muzzled eight-pointer with a outside spread of 18 1/2." and he would tip the scales at 200 pounds. Judging from the buck's well-worn teeth, his gray muzzle, and the structure of his nose, the man at the registration station determined that the buck was an old timer that had reached his prime a few years back and was now on his way downhill.

The more I think about it, the more I'm convinced that this buck is the same buck I saw four years earlier. Both bucks carried a low wide rack with the same type of short points, and I'd nailed him less than fifty yards from where I'd seen the other buck. If it wasn't him, this buck had to be from the same bloodline but I guess I'll never know for certain.

To some deer hunters a buck like this old boy would be considered little more than a mediocre buck. To me however, that old buck and the hunt that he provided for me are something I'll always treasure and remember for the rest of my life.

The Coupe

I've always been a man with many interests. Old arrowheads, old guns, old photos, old stories, and old cars have all played an important role in my life since I can remember.

My grandmother had a matchbox full of Indian arrowheads she always kept in the drawer of her old treadle sewing machine. They stirred such an interest with me that I developed an almost insatiable desire to search out ancient village and campsites sites. I would discover over one hundred such sites before my interest became satisfied and eventually quit looking.

My interest in old hunting photos led to a number of things. Collecting old photos led to me into wanting to know more about what took place in the hunting and trapping camps of long ago so I conducted research. That in turn led to interviews with old hunters and trappers which provided enough information for me to write six books in an attempt to preserve not only the photos but the history associated with them.

My grandfather's old double barrel shotgun spurred an intense interest in old guns. I collected old rifles for nearly fifty years until I eventually sold the collection in order to finance another of my many interests; old cars.

Old cars have been a part of my life since I can remember. My first car was a fully customized 1949 Mercury convertible that I bought in Minneapolis for $150.00 when I was fourteen years old. Three years later I sold it for $375.00 and figured that I'd really ripped the guy off. Had I kept it, it'd take $50,000.00 to buy that car today.

I started collecting old cars before I was sixteen. I had a '32 Ford Tudor that I paid $10.00 for, a '26 Model T Ford coupe I spent $3.00 on, and a '29 Oldsmobile coupe that I had $25.00 invested in.

Back in 1957, I bought a wrecked '56 Ford Fairlane Club Sedan for $350.00. My dad was a body man from the

The buck of 2003

old school and was more than willing to take on the project I had in mind; switching bodies and putting a car back together again.

We headed over to Minneapolis, bought a junked '55 two door, and had it hauled back to Wisconsin. Dad and I dove into the project headfirst and worked many nights in order to get the car back on the road again. I was soon driving a car less than a year old with less than $1200.00 invested.

That hands-on project was a real learning experience for me. During the project, my dad taught me a great deal about cars and because of what he taught me, my interest in this particular hobby has never subsided. I have built seven cars from the ground up since that time.

Since the day I turned fifty, I have described myself as an eighteen year old kid trapped in an old man's body. This feeling really became apparent after the recent problems I had with my health. I realized that I had things to do that I'd better get done as chances were I wasn't going to be around forever.

I'd wanted to own a hot rod since the day I bought my first "LITTLE PAGES" and saw my first real hot rod. Fifty years later I was still determined to own one.

I had owned two stock '33 Ford five-window coupes over the years. Foolishly I let them slip out of my hands. What I wanted for a hot rod was another a '33 or a '34 Ford coupe, chopped and channeled with some sort of a souped-up engine. (There's always been a certain mystic about owning a car with suicide doors, the kind of car with doors that open to the front rather than to the rear.)

I started saving my money and looking for just the right car. Two month's later I was sitting at the kitchen table looking over my saving's account, realizing that the car I wanted was totally out of my price range. I never would be able to afford a coupe with suicide doors. I found myself admitting defeat.

Mulling over my predicament, feeling somewhat sorry for myself as I looked over photos of various coupes I had lifted off of the Internet, it suddenly hit me. "YOU DUMB CLUCK!" "YOU'VE GOT WHAT YOU NEED SITTING DOWN IN THE GARAGE!", "YOU CAN BUILD THE COUPE YOU WANT!" Off I headed to the garage with tape measure in hand.

A most unlikely looking candidate greeted me down in the garage, a 1929 NASH 4-Door Sedan. Now a NASH in any form is not a thing of beauty in anyone's eye, unless of course they have their head turned away from it, but the sedan was a means to an end for me. It was a way for me to reach my goal in a way that I could afford.

To even try and begin creating a coupe from such a beast would be an insurmountable task for many people but to me, being as desperate as I was, I reasoned that if the task was impossible, it would just take me a little longer.

The old sedan donated it's frame, hood, cowl, front doors, and the curved portion behind the rear seat for my upcoming project. They would became the basis for the 3-window coupe I had in mind. Reincarnation was about to begin.

To update the running gear, I went for the front end from a Mustang II. The rear end from a S10 Chevrolet pickup hung off of a pair of Chevrolet Astro fiberglass leaf springs. For an engine I chose a small Hemi from a 1953 DeSoto to turn the wheels. All of this was put together by my long time friend Glenn Thompson.

The creation of the coupe's body was accomplished by the joint efforts of my newly recruited friend Mark Nelson and I. As I formed most of the pieces and panels used in the construction, Mark welded them together to create the coupe.

Mark and I learned a lot by trial and error and found that the toughest part of the entire construction was to install the suicide doors I'd always wanted. It took us a combined effort of 40 hours to complete the task.

After only fifty years, with a little ingenuity and a great deal of help on the part of my friends, I finally reached my goal. I have a hot rod like I always wanted.

The best part for me is, it got done in time to teach my grandson Trey the word "HEMI" to add to his street rodding vocabulary.

So that's how I managed to find time to write again. In the words of Paul Harvey, "Now you know the rest of the story."

Table of Contents

Dedication v

Author's Note vi

Foreward vii

Who Can I Blame But Myself vii

A Palace in the Popples ix
    Preface ix
    The Buck ix
    The Coupe x

Table of Contents xii

The Annual Corn Feed 1

The McCracken Family Album 5

The Life and Times of Silas McCracken 1808-1893 18

The Rendezvous 30

A Day in the life of the Mountain Trapper 32

Trapping and Home-Made Traps *from Outing Magazine by Ed.W. Sandys* 33

The Fur Trade *by J.H. Crooker* 41

Rivière Des Sauteux *(The Chippewa River)* 43

Charles R. McCracken 1831-1919 50

The Ice Fishing Trips 70

Charlie, the Trapper 72

Hunting with Hounds 77
    Deer-Hunting On The Au Sable *by W. Mackay Laffan, Scribner's Monthly* 77

We Lit Out After Them 86
    Departure from Home 86
    Getting the Hounds to the Hunt 89
    Success is Ours 90
    Dinner Time 95
    Arriving Back Home 102
    Our Hunts by Canoe 104

When Brown was Down 108
    The Ways we got 'em Back 108
    Wheels Enter the Picture 117

Our Success 122
    From Harper's Weekly, Saturday February 6, 1886 123

Other Hunts 128

Grandma glanced at the next group of loose photographs and began commenting about them to the group. "Your Dad and his cronies did an awful lot of trout fishing back then, all that they could. There were hundreds of smaller trout in every little trickle of water they came across. They had to get back in a mile or so off the main road if they wanted to catch the big ones."

"Just look at the number of trout they caught Hank!" Glenn exclaimed. " I haven't caught as many trout in an entire season, maybe even a lifetime, than they caught in a day's time."

"Your Dad and his trout-fishing buddies never wasted a single fish they ever caught either," Grandmother added. "They'd take a cast iron frying pan and plenty of fresh churned butter with them to fry the trout in. Your Dad was the cook for the bunch and he'd fry those trout to a golden brown, spread a slice of bread with a layer of butter, and make a sandwich out of it. They'd eat trout three meals a day."

"They always took more than enough bread with them just in case the trout weren't biting. That way they'd at least have some bread to eat. I can remember only one time that happened to them."

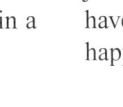

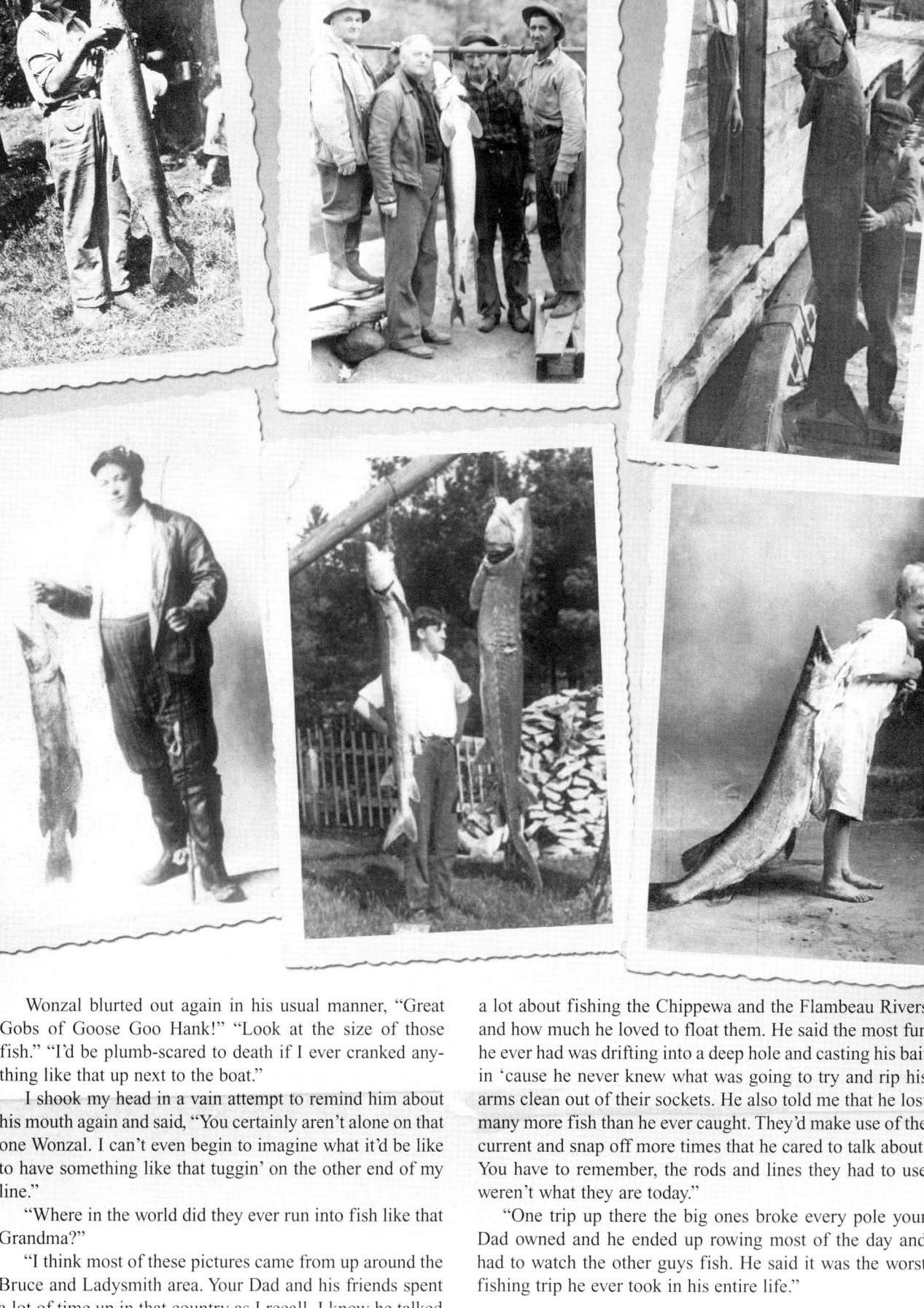

Wonzal blurted out again in his usual manner, "Great Gobs of Goose Goo Hank!" "Look at the size of those fish." "I'd be plumb-scared to death if I ever cranked anything like that up next to the boat."

I shook my head in a vain attempt to remind him about his mouth again and said, "You certainly aren't alone on that one Wonzal. I can't even begin to imagine what it'd be like to have something like that tuggin' on the other end of my line."

"Where in the world did they ever run into fish like that Grandma?"

"I think most of these pictures came from up around the Bruce and Ladysmith area. Your Dad and his friends spent a lot of time up in that country as I recall. I know he talked a lot about fishing the Chippewa and the Flambeau Rivers and how much he loved to float them. He said the most fun he ever had was drifting into a deep hole and casting his bait in 'cause he never knew what was going to try and rip his arms clean out of their sockets. He also told me that he lost many more fish than he ever caught. They'd make use of the current and snap off more times that he cared to talk about. You have to remember, the rods and lines they had to use weren't what they are today."

"One trip up there the big ones broke every pole your Dad owned and he ended up rowing most of the day and had to watch the other guys fish. He said it was the worst fishing trip he ever took in his entire life."

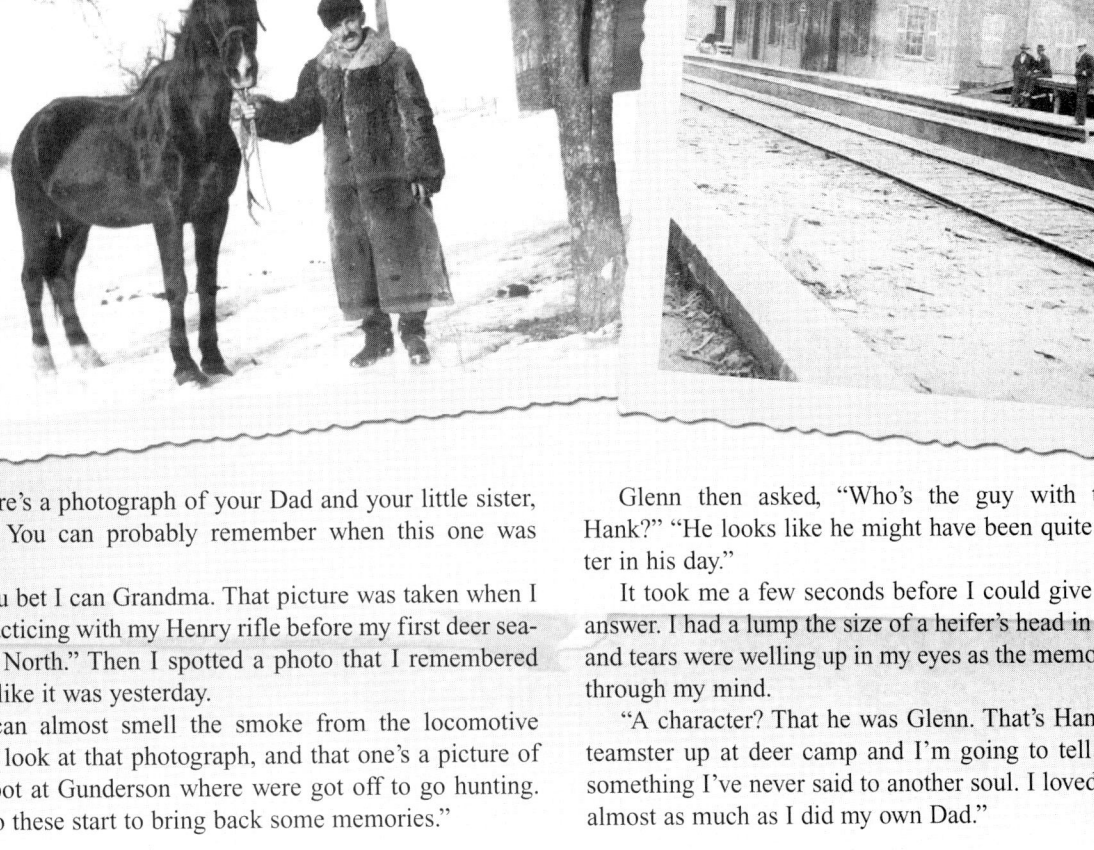

"Here's a photograph of your Dad and your little sister, Hank. You can probably remember when this one was taken."

"You bet I can Grandma. That picture was taken when I was practicing with my Henry rifle before my first deer season up North." Then I spotted a photo that I remembered seeing like it was yesterday.

"I can almost smell the smoke from the locomotive when I look at that photograph, and that one's a picture of the depot at Gunderson where were got off to go hunting. Man do these start to bring back some memories."

Glenn then asked, "Who's the guy with the horse Hank?" "He looks like he might have been quite a character in his day."

It took me a few seconds before I could give Glenn an answer. I had a lump the size of a heifer's head in my throat and tears were welling up in my eyes as the memories raced through my mind.

"A character? That he was Glenn. That's Hans, our old teamster up at deer camp and I'm going to tell you guys something I've never said to another soul. I loved old Hans almost as much as I did my own Dad."

"Between the two of them, they taught me more about deer hunting my first year up there than I've learned in all the years since. As a matter of fact, Hans was the first one to see the first buck I ever got. He was nearly as excited about me getting it as I was."

" I never will forget the day word came down to us that old Hans was gone. It was one of the saddest days I can remember. The train crew found him out near one of his old sheds still hanging onto a great-horned owl he'd shot 'cause it was killing off the mice around there. Hans always thought of those mice as his friends 'cause he didn't see many people up there where he lived."

"Wow, he really was a character wasn't he Hank"

"That he was Glenn." "That he was."

"This is a picture of our old deer camp and the first crew I ever hunted with when I was a kid. Talk about a bunch of characters, that huntin' crew was full of them. One of the guys hunted with the next thing to a cannon and then bragged that any deer he hit went down and of course he was right, it did. There usually wasn't enough of it still held together so it could run anywhere."

"The member of the gang that I think about the most was an old guy named Selmer. He didn't have a single, solitary tooth in his mouth and when he let loose with a good belly laugh, you couldn't help but laugh harder than he did. Every year when we were packin' up to head home he'd go around to all the guys to see if any of them was willing to trade deer with him. It didn't matter to him if he had the biggest buck in camp, he was more than willing to trade it for a yearling just in order to have some venison he could gum and eat."

"That picture shows us breaking up the camp at the end of season. It was a camp we had a few miles East of Draper, Wisconsin . It was taken just before we headed for home."

"To me, the closing of camp was the worst day of the entire year. I just dreaded the day we had to pack up 'cause I knew it'd be another whole year before we got back up to camp again."

"Those pictures make it look like it was an awful lot of fun, Hank."

"It was an UNBELIEVABLE amount of fun Glenn." "It truly was."

"I can remember several deer hunting gangs that not only took the train up to deer camp but then they'd rent a boxcar from the railroad for their camp. They'd get dropped off at an old siding that had been used to pick up logs years back that was located way out in the middle of the woods. They'd hunt right out of the boxcar then. Our bunch never did try that. We always felt it would restrict us too much as to where we could hunt. If there weren't any deer in the area we just couldn't up and take off and hunt somewhere else if we wanted to."

"About the only thing I can say that I enjoyed on the day we broke camp was getting the deer out of the woods and hauled to the railroad siding to load them on the flatbeds. It gave us a chance to see how some of the other gangs that we never would have run into otherwise had done."

11

"There'd be some deer brought in that were so tiny that I swear if you looked at them hard enough you could still find spots on them. Had it been up to me, I'd have left them running around in the woods. Then you'd see others that were so huge and with such monstrous racks that it'd make me wonder how they even managed to make it through the woods."

"Our gang always stood out from the rest of the gangs because we never took anything bucks unless they were racked bucks. That doesn't mean that it was beyond us to shoot a doe or maybe even a yearling. We'd roll as many of them over that we needed for camp meat. Sometimes we'd eat maybe four or five a year but we never wasted enough to make a brush wolf lick his lips over."

"Look at here will you!" I said. "My dad even put a 1917 deer tag in here. He must have picked it up off the loading dock after one of those city slickers from Milwaukee threw it away after they'd gotten skunked."

"Those tags ticked my dad off so bad that it wasn't even funny. Somebody down in Madison came up with the bright idea of making those of us that took the train up to go hunting tag our deer so they could get a count of the deer that were taken. If you lost it or misplaced it you were just plain out of luck. The main problem wasn't even that. If a deer didn't get a ride home on a train, they never got counted. How accurate a deer count do you suppose they got from that?"

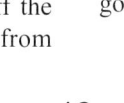

"These four photos were all taken up at Draper, Wisconsin. Draper was smack dab in the middle of some of the greatest deer hunting that there ever was. We started hunting up there a few years after the logging ended. Thousands of acres of white pine had been logged off around Draper before the turn of the century and with all the slash for cover and new growth that sprouted up, there were deer around by the thousands. The woods was practically crawling with them. Back in it's heyday, the area around Draper had some of the finest deer hunting Wisconsin ever knew."

I didn't realize until my Grandmother cleared her throat a few times that I had monopolized the conversation since she first opened the cover of the album . It was her way of demanding her time on the floor.

"Now you may be quite familiar with what took place during the past twenty-five years Hank, but now it's my turn to get in a few licks." The guys all laughed, I blushed, and Grandmother just grinned. It was my turn to sit back and listen for awhile.

"Your Great-Grandmother Elna and your Great-Grandfather Silas McCracken were quite old by the time I met them. They had to move in with your grandparents when they were unable to manage things on their own any longer. It was either that or the poor folks home for them and your grandparents weren't about to let that happen. You can't imagine how tragic it was to see fine folks like them that had worked their entire lives away and then ended up having absolutely nothing to show for all their work except a crippled body and a broken spirit. That pretty much describes your great-grandparents."

"I know from talking to your Great-Granddad that he would have loved to have had more time to spend hunting and fishing but spare time wasn't a luxury he ever knew. All that man ever knew was work which he did daybreak to dusk, day in and day out, just in order to provide for his family. Most all of the hunting and fishing he ever did was done out of necessity in order to put food on the table for his family."

"However, it could never be said that your great-granddad never got to spent time in the outdoors during his lifetime. He trapped out West for nearly ten years and after he got married, he trapped during the Fall and Winter to supplement his income. Some of those years they would have never made it if it hadn't of been for the fur money. I must say, your great-granddad was a darned good trapper too."

"You'll see that your Great-Grandfather Silas contributed to this album in his own special way. You probably already know that folks weren't much able to take photographs back in his day like they do today so he left behind stories of hunting, fishing, and trapping in his own manner.

Silas read every *HARPER'S WEEKLY, NEW ENGLAND MAGAZINE,* and *OUTING MAGAZINE* that he could get his hands on. As a matter of fact, he read about anything that had to do with the outdoors. Then he'd sit and cut out every picture and article that was of interest to him and glue them into the album."

"Once he had that done, Silas would sit back in his rocking chair, close his eyes, and let his mind drift off. It would take him on all kinds of hunting and fishing trips he knew he'd never have the chance to take part in."

"He told me once that it was even better when he drifted off to sleep. Then he could dream for hours on end about the things he had in this album."

"Your Great-Grandfather got a great deal of pleasure out of dreaming Hank, especially as he grew older and couldn't get around well anymore."

When she was through I asked, "Isn't it a little unusual for a person to dream like that Grandma?"

"Heaven's No!" she replied. "Folks have to dream,"

"There'd be no goals if there were no dreams."

13

"This photo was taken at the Draper, Wisconsin back in 1914 by the Dennison Studio located in Barron, Wisconsin.

DRAPER
WESTERN UNION
TELEGRAPH
& CABLE OFFICE
AMERICAN
EXPRESS CO.
AGENCY
Money Orders
Foreign Drafts

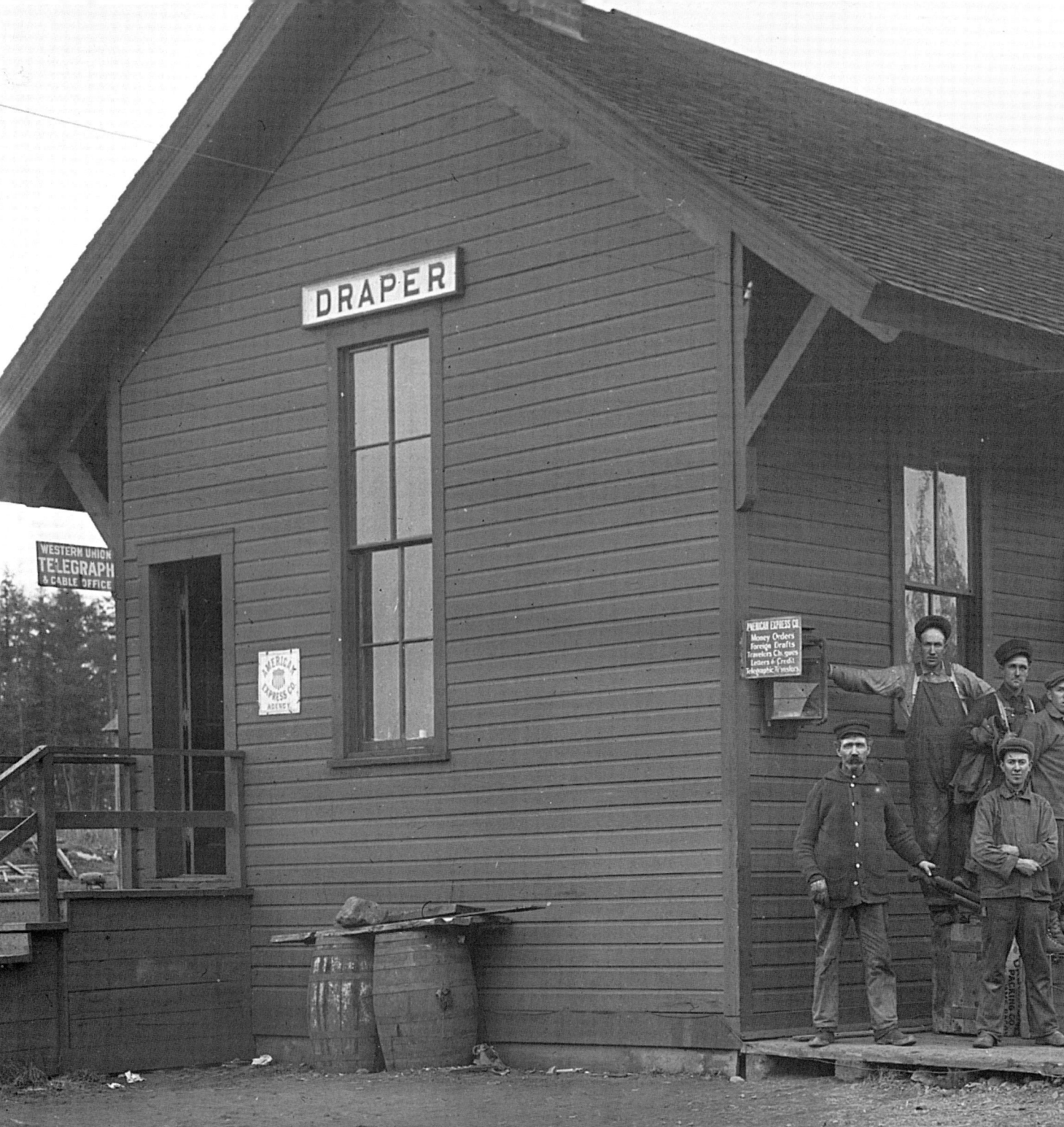

"The depot at Draper was a primary drop-off and pick-up location for hunters who traveled to deer camp by means of the railroad until the roads became good enough and the automobiles dependable enough for them to travel by car."

The Life and Times of Silas McCracken 1808 - 1893

"You were only a year and a half old the only time you ever saw your Great-Grandpa Silas so I doubt that you remember anything about him Hank. I do remember that he scared the livin' daylights out of you that day what with his wrinkled old face, his white beard, and his gruff sounding voice. He felt really bad when it happened 'cause he didn't mean to scare you any. He was really a very nice man when you got to know him. It's a shame they lived such distance a way that you couldn't have seen him when you were a little older."

"No Grandma, I can't say that I remember a solitary thing about him," I said. " He must not have scared me so bad that it did any permanent damage to me."

Wonzal piped up and said, "Maybe you don't think it damaged you none Hank but you'll never be able to convince the rest of us that it didn't."

It took a couple of minutes to quit laughing before we could get back to the subject at hand.

"As I mentioned, Silas may have come up short as far as his hunting and fishing experiences after he was married but he more than made up for it before he was married with his trapping experiences. He did more trapping in a few short years than most men could do in two lifetimes."

"Silas left home and headed West when he was fifteen years old, bound and determined to make a better life for himself than he'd had when he was growin' up. He set his goal at becoming a mountain man, living off the land, and trapping and selling fur to make his way. He just might of reached his goal if he hadn't crossed paths with the young daughter of a settler named Elna. You might say she put the kibosh to his dream."

Beamer was just kidding when he tossed in his two-bits.

"Yeh, and I always wanted to own a dance hall with a dozen good-looking women working for me. Then I up and met my wife. She went and squelched the whole idea for me."

I'm positive Wally believed every word Beamer said. "WOW!" he exclaimed. "Now that's a lifetime goal if I ever heard one. I'd be more than willing to suggest to your wife that she reconsider her decision if you'd like me to."

Beamer snapped back. "Don't be so damned ignorant Wally." "If my wife thought for a minute that I was serious about running a dance hall with a bunch of half-dressed young ladies running around, the next thing you'd be attending after this corn feed would be a funeral. My funeral."

Another two minutes were spent before we could continue. Even Grandma needed a sip of water before she could get started again.

"There was a neighbor kid named Eldrid Olesen that Silas had befriended and he decided to join up with Silas on his new venture. Eldrid had trapped some around home and Silas had run across a couple of his sets while out checking his own line. It looked to Silas like the kid knew exactly what he was doing so he figured they could trap twice the territory once they got started. Besides that, Eldrid enjoyed skinning, stretching, and getting furs ready for sale so he would definitely pay his way by doing that The two lads met up one morning and took off on their new adventure. Silas told me that neither of them ever even bothered to turn around and look back."

"Beaver hides were the most valuable fur at the time so naturally that's what the two boys went after. Silas had trapped a few beaver back home so he was pretty well acquainted with their tunnels, runs, slides, dams, feed beds, and houses. He began out trapping Eldrid about five to one

18

as Eldrid just couldn't seem to get the hang of it so Silas suggested to Eldrid that he become the skinner and Silas would do the trapping. That sounded like a good arrangement to Eldrid so that's what they did from then on."

"Eldrid got caught up skinning and stretching beaver pelts one day and had gotten the carcasses disposed of, he decided to try his hand at setting a beaver trap or two again. He wandered on down to the creek and must have scouted for awhile until he came across an area where there were some fresh beaver cuttings. Eldrid then decided to make a set down by the creek where the beaver had been coming up on shore. When Silas got back to camp, Eldrid was nowhere in sight so he went looking for him."

"When Silas got to the area with the fresh cuttings, he noticed a huge popple tree that looked like it had just fallen. The beavers hadn't even started trimming off the branches on it yet so he went over to investigate a little more. He looked down in the creek where the top was laying and spotted a boot and a pant leg just below the surface of the water. It was Eldrid. The popple had nailed him right where he was setting his trap and had him pinned to the bottom of the creek in about two feet of water. Silas figured that Eldrid must have frightened the beaver off when he walked up to the area, just moments before it was able to fell the tree. The breeze blowing that day had been enough to cause the popple to fall. Eldrid probably never knew what hit him."

Glenn muttered, "Good Lord, what a way to go." and C.J. added, "Talk about being in the wrong place at the wrong time!" We all just stood there and nodded in agreement.

"After Silas got Eldrid put in the ground, he was pretty broke up over what had happened so he decided to call it quits and head back home. He packed up what traps and supplies he could take with him and started heading back East. However, after a good night's rest and a few hours to do some thinking, Silas had a change of heart. He figured if he called it quits he would have just wasted all the time he'd spent and he never would reach his goal so he up and turned around and started heading West again."

Grandma paused for a moment then and said, "That's something that's always bothered me since I was your age. How do you explain why things happen the way they do? You know what I mean, how things seem to happen for a reason?"

" If you ever just sit and think about it, if one little thing had happened differently how it would have changed the entire outcome of your life. Things seem to happen for a reason, and the older you get, the more you begin realize that."

"Here was Silas, headed East and then he up and decides to head West. If he hadn't, he'd of never met Elna. If he'd never met Elna, I never would have met your Granddad Erlin. I wouldn't be sitting here today and you certainly wouldn't be standing where you are today Hank. It's eerie how things work out isn't it."

We all had to agree with her.

"Silas kept moving Westward until he finally reached the foothills of the Rockies, some where out in Montana. There he ran into a couple of trappers who were all het up over trapping bear. Bear was one of the few critters that Silas had never laid steel out for so he was more than willing and eager to learn what ever he could when it came to pinning a bear down. Little did he know until he got started that pinning one down was exactly what he would be doing. He wasn't going to be laying out any steel for them."

"Silas told me that one of the bear trappers answered to the name of Lefty because his right hand had ended up between the jaws of a big old boar bear. It'd got a hold of him and had his way with Lefty's right hand until it had his hand crushed almost beyond recognition. About the only thing the poor devil could use it for was to wipe his runny nose on a cold morning."

"The other fellow hadn't fared so well either. He went by the name of Pinky because the little fingers on both hands were completely gone. Both of them had been whacked completely off when a trap he'd set went off accidentally. Now this accident didn't happen to both of his little fingers at the same time mind you, but on two separate occasions!"

Grandma then added, "If something like that had happened to me once, I don't think it'd ever happen to me a second time. That fellow must have been running around the woods without a full stringer of fish if you ask me."

Grandma got a good roar out of the entire bunch of us with that line.

"The two trappers went to work and showed Silas how to go about rigging up deadfalls and he took right to it. The amazing thing about deadfalls was the fact that they didn't cost any money, they could be constructed out of materials laying nearby, and they could be used to trap anything from chipmunks to grizzly bears. Besides that, it didn't take a genius to set one up either. That's probably the real reason why those two decided to use deadfalls to do their trapping."

My Grandmother was beginning to show a sense of humor that I'd never seen before.

"Silas kept a notepad with him and sketched all the different setups that they used to make deadfalls. In time he added a few wrinkles of his own that made the deadfalls even more effective, or so he said."

"After a year or so of doing what he figured was more than his share of the work and having to split the gains made off of the trap line three ways, Silas grew tired of Lefty and Pinky's company so one day when he set off to check his traps, he just up and kept walking. I suppose the other two figured he'd got lost, that he'd drowned crossing a creek, that he was laying dead somewhere, or a big old boar bear had snuck up from behind and had him for lunch, cause they never saw him again."

"This tintype of Silas and Eldrid was taken prior to their departure on their trapping venture out West. They made a good-working team for the short time they worked together before Eldrid's untimely death. Silas teamed up with Lefty and Pinky and learned a great deal about trapping with deadfalls from the two of them."

"Silas moved about trapping whatever furs he would run into and when the fur started to run out in an area, then he'd move on again. He told me once that the further and further he got into the mountains, the more he had to watch over his shoulder for hostiles or other trappers that might not take kindly to having him move in on their territory. He said he had only two close calls in all the time he spent in the mountains but the two were enough to last him a lifetime. Strangely, both of his close calls happened when he was wading near shore in the shallow waters of a river."

"The first one happened when he was not being as cautious as he should have been. He admitted that to me. His attention had been focused on looking for the best place to set the few traps he had with him. He told me that he recalled hearing a rustle in the nearby rushes but assumed it was either a marsh rat or a mink scurrying away. The next thing he knew he had an Indian leaping through the air and onto his back with his arm firmly around Silas's neck, intent on seeing to it that Silas would never set another trap again."

" The only thing Silas had in his hand for a weapon were the six traps that he was holding onto by the chains. Silas swung his right arm up as hard as he could and caught the Indian square on the head and across his eyes with the traps. The Indian screamed, went limp, and the death lock he had around Silas's neck began to loosen until he finally lost his grip and fell face down into the river. He remained in that same position as he drifted away and then disappeared from sight around a bend in the river."

"Silas knew where there was one Indian there would more than likely be others so he eased himself up onto the bank or the river, covered himself up with dead rushes and waited for nightfall. Then he slipped back into the river again, found a log that was hung up on a sandbar, and laid beside it drifting with the current until daybreak. By then he was far enough from where it happened that he felt safe to go ashore."

"Oh by the way, I forgot to mention. Your Great-Granddad said that during the middle of the night as he was drifting down the river he bumped into something soft. When he reached out to see what it was, it was the dead Indian."

Wonzal broke his spellbound silence again with, "Balls on a frog, Hank!" He then apologized to my Grandmother again.

"Who would of ever guessed that anything like that had ever happened in your family, Hank? I'm sure glad we don't have to worry about things like that happening to us when we go hunting and fishing now days."

I hated to even admit it, but Wonzal couldn't have said it any better.

"You said that he had two close calls Grandma. What else happened to him?" I asked.

"Silas had to leave most everything he owned behind when he left in such a hurry like that. He kept his Hawken with him and some powder and shot. Without any steel traps, he had to resort to using deadfalls and snares that he could rig up for mink and beaver in order to start trapping again. This he managed to do quite well and soon had a sizeable catch of fur together."

"Furs weren't worth anything until they were either sold or traded so Silas set off in search of a trader or trading post where he could get rid of his fur. The only way he dared travel with a bundle of furs was to travel at night. If he were to be spotted by Indians or other trappers with a bundle of furs like that , he and his furs would both be fair game. He reasoned that if he stayed near the river he would eventually come across a trading post so that's what he did."

"One morning, just it was starting to get light, Silas started looking for a good place to leave the river and set up camp so he could rest until nightfall. There was a well-worn deer trail that came down to the river that was either a major crossing or a place where the deer came down to drink. He decided that would be as good a place as any to get himself out of the water."

"Just as he started to work his way towards shore and was about to step down with his right foot, he happened to glance down at what appeared to be a flat rock. Suddenly he realized that it wasn't a rock at all, it was the pan of a huge bear trap instead. He managed to drop his bundle of fur and then pitched himself sideways into the water in order to avoid the trap."

"He said that water flew in all directions when the fur bundle hit the pan and set the trap off. Fortunately for him, only the very bottom of several furs in the bundle were gripped by the jaws of the trap. After a few fruitless attempts to free the fur from the trap, Silas realized it waste of time to try and free the fur as the toothed jaws on trap had already done their damage. Reluctantly, Silas drew his knife from it's sheath and did what he had to do."

"Even many years later, Silas would still chuckle to himself every time he'd think about what the man who set the trap must have thought when came to check on it and saw the strange catch he'd made."

He always said, "If only I would have dared stay around long enough to see the look on the guy's face," and then he'd laugh again.

"The only thing that really bothered Silas about the whole incident was that he would have liked to know what the guy was after when he set the trap. Was the trap set to catch deer, or was it meant to be a man-trap? Silas never knew for sure."

"Silas came across a trading post a few miles downstream where he sold and traded his furs. He got the supplies he needed and then set off towards the mountains again to go about his trapping.

Several days later he was miles back into the mountains looking for a place to make camp and trap for awhile. One

morning quite by accident, he came across a dead pine marten caught in a deadfall. As any good trapper would do, Silas decided to make a wide berth around the deadfall so as not to disturb it any until a jaybird, a camp robber I believe he called it, landed on the marten and started pecking away at it."

"He knew a jay wouldn't go to work on a fresh caught animal so he walked over to check things out a bit better. Sure enough, the marten had been there so long that it was barely hanging together. The fur was slipping on it and it's eye balls were sunk halfway back in it's head."

"Silas thought to himself, "Either the man that set this trap is a mighty poor trapper or something musta happened to him. Nobody in their right mind leaves traps unattended this long.""

"Silas kept working his way along the side of the mountain and in a very short time came across three more sets with dead animals with spoiled furs in them. By then there was no doubt in his mind that something wasn't right. He kept moving in the same direction until late in the afternoon when he looked up ahead and spotted an old trapper's shack."

"There was no smoke coming out of the chimney and no one answered when he called out to announce his presence. Cautiously he worked his way over to the cabin fearing that he might get shot, called out a couple more times, and then pushed the door open. Sure enough, it was a trapper's shack, complete with a trapper."

" The old guy was laying on the floor and wasn't in a whole lot better condition than the pine marten was that the jaybird' been working on. At least the old trapper had had the decency to fall over onto a bear hide he'd been fleshing when he called it quits. Silas said that the bear hide was in better shape than the trapper was so he wrapped the bear hide around the guy and then pulled the wholes works out the door. By then it was getting too dark to bury the guy so he left him laying outside the door of the shack. Silas knew he'd be there in the morning 'cause he wasn't going anywhere."

"Grandma!" I said. "I can't believe that you can sit there and tell stories like this with so little emotion. Doesn't it bother you any?"

"Of course it bothers me Hank, but by the time you're as old as I am, you've seen so much death and heard so many such tales that you learn to take it as a matter-a-fact."

"Glenn interrupted us, which was a rare thing for him to do, and said, "I don't know about the rest of you, but this story is givin' me the Willies, but I'm not about to stop listening." "Go ahead Grandma.""

"Silas said the old guy had left a half a pot of coffee on the stove which he heated up once he got the wood stove going and some jerky the trapper had drying on a wire above the stove so he sat down and ate and drank his fill before he retired for the night."

"Crawling in the guys bedroll was the only part of the whole ordeal that bothered him any but he said he, "slept like the dead once he fell asleep.""

"I'll tell you one thing about your Grandfather Silas Hank. He had a genuine sense of humor. I could tell by the big grin he had on his face when he told me that part of the story."

"Silas said there wasn't a whole lot left of the guy to bury so it didn't take him near as long as he thought it was going to. When he had the body covered up, he rolled a big pile of stones on the grave to discourage the critters and then he marked it with a cross with one of the old trapper's busted traps hanging on the top of it. Silas figured that if he kicked the bucket and someone did as much for him he'd be pleased, so he left well enough alone."

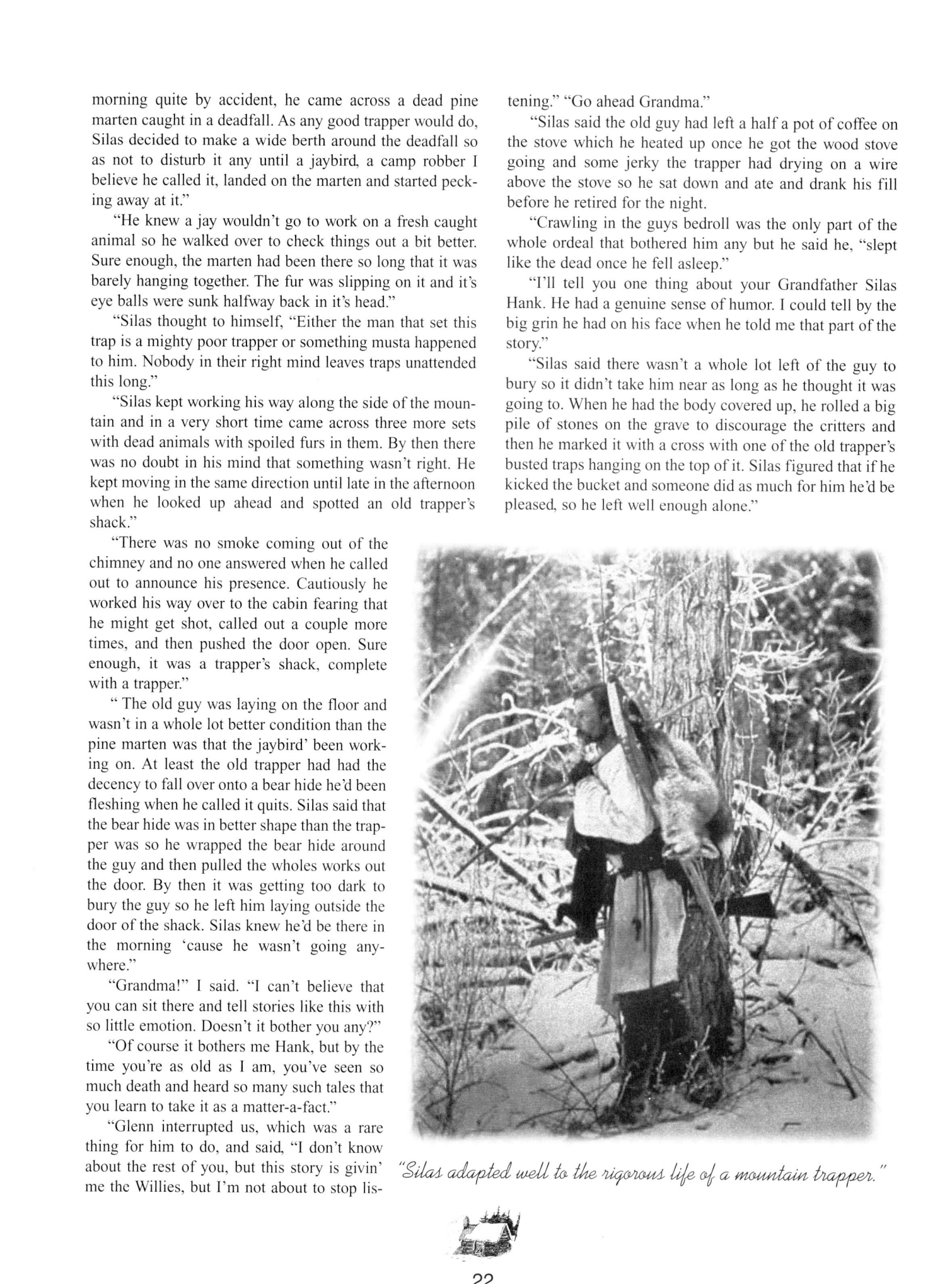

"Silas adapted well to the rigorous life of a mountain trapper."

"You might say that Silas just moved in and took over. He used the old trapper's shack and the same deadfalls that the guy had used. He also laid claim to what steel traps the old guy had left laying around. He said he found a dozen or so more of the guy's traps by walking around and listening for the crows and ravens that were working on whatever had been caught in them."

"Silas did extremely well with his trapping up there, so well in fact that he started getting further and further behind in his skinning and stretching until it had gotten to the point that in order to keep up he was making it on less than four hours of sleep a day. He didn't dare stay off the line for even for a day however, because if deep snow were to come he never be able to find all of his sets and then he'd be no better off about leaving fur in the traps than the trapper before him was."

"To add to the problems he had already, one day when he set out to check his trap line he ran into some trouble that he'd never had before. When he got to his first deadfall, he had caught a big male pine marten in prime condition. The only problem was that it's head and half of it's body had been eaten and what was left of the rest of it had been ripped to shreds. He cleaned up what mess there was, reset the trap, and moved on down the line to his next set. It was a complete repeat of the first set."

"What on Earth was going on Grandma?" I asked.

"Well Hank, Silas was beginning to wonder the same thing, she said." "By the time he reached his third set and the same thing had occurred, he pretty well had it figured out."

"Back at the fur post when he was trading off his furs, an Indian came in and threw a fur on the counter that he didn't recognize. Puzzled as he was, he walked over closer to get a better look. As he stroked the fur, he turned to the Indian, shook his head and shrugged his shoulders. In broken English the Indian said, "Stink Bear."

"Your Granddad nodded to the Indian and then walked back to his bundle of fur and waited his turn."

"When the trader came over to check out his fur, the first thing Silas said to the trader was, "What's a Stink Bear?"

"The trader looked up at him and replied, "Stink Bear. That's the Indian name for a wolverine. A Stink Bear is something you don't never want on your trap line son. In fact if you're a God-fearing man, I'd suggest that you say a little prayer each night that you never run into one. It might help some."

"A stink bear isn't satisfied just makin' a free meal out of whatever you catch. His greatest pleasure is to follow you around your whole trap line and do anything he can to mess up your traps, mess with your mind, and make your life as miserable as he can."

"When he's done tearing your set completely up, his final insult is to take a crap on your trap and then spray his stink all over the place."

"And just because they aren't big, you'd better learn right now to give them the credit they deserve. They've been known to make a cougar or even a grizzly bear back off from what they were eating on if they decided they wanted it. Despite their size, they have the strength and the temperament of the nastiest old boar bear you'll ever see."

"That's the reason why the Indians call him, Stink Bear."

"There wasn't an animal alive stupid enough to move in on a wolverine until it had eaten it's fill and moved on."

"Very few trappers who experienced the misfortunate of having a wolverine move in on their trap line ever outwitted the creature. Instead, the trapper would move on and put as much distance between the two of them as they possibly could."

"It's ground-hugging body structure makes a wolverine one of nature's finest attack animals. It rushes an intruder with lightning-fast speed and goes for the throat or unprotected belly area of the unfortunate creature before it knows what hit it."

"Your Granddad Silas knew that if he didn't get the stink bear that he would have to pull up stakes and get as far away from it as he could, and even that wouldn't guarantee he'd escape it's wrath. They'd been known to follow a man for a hundred miles just to torment him."

"Good Gravy!" "What on earth did he do then?" asked Wally.

"Well Wally, Silas thought back to what the trader had said about a wolverine following a guy around on his trap line so he decided to lay and wait him out to see if the trader was right."

"The next morning, Silas set off to check traps again and sure enough, the wolverine had hit it again. Silas went about cleaning up around the set but this time he left some of the best meat bait he had in the trap and set the deadfall off himself. He moved on down the line and did the same thing to the second set. This time however, he didn't move on to the next trap. Instead, he walked about fifty yards as if he was headed to the next trap. Then he took a sharp right as soon as he spotted a tangled pile of branches he could climb into and be concealed. Then it became a waiting game."

"About five hours later, Silas caught movement off to his left that was headed straight for his baited deadfall. That was the first look at a real live stink bear that he ever had. He described it to me as a creature that just plain looked mean, almost like it had a score to settle with someone."

"Silas watched as the wolverine ate his bait and then it proceeded to rip the entire set up. He watched it do its job on the log and then spray the set with it's stink until it was satisfied. It climbed down from the deadfall and then started following Silas's track again."

"Silas waited until it reached a clearing so that it would present a clear shot for him. When it reached the position he wanted, Silas eased the hammer back on his Hawken to prepare to fire. The hammer made the slightest click, barely loud enough to be heard. At very the instant the hammer clicked, the stink bear stopped in it's tracks and turned to face whatever threatened it. Having no fear whatsoever, the wolverine came straight in Silas's direction."

"Silas said that the way the wolverine loped when it ran was almost comical, but there was certainly nothing funny about what was taking place. Your Granddad knew his one shot had better be good or he was going to end up looking like a shredded marten so he held his fire to the very last second."

"Just as the wolverine left the ground and was in mid-air headed towards Silas, he let drive. That fifty caliber caught the wolverine smack in the throat and it fell dead right at Silas's feet."

Somehow I knew what was about to happen. Wonzal let loose with a few more of his words of wisdom. "SON OF A, WHOOPS!" "Sorry about that Mrs. Jennings."

Wonzal had managed to catch it in mid-air just like the stink bear had. In fact, if he didn't change his ways, that was going to be his new nickname when we were in deer camp, "STINK BEAR."

The more I thought about it, "STINK BEAR" would be the perfect name for Wonzal up at deer camp for more than one reason.

At camp, when fresh venison and onions were being served, he would more than live up to that name.

C. J. said, "My heart's still racing from that story, but please continue Mrs, Jennings."

"One day when Silas was nearly back to the cabin, he was startled by what appeared to be a person outside of his shack. The closer he got, the more and more it appeared that he either had a guest or he had an intruder waiting for him at the cabin door. To make matters worse, the party had a huge, mangy, mongrel dog that looked capable enough to rip the rear end off of a grizzly bear if it ever put it's mind to it."

"When Silas got within fifty yards of the person he could see that it was a woman sitting there in front of the cabin. She appeared to be a half-breed, hard at work skinning and stretching his furs, and it looked like she knew what she was doing. He called out a welcome to her but she was unresponsive. Her dog was laying nearby and it didn't move or utter a sound either. In fact, it barely even acknowledged his presence."

"She was so intent on her work that she never even looked up until he was standing almost next to her. When she finally did realize he was there she jumped back with a startled look on her face. She tried to utter some words but very little sound came out of her mouth, certainly nothing that he could understand. As she opened her mouth again in an attempt to speak, Silas could then see that she had no tongue. It had been cut off some time ago and had healed itself over nicely. Such a practice was common back then if someone feared the person knew things that should never to be repeated."

"Silas looked down and saw that the woman was putting meat from the carcasses into two piles, one pile consisting of what would be considered the most choice and tender meat of the animals and the other the tougher parts that were no doubt being set aside for her dog. She was nearly starving but rather that go into the cabin and steal food from him, she had been willing to work for what she got for her and her dog."

"Silas saw a good thing in the making. If he could somehow convey to her that she was welcome to eat the same foods as he did in exchange for skinning and stretching pelts for him, they could both could benefit from the arrangement. He soon found that he was able to convey his plans to her by handing her a plate of fried mule deer tenderloin while at the same time sliding the two piles of meat together and then over towards her dog."

"This arrangement worked well for the both of them for the next two trapping seasons, until Silas decided it was time to move on again. Silas left the cabin, a few of the traps, and food enough to last the woman until she was able to trap some of her own and then headed on his way."

"Numerous pine martens had fallen victim to the deadfalls of the deceased trapper. By the time Silas found them, they had been in the trap so long that they were too far gone to be saved. However, once the animal was removed and the deadfall was rebaited, Silas could continue using the deadfalls as long as he wished."

"Silas found the old trapper's cabin to be well-stocked with most everything he needed to conduct a working trap line."

"The furnishings of the old trapper's cabin were by no means elaborate but gave Silas a place to tend to his furs, fix a something to eat, and catch a few hours sleep."

"The old trapper had build himself a cache to store his provisions and keep them out of the reach of most any animal except perhaps a marauding grizzly."

"Between the old trapper's deadfalls and the hand-forged traps that he'd used, Silas had all the traps he could tend to."

"It made no difference what the temperature was, Silas had to check his trap lines daily in order to keep the trails open and his sets operating."

"Silas used the legbones of deer as bait more often than not. The animals he trapped knew there was rich marrow inside the bone and would go after them with relish."

"The deaf, speechless woman that Silas found skinning his catch when he returned from his trapline one day proved to be a huge benefit to him. The docile cur-dog she had with her never left her side during her entire stay."

27

"Your Granddad Silas was not only taken in by the hide hunters but by a young woman named Elna. She spelled the end to his trapping days."

"Silas, like thousands of other men, spent winters in a logging camp in order to make ends meet."

"Silas may have been better off had he remained a logger instead of trying to eke out a living as a farmer."

"Silas and Elna had their hands full between trying to build up a homestead and tending to a passle of young-ones that seemed to show up at the rate of one a year."

"Now if Silas had truly intended to spend his life as a mountain man, this was where he made his big mistake. He left a good woman who could neither hear what he said nor talk back to him but was willing to work eighteen to twenty hours a day for him just so he could see what was on the other side of the mountain. He soon found out."

Wonzal's wisdom went on exhibit again, "If you ask me, your Great-Grandpa Silas couldn't have been just right in the head to let a woman like that go."

I glared at him for a moment and said, "I didn't hear anyone ask you Wonzal."

Wonzal just shook his head.

"To make a long story short, when he got down on the plains he ran into a couple of hide hunters who invited him

"Elna's mother moved in with them after her husband passed away and helped out by tending to the youngsters so Elna could tend to her outside chores."

"Farming meant no rest for the wicked. Silas and Elna were pretty much strapped to the farm nearly the year around."

"Elna had a big garden to take care of every year. What she canned and put away in the root cellar would last them through the winter."

"This was about as close to deer hunting as Silas got. He and some of the neighbors got together one Sunday and had their picture taken by a traveling photographer posing with a fake deer. Silas said that at least he looked like a deer hunter even though he didn't have the time to be one."

to follow them back to their cabin and have a home cooked meal with them, which he did. They neglected to tell him that their families were waiting for the back at their cabin. That's when he met Elna."

"One thing led to another and the next thing he knew he had a wife in tow and was headed back towards Michigan. They took up a homestead on an abandoned piece of slash and build a cabin. Silas became a logger and spent several winters in logging camps throughout the Upper Peninsula of Michigan. He certainly did his part to help log off the Pinery. His biggest downfall was that he tried to farm when he came back home in the Spring instead of finding some steady work in town like many of them did."

"That's where the two of them ended up spending the rest of their lives."

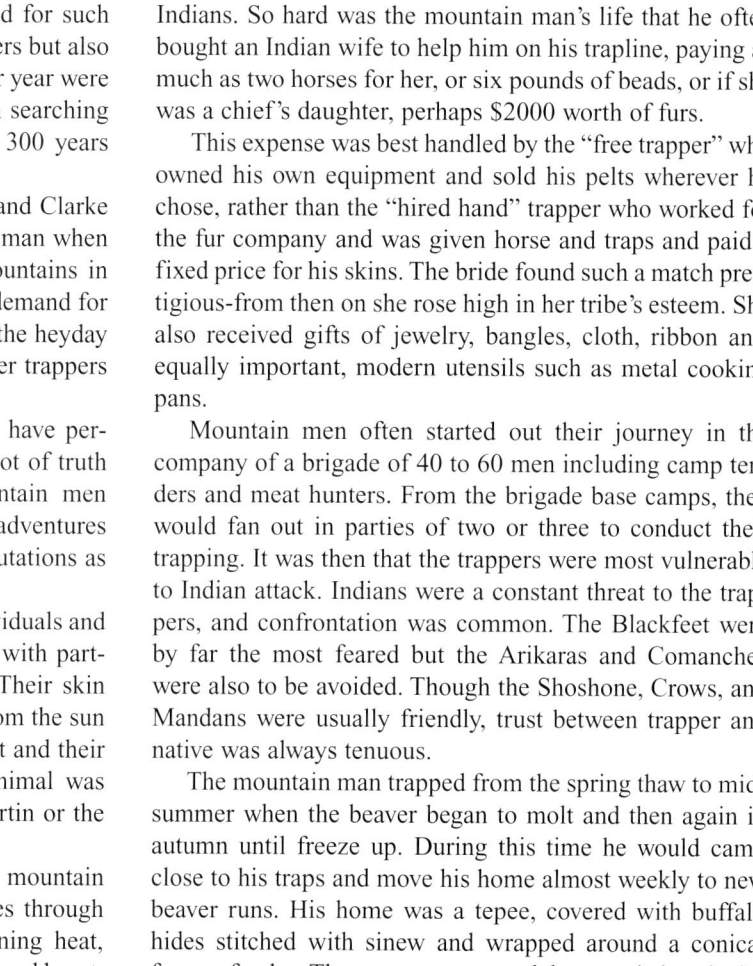

"This is about the time when your Great-Grandfather Silas began to realize that his dreams of hunting, fishing, and trapping trips were never going to be, so he began doing his hunting and so forth by reading. Several of the things Silas put in here were reminders of times and places that he was once familiar with. Other things you'll see in here are of places he wanted to visit or of things he wanted to do."

The Rendezvous

The era of the Mountain Man and the Rendezvous had its beginnings in a surprisingly civilized source: the production of hats made of beaver fur. The demand for such hats was led by not only sophisticated city dwellers but also the military. Upwards of 100,000 beaver pelts per year were being used in the hat industry. Hatters had been searching for a sufficient supply of these prized furs for 300 years before the Lewis and Clarks expedition.

John Colter, a former member of the Lewis and Clarke expedition became arguably then first mountain man when he ventured off on his own into the Rocky Mountains in 1806 to trap beaver in order to capitalize on the demand for fur. It is estimated that between 1820 and 1830, the heyday of the Rocky Mountain fur trade, that 1,000 other trappers roamed the American West in search of fur.

The legends and feats of the mountain men have persisted for decades, largely because there was a lot of truth to the tales that were told about them. Mountain men became a legend in their own time as their adventures became standard fare in the east where their reputations as invincible heroes grew with every story told.

Most of the Mountain Men were solitary individuals and even many of those who worked in brigades or with partners had an "every man for himself" attitude. Their skin was not unlike leather as it dried and browned from the sun and the elements. They were often quite unkempt and their clothing was made of the skins of whatever animal was available whether it was the noble fur of the martin or the pelt off of some lowly skunk.

The work was hard and the dangers many. A mountain trapper faced death on a regular basis-sometimes through the slow agony of starvation, dehydration, burning heat, freezing cold, and surprise attacks from both man and beast. His arms, legs, and feet were constantly wet and chilled from repeated immersion in icy streams and if somehow he managed to avoid pneumonia, he suffered from the aches and pains of the trapper's main complaint, rheumatism.

In order to survive the harsh wilderness in which they resided, they would often times adopt the ways of the Indians. So hard was the mountain man's life that he often bought an Indian wife to help him on his trapline, paying as much as two horses for her, or six pounds of beads, or if she was a chief's daughter, perhaps $2000 worth of furs.

This expense was best handled by the "free trapper" who owned his own equipment and sold his pelts wherever he chose, rather than the "hired hand" trapper who worked for the fur company and was given horse and traps and paid a fixed price for his skins. The bride found such a match prestigious-from then on she rose high in her tribe's esteem. She also received gifts of jewelry, bangles, cloth, ribbon and, equally important, modern utensils such as metal cooking pans.

Mountain men often started out their journey in the company of a brigade of 40 to 60 men including camp tenders and meat hunters. From the brigade base camps, they would fan out in parties of two or three to conduct their trapping. It was then that the trappers were most vulnerable to Indian attack. Indians were a constant threat to the trappers, and confrontation was common. The Blackfeet were by far the most feared but the Arikaras and Comanches were also to be avoided. Though the Shoshone, Crows, and Mandans were usually friendly, trust between trapper and native was always tenuous.

The mountain man trapped from the spring thaw to midsummer when the beaver began to molt and then again in autumn until freeze up. During this time he would camp close to his traps and move his home almost weekly to new beaver runs. His home was a tepee, covered with buffalo hides stitched with sinew and wrapped around a conical frame of poles. The cover was pegged down and closed with lodge pins except for an entrance hole that had a door flap. With smoke flaps for ventilation, the tepee was cool in summer and, facing away from the predominant winds, was windproof in the winter.

In November, as the streams froze, the trapper moved his campfire inside his lodge and both the trapper and his respected nemesis the grizzly bear went into hibernation. Buffalo robes helped to keep the trapper and his wife warm and total boredom would become their only enemy.

Often times during the winter when trapping was all but impossible, the trapper would either winter in the Indian village of his wife's people or he would gather with other trappers at one of the various forts in the area to share stories and swap lies and wait out the winter wither his own kind. Such life in a winter camp could be easy or quite difficult, depending on the weather and the availability of food.

The only exception to this scenario was if the fall trapping had been remarkably poor and he had few furs to show for his time, or if he was in dire need of food.

For several years, trappers found a major dilemma when it came to marketing their fur. They had to travel great distances with their furs to markets in St. Louis, Astoria at the mouth of the Columbia River, Santa Fe, or perhaps Fort Lisa at the mouth of the Big Horn River. On such a long trip the trappers had to encounter numerous hardships, among them having to travel through hostile Indian territory as a white intruder. It got to the point that they could not count on a fort being occupied from one year to the next.

General William Ashley came up with a solution to the problem in 1825 when he arranged to meet with all the trappers who wished to participate in the gathering at Henry's Fort on the Green River. There he would buy the trappers furs and provide them with supplies for another year of trapping. His idea was met with unbridled enthusiasm on the part of the mountain men and the yearly Rendezvous was born.

Since an animal's winter fur is far more valuable than it's lighter summer coat, trappers were basically off work in the summer and the Rendezvous became an annual party to end all parties. Besides the offer to purchase the trapper's fur, the traders brought with them mail, newspapers, gossip, and..., raw alcohol which they watered down and flavored with tobacco, ginger, or spices, and then sold as whiskey.

Weary of his harsh and sometimes lonely life, the rendezvous gave a mountain trapper something to look forward to each year. The brash, anything-goes revelry of the rendezvous gave the trappers a place to blow off some steam, rejoice in their reunions with friends that were rumored dead, enjoy the companionship of the Indian women, drink cheap, watered-down whiskey, participate in contests involving anything imaginable, and do most anything else he could manage to cram into the festivities.

In the meantime, while revelry was at it's peak, the trading was carried on. The merchandise given in exchange for the beaver skins consisted of knives, guns, ammunition, traps, blankets, clothing, salt, coffee, and etc.

A special type of trade goods for the Indians called foorawraw, included beads, mirrors, fish hooks, rings, bracelets, pans, and brightly-colored cloth and ribbons. It was said that as little as 12 cents worth of these goods would purchase a beaver skin worth from $5.00 to $8.00 in St. Louis.

What began as a practical gathering to exchange pelts for supplies and reorganize trapping units soon evolved into a month long carnival in the middle of the wilderness. The gathering was no longer confined to just trappers, but attracted women, children, Indians, French-Canadians, and travelers from around the globe. Mountain Man James Beckworth described the festivities as a scene of "mirth, songs, dancing, shouting, trading, running, jumping, singing, racing, target-shooting, yarns, frolic, with all sorts of extravagances that white men and Indians could invent." Tall tales were told, dirty jokes abounded, feats were held, and gambling of all sorts was carried on. There were horse races, fights, wrestling, songfests that were carried on all night and into the wee hours of the morning. With alcohol as a lubricant, everything else seems to have fallen under the heading of drunk and disorderly behavior.

An easterner gave his view, "mountain companies are all assembled on this season and make as crazy a set of men I ever saw."

(The image of a mountain man usually portrays him as an illiterate savage that harbored almost animal-like characteristics. While in rare instances this was a fairly accurate description, not all who attended a rendezvous came to see how much trouble they could find.

Many of the trappers who attended these rendezvous were educated men. Jedediah Smith, one of the more famous of the mountain men, was well read. He was also a very religious man and never went anywhere without his Bible in hand. Many of these men wrote legal documents and wrote letters for those who were not able to do so themselves. Many of the trappers who came exchanged well-worn books while others learned how to read during the long wait for spring.)

At the end of the rendezvous, the trapper, with a terrible hangover and most likely newly incurred debts to the traders, returned to the mountains with enough memories to get him through the year until the next rendezvous.

The final Rendezvous was held in 1840. Several things led to it's demise. By that time, the beaver had been all but trapped out. With less available beaver pelts available per trapper, there was less money available per trapper after the sale of his pelts at a rendezvous. The high prices charged for goods at a rendezvous combined with less money for fewer pelts sold brought an end to the rendezvous system due to simple economics. Also, the demand for beaver pelts diminished when a more fashionable and cheaper alternative came into popular use: Silk. Contrary to popular belief, trapping did not cease all together in 1840. The fur trade business continued and was conducted up through 1860 at numerous trading posts.

So ended a wild and exuberant chapter in history.

Above the mountain's frowning crest,
Where lines of rugged rock stand forth,
Where Nature bravely bares her breast
To snowy whirlwinds from the north;
High in the clouds and mountain storms,
Where first the autumn snows appear,
Where last the breath of springtime warms,
—There dwells my gallant mountaineer.

Credit - William T. Hornaday

A DAY IN THE LIFE OF THE MOUNTAIN TRAPPER

The beaver was more important to trappers than the anticipation of "hair-breath escapes" and "scenes of daring-do" is evident in the words of Zenas Leonard:

"When we first embarked in this business it was with the expectation that to ensure a fortune in the fur trade only required a little perseverance and industry. We were not told that we were to be constantly annoyed by the Indians."

These are scarcely the words and thoughts of an adventurer/Indian fighter, but if the truth be known few mountain men could be considered a "solitary" or a "free" trapper.

Large camps of trappers seemed to offer the most successful method for transporting men, furs, and equipment in an effective fashion.

Once the camp was set up: "The men were divided into messes, so many trappers and so many camp-keepers (skinners, fleshers, stretchers) to a mess."

The importance and presence of these camp-keepers seems to be one of the aspects of "mountaineer" life that is often overlooked. In a considerable company, half its numbers can catch as many beavers as all. But the half that keep guard, and cook, perform duties as necessary are just as important to the whole concern as the others."

Beaver is one of the most difficult of animals in North America to skin, but the hide can be taken off "dirty," leaving large amounts of fat and meat still attached to it in about ten minutes.

When properly fleshed a beaver skin has a white appearance, and is as clean as a sheet of paper.

After being fleshed the skins were then stretched to insure even drying. They are stretched round, either by pegging to the ground or by the common method of lacing them to willow sticks bent into a circular form.

Depending upon the weather, two to five days may be necessary for the skins to dry; they can then be folded, marked and baled.

The skins or plews were then marked for identification should they be stolen. Painting marks on them or scraping them in a particular manner were two of the most common methods used.

After drying and marking, the skins were folded with the fur inside and baled. It was their custom "to pack their beaver skins in bundles of about fifty pounds each, one of which was laid at night for a pillow, the rest were arranged in the most convenient manner possible for barricades of defense against the Indians."

The duty of the trapper during the trapping season was only to trap and how we went about that was our next concern.

An outfit for trapping was generally agreed upon as six traps, sometimes fewer, rarely more, depending upon circumstances, which cost the fur companies $2.00 to $2.50, first cost, but retailed in the mountains for a standard $12.00. Traps were bought by trappers, supplied by the companies, or loaned, and the 500% mark-up over first cost appears universal. These prices put the traps in with the more expensive gear of the trappers' outfit and comparable to rifles at $25.00 and blankets at $9.00.

These traps followed a few standard patterns, being generally five to six pounds and varying in minor details such as single or double spring, round or square jawed, but all were hand forged as mass production had not begun in the trap industry. Traps were supplied by various blacksmiths, gunsmiths and machinists.

Trappers scouted for "beaver sign," meaning dams, lodges, cuttings, slides, droppings or even smell, all of which gave evidence that the beavers were active and in quantity.

Sets were generally made at sundown and checked the following morning. When they went to make a set, the trapper found the place the animal came out of the water and set his trap in his path, about four inches under water, fastening his chain to a stake, which you put as far out in the water as its length will allow. He then dipped a twig in the bait to attract the beaver and placed it between the jaws of the trap.

The trappers prepared their own bait from the musk of the beavers themselves. Castors or scent glands used to mark territory or attract mates were saved by trappers and either used straight or prepared into baits using added ingredients. When the set was complete a small twig was dipped into the bait and placed either within the jaws of the trap, or just outside of them. When the beaver went to smell the castor, it was generally caught by the forefeet, flouncing over, and drowned in the water.

The business of eating for a trapper was not a very elaborate one, the sole article of diet being meat, either dried or roasted. By a certain hour all was quiet in camp, and only the guard was awake.

This daily routine took place in a yearly cycle and centered around the fall and spring hunts. The fall hunt began after rendezvous and lasted until freeze up in the winter.

During the course of the year a good trapper took an average of 120 skins which was worth about $1,000.00 and can be hired for about $400.00 payable at an average of 600% profit. Few trappers ever achieved the success they hoped for in the dangerous labor in the Rocky Mountains. But nevertheless many pursued the life as long as possible.

The decline of beaver prices caused many to realize that the fur trade was dead in the Rocky Mountains. Trappers became unable to support themselves which forced many of them to turn back to former occupations. Others found new ones as traders, guides or hunters at the new robe-trading forts.

Trapping and Home-Made Traps
From Outing Magazine
By Ed. W. Sandys

The art of trapping is as old as man. The prehistoric human lived in caves and chance-made natural shelters was surrounded by monstrous forms of life, some of which he fed in all probability, and others upon which he fed.

Time was when trapping consisted mainly of setting traps and taking the hides from the easily secured captives, but now it demands the closest study of wild creatures and their ways-has become, in fact, a strategic game between the highest form of reason and an instinct often so closely approaching reason that the dividing line is problematical. The very difficulty of successful trapping, the keen observation and close study it demands and the delightful contact with Nature's purest charms, form its greatest attraction. There is more excitement (of a certain kind), more pleasure and more genuine sportsmanship involved in trapping than in shooting game with gun or rifle, simply because the one demands more knowledge and closer and longer continued relations with Nature than does the other.

The successful trappers, the last few representatives of the hardy, picturesque race who blazed the trail for civilization across this mighty continent, know the ways of beast and fowl as a lawyer knows the intricate mesh of the net he will weave or disentangle from a disputed point. Such men can read the "sign" of forest, plain and sky with the utmost of accuracy.

I myself was a born trapper, and as my early life was spent in a small town from which the woods could be reached in a quarter of an hour, many and many a furred and feathered victim filled my snares. Fate led me to the grand old woods of Michigan's northern peninsula, and under the crowding, whispering pines and hemlocks, I and a scarred old waif from the western Rockies trapped together for two memorable seasons In those days ('75 and '76) wild pigeons nested in Oceana County, and at the close of the summer we took our full share of azure-backed, pink-breasted beauties with the nets.

Let us now consider a few useful traps. Let not the reader be disappointed with my devices, which include the easiest made, or set, and the most effectual of almost countless contrivances. Before we begin let us remember one thing. No trap should be set that will not be visited regularly at proper intervals.

The law of the land and the unwritten law of sportsmanship forbid the trapping of game, and while I knew well enough how to snare and trap deer, turkey, wild goose, duck, grouse and quail, I believe in "lead us not into temptation," and refrain from explaining.

In all likelihood few of my readers will ever penetrate the wilderness upon a regular trapping outing, so I need not devote much space to the capture of the greater carnivore. But for black bear, puma, wolf and lynx, several styles of traps are used. The best is the heavy dead-fall. It is sure enough, if properly constructed, and will kill animals as large as the black bear speedily, and without injuring the fur.

The best dead-fall is constructed as follows: In a swamp or bit of woods, where the "sign" says bears are working, build a pen about three feet wide, four deep and five high, of moderate-sized timber, for the cutting of which a keen axe is needed. Select soft ground and form the pen of three-inch saplings, pointed and driven firmly into the soil. When the pen is complete a couple of logs about six feet long are placed across the front. Outside, on either side of these logs, and in line with the sides of the pen, four stout poles are driven, as shown in diagram. The principle of the trap is that a heavy log shall fall upon the back of the bear and crush the body against the lower logs fixed across the front

"Heavy deadfalls could even handle a grizzly."

of the pen.

The heavy log, or "fall-log," should be nearly a foot in diameter and about twenty feet long. The working parts of the trap consist of a stout state (1) driven firmly just inside the "bed-piece," or short logs, and projecting above ground nearly three feet; a straight stick (2) about two and a half feet long and flattened slightly at one end; a "bait-stick," (3) notched at each end on opposite sides; two stout forks (4) driven firmly into the ground, and the short, straight cross-piece (5). The diagram will explain how the thing works. The weight of the "fall-log" rests upon the short projecting end of (2), which is supported by (1) and kept in position by the grip of the notched "bait-stick," (3) the reverse notch of which grips the cross-piece (5) held down by the forks (4). The bait, either a bit of smoked fish or flesh smeared with honey, is fixed near the lower end of the "bait-stick" (3). In order to reach the tempting morsel bruin must enter the trap at least halfway. A slight forward pull at the bait will release the lower end of (3), which at once allows the fall-log to crash down across the back of the unfortunate black fellow, who will possibly think the burden that lays upon him is greater than he can bear. In any event his career will be seriously incommoded by limits when he is once pinned between the logs. There are many other methods by which the fall-log can be worked, an excellent one being the figure 4, but perhaps the one described is the best, all things considered. As will be noticed in the illustration, the weight of the fall-log can be increased by resting one or more logs on it.

A good trap for taking coon, mink, squirrel, and the smaller furred creatures, is the little dead-fall. It is much used by professional trappers, and, of course, much lighter timber is employed in constructing it, as the animals are more easily killed than a bear cub. The pen can be made of small sticks and the fall-log can be eight feet long and about six inches in diameter. A useful method of setting it is explained by the illustration. The forked bait-stick is about a foot long and the fall-log is released by the animal pulling at the bait. The cross-piece upon which the fall-log rests is about fourteen inches long. The best baits are: for mink, a fowl's or bird's head, or a bit of fish; for muskrat, bits of carrot or apple; for skunk and coon, part of a dead fowl or bird, the first preferred.

"The real work began trying to remove the bear from the deadfall."

"Skinning an animal the size of a bear was an art in itself. A great deal of care was needed to make certain the hide was not cut as the price would be reduced with each and every bit of damage."

"Once the bear pelt was hung up to dry, it was time for a well-earned break."

"Every trapper's cabin bore evidence of his skill."

"The final destination for the trapper's catch was the fur buyer's trading post. There the trapper's furs were either sold or exchanged for supplies he needed to make it through another season."

SCENES IN THE LIFE OF A TRAPPER.—[Sketched by W. M. Cary.]

"Injuns, by gosh."

WINCHESTER RIFLES.
Model 1866.
Sporting.
Fig. No. A5247.

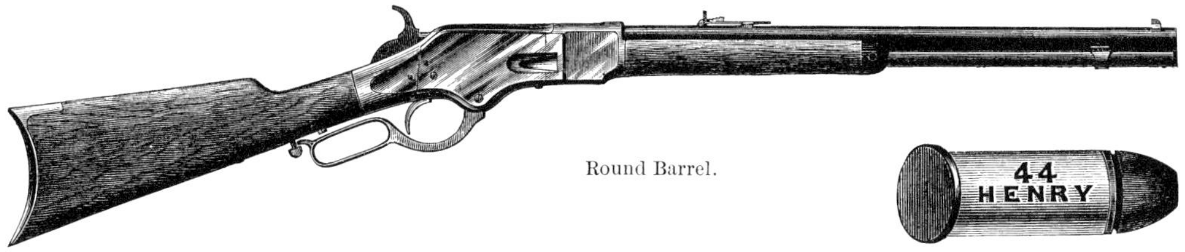

Round Barrel.

Sporting Model 1866—Round Barrel, Rifle Stock, Plain Trigger; Length of Barrel, 24 in.; Caliber, 44-100; 17 Shots; Weight, 9 lbs., $22.00
Sporting Model 1866—Octagon Barrel, Rifle Stock, Plain Trigger; Length of Barrel, 24 in.; Caliber, 44-100; 17 Shots; Weight, 9½ lbs., 23.00

Model 1873.
Sporting, Gun Stock.
Fig. No. A5248.

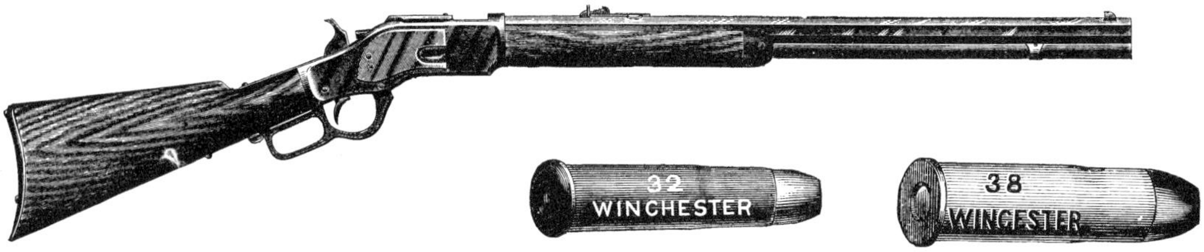

Octagon Barrel.

Sporting Model 1873—Octagon Barrel, Gun Stock, Plain Trigger; Length of Barrel, 24 in.; Caliber, 32 or 38-100; 15 Shots; Weight, 8¾ lbs., $27.00
Sporting Model 1873—Round Barrel, Gun Stock, Plain Trigger; Length of Barrel, 24 in.; Caliber, 32 or 38-100; 15 Shots; Weight, 8 lbs., 25.00
Sporting Model 1873—Half Octagon Barrel, Gun Stock, Plain Trigger; Length of Barrel 24 in.; Caliber, 32 or 38-100; 15 Shots; Weight, 8¼ lbs., 27.00
Set Trigger, extra, 4.00

Sporting, Rifle Stock.
Fig. No. A5249.

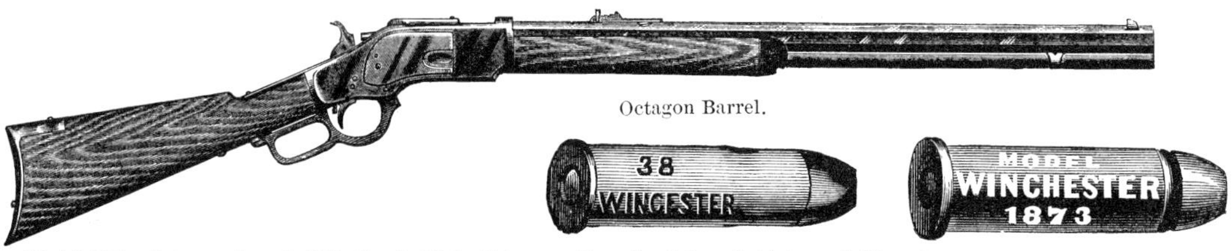

Octagon Barrel.

Sporting Model 1873—Octagon Barrel, Rifle Stock, Plain Trigger; Length of Barrel, 24 in.; Caliber, 38 or 44-100; 15 Shots; Weight, 9 lbs., $27.00
Sporting Model 1873—Round Barrel, Rifle Stock, Plain Trigger; Length of Barrel, 24 in.; Caliber, 38 or 44-100; 15 Shots; Weight, 8¾ lbs., 25.00
Sporting Model 1873—Half Octagon Barrel, Rifle Stock, Plain Trigger; Length of Barrel, 24 in.; Caliber, 38 or 44-100; 15 Shots; Weight, 8¼ lbs., 27.00
Set Trigger, extra, 4.00

Sporting, Models 1866, 1873 Short Magazine, same Price as Full Magazine of Corresponding Style.

Carbines.
Fig. No. A5250.

Carbines, Model 1873—Plain Trigger; Length of Barrel, 20 in.; Caliber, 44-100; 12 Shots; Weight, 7¼ lbs., $24.00

(1320)

WINCHESTER RIFLES.
Model 1876.
Sporting.
Fig. No. A5252.

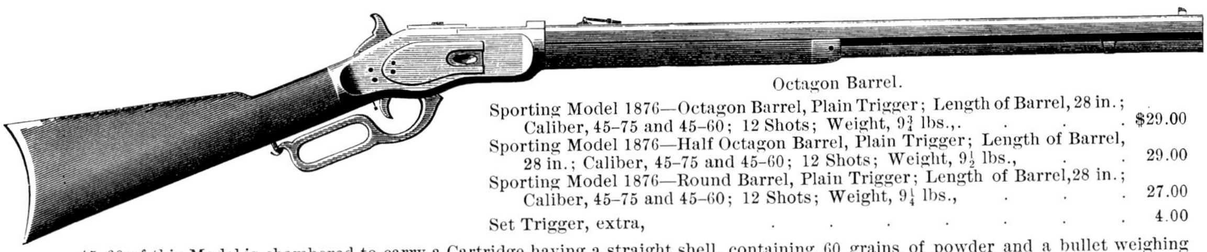

Octagon Barrel.

Sporting Model 1876—Octagon Barrel, Plain Trigger; Length of Barrel, 28 in.; Caliber, 45-75 and 45-60; 12 Shots; Weight, 9¾ lbs.,	$29.00
Sporting Model 1876—Half Octagon Barrel, Plain Trigger; Length of Barrel, 28 in.; Caliber, 45-75 and 45-60; 12 Shots; Weight, 9½ lbs.,	29.00
Sporting Model 1876—Round Barrel, Plain Trigger; Length of Barrel, 28 in.; Caliber, 45-75 and 45-60; 12 Shots; Weight, 9¼ lbs.,	27.00
Set Trigger, extra,	4.00

45-60 of this Model is chambered to carry a Cartridge having a straight shell, containing 60 grains of powder and a bullet weighing 300 grains. It has greater power and range than Model 1873, but less power, range and recoil than the regular Model 1876, 45-75.

Sporting Model 1876, Short Magazine, same price as Full Length Magazine of corresponding style.

Target.
Fig. No. A5253.

Cut shows Target Rifle complete with Pistol Grip, Vernier and Wind Gauge Sights. It can be made to order from any of the Standard Winchester Rifles by adding the following

Extras.

For additional length of barrel and magazine, add to price $1.00 per inch over the regular lengths, as quoted in pages 1320 and 1321. Extra heavy barrels, round or octagon, increasing the weight of the gun from 1 to 2 lbs., furnished at an additional cost of $5.00. Engraving from $5.00 to $100 additional, according to style and quality.

Full Nickel Plating, $5.00; Nickel Plated Trimmings, $3.00; Silver Plated Trimmings, $5.00; Gold Plated Trimmings, $10.00; Set Triggers, $4.00; Fancy Walnut Stock, $5.00; Checking Butt Stock and Fore Arm, $5.00; Pistol Grip Stock, Fancy Walnut, Checked, $15.00; Case Hardening, $1.00; Swivels and Sling Strap, $1.50.

Carbines.
Fig. No. A5254.

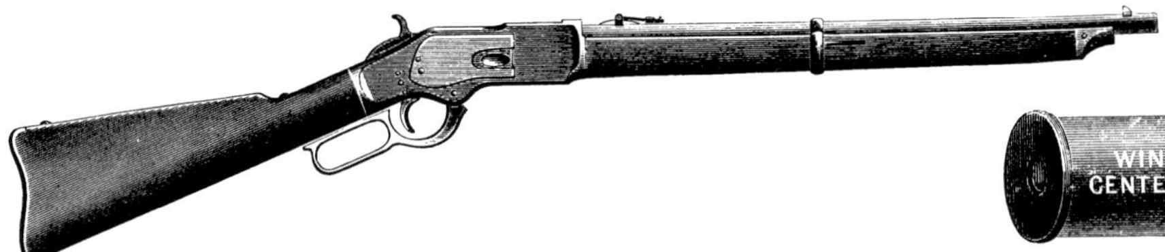

Carbines, Model 1876—Length of Barrel 22 in.; Caliber, 45-75 and 45-60; 9 Shots; Weight, 8¼ lbs., . . . $25.00

Express.
Fig. No. A5255.

Round Barrel.

Express, Model 1876—Round Barrel; Length of Barrel, 26 in.; with either Short or Full Length Magazine,	$35.00
Express, Model 1876—Octagon Barrel; Length of Barrel, 26 in.; with either Short or Full Length Magazine,	38.00
Express, Model 1876—Half Octagon Barrel; Length of Barrel, 26 in.; with either Short or Full Length Magazine,	38.00

(1321)

SIGHTS.

Fig. No. A5256.

Globe.
Cut Showing Sight Closed.
Winchester Globe, each, $1.50

Fig. No. A5257.

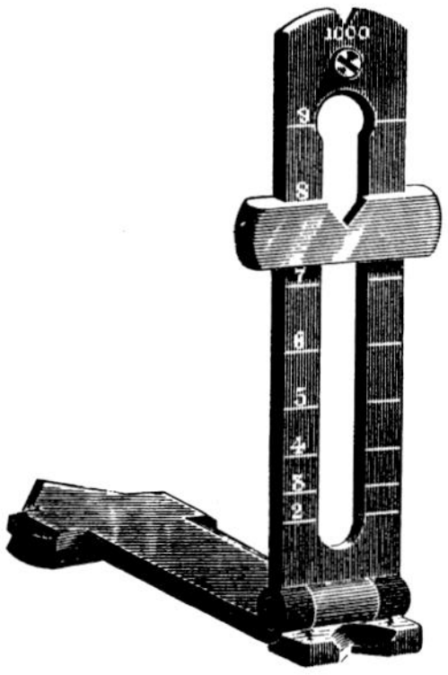

Fig. No. A5258.

Fig. No. A5259.

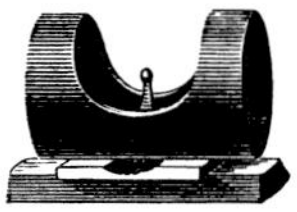

Globe.
Cut Showing Sight Open.

No. 2.   Lyman's, with Base.

No. 2—Sporting Leaf, Graduated 100 to 1000 yards; Model, 1876, ... each, $1.75
Lyman's Patent Combination; Complete, with Base, each, $5.00; without Base, . . . " 3.00

Fig. No. A5260   Fig. No. A5261.   Fig. No. A5262.

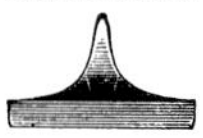

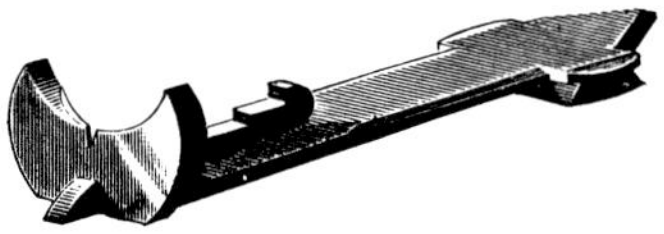

No. 4.   No. 5.   No. 6.

No. 4—Sporting Front, ... each, $ .40
No. 5—Sporting Rear, Graduated from 50 to 300 yards, ... " 1.00
No. 6—Carbine Rear, Graduated to 300 yards, ... " 1.00

Fig. No. A5263.

Beach Combination, ... each, $2.00
Any of the above Rear Sights will be furnished to order with Clover Leaf, Buckhorn, or any desired shape.

Fig. No. A5264.

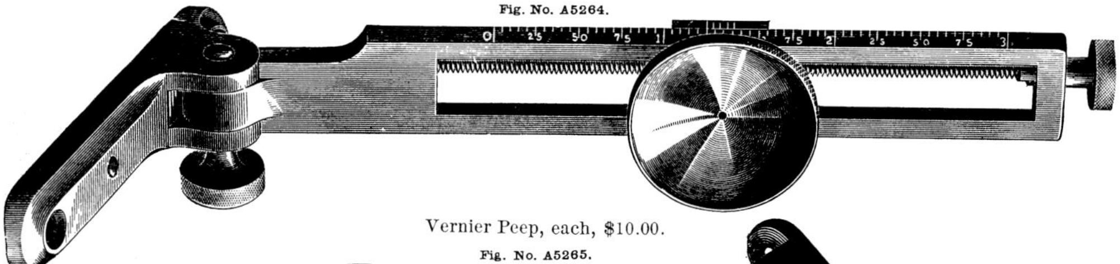

Vernier Peep, each, $10.00.

Fig. No. A5265.

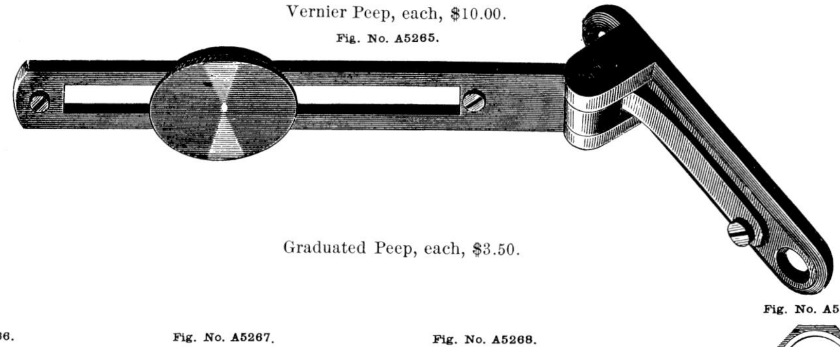

Graduated Peep, each, $3.50.

Fig. No. A5266.   Fig. No. A5267.   Fig. No. A5268.   Fig. No. A5269.

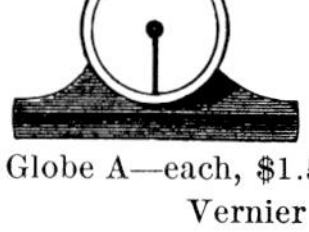

Globe A—each, $1.50   Globe C—each, $1.50   Globe M—each, $1.50   Wind Gauge, with Spirit Level, $8.00

Vernier and Wind Gauge Sights, with Spirit Level, Extra Disc., etc., complete in Morocco Case, $18.00
CUTS FULL SIZE.

(1322)

40

The Fur Trade
by J. H. Crooker

The very first white men to enter Montana so far as we know, were French voyageurs, about 1742, who in the interests of the fur trade, went westward with Indian guides, from the head of Lake Superior. They are said to have gone as far toward the setting sun as the Rocky Mountains (near the Canadian line), which they first saw on New Year's 1743. From this time forward, priests and traders traveled parts of the territory now known as Montana, some going westward from the great lakes, and others later coming eastward from the fur-trading centres on the Pacific coast, where Astoria was afterwards located (1811). The Lewis and Clarke expedition went and came through this territory in 1805 and 1806, discovering the sources of the Missouri, but just missing the Yellowstone Park. If they had entered that wonderland, who then would have believed the report? The American Fur Company in 1829 pushed its outpost forward to the mouth of the Yellowstone, where a stockade, two hundred feet square, called Fort Union, was built that year. The first steamboat, the Yellowstone, made its way up the Missouri to this point in 1832.

A few years more carried the white men four hundred miles farther up the great river, to a point where Fort Benton was built in 1846. This post, after being an important headquarters of the fur trade for fifteen years, became, in the early sixties, the busy center of trade and travel for the gold seekers entering the country by the river route. Over thirty boats from St. Louis landed there in 1866. In all those early years the motive which led to adventure, enterprise and sometimes to bloodshed was the fur trading ambition. There was a constant clash between the agents of the Hudson Bay Company and the American Fur Company. The Indians were often instigated by the traders to massacre the agents of the opposing company and their Indian allies. It is only recently that historical students have begun to appreciate how important as pioneers of civilization the fur traders really were.

It is impossible to overstate the importance of the North-American fur trade. For nearly three hundred years it was the principal-often the only-business transacted on the frontier, the incentive for most American exploration, and a prize over which France and England waged one hundred years of colonial war.

The business began in the sixteenth century as simple barter. The first European explorers traded trinkets to the Indians for pelts- an exchange in which neither side had much respect for the good sense of the other. The white strangers obtained valuable furs for what they considered trifles. To the primitive Indian economy, however, blankets,

THE FUR TRADE.

cloth, pots and pans, knives, and hatchets were hitherto unknown luxuries. Each side gave to the other something valued lightly for something prized highly, and both sides were happy. The simple approach didn't last long, though. Over the period of two hundred years the organization and methods used in the fur trade became standardized and streamlined by experience.

The furs both licensed and unlicensed traders sought came roughly in two classes-fine and coarse. Fine furs included those from which luxury garments were (and still are) made: mink. fox, raccoon, otter, muskrat, and, above all, beaver. The prime beaver skin, source of felt for men's tall hats-the rage of European fashion-was the common unit of exchange. Such a pelt was worth about six dollars at the top of the market in the 1820's. Coarse furs, suitable for lap robes, heavy coats, and winter boots, included buffalo hides and deer and bear skins. The traffic in bear skins expanded into a minor but flourishing market for tallow that put a new word into the English dictionary. Bear fat was the principal ingredient in a men's hair pomade called- for no apparent reason except as an exotic sales pitch-Macassar Oil. It was great for keeping natural hair slicked down, but it was greasy and left unsightly smears on the backs of chairs. Disgusted housewives retaliated by pinning doilies to the chair backs-and the antimacassar was born.

The actual purchase of furs took place at the wilderness posts. If a trader had no competition, all he had to do was to wait for his Indian customers to come to him. If there was competition, he would lead or send small parties into the Indian villages.

Trading posts were fairly standardized. The average post consisted of a cluster of log buildings around a canoe landing. Typically, there was a store, warehouse, and living quarters for the trader and his "family" of employees, called "engages".

Trading took place at the store. Here the trappers brought their winter catch, which was displayed and valued, pelt by pelt-a bargaining process the Indians enjoyed and at which they could hold their own when not dulled by firewater. Following this inventory, the trapper selected the goods he wanted from the shelves, and purchases were entered against the previously established credit.

Furs were assembled into packs for ease of storing and shipping. Each pack was a standard size. The pelts were tightly pressed and wrapped for protection. Each pack weighed about one hundred pounds and contained a fixed number of one kind of pelt-eighty beaver, sixty otter, one hundred twenty fox, fourteen bear, ten buffalo.

Charles Langlade probably never realized it, but when he brought his family to Green Bay he drove the first nail into the coffin lid of the fur trade in Wisconsin, though the inevitable end was long in coming. The state had a white population of fewer than 700 in 1820. A decade later the figure had grown to 3,000. By 1840 there were 30,945 Wisconsinites. When the total hit 305,000 in 1850 the fur trade already was dead.

The settlers who followed the trails of the trappers and traders destroyed the sources of the furs, forcing the fur traders ever deeper into the wilderness. The cycle repeated itself until a continent had been spanned and conquered.

"Strong natures and rugged types met in a free and unconventional competition. The wildness of the frontier life fostered liberty; the hardships developed sympathy; the newness stimulated originality; the glorious climate put vigor into the blood". J. H. Crooker.

A FUR-TRADER IN THE COUNCIL TEPEE.

Rivière Des Sauteux
(The Chippewa River)

One of the most intriguing bits of history is the journal of Francois Victor Malhiot who was a clerk for the North West Company and wintered at Fort du Flambeau in 1804-05. At that time it was a policy of the North West Company to require its clerks in charge of a post to keep a journal of the proceedings. His journal, which relates his experiences at Lac du Flambeau is a good example of its kind, too extensive to be repeated here, a few excerpts will prove of interest:

"12th of July, Thursday. I started this morning at four o'clock. I met an unloaded canoe of XY, but could not find out where it was going."

"22nd, Sunday. I was unable to have the canoes put in the water before three o'clock, because the lake was too rough for a long while. At 11 o'clock I arrived here at La Pointe, Mr. Cadotte's Fort. I decided to spend the remainder of the day there to give the men time to make themselves shoes for crossing the portage. I obtained eighteen white fish from the Savages in exchange for tobacco. I expressly forbade my people to trade their corn for fish."

"24th, Tuesday. This morning I started at 9 o'clock and at 11 I camped at Mauvaise Riviäre (Bad River). There are many pigeons here. I killed 24 (1)."

"25th, Wednesday. I heard from one of 'le Genou's' brothers, who left Lac au Flambeau a week ago, that the Savages have been on the warpath, that they are now hunting and that our people who spent the summer in the interior were to start four days ago to come and meet us."

"27th, Friday. Our people from Lac au Flambeau. They are thin and emaciated like real skeletons. They say they were more ill-treated then ever by Gauthier; that half the time they had nothing to eat, while he never passed a single day without having a good meal. How weak they are!! I gave each of them a drink of shrub, two double handfuls of flour, and two pounds of pork and they began to eat with such avidity that I was twice obliged to take the dish away from them, and notwithstanding this, I feared for a long while that injurious consequences would result; fortunately they all escaped with slight twinges of colic."

"August 2nd, Thursday. I started at 4 o'clock this morning and arrived here at Fort du Flambeau at 3 o'clock in the afternoon. I calculated that there were three packs of furs; besides these were thirty deer, six beaver, one otter, one bear and twenty-four muskrat skins."

"3rd, Friday. I got all the meat and furs Chorette's brother-in-law could have, and my men learned there was a rumor that the Savages wanted to go on the war-path."

"8th Wednesday. Until now, owing to lack of time and to sickness, I have been unable to make any observations on the country and the Savages, but as I am better today I will begin by saying that of all the spots and places I have seen in my thirteen years' of travels, this is the most horrid and most sterile. The Portage road is truly that to heaven because it is narrow, full of overturned trees, obstacles, thorns, and muskegs. Men who go over it loaded and who are obliged to carry baggage over it, certainly deserve to be called 'men.' "

"This vile Portage is inhabited solely by owls, because no other animal could find a living there, and the hoots of those solitary birds are enough to frighten an angel or intimidate a Caeser."

"As to Lac du Flambeau it is worthier of the name of swamp than of lake and at this season it would be easier to catch bullfrogs in the nets than fish. I have had the nets set three times since my arrival without catching a fish."

"9th, Thursday. We had a great deal of trouble last night owing to the liquor. They quarreled among themselves; we quarreled with them and almost came to blows. They made many apologies to me in the morning, saying that such a thing had never happened to them, that they were too drunk-the usual excuse of such black dogs!"

"24th, Friday. We are threatened with a famine because the Savages absolutely want to go on the war-path; consequently they will put the greater portion of their rice in caches, and we shall have to purchase at its weight in gold."

"14th September, Friday. Yesterday I got 4 sacks of rice from Folle Avoine for which I gave him half a keg of rum and half a brasse of tobacco. The rum was drunk last night at the lodges of Lac du Flambeau."

"5th October, Friday. I have just taken an inventory of the furs I have traded since my arrival here and I counted: 528 deer skins, 840 muskrat skins, 107 lbs. Beaver, 44 otter skins, 16 bear skins, 7 marten skins, 1 mink skin-the whole making probably sixteen packs. This autumn trade has greatly reduced my stock of goods so that I am unable to send any into the country of the River of the Sauteux."

RIVIÈRE DES SAUTEUX.

"14th, Sunday. I learn from two young men who have just arrived that 'le Muffle d'Orignal,' one of the Savages I gave a coat to last autumn, starved to such an extent that he had to eat his pack, his dogs, and even his gun-cover."

"10th November, Friday. The war party that arrived here the day before yesterday to the number of 17, went to Chorette's, killed his dogs and, this afternoon, are feasting on the same dogs. After making me eat some, they left us, to my great satisfaction, for my provisions are diminishing rapidly. Today I am sending 3 men to Chorette's to get my canoe. He is always extravagant as usual, and gives a brasse of cloth for one otter or two beaver skins."

"I am expecting another war party from day to day. I am alone to guard the Fort with Gauthier. My people have not had a day's rest since my arrival here last autumn. Of all the men who may be in the upper country I do not think there are any who have worked as hard as mine."

"5th December, Wednesday. Today we are in sight of Lake Superior, my people having done 21 pauses yesterday and 20 today. Tonight we are eating our last corn cakes and tomorrow noon we hope to be at the end of the portage."

"8th, Saturday. I started today from the Montreal River and arrived at La Pointe, Mr. Cadotte's fort. While walking beside the lake, I found a white fish half eaten by the eagles and half rotten, but not sufficiently so to prevent my eating it after roasting it on a spit."

It is difficult to determine from Malhiot's journal the distances which he sent his traders out during the year to deal with the Indians, and exactly what territory they covered. It is evident, however, that they journeyed to Vieux Desert, touched certain points on the Wisconsin River, to the Pelican Lake region of Oneida County, parts of Iron County and possibly west down the Flambeau River. During the winter Malhiot's command at Fort Lac du Flambeau, the XY Fur Company and North West Fur Company combined, thus stopping competition. His records indicated the following listings during the year:

INVENTORY OF FURS-1804-1805

	Rec'd in trade by Malhiot	Rec'd by Malhiot from Gauthier	Claimed by Gauthier but taken by Malhiot	Total
Large bear	94	4	1	99
Small Bear	21	–	–	21
Deer skins	803	100	30	933
Muskrat	1,353	218	24	1,595
Beaver	122 plus 107 lbs	20 lbs	6	128 plus 127 lbs
Lynx	3	–	–	3
Otter	87	4	1	92
Fisher	9	–	–	9
Marten	153	6	–	3
Moose	3	–	–	3
Mink	9	–	–	9
Raccoon	1	–	–	1

It must be remembered also that the Indian at this time was utilizing the skins from moose, deer and fur bearing animals as clothing, and although the fur companies were trading him trinkets, hatchets, knives, etc., the Indian clothed himself with the skins of wild animals of the forests. Undoubtedly, a considerable amount of fur and hides was used in this manner.

RIVAL TRADERS RACING TO THE INDIAN CAMP.

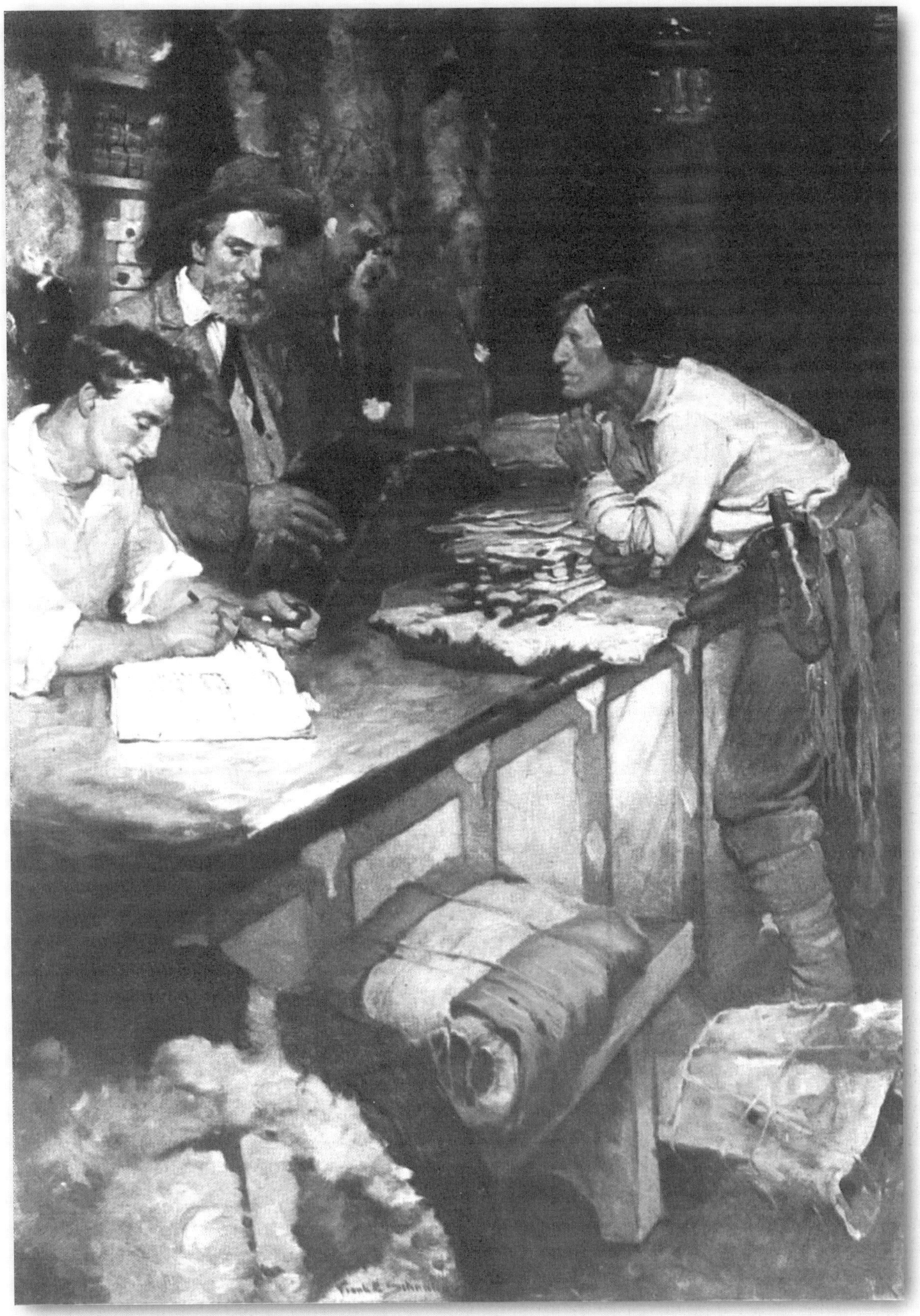

"Silas passed his trapping skills on to his grandsons. Silas is shown here with the boys and a badger they managed to capture."

"Silas carried a Winchester Trapper's Model with him most any where he went. Whenever he decided to use it, Silas wasn't known for his misses."

"It was a rarity for Silas to ever sit long enough to pose for a picture-taking session."

"It seems as though trapping is in the blood."

46

"It was extremely difficult for your Grandpa Silas and Grandma Elna to leave their home when they could no longer care for themselves after spending their entire married life in the place."

"Though the home was small and cramped, Silas and Elna managed to raise a family and entertain their grandchildren inside those old log walls. A great deal of love and laughter made up for the things they never had."

"The years Silas spent on his trap line took their toll on his health as he grew older. A person's body can take only so much icy water and frozen hands before the rheumatism and arthritus begin to take over."

"It was tragic to think of how hard Silas had worked and how little he'd gained from all of the years he'd spent trying to eke out a living on that run-down old farm."

"Your Granddad Charlie might be wearing a hundred dollar suit but if he felt like fishing, he fished."

Wonzal turned and said to me, "We've only seen the very beginning of your family album so far Hank. Are you glad I came as early as I did today?"

I relied, "I owe you one Wonzal, I really do."

Grandma spoke up and said, "Let's take a ten minute break to stretch and have a cup of coffee and then we'll take a look at the life of Hank's Grandfather." With that said, we adjourned for a short break.

Once we had all gathered back around the table, Grandma began by introducing us as to who my Grandfather Charlie McCracken was, where he lived, and how he'd spent most of his life.

"You can probably remember quite a bit about your Grandfather Charlie, Hank. You were quite a bit older and saw him several more times than you ever saw your Great-Grandpa Silas."

"Yes I do Grandma. If I close my eyes I can still see him without even looking at these photos."

Wonzal said, "You couldn't have been very old when he was around Hank, so he must have made quite an impression on you whenever you did see him."

I realized at that moment that I probably never gave Wonzal the credit that I should have for his forethought and his in-depth thinking abilities. Perhaps the reason why I didn't was the fact that they occurred so seldom over such a long period of time.

"You hit that one right on the head Wonzal. I seldom saw him without a suit coat on and wearing a fine pair of shiny leather dress boots. Despite how he was dressed, it didn't seem to make a bit of difference to him. It certainly didn't hold him back any from doing whatever he felt like doing when he felt like doing it. I remember him playing catch with me, playing tag with us kids, and taking me fishing dressed just as he was. If he muddied up the knees of his pants playing tag or got the seat of his pants all stained green from sitting down beside me on the bank of the river, it didn't bother him a bit."

Grandma said, "Well that's a whole lot more than can be said about your Grandmother Marie then. At times he almost drove her clean out of her mind by pulling stunts like that. She always thought he had an image he was supposed to live up to being a banker and the big-shot in town like he was. There were times when she was mortified to death by the way he'd look when it came time for them to leave. I think she half-blamed you Hank for getting him to act like a kid again whenever they came to visit."

I then replied, "I'm sorry if Grandpa got in trouble because of me, Grandma. All I know is that he and I had one fine time together whenever they paid us a visit."

"Charlie was ready to fish at the drop of a hat and with that I mean, anyone's hat."

48

"Well your Granddad didn't always play the smartest games with you or do the most intelligent things that I've ever seen when he was playing with you. For example, do remember that dog cart the built for you that was pulled by a pair of collie dogs just so you could be in the Fourth of July parade?"

"I certainly do Grandma. That was some of the best fun that I ever had in my life. I bet we went up and down the street a hundred times with that old cart. It was nothing for a kid to have a pony cart, but a dog cart? We were the envy of every kid in town with that cart."

"That's right, you certainly were Hank, but do you also remember what happened with you and that cart during the big parade?"

"I can't say that I do Grandma. I'm afraid that it all happened so fast that the memory of it didn't have a whole lot of time to become etched in my brain. It's all like a big blur to me now. I'm afraid time has faded it from my memory."

"Did you just say the word "afraid" to me? You have no idea whatsoever what the word afraid means unless you were standing on the curb next to your mother and I during that parade Hank McCracken, which of course you weren't. Instead of that, you were the one out there on the street causing the whole ruckus and being the center of attention."

Of course Wally couldn't leave a sleeping dog lie. "What happened during the parade Mrs. Jennings."

"Well as long as you asked I'll tell you what happened. Some idiot in charge of the parade thought it was a good idea to put all of the animals towards the back of the parade so that the marchers wouldn't have to be walking in a bunch of "you know what." That was just fine and dandy except that they didn't take into consideration what might happen if things went wrong with the arrangement, which of course they did."

"Hank was at the very end of the parade with his two "finely-trained" collies when the two of them had the notion to find out what made the elephants up ahead tick. They started going faster in order to catch up to the elephants so they could get a closer look at them. The faster the dogs moved and the more they gained on the elephants, the faster the elephants went."

"They kept this up until pretty soon the dogs were stretched flat out going as tight as they could and the elephants were at a full gallop, if that's what you call it when elephants are running as fast as they can go. Hank was in the wagon swaying side to side, gripping the sides of the wagon that his poor little knuckles turned white and screaming at the top of his lungs while the elephants had people running as fast as they could in every direction trying to get out of their way. The only thing that saved Hank from getting crushed to death by an elephant was having the wagon turn over sideways so the dogs couldn't pull it anymore."

" Hank landed face first in a pile of elephant "doo doo" and then he made me, not his mother mind you, hold his hand all the way back home. I'll never forget that day as long as I live."

Wally spoke up, "Give us a big smile Hank." "We want to see if you still have some of that elephant between your teeth."

By then the guys were down on their knees laughing so hard they had tears streaming down their cheeks. I didn't think it all that funny.

When things settled down a little Wally said, "I sure wish that I'd of had a Granddad like that." " Then again on second thought, maybe not."

"For sheer entertainment, Barnum and Bailey should have hired you and your dog cart to travel around the countryside with them."

Charles R. McCracken 1831-1919

"Charlie and his cronies could well afford to stay in the finest hotels around but instead of living in comfort, they would set up and stay in some of the seediest camps you could ever imagine."

"Granddad Charlie was the picture of success no matter where he went or what he did."

Grandma continued with her story. "Whatever your Great-Granddad Silas did wrong, it seems like your Granddad Charlie did right. When he left home he didn't head off for the mountains on some pipedream, instead of that he headed off to the city where the real money was, bound and determined that he wasn't going end up with nothing which was the direction that old Silas was headed for."

"Your Granddad Charlie started out as a teller in a bank and then kept working himself up the ladder until he eventually was some sort of a big shot in the bank. Once he reached that level, he could pretty much do as he pleased, which is what he did mind you. If he wanted to go somewhere or decided to do something, he did it. He not only had the money to do it with but he could also make the time to do it."

"Whatever hunting and fishing that your Great-Granddad Silas felt that he'd missed out on in life, your Granddad Charlie more than made up for. Charlie and a group of his business associates hunted and fished all over the country. They even made their way up to Canada a few times as if the hunting wasn't good enough here in the states."

"They certainly could have afforded to stay in the best of places there were around but instead of that they liked to set up camp somewhere or rent some of the most lowdown places to stay in that you could ever imagine. Maybe they felt that they had the finest day in and day out and didn't need it when they went off to relax."

Wonzal could come up with some of the stupidest things you'd ever want to hear, and some you didn't.

"I never felt before that you were any better off than the rest of us Hank, but this has got me thinking. Your Granddad must have left you a whole pile of money 'cause we stay in some of the seediest places on the face of the Earth whenever we go hunting."

I didn't even bother to respond to that one. It wouldn't have been worth my time.

"On many of their trips they would pack in with little more than their cooking utensils and their bedroll. They'd set up camp with what ever they could scrounge up."

"It seemed as though the simpler the camp was, the more the men enjoyed staying in it. Brush shelters were one of their favorites. They were quick and easy to prepare and they were warm and cozy."

52

"Your Granddad loved this old camp. He'd hunt or fish out of that fallen down relic anytime he could."

"Here are some photos of the trout they used to catch. They'd usually throw ten dollars apiece in a pot and have a fishing contest between them. I'd have to think that your Granddad won more than he lost 'cause he was one good trout fisherman."

"This was one of those fishing trips when the trout were biting faster than they could fry them up and devour them. They had to quit fishing for two days so so they could catch up before the trout spoiled."

"This particular shelter served Charlie's bunch for many a deer season."

"More lasting memories were made in a place like this than anywhere else."

"This was one of their more elaborate fishing camps. When they set up a camp like this it usually meant that they'd be there for eight or ten days."

"Many business deals were made in a camp like this."

Photo Courtesy of Greg Gaar, San Francisco, CA

"Your Granddad and his cronies had a special place in their hearts for their kids and grandkids. They made a special trip up to camp just to retrieve an old rag doll that had been packed in one of their bags as a prank."

"They just threw it aside and forgot about it until they got home and had to face a very heart-broken child."

"Your Granddad ran into some very unique individuals on his travels as you can see here. He said that this particular group provided him with some of the best belly-laughs he ever had in his entire life."

"Your Granddad Charlie was always game when it came to a little adventure. Shortly after this photo was taken they got mired down so bad that they spent the rest of the day digging themselves out and never even got to wet a line."

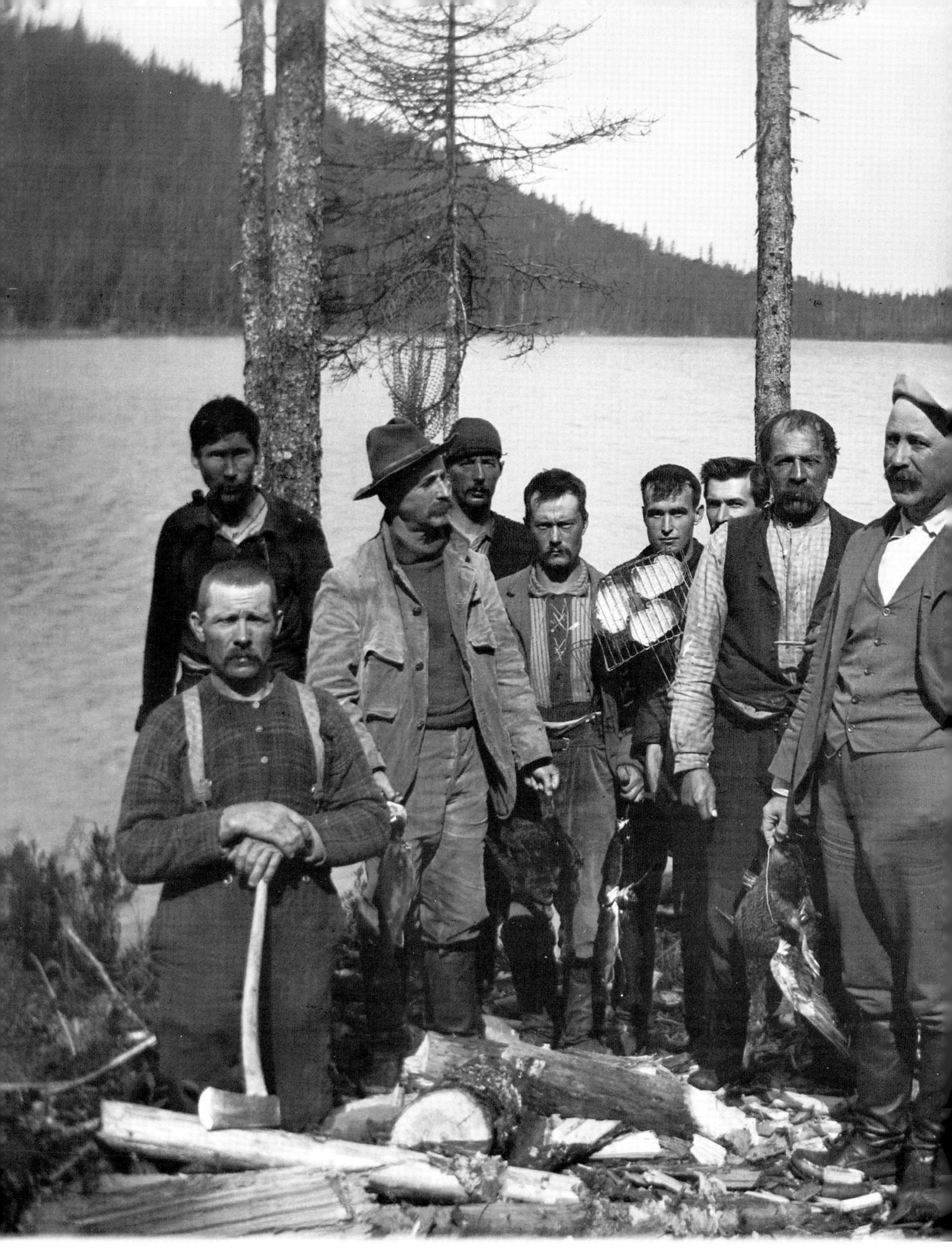

"This is a photo of the fishing guides that they used to hire whenever they went musky fishing up in the northeast part of the state near Rhinelander, Three Lakes, Boulder Junction, and Minocqua. I know that they caught some good sized muskies whenever they went up there. Of course they always came back telling about the big ones that got away."

"Charlie and his bunch spent more money hiring guides for their hunting and fishing trips in a year's time than many folks made in a years time but to them they always felt that it was money well spent."

"They didn't seem to care what kind of fish they went after as long as it would give them a good tussle. They caught some of the finest trout, musky, and pike that there were around."

"Your Granddad learned a tough lesson with this musky. He always told around when he'd raise a musky or have a follow. These fellows not only listened to every word he said, but followed your Granddad's directions to the tee. Your Granddad kept his mouth closed after this."

"Wilmar would have lost this musky for sure if he'd have been fishing alone. When he tried to net it by himself, he couldn't bend over far enough to get the net under the fish."

"Those who could afford it often had a painting done of their catch instead of being satisfied with a plain photograph."

"Menfolk used to get together a couple of times a year and have a catfishing contest. If you ask me, it was more of a contest to see who could come up with the foulest smelling bait."

"Everybody back then used to use ripe chicken guts. Your Granddad had to go one better than that. He used the innards out of the muskrats he caught after they'd cured in the sun. The smell definitely attracted catfish but he had all he could do to put his bait on the hook."

*"Your Granddad did everything he could possibly think of to avoid fishing anywhere near this man.
He was afraid of getting his eye shot out if the threads ever let loose on one of the guy's buttons."*

"Kids had to come up with their own entertainment back in those days so many of them turned to fishing. They were as bad as the men when it came to bragging and showing off."

"The kids headed to the nearest lake or pond the day school got out. They'd spend the entire day out fishing but at least they weren't getting themselves in trouble."

"A picture-taking session gave a man the chance to show off not only what he'd caught but every thing he used to make the catch. This is a prime example. That little musky fell victim to a shot between the eyes."

"I hate to admit it but when it came to fishing, it wasn't beyond a woman to do her share of bragging when the opportunity presented itself. Fortunately for them they did seem to know the secret as to just how far they could push a man before they wouldn't be asked to tag along the next time he went fishing."

"Women enjoyed getting out for a little quiet time and a chance to enjoy the outdoors every bit as much as men did."

"Sunday was often a day set aside to pack a picnic lunch and spend some time on a lake or a near-by trout stream with friends and neighbors. There weren't a great many things for them to do in an afternoon and still make it back in time for milking."

"There is a certain peace and solitude that one can find only on a quiet body of water. Most all of us can use a little of that every once in a while."

The Ice Fishing Trips

"Many times the men would haul a crudely-built ice shack out on the lake once they found a good spot to fish. With a small wood stove they could sit and fish in their shirt sleeves."

"Your Grandfather found that anything that would provide some shelter from the wind was enough to keep him warm."

"That dilapidated old shack that I said your Granddad loved so much? One of the reasons he favored that place was because of the lake that it was on. He and his cronies would head up there and go ice fishing in the middle of the winter mind you. I can't begin to imagine what fun it would be to chop a hole in the ice and then sit there all day long freezing to death and waiting for a fish to bite. It's completely beyond me."

"Northern pike was one of the most sought after fish there was. There was an abundance of them, they'd hit on most everything dropped in the water, and the action was fast and furious. Best of all, they went down good fried fresh or pickled. As you can tell by this photo, most groups weren't any to picky about the size of their catch, especially if they had their children with them. The more action the kids had, the more they wanted to go along the next time."

"They say that trapping runs in the blood and that may very well be true because your Grandpa Charlie loved to trap almost as much as his dad did."

" Of course he wasn't near as good at it as his dad was 'cause he didn't get started trapping on his own until he was practically middle-aged and he had to pick up what he could on his own."

"It was one thing for him to go off catching muskrats and mink but that must not have been exciting enough for him. He and his cronies got together one Fall up in one of those old cabins that they used and stumbled across an old bear trap that someone had stuck up between the purlins. For some fool reason, they decided that they were going to set traps for a bear that had been hanging around the place. Your Granddad would never admit it to me, me being a Baptist and a teetotaler like I am and all, but I've always suspected that the bear trapping idea may have been the result of a little tippling of some spirits among him and his cronies. What else would drive sane men to try something as insane as that?"

We just looked at each other and didn't say a word, one way or the other.

"The first thing they caught was the heel on Doc Prichard's new boot and it ripped the heel clean off. He had to walk around with one heel on and one heel off for the better part of a week. On the third night they finally did catch themselves a bear and then they didn't know what they should do with it once they had one. Nobody dared take it home because their wife would have known for certain they'd been drinking. At least that's what I figured."

Again, we just exchanged glances between ourselves and kept out mouths shut. That included Wonzal.

Charlie, the Trapper

"Trapping not only offers a person the opportunity for a little solitude,
but the challenge of outwitting one of the denizens on it's own turf."

"Finding the tunnels of a bank beaver was the most difficult part of river trapping but this German Shepherd had an uncanny knack for locating them as it walked along the bank. Few if any of them ever got past him."

"There was a great deal of work involved in the running of a trapline so most trappers wanted a picture taken of them with the proof of their success so they could remember the good years they had on the line."

"A twenty-two would dispatch a muskrat or mink with ease as long as the fur buyer was willing to ignore a little hole in the pelt."

"Your Granddad and his bunch of cronies found an old bear trap tucked away in the rafters of an old shack so of course they had to find out how well it worked."

"The group found out that the most difficult part about trapping bear was trying to get the trap set without one of them losing an arm or a leg in the thing. Getting a bear to walk into it once it was set was no big trick. The problem was, no one knew what to do with it once they'd caught one."

"No one insisted that they be the one to skin out the bear. As a matter of fact, the group drew straws to decide which one of them had to perform the duty."

"When it came to hunting bear, a good pack of hounds was hard to beat."

"Every so often a bear would be taken when it made the mistake of walking past a deer hunter who was on stand."

"Occasionally an ornery old bear found it easier to satis[fy] it's hunger by dining on a farmer's tame sheep rather than forage around in the woods. "Old Three-Toes" was [a] prime example. Three-Toes got himself pinched by a tra[p] once so he learned to avoid any trap set for him in no ti[me] flat. He also knew how to outwit any dog ever put on h[is] trail. When a dog was stupid enough to get within his reach, old Three-toes was more than happy to send it t[o] Hound Heaven. He earned quite a reputation as he terrorized the countryside for several years."

"This is what happens when a group of men have entirely to muc[h] time on their hands. They were, without a doubt, one of the first groups to practice catch and release. However, Doc Prichard foun[d] out that not all bears appreciated being confined in their blooming contraption. He had to stitch up a nasty bite on his own rearend when no one else in the group was willing to do it for him."

"A nice mix of fur. 1910."

"It was well worth the time to remove the pelt right out on the trap line rather than lug the entire carcass for several miles. Such was the case of the bobcat shown here."

"A line shack gave the trapper a place to get out of the weather and to tend to his day's catch."

"A dog not only made a good companion when out on a trapline, but also offered another set of eyes and a nose to warn the trapper of any danger."

"A good catch of canines."

"A nice catch of prime arctic fox."

"Many a good fox trapper went to his grave without revealing the secret of his success to anyone."

"A short, light, little rifle made a great addition to the trapline, especially when it came to tending to a skunk."

"There was a tremendous market for fur not only for hats, bu for stoles and coats made entirely out of fur. Not only were the warm, the fur wore well and was often the sign of very afflue people. Learning to care for a pelt in the proper manner was t difference between receiving top dollar for the hide or getting very little. A little extra time and effort was well worth it."

"Often times the caring of the fur was left up to the children of the trapper. That way he could remain on the line instead of having to stay home to skin, flesh, and stretch the pelts. It gave the kids the opportunity to learn some responsibility and to earn a little extra pocket money."

"One of the greatest sports, as far as your Granddad Charlie was concerned, was hound hunting for deer. He probably enjoyed doing that as much as anything he ever did. There wasn't much for deer around here to speak of, so he and his hunting buddies would get together every Fall and spent a couple of weeks chasing deer with their pack of hounds. They did real well at it too."

"A few of the men would leave a day or two earlier then the rest of the group. They'd gather up all the hounds, load them into crates they had on a wagon, and then take off for camp ahead the rest. Two days later the rest of the men would get on the stagecoach and take it up to the station nearest the camp. The men that had arrived earlier would pick them up at the stagecoach station and off to camp they'd go."

"Charlie ran across a couple of articles back in the seventies that he felt did a nice job of describing the way his bunch hunted. Rather than spend the time writing down all the details of how they went about their hound hunting, he just cut out the articles and put them here in the album. Perhaps he got the idea from looking at how your Granddad Silas's did it."

Hunting with Hounds

SCRIBNER'S MONTHLY.

VOL. XV.   APRIL, 1878.   No. 6.

Deer-Hunting On The Au Sable
by W. Mackay Laffan
Scribner's Monthly
Scribner & Co., New York
Vol. 15, No 6, April 1878

An invitation to a few weeks' deer-shooting in the wilds of Michigan was not to be foregone as there had been occasional rumors heard in the East of the winter sports of the Michigan backwoods.

I was to join a party of gentlemen, who for several years have hunted upon the Au Sable River in northern Michigan. We were all to meet upon an appointed day at Bay City at the head of Saginaw Bay.

The steamboat wharf at Bay City was full of bustle and activity. There were piles of baggage and numbers of anxious owners. Conspicuous among the parcels were the gun-cases, some made of new pig leather or water-proofing, and evidently out for the first time. Every object upon the wharf and about the freight office to which a dog could be tied had a dog tied to it, and all these dogs were rearing, and plunging, and tugging at their chains and giving vent to occasional sharp yells, in a condition of great excitement – a feeling more or less shared by the numerous higher animals who were present. The crowd was composed of hunting parties bound for the backwoods, of lumbermen going to the camps, of farmers going home, and of the usual variety of more or less accentuated Western types.

Our dogs, twelve in number, were safely bestowed between decks, and as remotely from the dogs of other people as possible; all our baggage was put away, and we moved off from the wharf with that sense of entire comfort that is incident only to well-ordered excursions.

A GENERAL SURPRISE.

77

We made some stoppages at points upon the shore, where seemingly unaccountable wharves projected from the outskirts of desolation. At these we took off people who might have been fugitives from some new Siberia, and debarked people who might have been exiles going thither.

At half-past eight we were cheerily hailed out of the darkness by a mighty hunter of the wilderness named Curtis, who had come down with his stout team to meet us and help to carry our multifarious traps. We disembarked amid a dreadful howling of the dogs, who charged about in every direction, dragging their masters in the darkness over all manner of calamitous obstructions, regardless of kicks, cuffs or vigorous exhortation. In half an hour we were comfortably ensconced in an inn with an enormous landlord, whose mighty girth shook with unctuous premonitions of an excellent supper. He produced half of a deer slain that very day, and gave us an earnest of our coming sport in the shape of a vast quantity of broiled venison, all of which we dutifully ate.

Our captain was Mr. John Erwin, of Cleveland, a gentleman at whose door lies the death of a grievous quantity of game of all kinds. We were under his orders the next day, and so remained until our hunt was over. He was implicitly obeyed; none of his orders were unpleasant; they simply implied the necessary discipline of the party.

We left Tawas in the early morning. We had two wagons, one of which carried nine of us, the other, Curtis's, had the heavier baggage in it, and was accompanied by the remaining three on foot. They had the option of getting into the wagon by turns, if tired, but they were all good walkers. We had twenty-five miles to make to "Thompson's," where we here to halt for the night, and on the following day proceed leisurely to Camp Erwin, six miles further.

As we left Tawas it rained, according to our nautical prophet of the previous evening, and it continued to rain during the entire day. There is nothing particularly exhilarating in driving in a drenching rain, even when it is done under particularly favorable auspices. Another dispiriting element was the road, of which a large part was what is known as "corduroy." The jolting we got over this was painful to a degree which it is disagreeable to recall. It jarred every bone in one's body, and embittered the whole aspect of life. It alternated with a series of diabolical mud-holes, into which we dived, and rocked, and swayed, and splashed interminably.

At last we emerged on a higher plateau of sand, and left the marsh behind us for good. The rain had become a milder and tolerable evil, compared to the swamp road. All was sand, but the wet made it "pack" beneath the horses' feet and the wheels, and we went over it at an excellent pace. Around us was the Michigan forest in all its wonderful variety of growth and richness, and in all its drear monotony and desolation.

The great fires that sweep across this region, leave hideous scars behind them. One sees for miles and miles the sandy plain covered with the charred trunks of the fallen forest. Great lofty pines, whose stems are blackened from the root as high as the fire has reached, huge, distorted and disfigured, stand gloomily above their moldering brethren, their white skeletons extending their dead and broken arms, in mute testimony of lost grace and beauty. Nothing could be more desolate than these "burnings," as they are called for they present an aspect of utter, hopeless dreariness , and such painful solitude beyond imagination.

The rain continued and wet us until we began to get on good terms with it. Besides, we got stirred up over the deer tracks in the sand. They were very numerous and fresh, and one or two rifles were loaded in hopes of a shot at one "on the wing." None came in sight, however, and the undergrowth and scrub-oaks effectually kept them from our view.

At half-past one, we came suddenly to the edge of a depression and there lay Thompson's. Here in the midst of the wilderness was a prosperous, healthy-looking farm, actually yielding vegetables and cereals, and having about it all manner of horses, cows, pigs, hay-stacks, barns, dogs to bark, pumpkins, and all the other established characteristics of a well-regulated farm.

We were met with a hearty welcome from Thompson, a bluff, hearty, backwoodsman, whom years of uninterrupted prosperity have made rich. He owns thousands of acres of timber-land, and his house is known far and wide as the best hotel in Michigan.

Mrs. Thompson is not exactly a backwoodswoman; indeed, she is quite as much of a surprise to one as is the place itself. She is an excellent lady, and her refining influence has been felt in a very marked degree in that wild region. She can shoot, though. Indeed, she handles a rifle with the greatest coolness and skill, — thinks nothing of knocking over a deer, and confesses to aspirations in the direction of bear.

We all sat down to a magnificent roast of venison, broiled chickens, and the most delicious of vegetables, for it seems that when one does get a bit of Michigan land which will consent to be cultivated, it turns out to be remarkably good land indeed. There were great glass pitchers of excellent milk upon the table, similar pitchers of real cream, and everything was neatly served. The table-cloth was fine and of snowy whiteness, the napkins (this in the heart of a Michigan wilderness!) ditto, and everything just as it should be, and just as one would least have expected to find it.

Thompson's hands came in the evening, — Canadians for the most part, and talking an inexplicable jargon called French.

Re-enforced by a few lumbermen and trappers, they were noisy, well-behaved, and good-humored, and they crowded around the stove and bedewed it pleasantly and copiously with infusion of Virginia plug. They spoke with loud, individual self-assertion, and there was a curious touch of defiance in every sentence that involved a direct proposition. This quality of their speech, coupled with a degree of profanity made a stranger feel as if a fight might occur at any moment, but there was no danger of anything of the kind. They only fight when the camps break up and the men are paid off. Then they congregate at the lake settlements and elsewhere, and get frightfully drunk for weeks, and shoot and stab each other liberality.

A strange thing happens to one who hunts this region for the first time. After a week of hunting, he finds himself impelled to the conclusion that he has shot the only small deer there are in the state. We could not meet a man in the country all about that had ever seen a small deer. The word fawn will soon be dropped from their language. It was always "the blankest biggest buck! blank me!" or "the blank, blankest blank of a blank of a blank doe! running like blank and blankation for the blank river!" That was all we could ever get; and when perchance one of these identical, peculiarly qualified animals happened to be shot, the speaker stood wholly unabashed and unconscious in the presence of his refutation. It must be in the climate.

We left Thompson's hospitable place the next morning after an early breakfast. Curtis and his team carried all our traps, (luggage) and after a tramp of two hours or so over the wet sand and through the desolate "burnings," we arrived at Camp Erwin.

CAMP ERWIN.

Camp Erwin is a deserted logging camp. The building on the left in the little sketch I have made is a rickety old barn; behind that it is a blacksmith's shop, and the remaining house is that in which we had our quarters. It contains, on the upper floor, one large and finely ventilated apartment; and below,

ON THE AU SABLE.

the kitchen, dining and "living" room and two small bedrooms. One of these was occupied by Mr. and Mrs. William Bamfield, the latter of whom had engaged to cook for our party, while the former, a stalwart and extraordinarily powerful backwoodsman, chopper and blacksmith, "assisted," and made himself indispensable by his general handiness and utility, his readiness to do anything and everything, his good-humor and his entire novelty.

The stream in the foreground of my drawing flows a mile away into the Au Sable (pronounced up here Sawble, the Au, too, being generally dropped), and around the house, as far as one may see, is the everlasting "burning." In summer all is dry, yellow sand; in winter, a mantle of snow sometimes covers it charitably, and conceals some of the blackness and deformity of the dead pines.

The first day in camp was devoted to unpacking our traps and provisions, filling our ticks with straw, disposing handily of our various knickknacks, overhauling the rifles, and wasting ammunition under excuse of getting one's hand in. My share being accomplished at noon, some of us started down to take a look at the Au Sable River. After a walk of fifteen minutes or so, we came out of the forest abruptly on the edge of a high sandbluff, and there it lay about one hundred and fifty feet below us. It came around a short bend above; it swept around another in front of us, and below us it wound around a third. Its waters were the color of dark-brown sherry, and its current was silent, swift and powerful. This singular river is one that knows neither droughts nor freshets, which is always cold, but never freezes, and which will always preserve its wildness and its desolation, since, in the future, the wilderness through which it flows will be even wilder and more desolate than it is now.

The first evening in camp, around the council-lamp, was spent in discussing the prospects of the morrow, in shooting over again all the deer that had been shot upon previous occasions, in comparing the target shooting of the day, and in the assignment by the captain of each man to his position on the river.

Curtis and two of our party were to "put out the dogs," and the rest were to be stationed at the different run-ways. This explains the method of hunting. The river for a certain number of miles was divided into run-ways or points at which deer, when hard pressed by the dogs, would probably take to the water and afford a chance for a shot. The dogs, twelve in number, were divided among those who were to have charge of them for the day, and they took them in various directions into the forest. When a fresh and promising track was discovered, a dog was let loose upon it, or perhaps two dogs, and the deer, after a run of greater or less duration, took to the river in order to elude pursuit. If it went in at a guarded runway, it stood an excellent chance of being shot; but, of course, a large majority of the deer driven in entered the river above or below, or crossed it shortly after reaching it.

A tick filled with straw and laid upon the floor makes an excellent bed, and sportsmen's consciences are always good, for they sleep with exceeding soundness. The ventilation of the apartment was generous in the extreme. The roof was tight, but all around were the open chinks between the logs, and through these the stars could be seen by anybody that had nothing better to do than look at them. Up through the middle of the floor and out through a big hole at the ridge-pole went the stove-pipe, always hot enough to worry an insurance man, and an excellent spot to hang wet clothes. Elsewhere it was as cold as charity, and I supplemented my blankets with my heavy frieze ulster and went asleep to dream of giant bucks and a rifle that wouldn't go off.

The Michigan forests abound in a variety of game, but the animals that are valued for their fur have been thinned out by trappers, who, in turn, have disappeared to newer hunting-fields. One still finds the beaver, marten, fisher, lynx and others. Bears are quite numerous, and there are plenty of wolves. Rabbits and Arctic hares and ruffed grouse exist in great numbers. The elk has almost wholly disappeared from the peninsula, but I heard that some were occasionally found in the extreme northern portion, and I saw a magnificent pair of antlers, having a spread of nearly six feet, which a half-breed had found imbedded in the trunk of a cedar-tree. The skin of the head and the greater portion of the skull were attached, the remainder having been torn away and scattered by wolves.

The deer of the region is the Cervus Virginianus, or common deer of America. It probably attains its greatest weight in Michigan. I learned from credible sources of bucks which weighed over two hundred and fifty pounds. Judge John Dean Caton, speaks of having killed a buck in Wisconsin that was estimated to weigh two hundred and fifty pounds, and adds that the largest common deer of which he had any authentic account was killed in Michigan and weighed, undressed, two hundred and forty-six pounds. Of the deer killed by our party, there were no less than three that weighed over two hundred and twenty-five pounds.

A tremendous uproar awoke me at the moment with Mr. B., shouting, "Breakfast! Breakfast! Turn out for breakfast! The captain's up and waiting!" It was half-past four, and everybody woke up at the summons, as was indeed unavoidable. There was a scratching of matches and a discordant chorus of those sounds which people make when they are forcibly awakened and made to get up in the cold, unusual morning. Down-stairs there was a prodigious sizzling and sputtering going on, and the light through the chinks in the floor betrayed Mrs. Bamfield and her frying-pans and coffee-pot, all in full blast.

Somebody projected his head through an immature window into the outer air and brought it in again to remark that it rained. A second observation made it rain and snow, and rain and snow it was, — a light, steady fall of both. We were all down-stairs in a few minutes and outside making a rudimentary toilet with ice-water and a bar of soap. Breakfast was ready,—plenty of rashers of bacon, fried and boiled potatoes, fried onions, bread and butter, and coffee, hot and strong.

A TALE OF LOVE, JEALOUSY AND DEATH.

These were speedily disposed of. Coats were buttoned up, rubber blankets and ammunition belts slung over shoulders, cartridge magazines filled, hatchets stuck into belts, rifles shouldered, and out we sallied into the darkness through which the faintest glimmer of gray was just showing in the east.

Half an hour or so later, by the time we had gotten to our runways, the dogs would be put out. Off we trudged over the wet, packed sand of the tote-road, the gray dawn breaking dismally through the wilderness. Leaving the road, we struck into the pines, and a walk of a mile through the thick sweet-fern, which drenched one to the waist, brought us to the edge of the cedar swamp by the river. The narrow belt of low bottomland on each side of the river is called Cedar Swamp. It is a jungle through which it is extremely difficult to progress, and in which one may very readily lose one's bearings. Great cedars grow in it up to the water's edge and as thickly as they can well stand.

Among them lie fallen trees in every stage of decay, heaped one upon another in inextricable and hopeless ruin and confusion. There are leaning cedars that have partly toppled over and rested against their stouter fellows, and there are cedars that seem to have fallen and only partly risen again. Sometimes the walking is treacherous, and the giant ferns that lie about are hollow mockeries and deceptions beneath their pretty wrapping of green. Standing upon one of these and doubtful whether to adventure a leap or more circumspectly climb to my next vantage point, I executed a sudden disappearance, much after the fashion of a harlequin in a pantomime. A hole opened beneath my feet and I shot through that hollow shell into the swamp beneath, leaving my broad-brimmed hat to cover the aperture by which I made my exit.

After a couple of hundred yards of climb, crawl, and tumble through one of these swamps, my companion took his place under the shelter of the cedars and indicated mine at a little distance up the river. It was one of the best of our runways,—a long stretch of open bank, where the cedar swamp did not reach the river's edge. I got there, took my stand, and indulged in expectation. The exertion of getting through the swamp had warmed me uncomfortably, but I soon ceased to regard that as an objection. The place was exposed; there was no shelter; the cold wind and the driving snow and rain had it all their own way with me. My hands became numb, and the metal of my rifle stung them. I did not put on my heavy gloves, lest a deer should come and they should prove an awkward impediment. I stood my rifle against a tree, stuck them in my pockets, and watched the river, while my teeth chattered like miniature castanets. The wind howled down through the trees, and clouds of yellow and russet leaves came sailing into the river and hurried away upon its surface. I was undeniably, miserably cold. But hark! I seized my rifle.

HUNG UP.

Yes, there it was, sure enough, the bay of a dog in the distance! I forgot to be cold. Nearer it came, and nearer and nearer, and each moment I thought would bring the deer crashing through the thickets into the river. Nearer and nearer the dogs came, until their deep bays resounded and echoed through the forest as if they were in a great hall. But no deer appeared, and the dogs held their course, on down, parallel with the river. "Better luck next time," I said to myself, somewhat disconsolately; but I was disappointed.

Presently the sharp, ringing crack of a rifle rang out and reverberated across the forest; another and another followed, and as I began to get cold again, I tried to console myself by meditating on the luck of other people. I stamped my feet; I did the London cabman's exercise with my hands and arms; I drew beads on all manner of objects; but steadfastly I watched the river, and steadfastly I listened for the dogs. The snow and rain abated, and the hours went by; and stiff, and chilled was I when, at half-past twelve, young Curtis's canoe came poling up the river to pick up deer if any had been shot above and had lodged in the drift-wood, instead of floating down to his watching-place, three miles below. The dogs were all in, he said, and the doctor had shot a big buck and a fawn.

At camp the doctor was the center of an animated circle. He was most unreasonably composed, as I thought, and told us, with his German equanimity, how Jack and Pedro had run in a large buck which immediately swam down the middle of the river. He fired from his place on the side of a bluff and missed. At the second shot he succeeded in hitting the deer in the neck just below the mastoid something or other. As if this were not sufficient, there presently appeared and crossed the river a very pretty fawn, whose young hopes were promptly blighted. They said it was not always that the first day yielded even one deer, and it was an excellent augury. During the afternoon, Curtis brought both deer up to camp and dressed them. The buck was finely antlered, and was estimated to weigh over two hundred pounds.

The next day I was appointed to the same runway, and I took my stand and, acting on the advice of others, built a brave little fire. Deer being driven into the river or swimming down it pay no attention to a small fire, and the making of it and the keeping it alive furnish excellent occupation. Indeed, there is something quite fascinating about building a fire in the woods, and it is quite inexplicable what a deep concern all the little details of its combustion create in even really thoughtful minds. My fire burned cheerily and blew lots of sharp smoke into my eyes, with the aid of the fitful wind; but I was not called upon to shoot any deer. I did not even hear the dogs, and at two o'clock I went home to camp persuaded that I had not yet learned to appreciate our style of hunting. Our captain had a handsome young buck and was in a wholly comfortable frame of mind.

We had a larded saddle of venison during the afternoon for dinner. It was flanked by a dish of steaming bacon and cabbage, and quantities of mealy potatoes and fried onions. The fragrance that filled the air of the cabin surpassed the most delicate of vapors that ever escaped from one of Delmonico's covers and we fell upon the table with appetites like that of the gifted ostrich. The air of the Sable would be worth any amount of money in New York.

The next day I passed in a meditative fashion on my runway. I was not disturbed by any deer, but Mr. M. and Mr. B. each scored one. The next evening, one of the dogs, footsore and worn out, remained in the woods. His master and one other sallied out into the inky darkness to look for him at points near which they deemed it probable he would have lain down. They took a lantern, without which it would have been impossible to walk, and after a fruitless search, extending to a distance of three miles or so, turned back. Suddenly they heard light footfalls in the tote-road, and with two or three beautiful bounds, a young doe alighted within the circle illuminated by the lantern, approached it in wide-eyed wonder and almost touched it with her nose. A young spike-horn buck followed her and both stared at the light, their nostrils dilated and quivering, and every limb trembling with mingled excitement and fear. There was an exclamation that could not be suppressed, a vain effort to shoot, and the deer were gone like a flash into the darkness. It was curious to hear both gentlemen, on returning to camp, protesting that to have shot deer under such circumstances would have been wholly unsportsmanlike.

It was upon my sixth day, when a dozen deer were hanging in the barn and I, quite guiltless of the death of even one of them, had gone to the river. The hours passed tediously up to noon, when I heard a splash and saw a deer take the water 300 yards or so above me. She was a large doe, and came down the middle of the river swimming rapidly, and looking anxiously from side to side. I felt unutterable things, and just as she got abreast of me I brought up my

Winchester and fired. She sank, coming up again some little distance down, and floated quietly away out of my sight around the bend. This performance produced a sense of pleasant inflation. All my fears were dispelled and I felt a keen desire for the presence of others to whom to impart the agreeable fact. It was one of those things about which one always feels as if he could not, unaided, sufficiently gloat upon it. At half-past twelve, the canoe came around the bend, and I prepared to be indifferent, as should become a person who could shoot deer every day if only he were so minded. Strange, I thought, that the legs do not project over the side of the canoe, and how is it that—At this moment the canoe gave a lurch, and I saw young Curtis's coat with painful distinctness lying in the bottom if it,—nothing else. I immediately inferred that he had missed the deer among some drift-logs as he came up. He protested he had not, but agreed to go back and search. I went with him and just a few yards around the bend we found in the oozy bank tracks which indicated that the animal had fallen to its knees in leaving the water, and up the bank to the top a trail marked with blood. The remarks of Mr. Curtis, though fluent and vigorous, were inadequate to the occasion. I was in a condition of unbounded exasperation. For

A CLEAN SHOT.

ON THE RUNWAY.

A TORCH OF THE AU SABLE.

a little distance through the grass and the bushes the marks could be seem plainly enough, but there they disappeared and that was the last I saw of my deer. The captain put two dogs out on the trail that afternoon, but the wounded animal had probably died in some dense thicket, for they soon returned without having run any great distance. Four fine deer were killed the next day, without any participation upon my part, and in the evening some of us with lanterns went down to the river to secure one that had lodged somewhere in the drift-wood. We found it by the light of the birch-bark. As we made our way along the bank, our backwoodsman would pick out here and there a large white birch and apply a match to the curling ringlets of bark at the foot of its trunk. In a minute the whole stem of the tree was in a roaring blaze that lit up the river bank all round about and made the great cedars look like gigantic skeletons. Each birch was a brilliant spectacle, while it burned in a crackling, sparkling column of flame, sending showers of sparks through the forest and then dying out in an angry red, and a cloud of murky smoke. Our deer was found, dressed, and hung up on a dead cedar, out of the reach of predatory animals, and we went home to camp by the light of our lanterns.

Next morning I was at my place, still unsubdued and hopeful. I heard a shot fired on the river below me; I heard the baying of the dogs and listened to it as it died away in the direction of some other runway. But I watched steadily. And as I watched I saw the brush about some cedar roots open, and out there sprang into the shallow water a noble buck. He was a stalwart, thickset fellow, his legs were short and compact, his fur was dark in its winter hue, and his antlers glistened above his head. He bore himself proudly as he stood in the water and turned to listen for the bay of the dogs he had out-run. I hesitated a moment, doubtful if I should let him get into the stream and swim down, or shoot at him as he stood. I chose the latter, aimed quietly and confidently, and fired. He pitched forward; the current seized him, and he floated down with it and past me, dead. In eight minutes, by my watch, Mr. M.'s "Jack" came to the bank, at the spot where the buck had come in and howled grievously over the lost scent. He was worn out and battered, and he came to me gladly when I called him. I had brought some luncheon down with me that morning, and I must confess that I was weak enough to give Jack every bit of it.

That afternoon when I reached camp, I found that I was the last to come in, and that my buck had already been seen and his size noted. I was received with acclamations, and a proposition to gird me, as a measure of affected precaution, with the hoops of a flour-barrel, was made and partly carried into execution. There were sung, moreover, sundry snatches of the forester's chorus from "As you Like It:"

"What shall he have that killed the deer?"

Of the Au Sable as a navigable river, I am pained to state that I cannot speak in a way calculated to allure people thither for the purpose of sailing upon it. Three of us were induced by our backwoodsman to embark upon a raft and make a run of fifteen miles to Thompson's. We did so, and failed to acquire upon the journey any marked prejudice in favor of that particular form of navigation.

THE BEAUTIES OF RAFTING.

Cedars growing at the water's edge have their roots more or less undermined, and some of them fall gradually outward over the river, their branches hanging in the current and becoming denuded of their foliage or dying. The trunk or stem of the tree is in some cases parallel with the water's surface, and in others it dips below it or inclines gradually upward from it. These trees have been named, with a nice sense of the fitness of terms, "sweepers." We found them such. Our raft was guided by poles, one aft and the other forward. A vigorous use of these might have had something to do with determining the course of the craft, but one was dropped and another broken, and she forthwith proceeded to work her sweet will of us. She seemed possessed of a mischievous intelligence, and if an obstruction came in view, made directly for it. There was generally room for her to pass beneath a "sweeper," which she always did; but it was different with the passengers, who, with a couple of unhappy dogs, were rasped from one end of her to the other, sometimes into the water, and sometimes only half into it, but always holding on to the logs with grim desperation. It was only by a united effort that the runaway was ultimately turned into the fence, so to speak, and held there long enough for us to jump off.

When the day arrived for breaking up camp, we had hung up in our barn twenty-three deer, my buck being accorded the place of honor at the head of the line. Our dogs were in, looking, it is true, rather the worse for wear, but all there, which is something unusual at the end of a hunt in this part of the country. The fact is, the natives discourage hunting with dogs, if not, indeed, all hunting in which they themselves do not participate. They place meat which contains strychnine on the deer-paths, and also, when occasion offers, shoot the dogs. A party of gentlemen from Bay City came into our neighborhood, a few days later than we did. They contemplated a three-weeks' hunt, but during the first three days had two dogs shot and three poisoned. They were discouraged, and left, their leader, Colonel Fitzhugh, offering three hundred dollars reward to any one who should afford him a few minutes' conversation with the individual that had done the mischief. Colonel Fitzhugh is a gentleman with whom a conversation of the kind would be preferable for being conducted vicariously. Some years ago a party of Ohio people lost their dogs in the same way, and unluckily for the active toxicologist, they found out who he was. When I passed that way he had rebuilt his barns and various out-buildings, and it was thought that until the region commanded the services of a reliable insurance company he would abstain from the use of strychnine. The immunity our party enjoyed had been gained somewhat as an ancient proprietary right, they having hunted there for so many years. Besides, they had in various ways rendered themselves popular with the natives; no visitor ever left the camp hungry—or thirsty, and the Herr Doctor's periodicity was a matter of importance to a widely spread, if not numerous, community. They saved up fractures of six months' standing for him, and events of a more strictly domestic nature seemed to happen adventitiously during his hunting sojourn.

We brought out our venison safely and in good condition,—a ton and a half of it or thereabouts. At Detroit we went our ways, ending an expedition which had in it, luckily, no mishaps to mar it, but plenty of wholesome recreation to make one's recollection of it wholly pleasant.

A TON AND A HALF OF VENISON.

We Lit Out After Them

Departure from Home

"Taking the stagecoach proved to be the most efficient way for the men to get themselves and all of their gear to the general area that they were going to be hunting. Once they arrived, a pair of hired teamsters would be waiting to take them the rest of the way into the woods."

"The men were never satisfied unless they were a considerable distance off of the beaten path. Their chosen destination would always be somewhere that few others ever traveled."

"It didn't take long for nature to try and reclaim the grounds around the cabin. Each year, shortly after they arrived in camp, the men arranged themselves shoulder to shoulder and tramped down the entire area before they settled in. It was much like lumberjacks did if they needed to open up a new skidding trail in deep snow. It didn't take long for them to show nature who the boss was, at least for a little while."

"Once camp was set up, both the men and the hounds grew increasingly anxious as they anticipated the excitement that was about to be theirs."

Assignments are Made

"The men divided themselves into two groups and then chose a group leader for the hunt."

"The standers prepared themselves mentally whatever might con... crashing of the brush."

"Every stander had their own favorite stand they wanted to be on when the hunt started in the morning."

"Doc Prichard's favorite stand overlooked a runway that skirted the shoreline of the lake. Doc figured that any deer worth taking realized it was a whole lot faster running around the edge of the lake rather than swim across the lake only to have the entire pack waiting for them when they reached the opposite shore."

"This particular bend of the river was the favorite crossing for every deer in the area. It was a natural stand and every year it produced well for the group. The men went to great lengths to find themselves the most advantageous position for a shot even at the risk of a chilly dunking in the cool waters of the river."

"Any man who owned a well-trained pack of hounds deserved all of the praise he heard."

"Once they arrived in camp it was pretty much all business according to your Granddad.

First the men chose a group they wanted to hunt with. The group leaders would draw straws to see whether their group would be standers or hound men running the pack the first day out. (After that they would alternate between standing or running the hounds every other day.)

The group of standers would decide among themselves which stand they'd be on in the morning.

Then it was early to bed and early to rise."

88

Getting the Hounds to the Hunt

"On very rare occasions, the group was treated to a brief background of snow that gave all who were involved in the hunt an extreme advantage, except the deer."

"After the deer had been pursued a few times, they often sought refuge on one of the large islands in the area. A boat was then used to transport men and hounds to the hunt. Each boat could handle three men and a pair of hounds with ease."

"A lead hound like Dusky was well worth his weight in gold."

"Trying to get a pack of hounds back into the woods be turning them loose had to be a trick in itself. Charlie said that was the only time that ten dogs could take off in fifteen different directions at the same time. At times it must have been nothing short of pure chaos."

"Success not only depended on a good pack of hounds but on having a master hound man. When a good master hound man barked an order, not only did he have the attention of the hounds, but of every man within earshot."

Success is Ours

"Hunting deer with hounds wasn't all fun. The work started after the horn sounded that signaled the end of the hunt. It depended a lot on the weather but most of the hunts started in the early morning and ended around noon. They didn't want the hounds running in the heat of the day, it would take most of the afternoon to get the hounds rounded up again, there were deer to get back to camp, and no one wanted to get lost in the dark trying to make their way back to camp."

"Once the hunt was over, the houndmen had the responsibility of rounding up the hounds and getting them back to camp. The standers were responsible for getting the deer dressed out and hauled back to camp. Neither one of the jobs was an easy task."

92

"There were those rare occasions when the men, hounds, and their quarry had to make the trip back to camp together, as seen in this photograph."

93

"Old hunters and old hounds often tuckered out at the same time."

"In a case like this, both man and hound appeared to have a mutual understanding that neither of them should make a sudden move."

Dinner Time

"A big part of any hunting or fishing camp was eating. Charlie said there wasn't a soul alive that could keep from asking the cook what they'd be having for supper or could walk past a pot cooking on the stove without lifting the cover and taking a good whiff. Your Granddad Charlie's camp was no different."

"Black powder did a number on the finest of rifles. A conscientious hunter would clean his rifle before he ever thought of sitting down to eat."

"A cup of coffee helps top off a belly-full of beans and venison steak."

*"Who can argue with success.?
This photo says it all."*

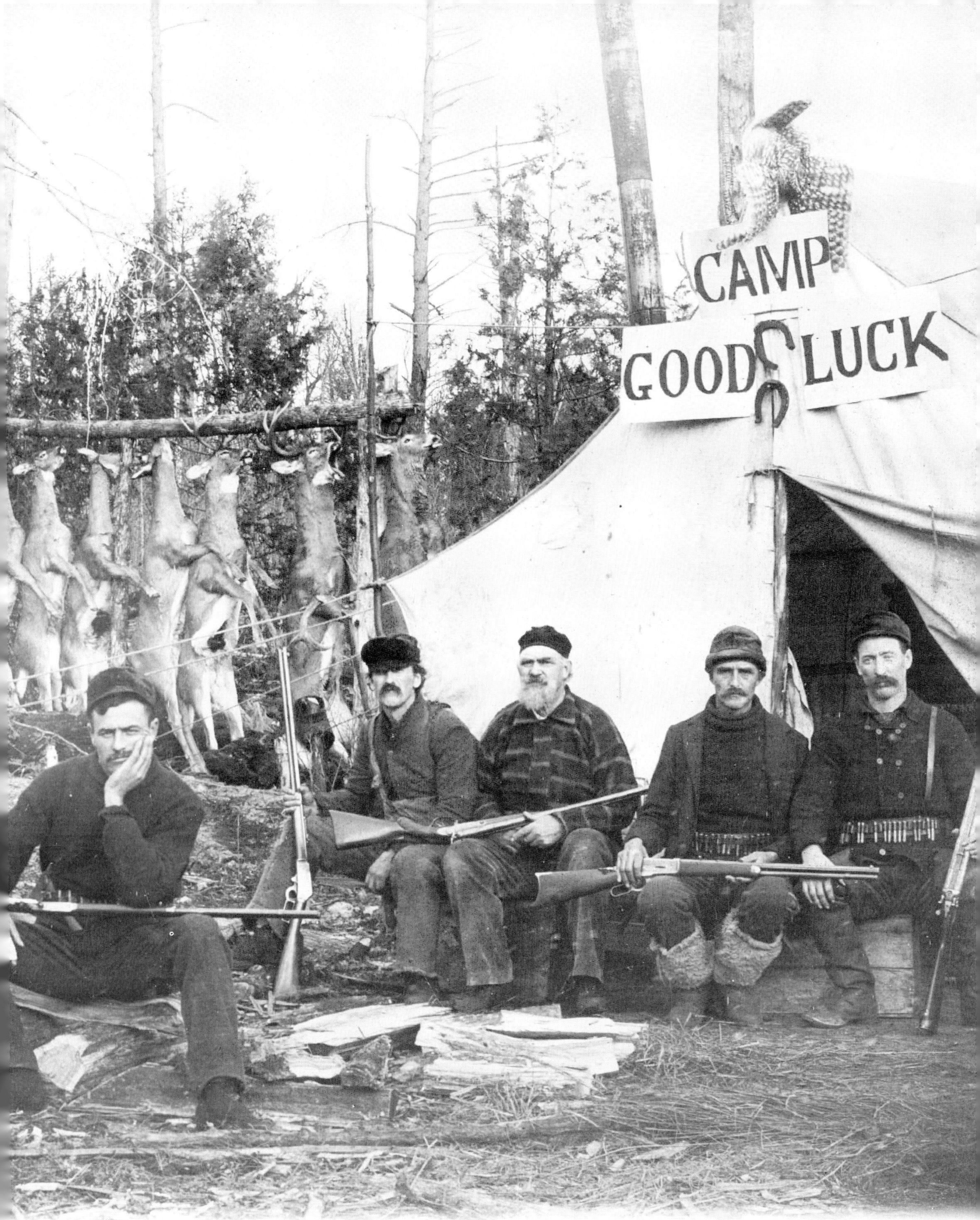
CAMP
GOOD LUCK

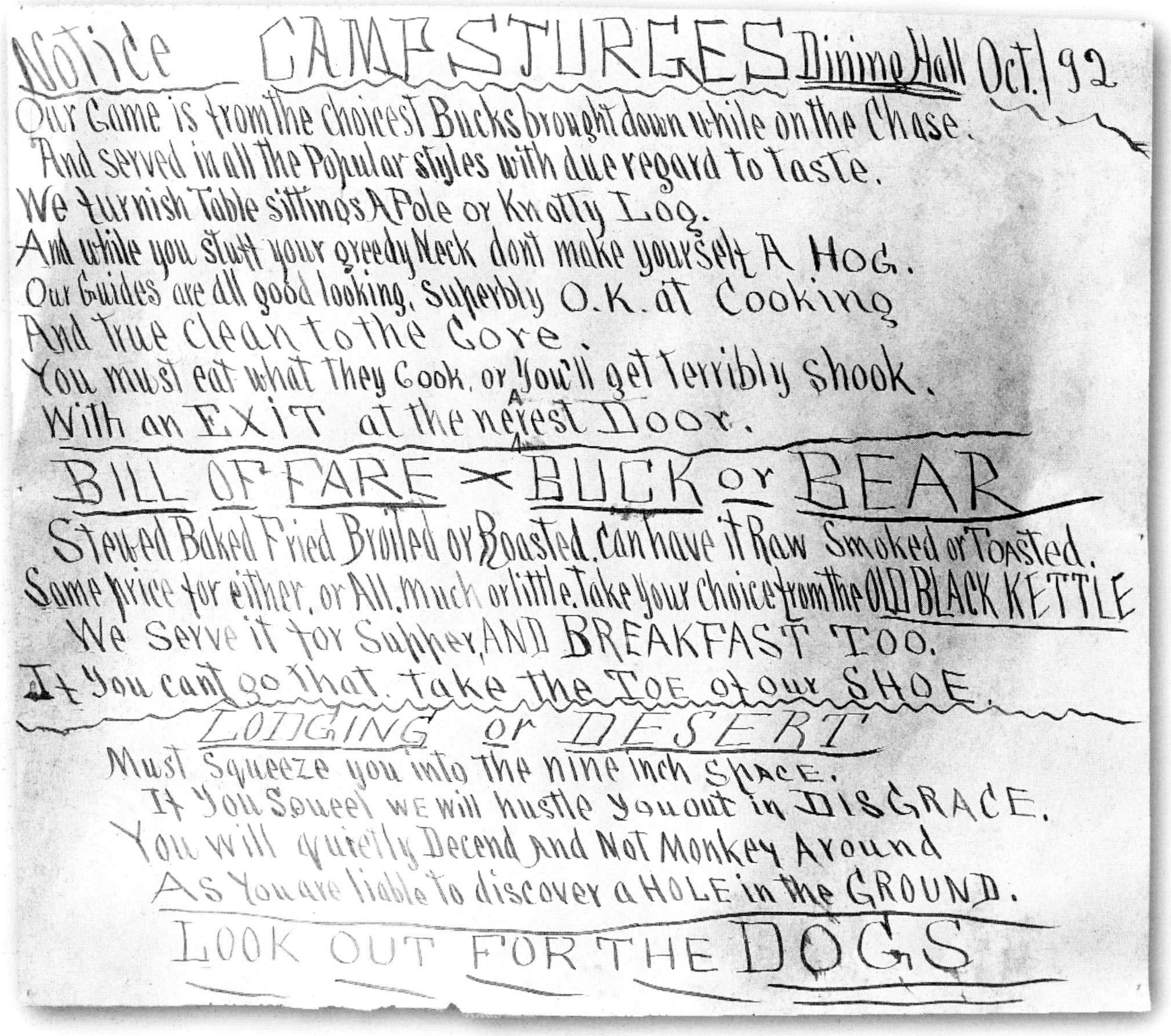

Notice — CAMP STURGES Dining Hall Oct./92

Our Game is from the choicest Bucks brought down while on the Chase.
And served in all the Popular styles with due regard to taste.
We furnish Table sittings A Pole or Knotty Log.
And while you Stuff your greedy Neck don't make yourself A Hog.
Our Guides are all good looking, Superbly O.K. at Cooking
And True clean to the Core.
You must eat what They Cook, or You'll get Terribly Shook.
With an EXIT at the nearest Door.

BILL OF FARE × BUCK or BEAR

Stewed Baked Fried Broiled or Roasted. Can have it Raw Smoked or Toasted.
Same price for either, or All. Much or little. Take your choice from the OLD BLACK KETTLE
We Serve it for Supper, AND BREAKFAST TOO.
If You can't go that, take the TOE of our SHOE.

LODGING or DESERT

Must Squeeze you into the nine inch Space.
If You Squeel we will hustle you out in DISGRACE.
You will quietly Decend and Not Monkey Around
As You are liable to discover a HOLE in the GROUND.

LOOK OUT FOR THE DOGS

"One year the camp cook got so tired of answering the same old questions twenty times a day that one year he made up a menu and hung it on the wall of the cook tent. The menu seemed to answer most of the questions that were being asked."

"Besides making a journal, the men tried to take a photograph at the end of a hunt as a means of recording what had been taken. Unfortunately, this was often a difficult thing to accomplish.
All too often it would be nearly dark by the time the men and hounds made their way back to camp, it was quite difficult to get a group of tired men and hounds to sit still long enough to take a picture, or the weather might not want to cooperate with them. The group would record each hunt by writing a description of each day's activities, the location of every kill, and the overall success for each hunt in a journal. A quick glance at the journal made it quite obvious which of the stands were the most productive."

"The group didn't restrict themselves to just taking deer. The raccoon population was reduced considerably by the time the group closed up camp."

"While in camp, the men ate the choice cuts and the hounds were fed the scraps. By the look on their faces, neither group was dissatisfied with such an arrangement."

"A good day's take."

"A proud moment for this hunter and a member of the pack."

Arriving Back Home

"It seemed like half of the townsfolk turned out on the day that the stage brought the hunters back. The children would climb aboard to see what the coach was like and then they'd argue over who's dad or grandpa had gotten the biggest buck. The wives could be heard asking, "What are we going to do with all the meat?" and then they'd say "You're going to spent an hour in the tub tonight before you even think about going to bed," and the sight of the hounds sent all the cats in town headed for the nearest cover. It was all quite a big to-do."

Our Hunts by Canoe

Credit - Roland Reed

"I have to believe that your Grandpa Charlie got the idea to hunt deer from a canoe by talking to some of the old Indians who used the practice. They were extremely successful hunting deer by canoe. Both would keep watch for a deer standing or bedded down on the river bank and then the man with the paddle would move the canoe closer in for the shot."

"He also read many of the same old magazines that his father had. He found this next old print in a book of Currier and Ives paintings. Those two fellows preserved a great deal of our countries history in the paintings that they did.

"Early explorers who travelled the riverways hunted deer from a canoe from the very beginning. Canoe hunting was without a doubt the most productive way to get a deer in many areas, particularly in light of the fact that there were very few roads to travel by.

"Currier and Ives did a number of color paintings which portray the sport of deer hunting. The paintings were used as framed prints and calendar heads for many years."

"There were others who carried on practices back then that your Grandfather would have no part of for he was a man that believed in fair chase Some thought nothing of shooting a deer when it was helpless as it swam in deep water despite the fact that it had no way to escape."

"Another practice used by some of those so-called "hunters" was jack-lighting. That method bothered your Granddad probably as bad as anything ever would. The men would slip into a canoe in the dark of the night and then drift in the current or use their paddle as little as needed. They carried with them a pine-pitch torch and they'd watch for the refection of an animal's eyes as it stood in the water staring at them. Then they'd shoot the blinded animal and return bragging about what they'd taken. That practice bothered your Granddad more than anything else."

"The areas that your Granddad and his bunch hunted were quite remote so there were few stretches of the river they could put into and get picked up again at the end of the hunt because of the lack of roads and bridges. Because of this they would have to hunt the same stretch several times in a season so they'd never float the same stretch of river two days running. They always gave a stretch a couple of day's rest so as not to rile up the deer too bad.

"More often than not, the easiest part of the hunt was the downing of the deer. The most difficult part of the hunt began when it was time to get the deer back to camp."

The exciting part of such a hunt was that they never knew what would be standing around the bend. There were times that they never saw a solitary deer and the other times when they'd drop all that they dared carry in the canoe and have to pass up several before the float ended."

"Crossing large bodies of water in a fully loaded canoe was a normal part of the hunt so the hunters took it in stride. According to most of your Grandfather's group, the adventure of such an undertaking was well worth the risk."

106

"Of all the things that bunch of your Granddad's would hunt or of all the ways they went about their hunting, Doc Prichard's favorite way to hunt was by canoe.

He said that nothing he ever found could duplicate the quiet and solitude that they enjoyed as the floated quietly down a river."

"Whether anything was bagged or not, Doc always let it be known that any float trip he ever took down the river was always "A OKAY" in his book."

"The boys took whatever game they wanted to back in those days but they also made use of everything they shot."

When Brown was Down
The Ways we got 'em Back

"Snowshoes were a great thing for the men to use in order to get back in where the deer were. Trying to wear them on the way out when dragging a deer was an open invitation to a face full of snow when their feet got tangled up."

"Snow proved to be a real boon when it came to getting a large deer out of the woods. Charlie always knew when he had a better than average buck by the number of times he had to stop for a breather on the way back to camp."

"Your Granddad's bunch and several other gangs came up with a number of ingenious ways to get their deer back to camp once they had them down. The method they used would depend on several things; whether they were alone or had help, if there was snow on the ground, the lay of the land they were hunting, and so forth."

"If there was a good layer of snow they might decide to just drag them back by themselves."

"If there's wasn't enough snow cover to drag 'em on, they might decide to carry them in. Your Granddad told me that the toughest part of carrying a deer was always trying to get them up and balanced. Once they managed to do that, it was usually far easier for them to carry the deer back to camp than it was to drag them in."

"Any man who was willing to risk his shirt by carrying a deer around had to be single, widowed, very sure of himself, totally insane, or completely immune to pain."

"Hell hath no fury like a woman who discovers a bloody shirt tossed in with a load of wash."

"The enthusiasm of youth is ofttimes overshadowed by experience."

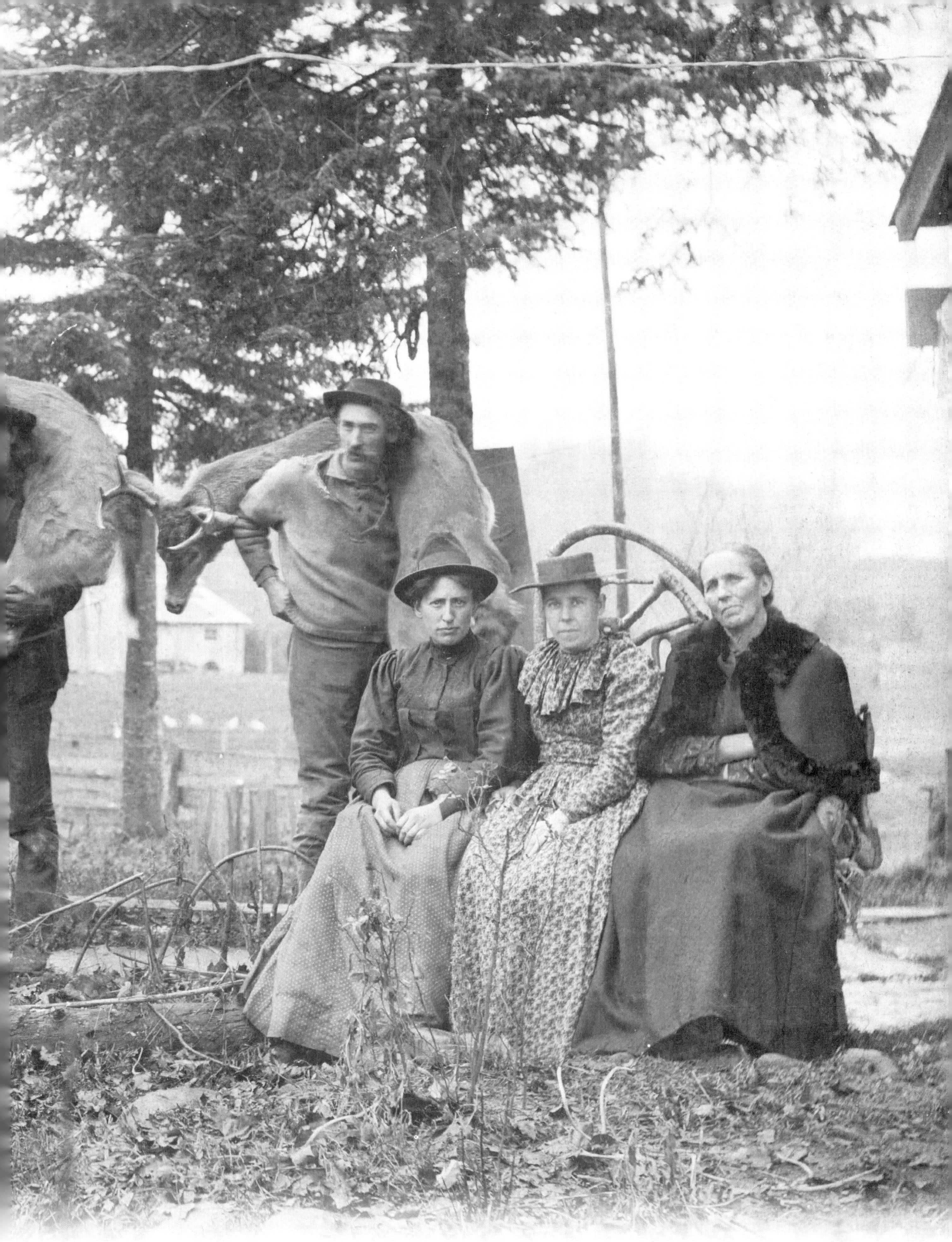

"Packin' 'em in. The hunt of 1906."

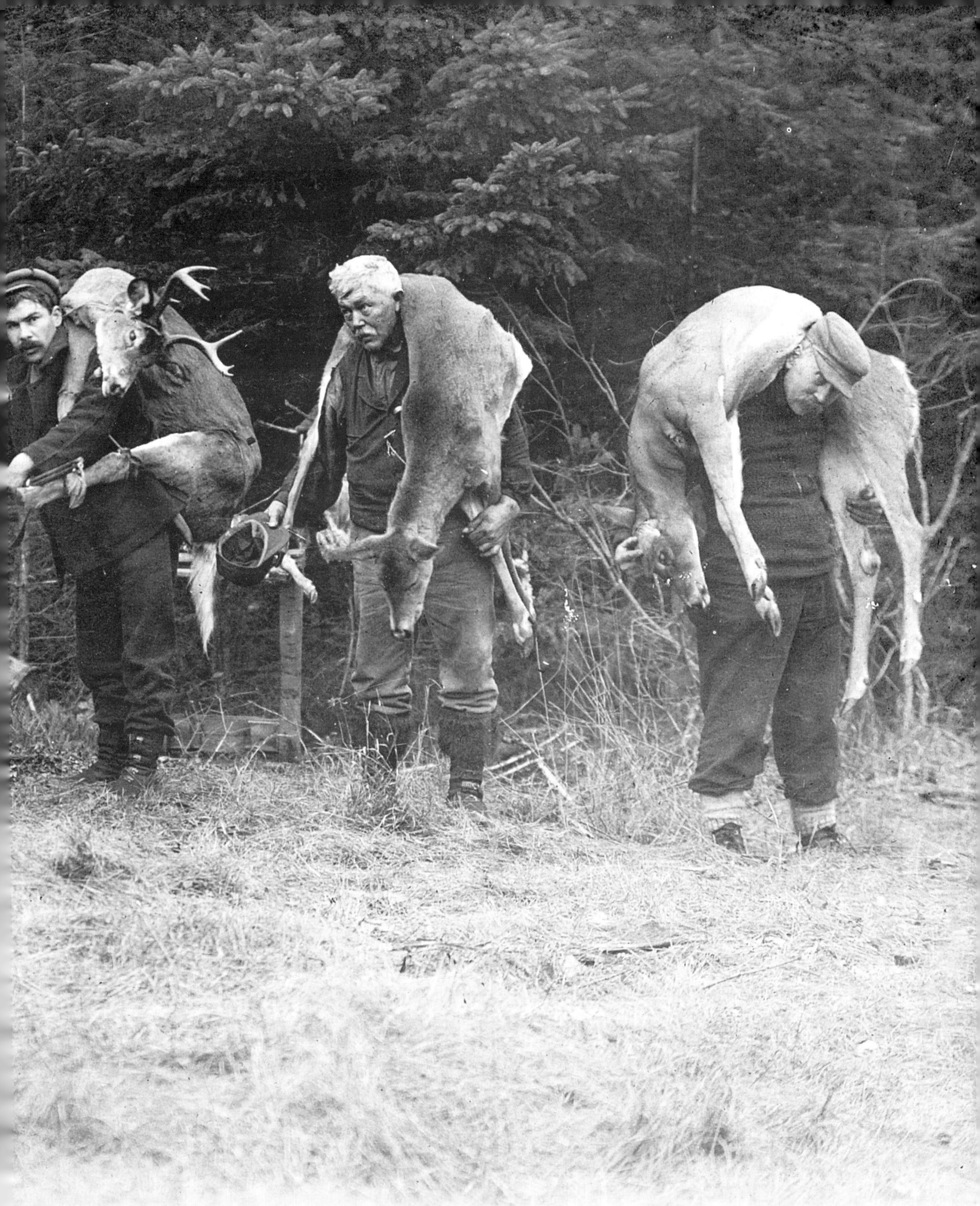

"At times the size of the deer, the lack of snow, or the type of terrain would dictate another type of carry if at least tw hunters were together. They'd cut a sapling down and then cut a ten or twelve feet long pole from it. Then they'd tie the deer's legs together with the pole between the legs."

"Getting the deer up wasn't as bad as trying to keep it from swinging back and forth on the pole. If it started doing that they had to put it down and start over again."

"Sometimes, rather than carry a deer out on such a pole, they'd modify that idea and use two poles fashioned together as a litter and carry their deer out."

"Some of the men came up with the idea of building a sled that they could pull into camp with their gear on and then when necessary, it could also double as a deer sled to help them get their deer out of the woods."

"There were three tricks involved when transporting deer in a canoe: 1) Don't puncture the bottom with a horn. 2) Make certain the load is balanced perfectly. 3) Make no sudden moves over deep water.

"Your Granddad always had a twinkle in his eye whenever he told us about the rule they followed when they hunted by canoe."

"We use the same rule that girls followed when we took them to a dance years ago." "You go home with the one what brought you."

"The only difference that I can see is that we usually didn't turn the buggy over on the way home if it wasn't loaded just right."

"If the gang brought a horse to camp it took little effort to drag their deer behind or toss it across the back of the horse."

"For a few extra dollars and if their hired teamster was willing and able, the life of the deer hunters became much easier. Deer were very often just left in the woods where'd they'd been shot until the end of season. They'd be hung up to cool and to keep them out of the reach of wolves and then left where they were."

"At the end of season they'd send a horse and sled or sleigh in to pick up their deer. With a horse, a much larger sled could be used to pull several deer out of the woods at one time."

Wheels Enter the Picture

"A horse and a high-wheeled wagon made getting deer back home an easy task."

"A good ox was worth his weight in gold. He was willing to plow the field, skid the logs, make a shopping trip to town, take the family to church on Sunday morning, or in this instance make the long trip to deer camp."

"One of the many reasons that these became known as 'buck' boards."

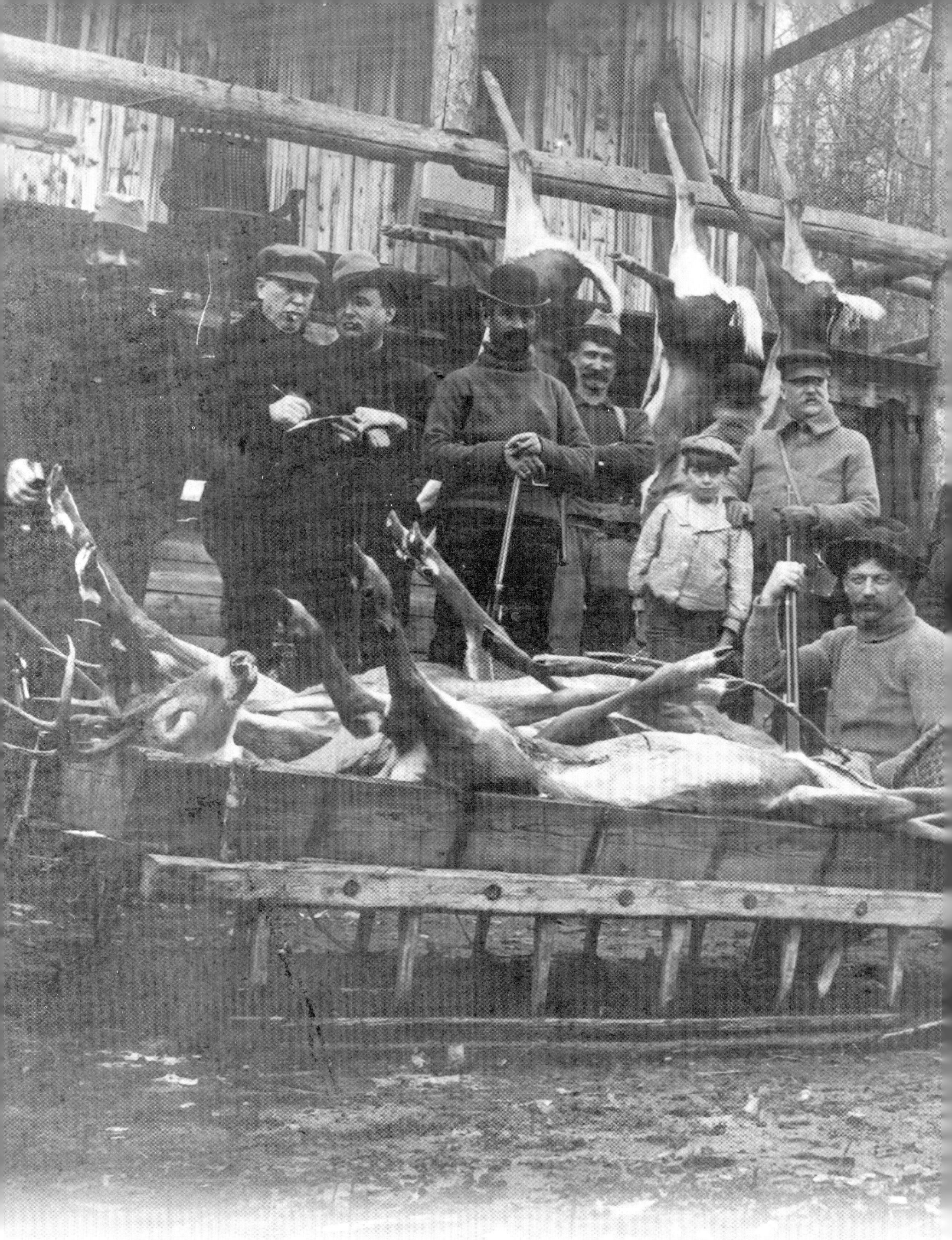

"The deer were often left hanging right in the woods where they were shot. When it came time to close camp, the teamster would take his horse and sled and go around through the woods and pick up the deer for the hunters."

"The end of a great hunt."

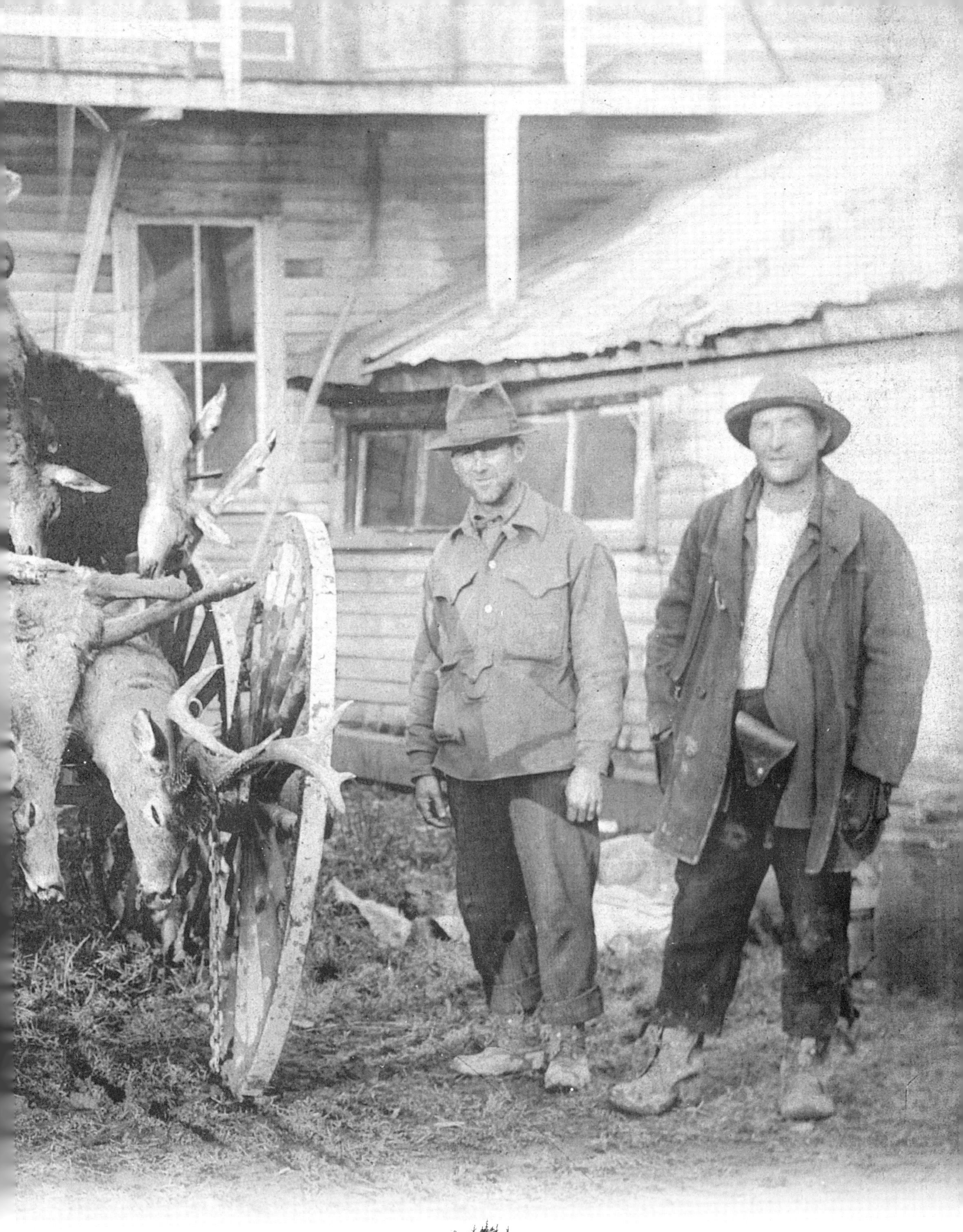

Our Success

"These next several pages should give you boy's a pretty good idea or what deer hunting was like back in Grandpa Charlie's time. Not only did they shoot a lot of deer, but they shot some pretty good sized ones too."

"Instead of spending the time to write down any stories of their hunts, Charlie found an article in an 1886 Harpers Weekly Magazine that came close to describing the ways many hunted back then. He cut it out and put it in here. It really makes for some interesting reading."

"You'll also notice that a few of the photographs have started to fade a little but most of them have held up quite well considering how old they are."

"Perhaps it helped by having the album up locked in the trunk all of those years and being kept out of the sunlight. I've heard tell that sunlight will fade a photograph much the same as it will a dyed cotton dress." Grandma's statement gave me the opening I needed in order to get back at the bunch for laughing at me.

"Now that's something you guys should know all about, wearing faded dresses. Especially you Wonzal."

I knew when I said that, that it wouldn't go over any too good. The punch I took in the arm proved it.

"Hunter's have always been a proud lot and you can certainly see it on the faces of Charlie's group. If you look real close, most of the time they have a look on their face as though hunting was the most serious thing there was in the whole world. If a person only knew the truth, the poor photographer probably had to take five shots to get one photograph they could use if that bunch acted anything near the likes of you Hun yaks."

From Harper's Weekly
Saturday, February 6, 1886

In the immense rugged forests of the lake-bound state of Michigan, where huge white pines and hemlocks tower above the more picturesque groves of maple and beech, is one of the great summer homes of the common deer. This is especially so in the upper peninsula, where the law permits them to be shot between the 15th of August and the 15th of November; while in the lower peninsula the open season is from the 1st of October to the 1st of December, and in Wisconsin only from November 1 to December 15. Owing, however, to the peculiar habit of the deer of migrating in scattering bands to upper Michigan from the central and northern part of Wisconsin at the approach of spring, the law prohibits their capture by means of pitfalls or traps, which could be successfully constructed in their paths.

After spending the spring and the early summer months in the vast wilderness, where they find a safe harbor and an abundance of food, they turn their faces southward about the beginning of August, and come rambling back to their winter-quarters in less bleak latitudes. Owing to the geographical construction of the country, their lines of travel run nearly north and south. In many places the diverging trails in the north concentrate as they approach Wisconsin. Occasionally the lay of the country causes them to converge and run almost parallel to each other within short distances, and these paths are known as main trails.

It is in such localities as these that the hunters have adopted a mode of destroying the deer that is unknown in other sections of the country. This method is called platform or scaffold shooting, and leads to the killing of hundreds of deer every season. As the paths run through a well-wooded country, the hunters have constructed brush fences by felling small trees and entwining branches and young sprouts in the rude barrier. These fences run diagonally across the trails, and at the southern end of the fences platforms are built, usually in the outspreading branches of the great pines, or sometimes at the top of log scaffoldings. The platforms are constructed about twenty-five feet from the ground, and are large enough to accommodate a couple of hunters.

From these elevated positions there is but little fear of the timid deer winding their human foes. Running from the end of the fence to the platform, avenues are cut in the young timber to allow the hunters a good view of the deer, and thus secure a good shot. Frequently, however, the hunters avail themselves of natural openings in the woodland, where they build their platforms, and to which they direct the lines of fencing.

When the first gleams of sunlight brighten the barkless tree-tops, the deer rises from his grassy bed. He shakes the dew-drops from his grayish-red coat, and taking several steps forward, drinks in the delicate aroma of the forest. Presently he is joined by others of his kind from branching trails. Sauntering slowly onward, and occasionally stopping for a moment to nibble some tempting blade of grass, or to lap the

FROM HARPER'S WEEKLY.

refreshing waters of some trickling rill, the leader winds his way, followed by the tripping does. The red glare of the sun dispels the morning dampness, and dead twigs begin to crackle beneath the delicate foot-steps. How quickly the buck raises his head, and pauses at these startling sounds! He no longer lingers on the journey; his steps come quicker, until he breaks into a graceful lope, and the pattering footsteps of the herd break the death-like silence. But the day is growing warm, and after a scamper of a mile or more the little band drop back into a walk again. Beneath scraggly, armless pines, across glassy glades, and through softwood groves, until the fatal fence is reached which lies across their path, they go on their way. They halt but for an instant, and then turning sharp to one side, they follow down the fence, often being joined by other deer from branching trails, until they reach the broad avenue at the side of which the hunters are awaiting their approach. Several deer have passed that way that morning, and when our little party stray in range of the hunter's stand, two faint puffs of smoke will drift through the leafy canopy, and two more trophies will be scored before the hunter's work is done.

Although the law in both Michigan and Wisconsin thus prohibits the shooting of deer except upon their migration southward in the autumn, deer are to be found in northern Wisconsin all the year round, and are at no season effectually protected by the game laws. The summer travelers on the Wisconsin Central may often see, close beside the track, the rude scaffolding partially concealed by a screen of withered boughs, and made accessible from the ground by a ladder, which constitutes a "deer-box." While the deer are in winter-quarters, though the venison cannot be safely marketed, deer are shot for their own use by the settlers and the loggers whose camps dot at intervals the wilderness of pine. A deer box is a very common adjunct of a loggers camp. When the weather is bitterly cold and the camp is snowed in, the venison this obtained is a very desirable addition to the camp larder. At such seasons it is not uncommon for the deer, forgetting their timidity in their need of food and shelter, to make their way to the camp and to crowd in among the cattle in the sheds. It is this mid-winter shooting that is depicted on the front page of this issue of the WEEKLY.

Credit - Currier & Ives

"Hunting stories were told when hunters arrived back home, but a photograph in hand was "frosting on the cake.""

"Whether a photograph was taken deep in the hunting woods or in the comforts of a studio, a photo-taking session was nothing short of serious business."

"A Flambeau River hunt near Ladysmith, Wisconsin during the late 1800's."

Photo by TIFFANY

125

"Memories will begin to fade in a short amount of time. Photographs tend to last far longer."

"A buck that every member of the group could brag about for many years to come."

"Venison for the table and furs to add to the income. Life can't get a whole lot better than that."

"Back when meat on the table was far more important than horns on the wall."

Wally spotted something that the rest of us had missed. "Did any of you happen to notice anything about that one deer on the last page?" We hadn't, so we just shook our heads.

"They gutted their deer a whole lot different back then compared to how we do it today. I wonder why they did it that way."

We flipped back to page 126. "Yeh, you're right," I said. "I see it now. They opened 'em up just barely enough to get the guts out. We split 'em wide open from the top of the ribs right down to their rear end. In fact, I even take my hatchet and split the pelvic bone on 'em."

Wonzal said, " That's the same way I do it when I shoot one."

I had to interrupt him of course. "I believe you meant to say that's the way you do it if you ever shoot one."

Grandma supplied the answer we needed to that question.

"There was several reasons why they gutted them that way back then. They were up there for two weeks so it helped keep the deer from drying out and it kept the jay birds and chickadees from pecking away at the inside of the cavity. However, the main reason they gutted their deer that way was to keep from getting their clothes all messed up when they went to carry a deer out of the woods on their back."

"There's something else you boys have missed on these photographs we've been looking at," Grandma added.

"What's that?" I asked.

"You boys should start watching for all the photographs that have horseshoes and white rabbits hanging around these camps. They're for good luck you know," she said.

Wonzal had to add his two-bits again. "Having a dead rabbit hanging around somewhere may have been lucky for the hunters, but it sure wasn't very lucky for the rabbit."

Excluding Wonzal, the rest of us had learned something new that day.

"This deer hunt took place in 'Indian Territory' during the 1800's."

127

Other Hunts

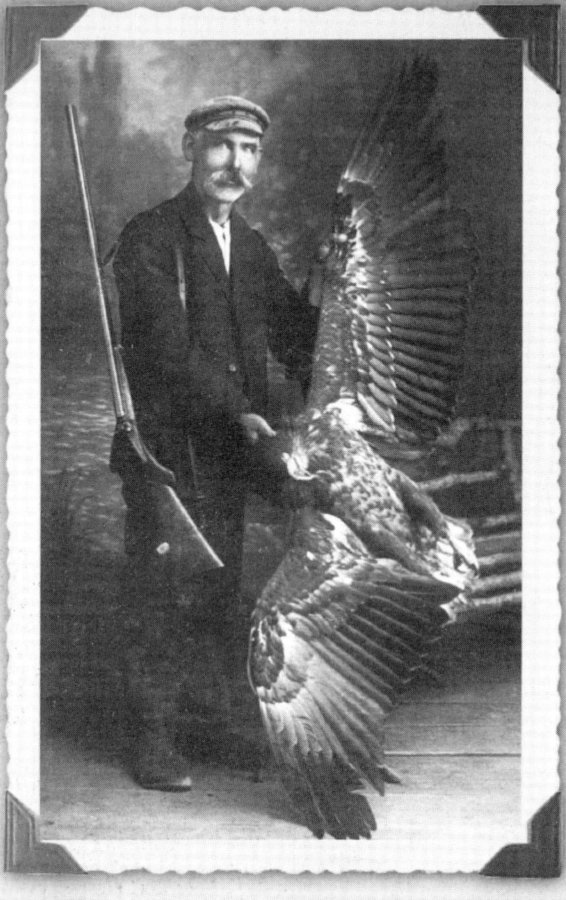

"As you see here, Grandpa Charlie and his cohorts chased more than just deer around They went after about any kind of game you can think of and probably some they never even mentioned. Snowshoe hares, cottontails, raccoons, fox, bobcats, wolves, grouse, ducks, geese, cranes, and shorebirds of all kinds. Some of them even went so far as to drop a hawk or eagle out of the sky if the poor devil was foolish enough to cross paths with them."

"Turkeys were a common sight in many areas and every pothole in the country held a flock or two of ducks."

"There was a time when there were so many rabbits that it took a group effort in order to try and reduce the numbers but the effort was only superficial."

"When it came time to truly reduce the population, Nature took over where man left off. Tuleremia was far less humane than any method used by man but it proved to be a far more lethal way of reducing the population than anything man ever came up with."

"Rabbits, and ducks were common tablefare for a good many countryfolks."

"A large group of mounted hunters gathered on a Sunday at the Hotel Bowler located near Green Bay, Wisconsin for their annual fox and brush wolf hunt."

"Anyone game for some rabbit stew?"

"A brace of partridge could be had with little effort."

"Even the best of hunters didn't come by a mixed bag like this every day."

"A fox in the henhouse. End of story."

"Success depended on having a good dog and being a crack-shot."

"Success in the woods of Northern Wisconsin during the early 1900's."

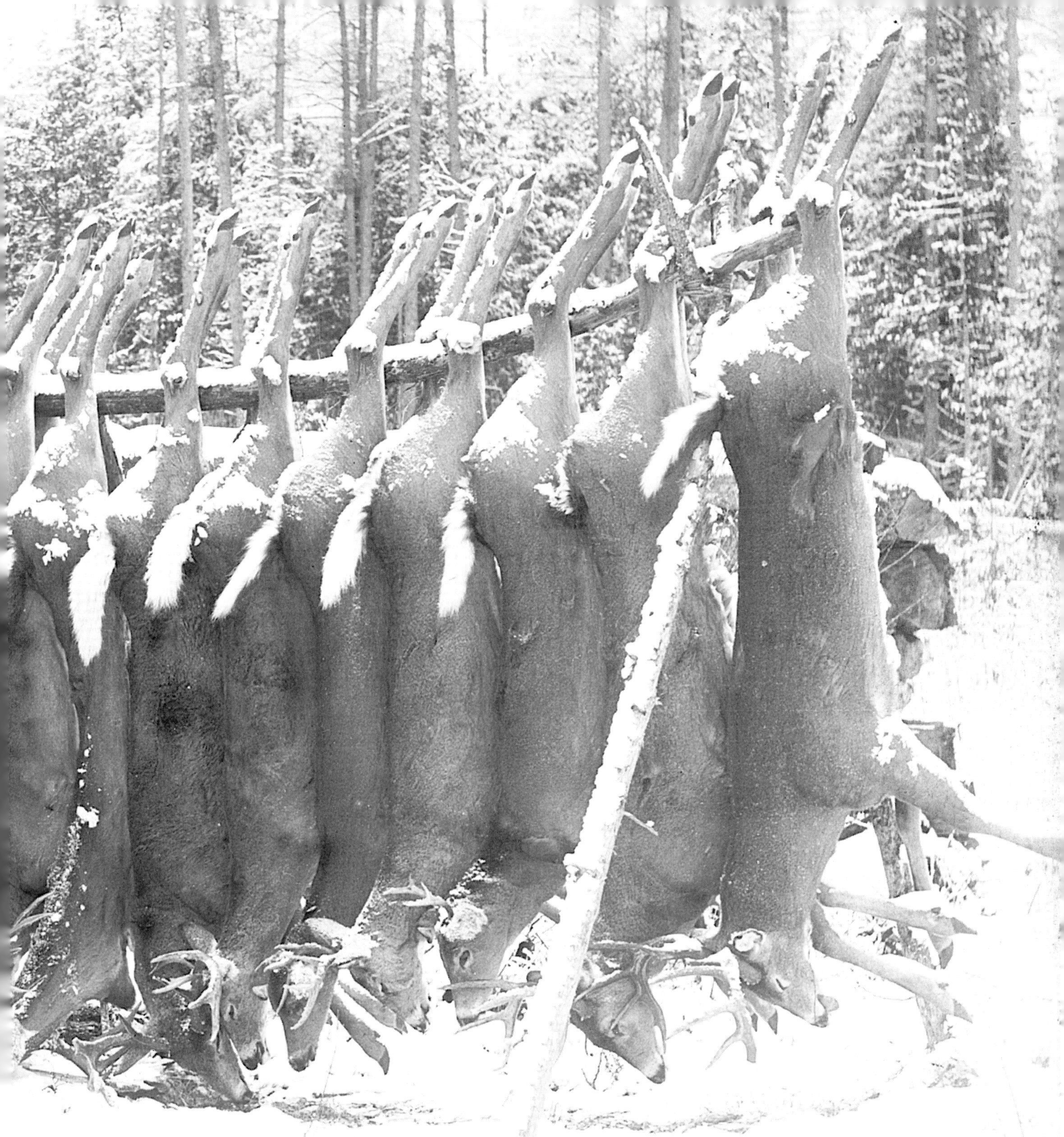

The Slaughter of the Buffalo

"The Taking of the Tongues." L. A. Huffman

Grandma then gave all of us a little history lesson for the day.

"To ensure the collapse of any possible resistance from the Indians, the idea of exterminating the buffalo was put into effect long before the Indian Wars ended. At first the indiscriminate shooting of buffalo was motivated by little more than the desire for "sport," or for the diversion of railroad hands and passengers, who might incidentally help to clear the tracks and curb a nuisance.

"In 1871, after it was discovered that buffalo pelts and leather could be marketed at a high profit, the slaughter was organized on a commercial basis. Now

"Fresh meat for the reservation."

professional hunters and skinners working in teams stepped up the butchery to three million buffalo a year. The advance of the railroads hastened the end of the herds."

"By 1878, the vast southern herd, the larger of the two main herds, had been wiped out. Five years later, when collectors tried to round up a few specimens of what had recently been the most numerous breed of large animals in the world, only remnants of the northern herd could be found in remote parts of Canada."

"The virtual extinction of the buffalo is the classic example of the white man's heedless rapacity in the exploitation of nature," she said.

"Life among the nomads underwent a drastic change."

134

"Hide hunters cutoff every avenue of escape for the few that survived."

"Time to start peeling the hides."

"Stacks of buffalo hides ten foot deep awaited the trip to the tannery."

The End of an Era

"By 1887, the State of Wisconsin was practically overrun by resident and nonresident game hogs who cared little about leaving anything for the next generation. Something needed to be done before the game was completely gone so the State hired a group of four game wardens and assigned them to duty."

"The warden's job was to try and enforce the few laws that pertained to wild animals and despite the few laws that there were, it was still a very difficult task to do. Relatives protected relatives and neighbors protected neighbors when it came to game violations. Besides that, it was an

"This is a prime example of the gamehogs disregard for game laws. Written on the back of the photograph was, 'The ones we got for the 4th of July Barbecue.'"

"Anything that flew was fair game for the market."

unwritten rule among the wardens that they turn their heads if game was being taken by a violator for their own personal use. The ones they were really after were the poachers and violators that were illegally taking game and then selling it on the market."

"Your Grandfather always referred to 1897 as, "The End Of An Era" because a big change took place that year. That was the first year that the State of Wisconsin required hunters to buy a license if they wanted to hunt deer."

"By now you know that the dollar they charged for a license didn't bother Charlie and his group any. After, all, what did a dollar mean to that bunch? Absolutely nothing."

"It was the common man, the farmers and the loggers

"Winnebago duck hunters."

who didn't have a spare dollar to part with that it really meant something to. Besides that, most folks felt that the game that was on their property was theirs, and it was a God-given right of theirs to take what they wanted when they wanted off their own land."

"Charlie understood their feelings but the real ones that he took pity on were the Indians. Here we'd moved in on them and now we were imposing laws on them to prevent them from hunting like they'd done for centuries before we ever showed up."

"For years they'd managed to survive off of what the land provided for them but as more and more white people moved into the territory, the less room there was for the Indian to gather what he needed in order to live."

"Your Granddad was a good man, and he always went out of his way to help the Indians whenever he could. He was one who shared what he had with those who had nothing."

APPLICATION FOR RESIDENT DEER-HUNTING LICENSE.

STATE OF WISCONSIN.

To the County Clerk of _Forest_ **County:**

I hereby apply for a resident's license to hunt deer as provided by law and declare the following statements by me made to be true:

Name _George Ogomoss_

Residence _Armstrong Creek_ County of _Forest_ State of Wisconsin.

Have you resided in Wisconsin for a period of a year immediately preceding the date of this application? _yes_

Age _24_

Height _5-8_

Weight _168_

Color of Eyes _Brown_

Color of Hair _Black_

Distinctive marks _Lost two front upper teeth and two rest filled with Gold_   _Indian_

Hunting season for which license is applied for—189 _7_.

Dated, this _30_ day of _October_ A.D. 189 _7_.

George his + Ogomoss mark

State of Wisconsin, } ss.
County of _Forest_

George Ogomoss being first duly sworn, on oath says he is the applicant for a license to hunt deer whose name is signed thereto; that he has not and will not make application for license of any other county clerk in the State of Wisconsin during the period covered by this application; that he knows the contents of the above application and that the same is true.

Subscribed and sworn to before me this _30_ day of _October_, A.D. 1897.

George his + Ogomoss mark

Court Commissioner

"A squaw and her cradled papoose."

"An Ojibwa elder, her grandchildren, and their lodge near Milacs, Minnesota."

"Ojibwa youngsters pose near their bark-covered lodge, somewhere in Wisconsin."

"Crafts were peddled to travelers in order to supplement their meager income."

"An Ojibwa maple sugar camp in northern Wisconsin."

"Two or even three generations often shared the same lodge."

"Government housing was provided but many of the reservation residents found it difficult to part with the old ways."

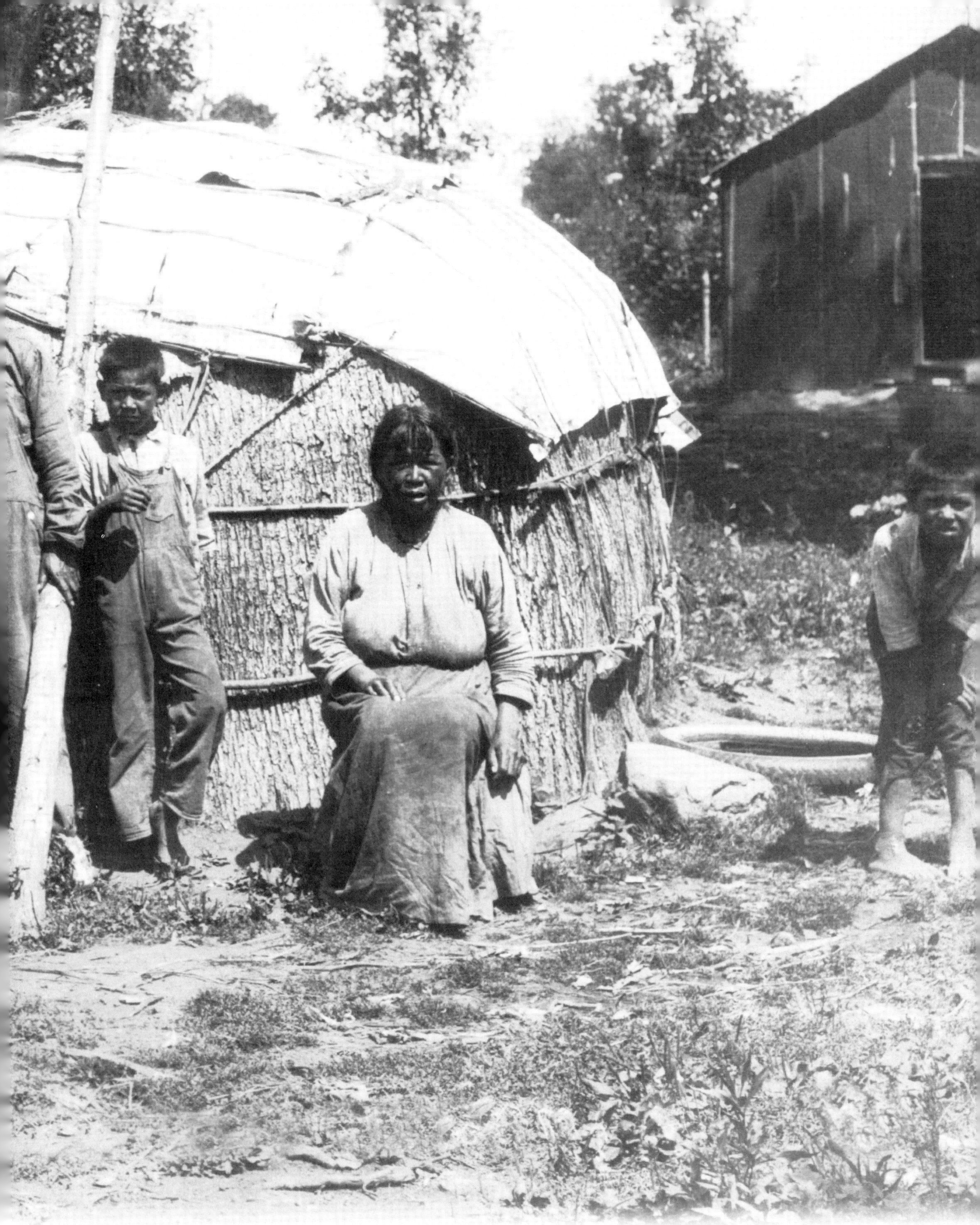

Women Join the Hunt

"Your Granddad and his sidekicks saw it coming years before it actually did, so it wasn't a big surprise for them when it happened."

"What was that?" I asked.

"The womenfolk wanted to join in with the men and do some hunting and fishing like the men were doing. Women loved the outdoors just as much as the men did and they'd grown tired of sitting at home while their men folk were out gallivanting all over the country. In order to keep a little peace and quiet around home, the men slowly began to give in and make room for the women on their outings."

Glenn was awestruck. His knees went weak on him and he had to grab a chair and sit down.

"Whatever you do Hank, don't ever let your wife have a look at this album or we'll all be doomed!" For some reason, I didn't feel the same way.

"I don't know about that Glenn. It wouldn't hurt anything if we saw to it that our wives got out with us just to see what we were up to and why we enjoy doing what we do so much."

" I'm almost certain that they wouldn't even want to do all of the things we do and it might even relieve some tensions that have built up over the years. Besides that, now that our kids are old enough to be going with us, I can't help but think that our wives would enjoy watching them experience new things. I know my wife would "

The boy's were a bit reluctant, but they tended to agree with me.

"It was inevitable. It was something that was bound to happen sooner or later. A great many women took as much pleasure in spending time outdoors as men did. Whether it was tagging along on a hunt, taking a leisurely hike over hill and dale, or spending a weekend of primitive camping in some desolate woods, women took to it like a tick to a hound's hide."

"These women were fascinated by an ancient Indian trail marker located deep in the middle of woods."

143

"Camping might be combined with a little fishing or hunting. The women learned quickly not to wince at the sight of whatever game might be taken on the trip."

"Staying in a tidy camp took some getting used to by the men. They were used to throwing things where they landed and stepping over them until it was time to head back home. Keeping a camp neat and clean was a carryover from the women's household duties."

"Conditions were not always favorable for wearing their finery into the woods or in the confines of a fishing boat. Blood, worm goo, and fish slime did a real number on many a fine outfit."

"There was no argument among the men as to who should assume the cooking chores. They were more than happy to delegate that chore to the womenfolk. If the women were willing to cook, it gave the men more time to spend fishing instead of wasting their time on kitchen duties."

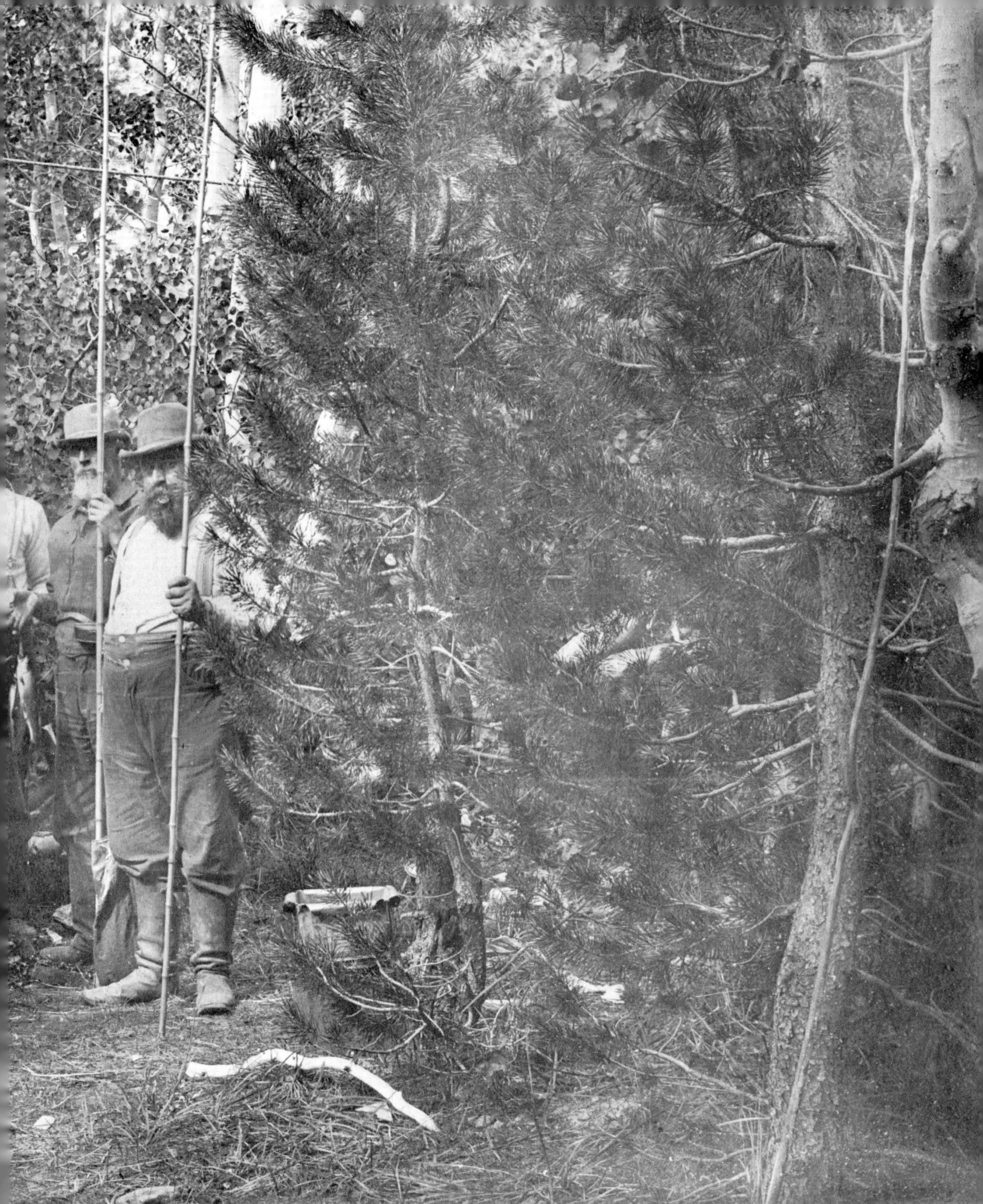

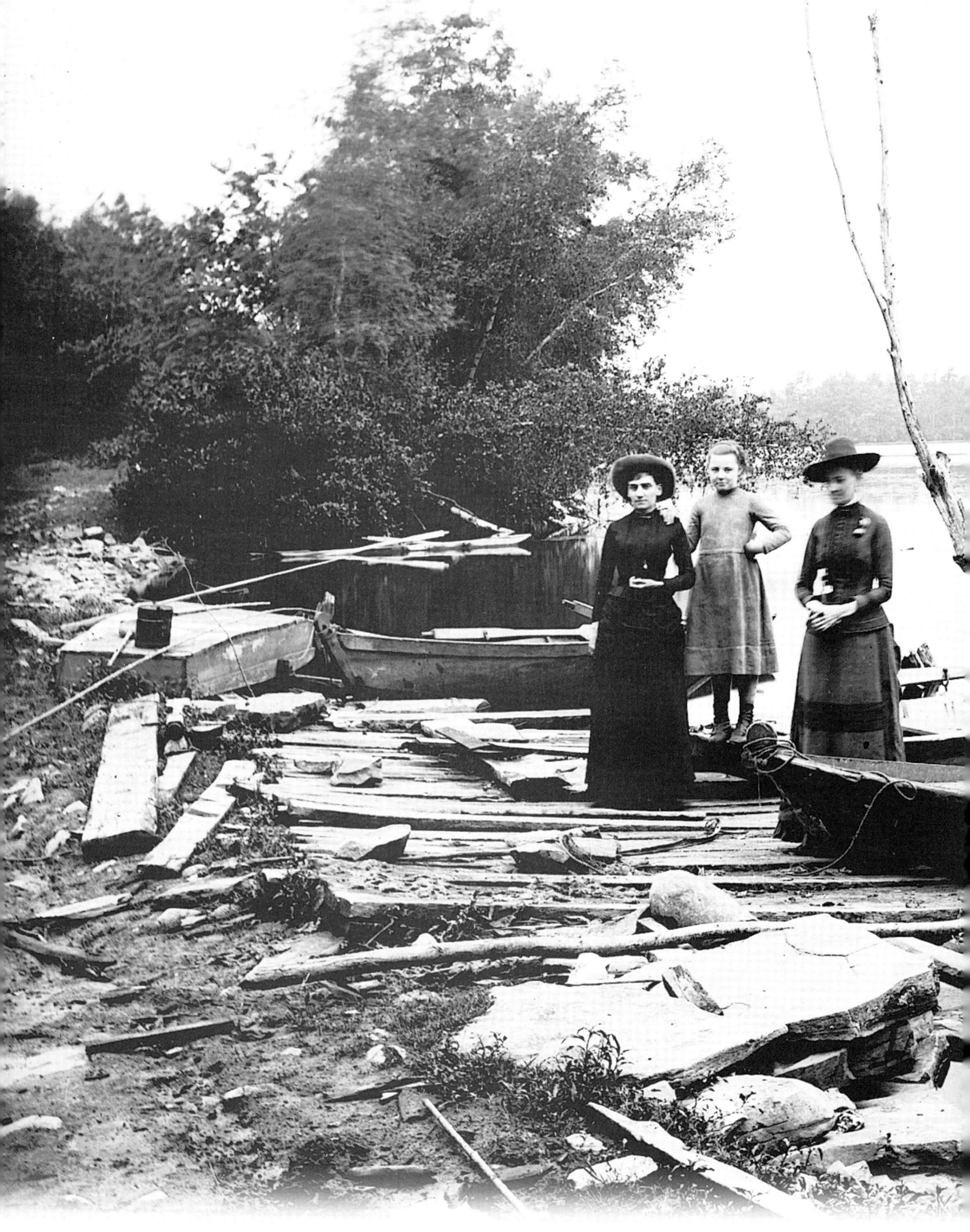

"No matter how their time was spent outdoors, womenfolk took a
special liking to the peace and quiet of drifting quietly across
the glassy surface of a sparkling blue lake."

"Before your Granddad and his cronies would agree with their wives and allow them to accompany the men on their outdoor adventures, the men all got together one day and laid out a few ground rules before they would even considered telling the women that they could take part in any part of their hunting activities."

"Fishing was one thing. There would be an occasional hook flying in their direction and a few of them would probably take a hook in the ear or have one get stuck in their hat or shirt sleeve, but the men all agreed that hunting was a completely different story. Not a one of them wanted any part of taking a woman into the field nor did they want to be anywhere near any woman that didn't handle a gun as well as any one of the men did."

"Your Granddad compared trying to teach your Grandmother how to handle a gun properly to trying to teach a new pup not to piddle on the kitchen floor. He said about the time he thought he had her undivided attention, she'd be off talking to one of her friends or involved in some sort of horseplay. He had to correct her time and time again before he'd even consider putting a shell in the gun."

"When he finally did get nerve enough to hand her a loaded rifle, the first thing she did was swing around with it pointed in his direction and ask him what was next. Then he had to start all over again."

I couldn't help myself. "That sounds a lot like you Wonzal. Not the part about mishandling a rifle but the part about trying to break a habit of piddling on the floor. That's a tent we stay in at night you know, it's not the great outdoors."

The result was another well-deserved punch in the arm.

"Hank McCracken." "You quit your pickin' on Wonzal right now whether he deserves it or not!"

Over the years I had learned that when my Grandmother spoke, I jumped.

"Your Grandmother Marie finally learned the proper handling of a gun and Charlie felt as good about being around her carrying one as anybody. It may have had a lot to do with her seeing what was left of a rabbit she shot with her deer rifle. She knew right then that she never wanted to see a single soul ever get shot with one."

"The old saying, "Practice makes perfect," was certainly true when it came to handling guns and learning to put a bullet in the middle of a bulls-eye."

"Patience is a virtue."
"A great amount of it was required when it came to teaching someone how to safely handle a rifle."

"Once the women had learned how to handle and shoot their rifles properly, the men had the women join them in their shooting club. Many of the woman became good enough shots that it put some of the men on their toes and forced them to sharpen up their own skills a bit."

"At first the women didn't take the training any to serious. As soon as your Granddad turned his back, your Grandmother would be off horsing around with one of her friends."

"As impossible as it appeared, the women began to get the drift of it all and became some very good shots."

"It was a hard pill to swallow when a wife, year after year, kept shooting bigger bucks than her husband. After a while he could no longer attribute her accomplishments as beginner's luck."

"Occasionally the competition would start to get to one of the men. One day the fellow in the back was heard to say, 'Today the women are going to drive' which was an okay thing to say except under his breath he added, 'me nuts.'"

"While still considered to be a dress, her hunting outfit did not hinder the efforts of this young lady. Her brother, knowing that he'd pushed the doe to her, wears as big a smile as she does with her first deer ever."

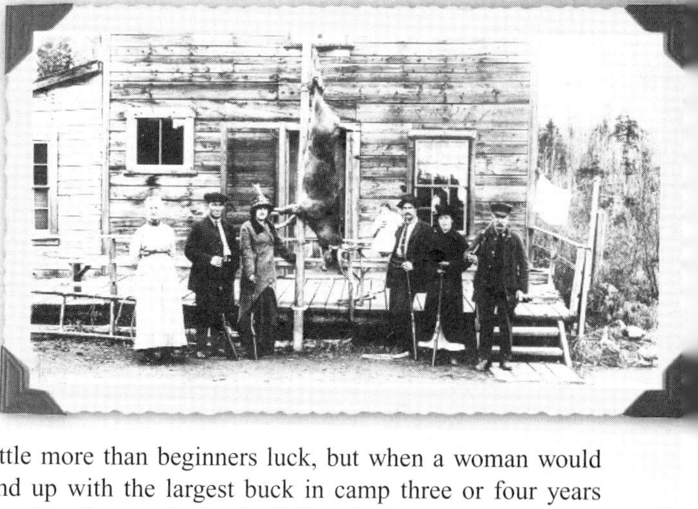

"Women took to hunting like a duck took to water, and not only enjoyed hunting rabbits, squirrels, ducks and game birds, but had a special thrill when they were given the opportunity to hunt deer."

" Women were surprisingly good at deer hunting too. Many of the men attributed a woman's success to being little more than beginners luck, but when a woman would end up with the largest buck in camp three or four years running, the men had to look for other excuses."

" I myself feel that a great deal of their success had to do with their desire to prove themselves among the men and that they were truly worthy of being called a hunter."

152

"The men marveled at how the women could manage to venture into the woods with their long dresses and petticoats and then walk back out again virtually unscathed. Any good hunter would take great pride in taking a buck like this. A photograph would preserve the memory for many years to come."

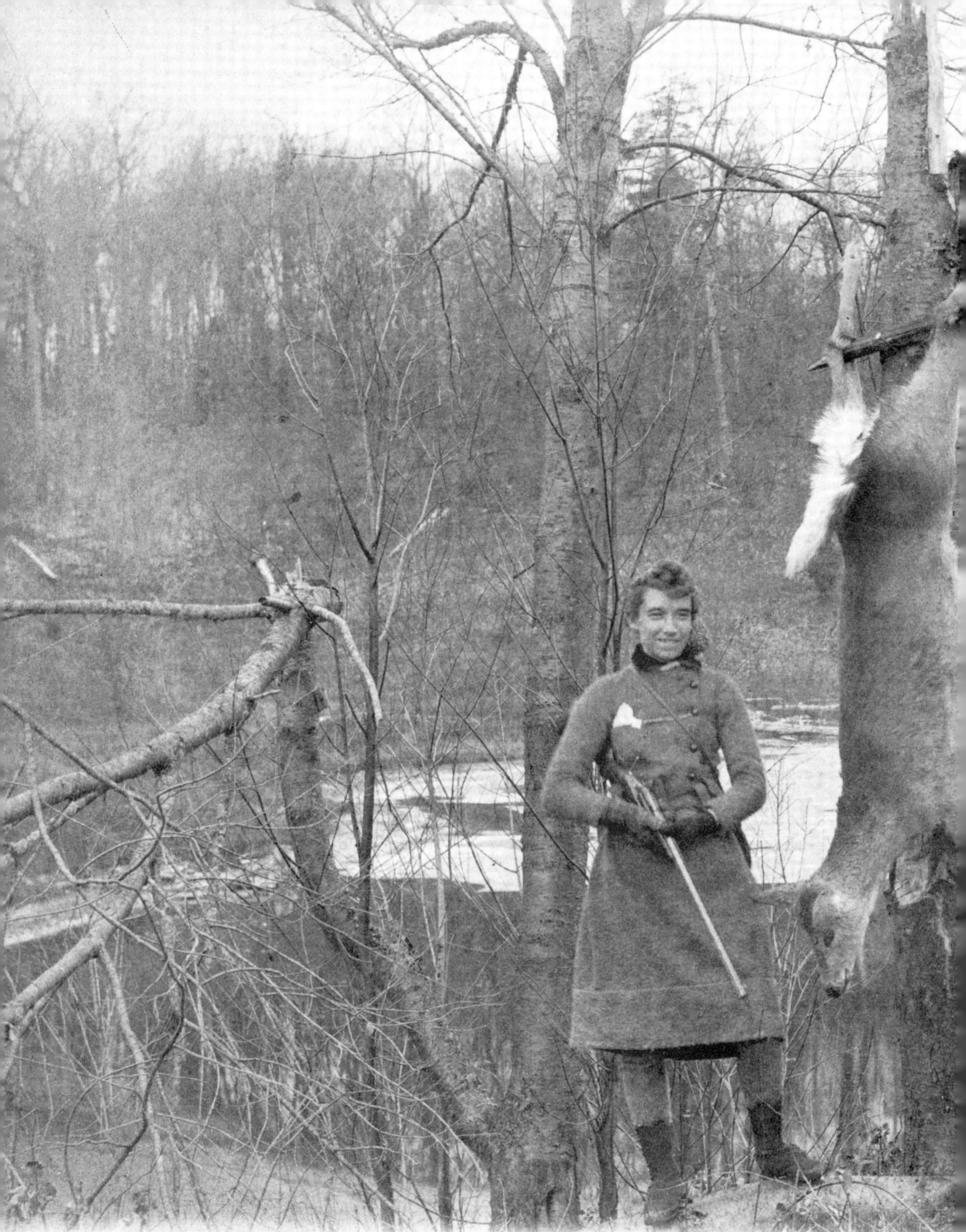

"While still considered to be a dress, her hunting outfit didn't hinder the efforts of this young lady. Her brother, knowing that he'd pushed the doe to her, wears as big a smile as she does with her first deer ever."

"Aunt Agnes with her high-grade Winchester and a buck to match. It doesn't get any better than that."

"Late one Fall your Granddad got the idea in his head to take a trip out West by rail. He'd been out West once before years back but your Grandmother Marie never had been out there so she had no idea what it was like. When she was a youngster growing up, her family didn't have the means to ever take a trip like. Your Granddad thought it'd be a real treat for Marie to see the desert and the mountains and so on."

"He had an ulterior motive however. He planned to line up a big game hunt out there so that he and some of his group could hunt for elk and mountain sheep and so forth the next Fall. He thought by taking her along that he'd kill two birds with one stone."

"While it was a nice thought on his part to take Marie out there with him, he had neglected one thing. He hadn't thought of how the weather would be out West that late in the year. His only other visit out West had been in the late spring when the flowers were in full bloom up in the mountains. He said that it was simply breathtaking. I guess you might say that it was breathtaking to Marie too."

We just looked at each other again. We had no idea what was in store.

"The two of them left early one morning for the ride to the railhead. They arrived with time to spare, picked up their tickets at the station, turned over their baggage to the depot agent, and then made arrangements with the livery to care for their horse until they arrived back. Then they checked in at the railroad house and got their room. They got their room straightened around and Charlie wined and dined Marie in the hotel restaurant. She told me she felt just like she was on her second honeymoon that evening. Little did Charlie know that it could have been the beginning of the end for the two of them, in more ways than one."

By then we were all ears.

"They got and early start the next morning and within two hour's time they had traveled enough distance so that everything Marie saw as they passed by was new to her. She'd never been that far away from home before."

"Marie "OOHED" and "AWED" at everything she saw and kept poking Charlie in the ribs so often that the poor devil couldn't even take a nap. She kept that up until nightfall and it was finally to dark to see anything out of the coach window any longer."

"After they'd eaten they retired to the sleeping car, and fell asleep to the gentle rocking of the car as it traveled the flatlands on it's way West."

"When Marie awoke the next morning and opened the curtains, she "OOOOOOHED" and she "AWWWWWWED" all over again, but this time for a much different reason than the day before. During the night they had left the flatland and they were working their way into the mountains. Marie would look out one side of the car and see nothing but solid rock as they passed a few feet away from it. On the other side of the car she could look down into a gorge that was so deep that she couldn't even see the bottom of it."

"A little later on that day she woke up from a short nap and when she glanced out the window, and saw nothing but blue sky. She quickly sat up to take a closer look and then she found out why. They were on a trestle several hundred feet above a gorge. The river that ran through it was so far below them that it appeared to have no more water flowing in it than a trickle out of the well pump. Marie suffered from a fear of height as it was, so such a sight put her on the floor of the coach digging her fingernails into the carpeting."

"What finally broke the camel's back for her was when the train came to a complete stop out in the middle of nowhere with the locomotive stopped on top of a rickety old wooden trestle. The section crew had found a couple of cracked timbers so they wanted to make certain that the timbers could handle the load before they'd allow the passenger cars to pass over it. By that point Marie was bound and determined to get out and walk across but neither the conductor or Charlie would hear any part of it. That really opened up her damper. She was furious."

When they been dropping grade for quite some way when Marie looked out the side of her window only to see a woman on the track next to them traveling down the track riding on a single-pump hand car carrying a lunch bucket in her hand. Marie was absolutely awestruck.

"What on Earth is she doing, Charlie?" Marie asked.

"She's just on her way to work, Marie." "I imagine she's the only school marm there is in these parts so the railroad is kind enough to let her ride the rails to work. Aren't you glad that you don't have to be doing that this morning, Marie."

"Marie never even answered him. Her mouth was hanging too far open, according to what Charlie said."

"They finally left the mountains and a few hours later were traveling through a portion of the desert. Marie by that time had managed to settle down some now that her feet were closer to the ground than they were when she was on top of that trestle."

"Charlie glanced out the window and spotted something up ahead that Marie probably didn't need to see so he tried to get attention so she'd be facing away from the window. What it was, was the remains of a buggy and the horse that had been pulling it. There was nothing left of the horse but a pile of bleached bones with the harness laying on on top of them.

"It almost worked, but the Marie suddenly turned her head and looked out the window."

"What on Earth is that Charlie?" she asked .

Charlie's casual answer to her was, "I'd say by the looks of things that they didn't make it all the way home Marie."

"Marie let out a scream. She was completely horrified."

From where I was standing, so was Wally. I swear his eyeballs were rolling around in his head.

"The railroad hotel where we stayed".

"The depot from which we departed."

"The engine on our train."

"The caboose and train crew."

"Departure time."

"The dining car where we ate."

"Rails alongside the river."

"Winding our way through the gorge."

"Climbing our way up the Great Divide."

"A school teacher on her way to work."

"Tracks on the side of a mountain."

159

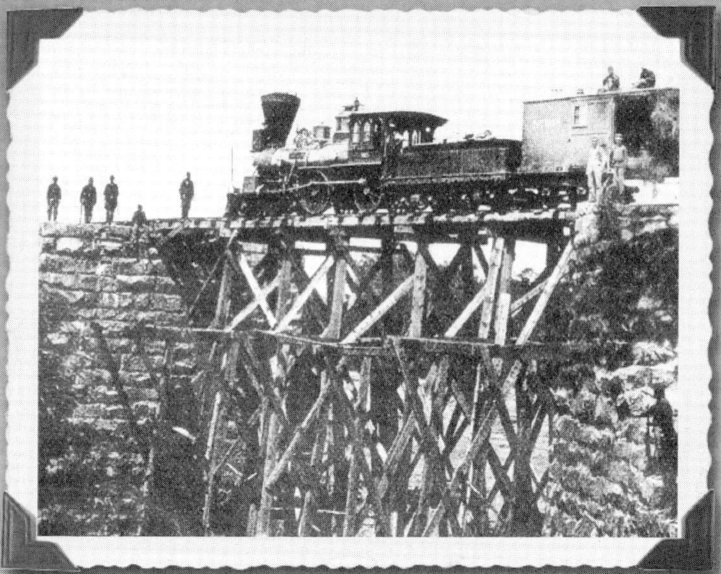

"Stopped on a trestle. A fine place to check and see if it's safe."

"Hundreds of feet above the gorge with nothing but sticks between us and certain death."

"The horse and buggy that never made it. Whatever happened to the driver?"

"An Indian's way of meeting his maker."

"A wagon train makes it's way across the desert. Where a break down or a lack of water meant an untimely death."

"When they finally reached their destination, Marie was terrified by the group of men that had come to pick them up and take them to the cabin where Charlie wanted to hunt. According to her they were all armed and looked like a bunch of outlaws."

"She had Charlie ask one of them why they were carrying rifles with them like that. The guy turned to answer Charlie but before he said anything he spit a big wad of chewing tobacco onto the ground .

"Hostiles, renegades, highwaymen, whatever."

Grandma then added, "I heard tell that he winked at Charlie when Marie put her hands over her face and then he whispered so she couldn't hear him. " There's a big buck that hangs out around here. We've been after him for two years now. Keep your eyes open for him will 'ya?"

"On the way to the cabin the men tried to assure Marie that the guy was just pulling her leg when he said that and that she'd probably end up getting the big buck. That didn't even convince her."

"When they finally arrived at the cabin, Marie was overjoyed to see that there was at least one more white woman in the country. She was the wife of the rancher on who's property they were staying. She was the one that was finally able to convince Maria that she would be quite safe up there."

"According to what Marie said, the scenery surrounding the cabin was absolutely beautiful and teemed with wildlife. According to the rancher's wife, if Marie wanted to shoot a deer, she'd have every opportunity in the world to shoot one up there even if she hunted right around the cabin."

"Your Grandmother Marie decided to do some hunting on her own rather than tie Charlie up guiding her around. He could go with the ranch hands and do some scouting so he could learn the lay of the land. That way he wouldn't have to do it should they return some day to hunt mule deer again. He'd be able to spend his time hunting."

"Being that it was the first time she was out on her own, Marie decided to stay within sight of the cabin to do her hunting so as not to get lost and she still fared quite well. She ended up shooting a goat of some kind her first day out and then shot a doe and a small one-horned buck the next day so her hunt was quite successful and overall they were all did quite well."

"Our escorts to the cabin."

"A cabin nestled in the pines."

"The accommodations where we stayed and the rancher's wife. Thank Heavens another woman amongst all these

"The scenery as we viewed it out our bedroom window. A great place to hunt and close enough not to get lost."

"The rancher and his wife admire my deer. Neither could believe I had it in me."

*   *   *   *   *

"So far it sounds like a pretty nice trip for the two of them. I thought when you started telling the story that it could have been the end of the two of them." I said.

Grandma turned around, looked up at me, stared me straight in the eye, and then said, "They aren't home yet are they Hank" That's all she said.

"The day they were going to leave, your Grandmother wanted to clean up the cabin so she went around and tidied things up a bit. While she was doing that, she happened to look underneath an old calendar hanging on the wall and spotted something that caught her eye. It was an old Currier and Ives print that someone had taken from it's frame and hung up there on a nail."

"What was on it?" I asked.

"It was a picture of a train stuck in the snow and people shoveling frantically trying to dig it out. It was called, "AMERICAN RAILROAD SCENE -SNOW BOUND."

Marie said her stomach suddenly turned into a knot and she felt faint. She told me later that at the time it felt as if it was an omen of some kind, a bad omen. As it turned out, she was right."

"The ranch hands got the two of them down to the railroad station all right but then just before they left the foreman said, "I hope you don't run into snow when you get down on the plains. They can get some pretty nasty storms out that way, especially this time of year. With that, they were on they're way."

The trip out of the mountains was uneventful but no sooner than they reached the plains, it started to snow, and did it ever snow. Both Charlie and Marie had lived through what they had thought were some pretty bad snowstorms in the Midwest but what they'd seen was nothing compared to what they were running into now. They couldn't see a foot beyond the windows of the coach and the wind was blowing so hard that it was whipping the snow into huge drifts right before their eyes."

"They both felt the train begin to slow down as it bucked it's way through the huge drifts until the wheels on the locomotive began to spin on the wet and slippery rails. The train continued to slow down until it was barely moving. Then it stopped moving all together."

"They felt the train lurch and rumble as the engineer backed it up for perhaps two hundred yards. Then it began moving slowly forward, the engineer intent on ramming his way through the deep drifts that lie ahead. The attempt proved fruitless. They were snowbound, just like the train on the Currier and Ives print."

"The train crew soon came though the coaches and recruited all the able-bodied men to man a shovel and help dig the train out of the snowdrifts."

"Move, and move fast," they shouted. The longer we wait the less chance we have of digging our way out."

"In a situation like that, a person's status made no difference whatsoever. The fireman worked beside cowpunchers, the conductor worked with storekeeper, and a hobo worked alongside a banker that day."

" The winds picked up and snowdrifts formed faster than the men could shovel.

"Their effort proved to be a waste of time. All they could do then was wrap themselves up in whatever they could find and wait it out. It was a day later before the snow plow managed to break through and reach the stranded travelers. By then, Marie was a complete basket case"

"The engine fought through the drifts until it finally bogged down."

"The men got out and tried to shovel the track clear. It was an impossible task."

"It took three locomotives with snowplows to clear the tracks."

"Thank The Good Lord we made it home!"

It didn't help matters out any either when the finally started moving down the track and the were finally on their way home. Charlie opened up an old newspaper he found jammed beneath his seat and started reading the headlines to Marie.

"Look at this Marie. There's a story in here about some guy that shot and killed a robber in Kansas City, Missouri back in June. He got shot himself but still managed to shoot the holdup man a couple of times." Charlie then proceeded to read all the details to her.

Edited from the local paper
KANSAS CITY, MISSOURI

J. A. Foster was working behind the counter visiting with Miss Lillian Campbell, owner of the cafe, when a well-dressed young man entered the cafe and ordered a cup of coffee.

Miss Campbell started to get up to get a cup for the man but J. A. Foster volunteered to get the coffee for her instead. Foster walked over to the corner of the cafe, picked up and urn of coffee, and poured a cup for the man. Foster returned to the smaller counter and had no more than turned around to start work again when the young man bellowed, "UP WITH 'EM."

Miss Campbell started to lift a stool to confront the robber with but saw a revolver in the young man's hand. so she set the stool down and raised her hands empty.

Foster did not put his hands up fast enough to satisfy the robber who then opened fire on Foster almost simultaneously with the command he'd given.

The bandit's first shot went wild but his second shot hit Foster in the cheek, dropping him to the floor behind the counter. (It was a quirk of fate that found Mr. foster armed that evening. J. A. Foster would have been left empty-handed but earlier that evening he had gone to his apartment to put on a new pair of socks as one of his other socks had a hole in it. While he was there he grabbed his revolver, thinking he might have use for it if he was going to be working for Miss Campbell that evening. When he returned to the cafe, he had placed the revolver on a shelf located behind the counter.)

As Foster fell to the floor, he reached for his revolver and fired at the bandit between the aisle that separated the two counters, but he missed.

Foster's second shot obviously struck the bandit for he screamed as he backed out of the cafe towards the door. A third shot from Foster's revolver struck the would-be robber who again screamed in great anguish, fell to the floor, regained his feet, and then fled out the door, running west on Fifteenth Street.

Foster then followed the man out the door where he saw another man run up to the wounded robber, yell something in his ear, and then run. Foster watched as the robber disappeared into the alley on the west side of Jackson Avenue at Fifteenth Street.

Police were summoned and as they entered the alley, they spotted blood on the tongue of a nearby wagon. As patrolmen David Bradley and B. D. Thomas approached the wagon,

165

Winfield fired at the police from the bed of the wagon where he had taken refuge. A gunfight between the robber and the two police officers ensued. and the robber, Julian Wingfield, was fatally wounded by Detective Bradley.

It was reported by Charles Walker, Bertillon clerk at police headquarters, who bent over Wingfield as he lay dying, that the bandit said, "I'm done. But I die with my boots on." Whereupon, having uttered this grandiloquent phrase, he succumbed.

James A. Foster who was shot through the head in a restaurant at 4305 East Fifteenth Street by Julian Wingfield, a highway robber, who in turn wounded Wingfield so seriously that he could not escape, was given a reward of $50 by the police commissioners yesterday.

AUTHORS NOTE: James Alexander Foster was born in Ireland on January 14, 1877 and moved to the United States with his parents where they settled in the vicinity of Armstrong, Iowa.

While most lads his age were still living at home, James left home and began working at very early in his life hiring on for a number of dangerous jobs and responsibilities

At the age of fifteen, James and his brother drove supply wagons from Liberal, Kansas to Guymon, Oklahoma.

He became a member of the Militia at the age of sixteen and served in Company G 2nd Infantry at Camp Goldfield near Victor, Colorado.

At the age of twenty-one, J. A. Foster became a deputy sheriff in Beaver County, Oklahoma Territory. and after a brief stay there, he started to move around the country spending time in Ochiltree, Texas; Strong City, Kansas; and finally in Kansas City, Missouri.

Courtesy of Ronnie and Kenny Bird, grandsons of J. A. Foster

The shooting of Julian Wingfield by J. A. Foster would account for only one of the notches on Foster's Colt 45. According to Foster's Grandson's, Ronnie and Kenny Bird, there are two other notches on the handle of his Colt that have yet to be accounted for.

Marie had listened to every word Charlie read to her and after he had finished she said, "Oh Good Lord, Charlie," "Do you mean to tell me that things like that are still going on out her?"

"Yes Ma'am, they Certainly do," Charlie said to her.

J. A. Foster

"Well thanks a whole lot Charlie McCracken, that's all I needed to hear right now," as she turned and stared blankly out the window.

"When they reached the station back home, Marie stepped off the train, dropped to her knees, and kissed the wooden dock that ran alongside the track. When she stood back up she turned to your Granddad and said, "Never again will you put me through anything like that Charlie McCracken. Never again."

"Much to your Granddad Charlie's relief, time has a way of healing. There was a better part of a year left for Marie to get over it before he planned on taking her back out West again."

"Good Heavens," C.J. said, "He was one lucky man." " My wife would have skinned me alive if something like that ever happened to her."

I couldn't speak for the rest of the guys but being skinned alive would be a minor discomfort compared to what my wife would have in mind for me.

Just before my Grandmother turned the page so we could have a look at the photographs she said, "Pardon my language Wonzal, but I should mention one more thing."

Wonzal asked, "What's that Grandma?"

"Marie always called her trip West, "The Trip From Hell.""

We lost it that time.

The Elk Hunt

"A couple of months passed by and Marie began to mellow some concerning the trip she'd taken out West. On occasion she would mention to Charlie how beautiful she thought the mountains had been and how strange it was to see a cactus growing in the desert. Charlie used his head and didn't push his luck any with her by bringing up the subject of taking another trip out West. He still had time before plans had to be finalized."

"One day, Marie left the door wide open for him when she said, "The more I think about it Charlie, the more I believe I'd like to take another trip out West and spend a little more time looking around out there that we did on the last trip. I'd be willing to go as long as I knew for certain that we'd never face another snowstorm like that again.""

"Charlie answered her with, "A group of us have been planning on going elk hunting out there early this Fall. I know for certain that at least two of the women want to go along and do some hunting and sightseeing so at least you wouldn't be the only woman out there. What do you say.""

"Marie turned, looked at her partner in life and said, "Count me in." Little did she know that he already had."

"Charlie and a group of his hunting partners had already made plans to do an elk hunt in the Rocky Mountains of Northern Wyoming. They had chosen that particular area because of an article Charlie had found in an old Harper's New Monthly Magazine. None of the group had ever participated in such a hunt so there was a great deal of excitement and anticipation amongst them. They would spend a month out there and hunt for elk, antelope, bear, mountain goat, and sheep during that time."

"Through one of his banking associates, Charlie had been able to line up an area where they could hunt and a place for them to stay while they were out there. Besides providing the accommodations for the group, the outfitter would also furnish wagons, guides, pack animals, and whatever else was necessary to make their hunt a memorable one. Plans were finalized and they were set to depart on the first day of October, eighteen ninety eight."

"It was mid-morning when the train pulled into the station. The wagons were waiting there for them just as promised but it took a considerable amount of time to get everything unloaded off of the flatbed and loaded into the awaiting wagons. The lodge where they would be staying was nearly fifteen miles away and so by the time they were done packing they had little time to spare if they were to get to the lodge before dark."

"The trip started out on the edge of foothills that changed rapidly into high hills. As they gained elevation, the high hills would gradually be transformed into a low level mountain range."

"Charlie informed me upon their return that when the group reached the top of the hills, the wagons came to a stop and that the drivers had climbed down from the wagons and then proceeded to uncork a bottle or two. They all took a healthy swig and then offered to pass the bottles around saying, "Go ahead. There's more where this came from. It appeared as though they were bent on getting drunk right up there on the ridge despite the fact that they were working on another group's time."

"It didn't take too long for Charlie and his friends to put a stop to that. They didn't care whether the driver's appreciated it or not. After all, Charlie knew that he had to prevent any problem before it got out of hand. He didn't need anything that might result in a repeat of Marie's earlier trip West."

"I'd suggest you put your bottles away now and get moving again," he said, " or we'll file a complaint with the outfitter when we do get to the camp."

"Evidently no one had ever dared buck the drivers before because that's all it took. They climbed back onto the seats without any argument and they proceeded on their way again."

168

"It was a good thing Charlie spoiled the party. They were about a mile from where they needed to switch from the wagons over to pack horses for the final leg to the lodge, the axle on the lead wagon separated and there they sat.' Charlie told me, "Thank Heavens the drivers were sober of we would have spent the night out there on the trail."

The drivers hoofed up the mountain, picked up the pack horses, and then returned with them to the wagons."

"Once the pack horses were loaded, it didn't take very long to see why the wagons had to be left behind. In a short distance, the road completely disappeared and there was nothing but a talus slope left to travel on."

"An hour or so later, a cabin appeared a short ways up ahead. Marie looked at Charlie and whispered, "That's not the lodge we're supposed to stay in is it Charlie? That little cabin isn't big enough for three or four people let alone a group this size. You don't really expect me to stay in a place like that with a group of men do you?"

"By Jove it better not be!" he replied. "They told me it was a lodge, not shack."

"One of the driver's over heard them and interrupted their conversation. "Don't work yourselves into a lather folks. That's the guide' quarters, not yours. If you look, you can see the lodge up ahead there."

"Marie looked a couple of hundred yards up the trail and there stood the lodge. It looked as though it might turn out be a good trip after all."

"Marie was able to sleep in the next morning but Charlie couldn't. He had places to be and things to see."

"One of the guides woke him quite early the next morning and once the group was together, the first thing they did was to divide the group into parties of four. Each of the parties was then assigned to a guide."

"Each of the guides then set about preparing a huge stack of flapjacks, bacon, and eggs breakfast for their party. After a hearty breakfast, each party left the lodge led by their guide and headed off into the high country to scout for elk and get a look at the country they'd be hunting."

"Each of the guides showed their party a park they would hunt and then gave each man a general idea of where they should take their stand the next morning."

"Charlie told me that the most fascinating thing he'd seen up to that point were the glaciers and ice fields found in the area. Such things were completely new to the men so they spent the rest of the day exploring them."

Our Guides

"No one saw a thing the next morning and when the parties got together for lunch around noon, they found out why. The guides informed them that there weren't enough elk to bother with in the area because they hadn't come down from the higher elevations yet. The weather was still to nice for them up there yet."

"One of the guides summed things up by saying, "If the elk aren't going to come to us, we'll have to go up after them."

"The parties headed back to the lodge to get what supplies they needed, turned around, and then headed for higher ground."

"The outfitter had several different base camps scattered around the area that could be used on remote hunts. Some of the camps were a bit more rustic than others but they served the needs of the hunters. All of them had the two things necessary to satisfy a tired hunter at the end of the day; a place to eat, and a place to sleep."

"One of the many parks we would hunt."

"The glacier with it's runoff water fascinated us."

"There's nothing colder or sweeter than the water from a glacier."

"The glacier and surrounding scenery were breathtaking."

"A strange feeling to have your feet freezing and your brow sweating at the same time. We all suffered from an unexpected sunburn."

"A natural bridge of solid ice. Truly one of the wonders of nature."

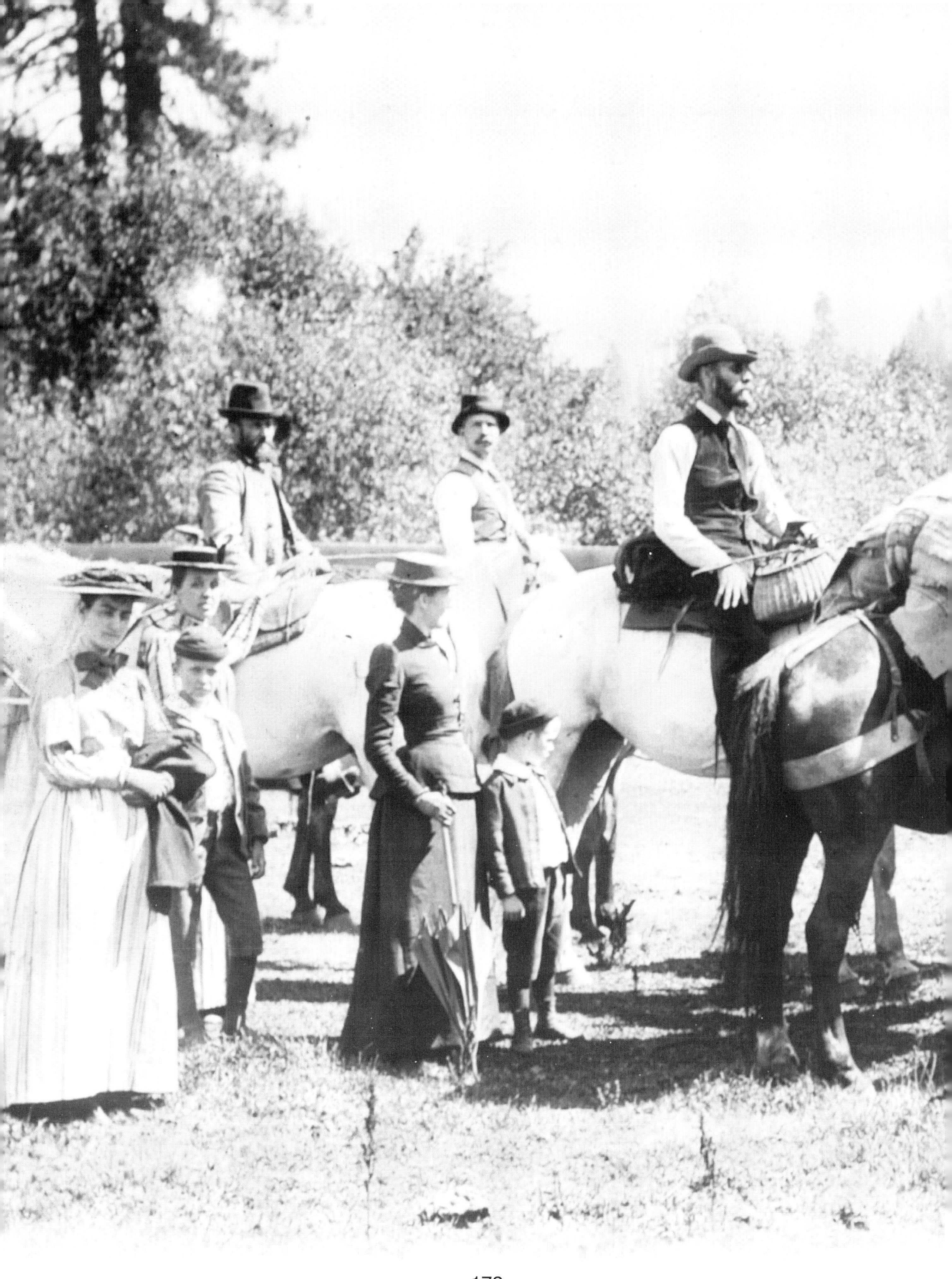

"The folks bid us farewell as we headed for what would hopefully be a more productive area to hunt."

"A perfect place to set up camp. We were surrounded by peace and quiet and game could be found a hundred yards from our tents."

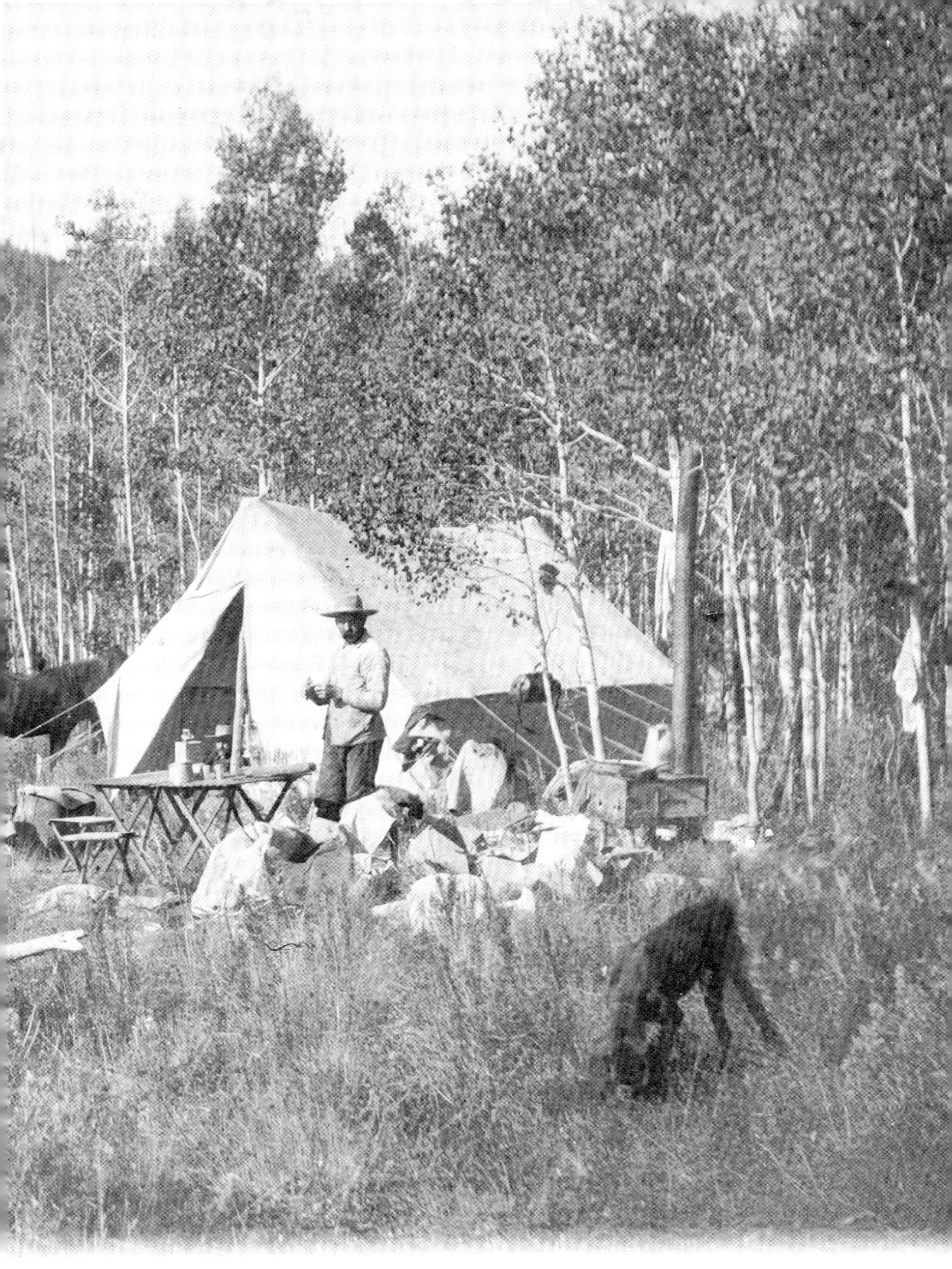

"Even though none of us city slickers knew what we were doing, the horses seemed to know exactly was was ahead of us every bit of the way."

"One of the more rustic remote camps that were available to us."

"Accommodations were far more modern in some of the camps than they were in others."

"No dining hall existed in any of the camps but at least we had a place to eat."

"The next morning all of the hunters in Charlie's party were on their stand an hour or so before daylight. Besides Charlie, the other members of the party consisted of Wallace Olson, Merl Lock, and Doc Prichard. None of the men had ever seen an elk close up so it would be a thrill for them just to see one, let alone get a shot at one."

"About 8 o'clock that morning, Doc heard a noise somewhere above him that sounded almost as though something was walking and moving about on the rocks above him. He couldn't imagine anything being able to climb up that high on solid rock, let alone be an animal of any size. Doc said he froze right where he was and never moved a muscle just in case it was an animal of some sort approaching."

"Doc stayed completely still until something up above him jarred a rock the size of a watermelon loose and sent it tumbling down the slope just barely missing his head."

"Shaken by the incident, he quick wheeled around to see what was up there above him and found himself staring eye to eye with a huge bull elk. As soon as the elk saw him, it turned and disappeared from sight. Doc never even had the chance to tell the others that he'd had a bull elk in his sights let alone fire a shot at one."

"After two hours of sitting, Wallace grew tired of staring at the same dull objects surrounding his stand so he decided to move around a little to warm himself up. At the same time he'd do a little sneak hunting."

"He made his way out of the dense pine growth that he'd been sitting in and worked his way into some mixed hardwoods that were scattered about the top of a ridge. He noticed that the ground he traveled on was literally torn up and upon closer inspection he saw that the snow was completely covered with tracks."

"He knelt down on one knee to check out the tracks and when he looked back up, he could detect movement moving through the trees a couple hundred yards in front of him. It was a herd of elk, and they were headed straight in his direction."

"Wallace didn't dare move but he really didn't need to. He had crouched right next to a stump that provided the best cover for him that he could of asked for."

"He saw that there were two lesser bulls towards the front of the herd and a six by six that was mingling among the cows towards the back of the herd. He decided to wait until the herd passed by and the big bull presented a wide open shot for him."

"As the huge bull stepped into an opening, Wallace took careful aim at it and squeezed off a round. The bull was visibly shaken as it slumped forward and stumbled a step or two. He knew that he'd hit it."

"However, the bull spun around and took off as though it hadn't been touched and ran on down the slope until it disappeared from sight. Wallace did the same thing that he would have done had he been hunting whitetails."

"He waited several minutes before he headed over to where the bull had been standing when he fired. Upon reaching the spot, he found blood sprayed all over the place. He'd not only hit it, he'd made a good hit on it."

"Wallace waited several more minutes before he started tracking. The bull had covered an awful lot of ground in a very short amount of time in it's desperate effort to escape, but after about two hundred yards the elk had slowed it's pace considerably. Wallace then slowed down his pace also."

"The elk had worked it's way down the south slope of the ridge where the snow had all but disappeared from the heat of the sun. Evidently the wound had started to plug up for it became increasingly difficult for him to follow the elk's tracks without the benefit of snow."

"Wallace knew he was close to the elk so he slowed himself down to a snail's pace. He'd spent a minute or two between each step looking around to see if he could spot the elk either laying dead or bedded down somewhere up ahead."

"He took another step or two and this time when he stopped, he noticed a group of branches that looked out of place among the deadfalls up ahead. It was his elk, and it was the first elk anyone in his bunch had ever taken."

"While Doc and Wallace were busy seeing elk, Merl was bust trying to catch a better glimpse of something that had been watching him. The first time he saw it was shortly after daybreak and whatever it was had darted between two groups of boulders down the slope from him. It moved so fast in the dull light of dawn that he had been unable to identify what it was."

"About an hour later after he had all but forgotten about it, there was a movement some distance below him and off to his left a little ways. He saw it move between the tangle of fallen timber on side of the slope and then it disappeared again. For a moment he wondered if he was seeing things but then something definitely moved again, but this time quite a bit closer to him than it was before."

"By now his curiosity had the best of him so he focused on the area that he had last seen the thing and waited. To his dismay, it never appeared again."

"He had agreed to meet the others at noon back over where his group had parted ways earlier that morning. As it was eleven-thirty, he decided it was time to get up and work his way over to the place where they were to meet.'

"Merl was about four hundred yards from his stand when he was suddenly overcome by a feeling that he was being watched. According to him it was the strangest sensation that he'd ever felt. He swung around just in time to see a huge cat-like figure disappear into the tall timber. The thing must have been following him from the time he'd left his stand. Startled as he was, Merl doubled his pace and headed straight for the spot they were to meet."

"The rest of the party were there by the time he arrived and by then he was so out of breath he couldn't speak. When Doc asked him if he'd seen anything, he was unable to answer him so Doc said, "What's the matter Merl? Did a cat get your tongue?"

"By then he'd caught his breath enough so managed to say, "That ain't as damn funny as you might think Doc and I'll tell you why it ain't." which he proceeded to do."

"I just had a cat watch my every move from sunup until about a half an hour ago. It even followed me on the way back over here."

"Charlie hadn't been listening and had no idea what was going on. He just walked into the middle of the conversation. "I don't know why you're so all-fired up about a cat following you home Merl. Hell, I've had a dozen cats at a time follow me home from the bank looking for a free handout."

"Not a cat like this you haven't Charlie. This ones eight feet long from the end of his nose to the tip of his tail and he wouldn't be looking for a handout to eat. More than likely he'd be looking for a hand to eat."

"Hiram, our guide, then stepped in and took over the conversation. "That was a mountain lion that was tailin' ya Merl. Some folks will call him a cougar, he's a panther to some, others call him a catamount, and a few refer to him as a puma. I myself call 'em a mountain lion.

"No matter what he's called, we don't want the likes of him hangin' around these parts. A cat like that'll spook the game right out of here and if'n he does and he can't find nuthin' else ta eat, he just might get it in his head to start sinkin' his teeth inta one of us. Twudn't be the first time it happened in these parts ."

"That was exactly what Charlie and his bunch wanted to hear."

"To ease their nerves a bit Hiram added, "One of the freight drivers in our outfit has himself a pair of pretty fair cat hounds. They'd be more than happy ta put the run on that cat." "

"And that they did."

178

"A big job ahead."

Credit - L A Huffman

"A nice 5 X 5."

"Doc and the bull he ambushed."

"Wallace and his prize elk."

It was C.J. that ended up asking the question that was on all of our minds. "Was the bull that Wallace shot the only elk taken by the group that year Grandma?"

"Heavens No," she replied. "I believe that was the year they ended up with all the elk they were allowed. They had more elk meat than they knew what to do with. They were up past their ears in it. As I recall, they ended up giving a good deal of it away."

"The near-toothless cat is loaded and ready to go."

179

"Hiram offers some stern advice to his dog not to mess with the elk."

"As I mentioned before, your Granddad Charlie's was a man who believed in sharing some of what he had with those folks who were a little less fortunate. Out there on one of his hunts he ran into a group of folks who were a whole lot less fortunate than any group of folks he'd ever come face-to-face with before."

Wonzal obviously hadn't quite caught the drift yet, evidenced by his next statement. "Who might that of been Grandma. Some of my long lost kin?" The rest of us just looked at him and shook our heads.

"No Wonzal, it wasn't any of your kin unless you're part Blackfoot Indian."

Then Glenn had to go and pipe up again. "Oh there's no doubt about it Grandma. Wonzal's a blackfoot for sure. He'll spend two weeks in deer camp and never even bothers to wash up and his feet get as black as the ace of spades."

That time it was Grandma who shook her head.

"To get on with my story you bunch of Hun yaks, Hank's Granddad Charlie had just shot a dandy bull elk. He was bent over it intent on getting it dressed out when he had the feeling he was being watched. He stood up and turned around to see if he was right and discovered he was! He nearly jumped clean out of his skin it startled him so bad."

"What'd he see that surprised him that bad?" I asked.

"There were two Indians on their ponies standing right next to him. He never heard them or their horses approach. He couldn't believe it. He told me if they'd of been hostiles he'd a been a dead man for sure."

"Well, one of the Indians spoke enough English so that Charlie could make out what he was saying. The Indian said they'd heard a shot and had come over to see what was going on. He then indicated to Charlie that if his group had more meat than they needed, he and his camp would take what ever was left. Then he added, "Tribe hungry. We no waste food like white man.""

"Charlie said that at the time he made his offer to the Indians it was more out of fear than it was out of generosity. He told them, 'Take this one here,' and then he held his hands up next to his head. He spread his fingers out and said, 'I want.' "

"Charlie watched to see the direction the Indians headed so the next day when one of his group took another elk, Charlie informed him that they would be taking the meat to the Indian camp, which they did."

"Charlie and the other fellow found the camp with little difficulty but both said later that they sort of wished they hadn't. What they rode into upset both of them more than anything they'd ever seen in their entire lives."

"The Indian had not told them the entire truth the day before. The Indians in the camp were practically starving and they were living squalor like they never knew existed. The rest of the meat they took that year went right straight to the Indian camp."

"It's hard telling how many lives they saved by doing that," I said.

"That's the same way I've always looked at it," Grandma replied.

Preparing to Move

A Family Group

Blackfoot profile.
"Man-Shot"

"Sopomoxo"
("Crowfoot")
Head Chief of the Blackfeet.

In winter costume.

Squaw & Papoose.

Warrior.

Remington

"The two Blackfoot braves that surprised Charlie."

"A Blackfoot village near the lake."

"A Blackfoot lodge and it's occupants."

"A child's curiosity, fascination, and appreciation with our visit to the village."

"Hiram displays a few trophies of the hunt."

"Several mounted trophies taken on our western hunt."
"It took more than one wall to display the trophies of our hunts."

"The day that they took the last elk they were allowed to take, Charlie's bunch got a notion in their heads to pull up stakes and move. That night seated around the campfire, they decided among themselves that it might be a good idea to move to a lower elevation and hunt for mule deer and antelope for a while, just for a change of pace. However, that decision was met by some stiff opposition from the guides."

"One of the guides told them, "If'n you put off huntin' goats and sheep when you got the chance, ya might not get the same chance a week from now.""

"Snow will put an end to gettin' back up here again. It can come so fast and fall so hard that you'd be chancin' it gettin' yurselve's stranded up here in the mountains. If'n that happened, ya might never make yur way back out again. Ya'd end up dying like the Donner's done a few years back, less'n you don't mind bein' cannibals.""

"The group decided that it might be in their better interest if they started hunting goats and sheep the next day."

"According to many in the group when they returned home, goat and bighorn sheep hunting was much like "a waiting game.""

" The guides took their party of hunters out each morning, assigned them to a vantage point, and then had them glass the slopes to look for goats or sheep. If they were fortunate enough to spot any, they would then have to stalk the animals before they could get a shot at them. More often than not there was quite an interval before they'd even see anything."

"Charlie said that many times after they had spent an hour or two stalking so that they were within shooting range, the animals had moved on to a different height and were further out of range than they were when the stalk began. Eventually however, each of the men managed to shoot themselves both a goat and a bighorn."

"They appreciated the fact that they were hunting with a reputable outfitter and knowledgeable guides because one day they ran into a game warden out there in those forsaken mountains, if you can believe such a thing."

"Charlie said if they hadn't been following the rules they would have faced a stiff fine and would not have been allowed to come back again. That would have hurt more than putting a dent in their billfold."

Our Goat Hunt

"The best weapon we had to reach out and touch a goat was the '95 Winchester shown here."

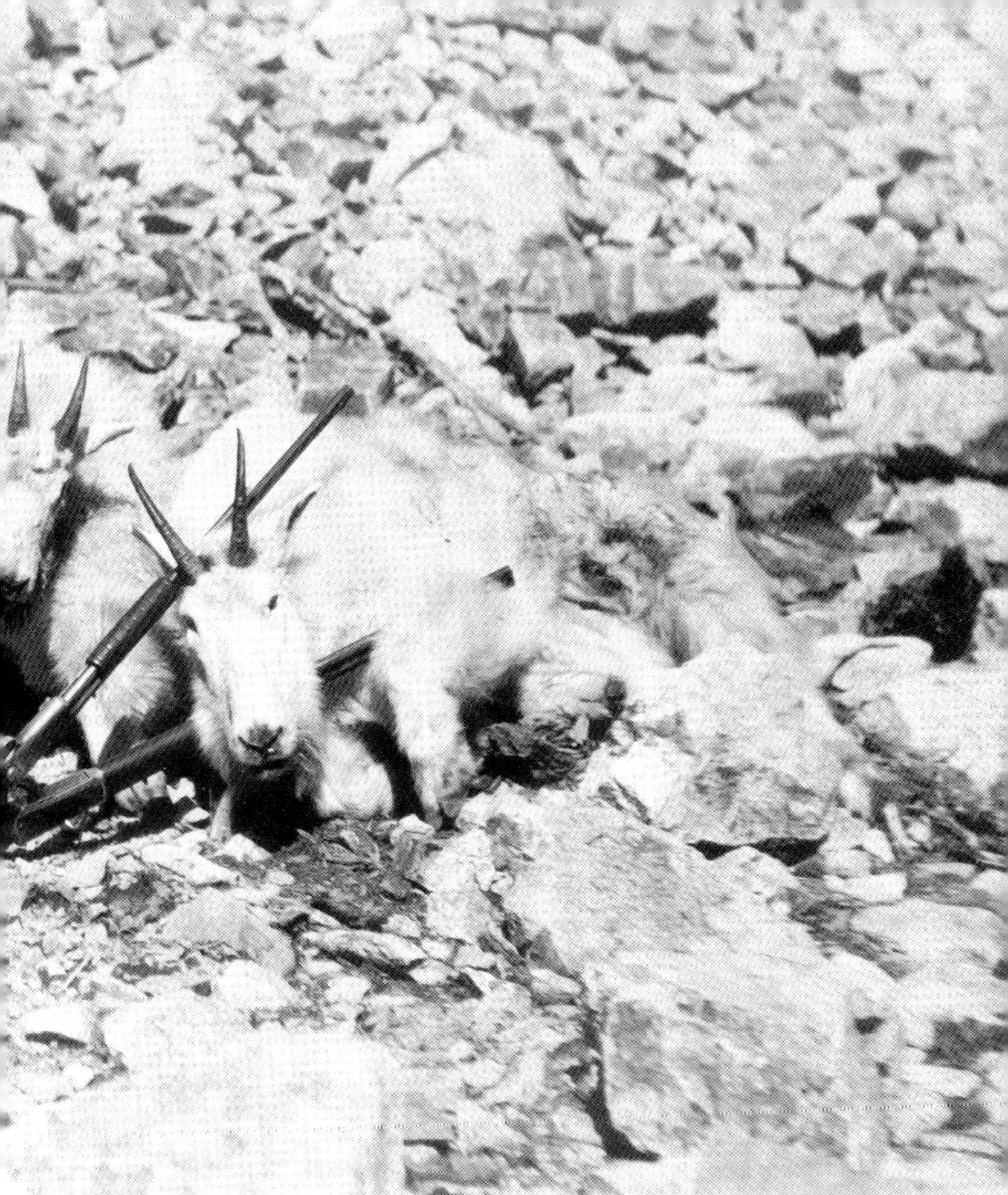

"To scout from a vantage point like this is hard to beat."

"Goats are amazing. They can navigate sheer cliffs with ease."

"A game warden pays Charlie and his guide a surprise visit. With tape in hand, the warden measured the goat while his assistant recorded his findings."

"The wardens recorded the weight of the cape to prevent thoughts of taking another goat."

Our Sheep Hunt

"Charlie glasses the slopes in search of sheep."

"Charlie's Model '95 reaches out for sheep too."

"Charlie admires his prize bighorn."

Credit - L.A. Huffman

"Hunting becomes a real challenge in knee-deep snow."

"Luck was on his side. One slip and his bighorn would have disappeared from sight."

"The skulls are skinned and fleshed and ready to start drying."

190

A Run-In with a Grizzly

"One of your Granddad's bunch almost didn't make the return trip home, at least in one piece. He ran into something he wasn't quite prepared to handle up there in the mountains."

(By then we knew better. None of us interrupted Grandma when she started a story like that. We knew she was going to finish the story for us.)

"This man Fredric came back to camp one night telling about the huge black bear tracks he'd run into up on the mountain near the timber line. He said, "I've seen some pretty big bear tracks in my life but none of the would even compare to what I saw this morning. They were so huge they took my breath away when I looked at them.""

"I went to put my hand in one of them and I'd say the track was at least four inches wider than my hand. I mean to say that it was four inches beyond either side of my hand!"

"And talk about long, you wouldn't believe it if you saw it. There was no sense in me trying to compare it to my hand. I swear it was half again as long as my foot."

"The rest of you can go ahead and chase a goat or a sheep tomorrow. I'm going after that thing. If I'm lucky enough to get it, I'll have myself a world record black bear for sure."

"Fredric was known to be a blow-hard and a teller of some pretty tall tales so the rest of the men generally just blew him off. The men just figured that this tale was just some more hair off the same dog's back. They nodded to him and said, "You're right Fredric, if the thing is as big as you say it is, you probably will have something to brag about if you get it.""

"The next morning he left camp early. He'd told his guide that he was going to get back on his stand and set up early so he could start glassing for sheep as soon as the sun came up. Had the truth been known, he was headed straight for the very spot where he'd last seen the monstrous bear tracks. He was bound and determined to shoot himself the biggest black bear there was in the entire world."

"The day before on his way back to camp, he'd come across a gut pile from a bighorn that another member of the party had shot. He reasoned that if the bear hadn't found it and had disposed of it during the night, it would surely find it in a day or two. He'd sit over the gut pile and wait for the bear to walk in."

"Fredric found a soft spot on the edge of the timber next to a tree that he could sit down by and rest his back against.

He made himself comfortable and began his hunt."

"About five hours into his sit, he grew weary of seeing nothing and closed his eyes just long enough to rest them a moment. Instead, he fell sound asleep."

"He was awakened by sounds of sniffing that were very nearby. He opened his eyes very slowly and there before him stood the source of the strange sniffing sounds. It was a bear, but it wasn't the one he was waiting for. This bear was large but it certainly wasn't big enough to be the one that had left the huge tracks he'd seen the day before."

"As he watched it, he noticed something else about the bear. It didn't sport the glistening coat of black hair nor did it have the white patch on it's chest that was common to a black bear. This bear's coat was more on the brownish side and it's long guard hairs were tipped with traces of silver white. That seemed curious to him."

"He sat and stared at the bear for some time until, from the far back reaches of his mind, he started to recall several articles that he'd read in Harper's Monthly Magazine regarding the bears of the West. He had also seen prints done by Currier and Ives that depicted an almost devil worship that the Indians of the West had towards this particular type of bear that lived in the West."

"One of the articles that he'd read in Harper's described the hunts of General George Armstrong Custer that had taken place in the Dakotas. He used a pack of long-legged hounds to track and run down his bear."

"Another article in Harper's described the hunts of Theodore Roosevelt in the territory of Montana. In both instances, the bears they hunted were not even a close cousin to the black bears of Minnesota, Wisconsin, and Michigan. Those bears were called grizzlies, bears that didn't run from the sight or smell of man, and showed fear of absolutely nothing, let alone man."

"There was something even worse than their having no fear of man. They were known to have actually hunted men down and killed them for food."

"Fredric suddenly developed the driest spot in his throat that he'd ever experienced, so dry in fact that he couldn't swallow. By that time, the bear had worked it's way over to the gut pile and had laid down right in front of it. The bear then began dining on the choicest parts and it appeared to be bent on staying right there until it devoured the entire pile of guts. Fredric knew he was in for a long sit."

"What seemed like an eternity but was probably less than five minutes, the gut-eating bear suddenly rose from it's prone position, turned, and then stood upright on it's hind legs. It had prepared itself to face an intruder that had suddenly appeared on the scene. Then, as quickly as it had stood up it dropped back down on all four, wheeled around, and lit out for the timber as tight as it could go. Fredric soon saw why it had decided to leave."

"The largest living creature he'd ever seen in his life lumbered into view. Fredric was now looking at the bear that had left the big tracks the day before."

"Fredric carried a Model '95 Winchester with him that was chambered in a 40-82. It was his pride and joy. The men back in camp, every last one of them including your Granddad, had ridden him pretty hard about that rifle. They'd told him his favorite piece was nothing short of overkill, and that he'd never need anything that big for what they were hunting for. His answer to them had been, "Better to much than not enough."

"He was about to find out who was right."

"The grizzly's head swung back and forth as it lumbered it's way in and headed towards the gut pile. Every movement it made was as though it was spoiling for a fight, like it would tangle with anything it saw at the slightest provocation. It's actions reminded Fredric so much of the neighborhood bully that he'd had to content with nearly every day of his life while he was growing up."

"Nobody ever dared confront the bully so he got by pushing everybody in the neighborhood around years. He did that is, until the day he finally pulled Fredric's trigger."

"That particular day Fredric's kid brother came home all bloodied up and it completely set him off. He actually went looking for the bully and when he finally found him, he waded into the kid with everything he had. By the time it was over, half of the bully's teeth were gone and Fredric left the kid with a cut over his eyebrow that never did heal quite right."

"It appeared to Fredric that history was about to repeat itself."

"Fredric, seated on the ground like he was, knew he was at a distinct disadvantage if the bear spotted him or caught his scent. He figured if he could just get in an upright position, he could not only aim better but he could also put a tree between he in the bear in the event it charged. He moved as slowly as he possibly could as he went to stand up but evidently it wasn't slow enough."

"Despite the fact that the grizzly had it's head half buried in the pile of guts, it must have caught some movement. It stopped eating, swung it's body around so it was facing Fredric, and than reared up on it's hind legs."

"It towered way over Fredrick as it held it's front legs out in front of it's massive chest. It then uttered a low, ominous growl, dropped back down on all four, and charged Fredric head on."

"When he got back to camp, Fredric told the men that the only reason he was still alive was because of pure instinct. The charge occurred so quickly that the only chance he had was to get his rifle up to his hip, pull the hammer back, and fire. That shot was the only shot he had time for."

"The 40-82 took the grizzly just below it's left eye and exited out the back of the bear's skull, but even a bullet through the brain wasn't enough to stop the grizzly in it's tracks. Fredric dove to the side in order to avoid being crushed beneath the massive creature."

"Later on that day there was talk among the group of perhaps trading guns and upgrading their firepower when they got back home."

"Fredric made believers out of some that day."

"Sioux warriors perform the Dance of the Bear."
Credit - Currier & Ives

"The taking of a grizzly by the Sioux was no simple task."
Credit - Currier & Ives

"We didn't really hunt grizzlies. We encountered them."

"Fredric confronts a grizzly on his terms."

"The grizzly was no match for Fredric's 40-82 Winchester."

"Fredric and the big bear's hide."

Our Hunt for Mule Deer

"With a limit of sheep and goats and a run-in with a grizzly behind them, the men were willing and eager to pack up and move camp on down to the foothills where they could then hunt for mule deer. If the were successful getting their limit of mule deer, they would then move their camp still further down the slopes to the flatlands and finish their hunt off pursuing antelope."

"The men in your Granddad Charlie's group were all veteran deer hunters and there wasn't a one in the bunch that couldn't brag about taking several nice whitetail bucks during their lifetime. However, they may have hunted deer before, but none of them had ever hunted deer that acted as strange to them as a mule deer."

"Those men had hunted whitetails before. They were used to hunting bucks that would put their head down and take off as tight as they could go until they reached the next county."

"Mule deer didn't do that. They'd stand and stare at a man for a few moments, take off, and then they'd stop again and turn their head for another look before they went over the ridge.

"And when a whitetail ran, it meant business. There was no doubt in anyone's mind that it wanted to put as much distance between it and the hunter in the shortest time possible."

"Mule deer didn't run flat-out like a whitetail did. Instead they would bounce from one side to the other like some sort of deranged jackrabbit. That completely rattled the men."

"Charlie said that while hunting for mule deer was both fun and exciting, it was something that definitely took a great deal of getting used to."

"The guides set up camp for the men in the lower foothills where they could either hunt an area consisting of brush and mesquite trees or an area of timbered country in the foothills depending on which direction they decided to ride on a particular day."

"For the first couple of days, most of the group were content to hunt the mesquite area near the camp. They spread out in the morning and hunted over a nearby water hole or they'd sit on either side of a shallow trickle of water that ran between the foothills and wait for the deer to come to them."

"Bucks were few and far between but there were numerous mule deer does that would appear at midday for a drink or be seen bouncing their way though the brush. Though they were legal, no one bothered to shoot one unless fresh meat was needed in camp."

"Charlie was off on one of his forays one morning, sitting and waiting for a buck to show up when he heard the sound of gravel being rolled beneath the hooves of some animal. He fully expected to see a deer come into view but much to his surprise it was a rider on horseback instead."

"He saw immediately that it wasn't any of his group and it wasn't one of the guides so he stood up and waved his arms in an effort to hail the rider down. The rider was as much surprised to see another man out there as your Granddad was."

"The fellow rode over to Charlie, introduced himself, and asked your Granddad what he was doing in those parts. Charlie explained that he was hunting for mule deer, told the man the name of the outfitter he was with, and then described to the rider where they were camped. All the time he was talking the rider had one hand on his pistol which made your Granddad quite uneasy."

"What was that guy doing out there in the middle of nowhere?" I asked.

"As it turned out," Grandma replied, "he was a ranch hand for the biggest ranch there was in those parts. He was riding around looking for rustlers that had been stealing cattle for the past month or so."

"That's right." Grandma replied. "He thought at first that Charlie might be one of the rustlers he was looking for. He was ready to shoot him if he made one wrong move."

"What happened then?" I should have known better than to ask. Grandma looked at me over the top of her wire-rimmed reading glasses with a look that only a grandmother can give and then she proceeded to tell us.

"Once he realized that your Granddad was okay, he started to talk hunting with him. He told your Granddad that they went through a pile of deer back at the ranch just to keep the men fed. He added that nearly all of the deer they took were does because they didn't seem to taste near as strong as bucks did. Besides that, there appeared to be a lot more does around than there were bucks."

"He told Charlie that if he wanted to keep his shootin' eye sharpened up that he was more than welcome to knock over a few does and bring them over to ranch. "With that bunch of hungry hands back at the ranch, it's nuthin' for us to put away at least a deer a day," he told him."

"Your Granddad was more than happy to oblige him. He told the ranch hand that he'd be bringing some venison over to him the next day. The cowpoke said, "Just follow the only trail there is out here and it'll lead you straight to the ranch." "With that said, he rode off."

"It was a good morning for a hunt. An inch or two of snow had fallen during the night and Charlie had something to hunt for even if there were no bucks to be seen."

"It didn't long for him to start rolling does over. When he had three of them down, he took his time as he gutted them out so the cook at the ranch would welcome more of them."

"With that chore out of the way, he rode until he reached the trail which he took and headed for the ranch."

"He rode for the better part of an hour and was beginning to doubt himself when he spotted a rider working his way down out of the foothills with a deer tied across the back of his horse. Charlie held up and waited for the rider to catch up to him."

"As the rider drew close, he hollered to Charlie, "It looks like we might be headed in the same direction.""

Charlie answered, "If you're headed to the ranch we are.

I was starting to wonder if I was headed in the right direction."

"You'd of got there sooner or later," answered the cowpoke. "I'll lead the way. You can follow me," and in a short while the ranch was in sight."

"The cook was nearly beside himself when he saw the does Charlie rode in with. "I usually end up trimming half of the meat away when one of the cowpokes comes in with somethin' he shot," he said. "Between their either blowing a big hole clean through the guts or dragging 'em through the dirt when they bring 'em here, I've got my work cut out for me when I try and get one ready to eat. At least you know what you're doing."

"He motioned to your Grandad to follow him over to the south side of the cook shanty. "Looka here," he said. "Cowpokes ain't even got enough horse sense to hang what they get in the shade. They hang 'em over here where the sun can get at 'em and then expect me to serve them something like they'd have if'n they were eatin' at a fine restaurant in Rawlings or Billings or Lord knows where."

"Hell's Bells, looky here," he said. "One of them yeh hoos blasted this bunch of birds and they went and hung 'em up with the innards in 'em. They must think they're in England or sumthin. Ya know, there's only so much I can do with what they brung in. I ain't no miracle worker. Yu'd think they'd know at least that much wouldn't ya? ."

"Your Granddad had to agree with him."

"After the deer were hung up to cool, the cook pointed over at the foothills towards the West and said.," If'n you and your group are after bucks, you'd stand a fair chance of seein' one if'n you spent a little time wandering around over there."

"Your Granddad thanked him, got on his horse, and headed back to camp again. He knew where he'd be spending the next day."

"Early the next morning, Charlie, Doc, Merl, and Wallace left camp and headed towards the foothills West of the ranch in search of some bucks. They rode up into the hills until they found a grassy open area where the horses could graze. They tethered the horses so that they wouldn't stray and they headed off in four different directions to hunt."

"They'd barely left sight of one another when a shot rang out over in the direction that Merl had taken. A short while later, another shot echoed through the foothills from the direction that Wallace had taken. Charlie had yet to see so much as a bird since they'd split up."

"It was about ten o'clock when the third shot was heard and then a fourth. Your Granddad thought to himself, "That had to have been Doc that time."

"He still hadn't seen anything."

"They'd agreed to meet back at noon where they'd left the horses. If they were fortunate enough to drop any, they figured by the time they got them packed up that it'd be time to head back to camp."

"There your Granddad was, the one who'd found the place to hunt and he hadn't seen a thing or fired a shot. He was a little put out to say the least."

"It had gotten to be about eleven thirty so he decided to head back and meet the others. Your Granddad was never one to give up or ever let his guard down which was a good thing for him."

"Every step he took was muffled by the lush growth of moss that grew in the shadows of the tall pines as he continued to sneak hunt on his way back to the horses. He'd pause every two or three steps and then scan on either side and in front of him. Then he'd take two or three more steps and do the same thing all over again."

"He was only a short distance from the horses when he paused once more. He glanced up the slope off to his right and did a double-take. There was a buck staring right back at him."

"However, as soon as Charlie started to raise his rifle, the buck took off up the slope bouncing this way and that between the trees as he quickly put some distance between the two of them."

"Your Granddad said that trying to follow that deer through the trees was like trying to shoot a partridge that was drunk on fermented berries except the buck did something that a partridge would never do. It stopped to take one more look at him before it went over the hill. That was all time your Granddad needed. He took aim just behind it's shoulder and dropped it right where it stood."

"Charlie finally ended up with a buck but not without taking a good razzing from the rest of his party. Their bucks all sported a fine set of highly polished antlers that a taxidermist could take great pride in preparing. The antlers on your Granddad's buck couldn't be mounted. His were completely covered in velvet."

"A few day's in the brush had us looking much like the guides: One Rough Crew."

197

Our Antelope Hunt

"According to the cook at the ranch, there were large herds of antelope on the flatlands East of the ranch. The cook also told them that no one on the ranch went out of their way to hunt antelope but if an antelope happened to get in their way they were more than willing to bring it back with them. Doc passed the word on to the guides who then rode off to check out the story."

"Upon their return, the guides wore a grin that could be seen a mile away. They reported huge herds of antelope that had little fear of a man on a horse. That was something seldom ever seen. Most of the time an entire herd would take off running at the slightest hint of danger. The guides attributed this lack of fear to the fact that they'd been hunted so little. They would pull up camp and move where they were closer to the herds."

"They set up camp once they found an area where they could find sufficient firewood for their campfire. However, where they found firewood there was no water. The only water they found was in a mud hole about half a mile from camp and every animal in the area used it as a watering hole. The water wasn't fit for humans to drink."

"For a short time the guides pretended that the camp would have try and get by on as little water possible which of course meant no morning coffee. However, there's and old saying that goes, "One only becomes thirsty when there is nothing to drink." That certainly held true that day."

"As soon as the first man complained about the lack of water, one of the guides said, "If'n any of you boys are thirsty, you better follow me." which they did.

"The guide strode over to a large barrel-shaped cactus that looked much like the wooden water barrel they were used to seeing back home. He pointed over to it and said, "There's your water"

"Then he took an axe, chopped a big hole in the top of it and sure enough, there was the water they needed."

Good old Wonzal came through for us again. "Wouldn't it be great if we could just walk up and chop a hole in a jack and have beer start pouring out of it?"

"Think of the work we'd save not having to haul it into camp with us."

Grandma was ready for Wonzal that time. Before he could even offer one of his weak apologies again she said, "Nothing you could say would surprise me anymore Wonzal so it's only fair for me to warn you about something Wonzal."

"What's that?" he asked.

Grandma was completely calm as she said to him, "A few years back when Hank's Granddad Jennings was still alive, a rabid skunk wandered onto our place one day. As you probably already know, there's no known cure for that disease either, so Hank's granddad up and shot the poor devil to put it out of it's misery."

If that didn't make Wonzal feel like the South end of a horse headed North, nothing ever would.

Grandma slowly turned another page of the album and continued, "Hiram rode out that day and showed the bunch how he hunted antelope. When he spotted a herd, he'd lay low in the saddle and then ride slowly towards them. Antelope are curious animals and as long as they aren't scared they'll stand there and watch a rider approach.

"When he got within range, he raised himself up real slow and took a shot before the herd got wise to him and ran off. Hiram's method worked so well that every man in the party had a dandy pronghorn or two by nightfall."

"The next day the party decided to modify Hiram's method a bit. They loaded themselves up in a buckboard and all but the driver laid down in the box until they were close enough to the herd to shoot. They'd wait until the driver signaled them and then they all sat up and fired at the same time."

" That method worked so well that they soon had all the antelope they wanted."

"Their limit of antelope ended their hunt that year, but others would follow," she said. "Your grandfather and your grandmother enjoyed their hunting trip out West more than anything they'd ever done and except for the following Fall, they headed out West to hunt for the next several years."

"Water was as near as the closest cactus."

"Our guides method of hunting antelope."

"Hiram dresses out his antelope."

"Charlie's pronghorn buck."

"Hiram shows how to transport his pronghorn."

"Our modified version for approaching a herd."

Guides that Led the Way For Us

"What'd they do the Fall after the hunted out West," I asked. "Did they stay in Wisconsin and hunt whitetails like they'd been used to doing?

"No they didn't," Grandma replied. "Your Granddad and his bunch weren't quite satisfied with what all they'd hunted yet. They felt that there was a lot more game for them to go after."

"One of his cronies had done some reading about hunting moose up in Canada so he suggested they try a hunt up there for moose before they all got too old to enjoy it."

"Your Granddad jumped at the opportunity of course. That man would have gone to Hades to hunt for a glass of boiling water if someone had suggested it to him."

"Being the banker like he was, your Granddad had connections all over the country and evidently quite a few in Canada too. It's a probably a good thing that no one ever suggested hunting elephants in Africa to him. He no doubt would have had connections even over there if the truth was known."

"That's all your Grandmother Marie would have needed, Hank."

"What's that?" I asked

"Oh, getting charged by a bull elephant, attacked by a lion, having a crocodile after her, or seeing some big snake hanging down out a tree smack dab in front of her."

"Lord knows what could have happened to her over there. She was a nervous enough wreck as it was. That would have completely done her in."

If a trip like that would have done her in, I could only imagine a trip like that would do to me. My wife would have found me curled up under the Christmas tree, gift wrapped in a straitjacket and babbling to myself for sure."

"Your Granddad knew from experience after his trip out West that the way to a successful hunt in strange territory was by having a good set of guides. Consequently, the first thing he did was check with some of his acquaintances that had hunted there before. He got the names of some really good outfitters and guides from them."

"It proved to be a wise move on your Granddad's part to check around before he started making arrangements for a hunt. Not only did he find out what to look for when it came to hiring guides and outfitters, he also found out quite a bit about moose hunting at the same time."

"He found out that a good outfitter would supply everything a party of hunters needed in order to have a successful hunt and the that only thing a hunter should have to worry about was his weapon and the clothes he wore on his back."

"As far as guides went, any good guide should know every aspect of the hunt, know the country like the back of his hand, and make the trip as enjoyable for his client as he could."

"One guy even went so far as to tell Charlie that the best advice he could give him was to make certain the guide could cook. A month is a long time in the brush."

"Another fellow gave your Granddad the best piece of advice that he possibly could have, which your Grandfather kept to himself."

"If you ever have your choice of guides, pick one that's as close to being a full-blooded Indian as you can. They know how to call in a moose better than anyone alive."

Currier & Ives

"Our fishing guides."

"Every one of our guides could have been a chef."

"A guide packs out a buck for his client."

"Having an Indian guide usually spelled success."

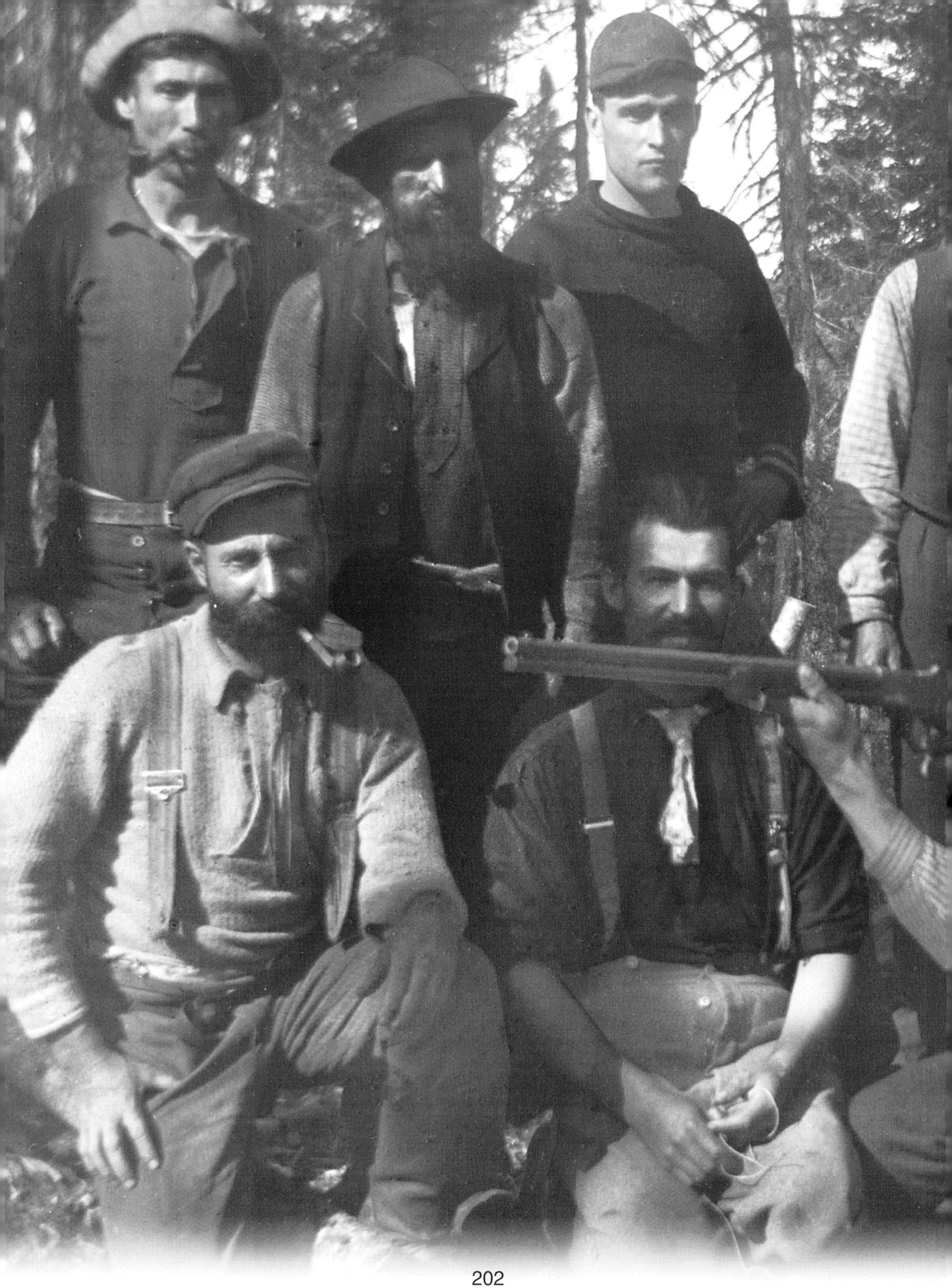

"Guides had to be good. Often our life depended on them."

The Moose Hunt

"What did Charlie find out about moose hunting itself?" C.J. asked.

(I fully expected C.J. to get nailed for asking her a question like that. To this day I've never understood why my Grandmother would look at me one way and look at someone else in another way when we'd both ask the same question. Perhaps she just expected more of me.)

"Charlie found out there was really three different times and several different ways to hunt moose. Moose could be called into close range during the rut, they could be hunted from a canoe by drifting down a river or by paddling in the quiet bays of a lake. Later on in the Fall and the early Winter they could also be tracked and ambushed. He reasoned that if they planned their hunt right, they stood a good chance of getting in on several different ways to hunt."

"The day finally came when eight of Charlie's hunting group were finally nestled in a primitive cabin in the back woods of Canada. Just getting there was a memorable experience in itself."

"To begin with, they had to motor their way for more than a hundred miles over some of the roughest, rutted, desolate roads that existed in North America. Numerous stops and several flat tires later, they managed to reach the Canadian Railroad that would take them into the far North woods where they would carry out their hunt."

"For ten hours the train rocked back and forth and leaned this way and that before it finally came to a stop in the middle of nowhere. Under the watchful eye of the brakeman, they unloaded their baggage as quickly as they could in order that the train could be on it's way again."

"There was an eerie quiet as they stood and watched the train as it pulled away, and grow smaller and smaller until it finally disappeared as a speck on the far horizon. They were as alone as they'd ever been."

"Charlie understood when he made the final arrangements that someone would be there to meet them when the train arrived but not a soul was in sight. He began to feel guilty and blame himself that things weren't going according to plans but there was little anyone could do about it other than to mill around and wait until someone eventually showed up."

"In the meantime, a visitor of sorts did stop by to pay the men a visit. Emil spotted it first and shouted to the others, "Well look who's coming down the track."

"The others glanced up and there it was, a full-grown cow moose, and it was headed right straight for them. Several of the men ran for cover as tight as they could but three of them stood their ground to see how close the moose would get before it would turn and ran away."

"Instead of running away, Charlie said the blooming thing walked right up to them and started licking the salt off their hands. When it was that close to them, they didn't dare turn their back on it for fear it'd get mad and charge one of them so there was nothing they could do but stand there and let the thing lick away to it's hearts content."

"About that time one of the guides made his appearance and shouted at the moose, "Get the blazes out of here or I'll be frying you up for supper."

"It was as though the moose understood what he was saying because it turned around, slowly walked off the railroad bed, and disappeared into the brush."

"That ignorant animal anyway," he said. "She started acting weird like that when a bear ran off with her calf this Spring. She's just lonely if you ask me."

"Doc was a little irritated as it was after standing around for an hour or so out in the cold so he said in a rather sarcastic tone , "If all the moose up here act like that one, I've just wasted my time and money coming up here. Who wants to go back home and brag about shooting a tame moose?"

"The whole group was caught off guard when the guide fired back at Doc but as Charlie said later, they were listening. "You start goin' around judgin' all moose by the way that one acts and one of these fine days you're going to wake up dead."

"There may be a few of 'em that act docile and stupid like that cow does but you get yourself anywhere near a bull that's crazed with the rut or one that you've gone and wounded 'cause you can't shoot straight, you'll have more trouble on your hands than you'll know what to do with. A moose ever gets in that mood, they'd sooner kill ya' than look at ya'."

"Needless to say, that changed Doc's tune in a fast hurry."

"Once his ruffled feathers settled back in place, the guide apologized for not being on time and being there when they'd arrived."

"The miserable rail lines up here don't run on a tight schedule like they do down your way. They really think they've done something when their train pulls within an hour one side or the other of when they're supposed to."

"Today they were early, the next time they'll be late. You just never know about 'em."

With that out of the way, the guide looked the group over and said what they'd been waiting to hear, " Let's go hunting."

"Word was when they got back home that the wagon ride into camp was a long one and the walk they had was a rough one but they all agreed when they got back home that it was worth every bit of the misery they had to go through."

"For being as far back in the woods as it was, the cabin proved to be more than any of them expected. The beds were clean and comfortable and despite the fact that the place didn't have running water, they had a makeshift setup there that enabled the men to take a hot shower whenever they wanted to."

"At supper they found out that the head guide also knew how to cook. Good food and plenty of it were most important to them after a hard day's hunt."

"After they'd eaten and the guide had cleaned up the mess, he called the group together and said,"

"I will be assigning each of you your own guide for the hunt. He will be responsible for your safety and will see to it that your hunt is as successful as it can possibly be."

"As the guides stepped into the room, Charlie was suddenly reminded about something his friend had said about taking on a guide;" "If you're given a choice, pick a guide that's as close to being a full-blooded Indian that you can."

"It seemed like sound advice to Charlie at the time so that's exactly what he did. He felt if he didn't it might come back to haunt him."

"Rather than wait and regret it later, Charlie spoke up before the head guide even got started. He told me that he didn't hesitate for a moment and he wasn't one bit bashful when he did it either. "

"Would it be all right with you if I picked my own guide out of the group? If you ask me why, it just might be that I just have a good feeling about one of them in particular."

"It was like a wounded bull moose almost looked forward to rearranging the anatomy of an unsuspecting hunter."

Fredric Remington

"Caution was the word of the day when it came to approaching a wounded moose."

A.B. Frost

"It was all but certain death whenever a hunter let his guard down."

B. Cory Kilvert

206

"The head guide replied, "I don't see nuthin' wrong with that if it's okay with the rest of your group. It don't make no difference to me one way or the tother." and so he did."

"As far as he could tell, Ishmay, Charlie's newly-picked guide was the nearest thing to a full blooded Cree that could be found in all of Canada. Charlie knew he'd made a good choice too, for the two of them bonded the moment they shook hands."

"Early the next morning, Ishmay woke Charlie with a gentle touch on his shoulder and whispered, "We move now,""

"Ishmay had Charlie's breakfast ready and waiting when he sat down to eat and while Charlie wolfed down his meal of fresh walleye and eggs, Ishmay checked over your Granddad's bag to make certain he had everything needed to spent the day. As soon as he was finished, they made their way down to the lake, slipped into their canoe, and headed for the opposite shore."

"Ishmay eased the canoe onto the shore and whispered to your Granddad, "Quiet now," "Moose good ears." With that he lead your Granddad into the dense spruce forest that bordered the entire lake and headed towards the East."

"For several hundred yards they stepped over countless fallen trees and walked around tangles of deadfalls until they reached a point of land that jutted a quarter of a mile out into a swamp overgrown with alders and red willows."

"No sooner were they seated than Charlie began to notice the wide trails that lead in and out of the swamp on either side of the point. About that same time, Ishmay whispered again. "Moose trail. You watch.""

"They sat there for perhaps half an hour without moving or saying a word to one another. Finally, Ishmay broke the silence. "Me call now." "Be ready.""

"Despite the fact that Charlie knew it was coming, the sound that came out of Ishmay's birch bark call startled him so bad that goose bumps chased each other up and down his arms and across the back of his neck. Your Granddad described it as a combination with the bellowing of a heifer in heat mixed in with a cow calling for it's calf. Ishmay called twice and then all was quiet again."

"Fifteen minutes later as your Granddad was looking off to his left and was concentrated on watching for movement in the willows below, Ishmay let loose with another of his strange sounding calls again. It was a repeat of the first time, but it still sent goose bumps off on their wild race."

"Five minutes later Ishmay turned towards Charlie and whispered, "Be ready. "Moose come now.""

"Charlie had all he could do to contain himself and keep from jumping clean out of his skin.
"What?" "Where?" "Which direction? raced through his mind but he knew better than to speak."

"Suddenly there was no need to ask questions. The answers could be heard coming from the swamp below as a bull thrashed around in the willows, challenging every single one of them to do battle with him."

"Then it grew very quiet and Ishmay said, "Me call again.""

"This time the sound that came from the birch bark tube Ishmay held up to his lips was barely loud enough to be heard. The call was so forlorn and begging that Charlie could barely even listen to it. Evidently it was having the same affect on the bull down in the swamp. He couldn't take it any longer either."

"Your Granddad told me that all he could think of when that bull charged out of the swamp, came up the end of the point, and headed straight for him was to be standing in front of a locomotive bearing down on him at thirty miles an hour."

"All your Granddad really remembered was the glazed look in the bull's eyes as it closed the distance between Ishmay and your Granddad."

"Ishmay was saying, "Shoot." "Shoot Now!" so your Granddad did.

"The bull was coming head-on as it raced towards them. Charlie's first shot caught it just below it's chin and then entered it's neck. The bull stumbled, caught itself before it went down, and then continued coming straight at them. Your Granddad fired again and this time connected a little lower than before. The bullet went between the brisket and the shoulder and lodged itself in the heart. The bull dropped but a few scant yards in front of them."

Wonzal blurted out, "Holy Balls," " If happened to me I'd be wettin' my pants right now."

Glenn had to express his feelings then too. "I'm with you on that one Wonzal." "The trouble with me is, I might mess myself up even worse than that."

We fully expected my Grandmother to give all of us a good chewing out after an outburst like that, but when she spoke there was no need to fear.

"I hate to agree with either one of you two Hunyaks," she said," but I'm afraid I'd be looking for the nearest two-holer myself right about now."

It was time for a break anyway.

"Happiness prevailed in this moose camp with one down and two to go."

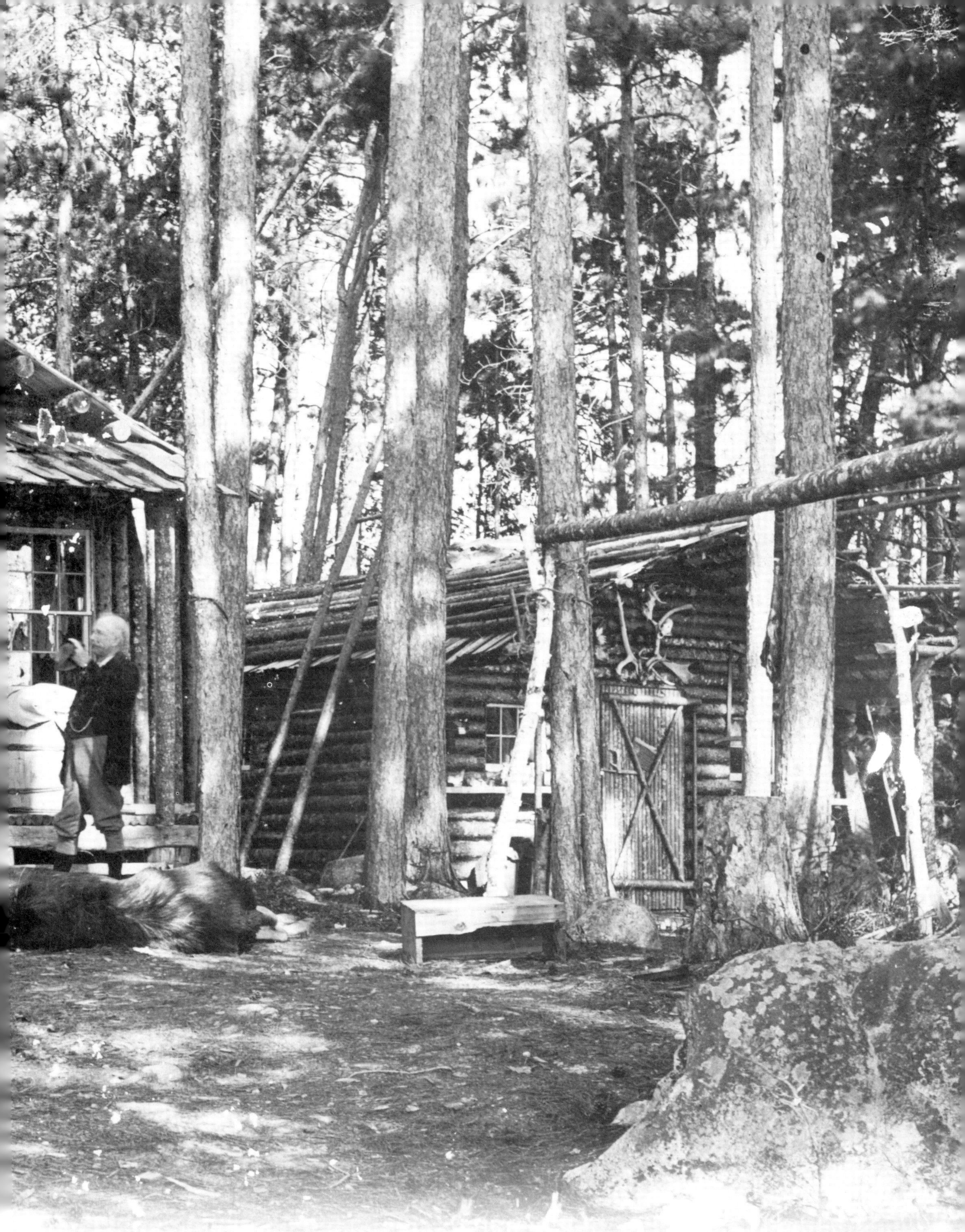

"Ishmay was a full-blooded Cree Indian who could lure the most cautious of lovesick old bulls into shooting range."

"There was no doubt in anyone's mind that this was a keeper."

"At times it was necessary to have a good tracking dog."

"With the harsh conditions and a roaming wolf pack, few bulls ever reached these proportions."

"More often than not a bull like this was a once-in-a-lifetime thrill."

"Antlers, skulls, and capes with a few jumpers thrown in."

211

Moose by Water

"Hugh Powers and his guide decided to try for moose by paddling around the shores of Kaitchie Lake in hopes of spotting a moose out in one of the bays eating water plants. The guides had told the men that if they hunted that way that they'd have to be watching close because a moose would often be half-submerged and dunking it's head under water like someone bobbing for apples at a Halloween party."

"A slow flowing river ran just below the cabin and emptied into the lake Hugh and his guide would be hunting that day. In the morning they would drift downstream to the lake where Hugh would spend the rest of the day looking for moose as his guide paddled around the lake. The only break they would take all day would be the shore lunch that the guide would fix for the two of them."

"Despite the fact it was slow moving, the river had enough current to make it difficult for one man to paddle against it. Upon their return that evening, Hugh would need to help the guide paddle upstream from the mouth of the river up to the cabin ."

"Bright and early the next morning, Hugh and his guide climbed into the canoe and set out on their float hunt. It was just a short distance down the river to the lake and Hugh was still shifting himself around trying to get comfortable when life along the river started to show itself."

"The guide had taken less than a dozen strokes on his paddle when a small flock of geese jumped out of the shallows near the bank. They honked and clamored their way into the air causing a general ruckus to the stillness of the morning before they disappeared into the mist."

"Under the steady flow of the current, they continued to drift silently down the river towards the lake. Then, just as they drifted into the only bend there was in that stretch of the river, everything broke loose at the same time."

"A huge moose stepped out of the dense brush and into the river only a few yards in front of them. Hugh said it was a toss-up as to which of them was the most surprised, but he always swore it was the moose."

"The cow turned and looked eye ball to eye ball with Hugh. Suddenly it realized it was probably in it's best interest to head for cover in an utmost hurry. Hugh said it was standing so close to the canoe that he and the guide ended up getting drenched when the moose took off."

"Being all legs like they are, it was almost comical to watch it's ungainly departure as it fought it's way against the current. Once it put some distance between the two of them, the cow slowed down and just waded over to the opposite bank, left the river, and disappeared into the brush."

"There was a great deal for Hugh to keep his eye on once they entered the lake. The entire bottom of the shallow lake was either solid bedrock that often was barely beneath the surface or it was littered with hundreds of huge boulders left by the glaciers that were strewn about the bottom, presenting obstacles that had to be avoided every few feet."

"The guide had also motioned to Hugh to keep an eye on the countless tiny islands that jutted out above the surface of the lake. Moose often swam out to an island to spend the night away from the wolves and would swim back to shore in the morning to feed."

"There was also the shoreline one needed to keep a watchful eye on. Moose moved freely back and forth on the shore as they came down to the water to feed and drink or would leave to seek shelter in the dense spruce that grew along the shoreline. Hugh felt he had every bit as much to do as the guide had paddling, perhaps even more."

"About an hour up the lake, Hugh spotted two objects some yards ahead. At first they appeared to be bobbing on the surface but as they drew closer, they appeared to be standing motionless out in the water."

"The two objects were only about fifty yards from shore but made they no effort whatsoever to get any closer as he sat there and watched them. Hugh then turned around towards the guide and moved his lips as if to say, "What's that up ahead?""

The guide whispered back to him, "Moose, cow and calf." "Look on shore."

"Hugh turned and looked towards shore. They blended so well with the background that it took a few seconds for him to make out the objects the guide had seen on shore."

"They were wolves, three of them, that paced back and forth, and were waiting for the inevitable to happen. They knew that sooner or later, the cow and her calf would tire and have to head for shore. That's when they would make their move."

"Hugh turned back to the guide. "Should I shoot?"

"The guide replied, "Up to you. It's your hunt."

"By the time he turned around to look back, the inevitable was about to take place. The cow and her calf were both exhausted by that time, so they headed towards shore to take their chances."

"The cow climbed on shore first and two of the wolves went after her right away. She was doing her best to hold them off but there was no way she could fight the two of them off and try and protect her calf against the other one at the same time."

"Then, as the calf struggled onto shore, the third wolf went after it with a vengeance, trying to hamstring it and bring it down."

"Hugh estimated the distance, raised his rifle, peered through his peep sight, and fired. Even from that distance, both of them could hear the wolf yelp in pain. In a last ditch effort to escape, the wolf turned away from the calf, staggered a few yards towards the spruce, and fell over dead."

"Hugh levered in another round, put his front sight behind the shoulder of the big wolf nearest to him, and fired again. That one dropped dead, right where it stood. By that time the third wolf realized there were better places for him to be and that's exactly where he headed. Hugh figured that two out of three wasn't all that bad"

"Hugh told me the cow walked over to her calf, licked it a couple of times, and then the two of them turned and faced the canoe. They both looked right at him and the guide. Then the cow nudged the calf and the two of them lit out for the spruce thicket."

"Hugh also said that when the cow and her calf turned and looked at him, it was the best feeling he ever had in all his years of hunting."

"What'd the guide say to him about shooting wolves and scaring every moose within hearing distance away?" I asked.

"Good Shootin'."

"They saw nothing for the next mile or so down the shoreline. Hugh feared that perhaps his compassion for the cow and her calf may have been the cause but it didn't matter to him in the least."

"Hugh was one of those rare people who justified everything he ever did. In this particular case, he felt the saving of a creature would last him far longer than the taking of a creature ever would."

"As the guide brought the canoe around a sharp point that jutted out into the lake he whispered, "Keep close watch on these next few bays. If we're going to see a bull today, chances are it'll be in this stretch up ahead."

"That was enough to bring Hugh to the edge of his seat. He began studying the shoreline looking for the outline of a moose to appear. Then he'd turn and survey the lily beds, trying his best to spot a moose standing out in the middle of one of the many patches as it fed on the tasty morsels growing beneath the surface, but there was no reward for all his effort."

"It was getting close to noon and Hugh's stomach was beginning to growl with the thoughts of a much needed shore lunch to satisfy his empty stomach and a chance to walk around and stretch his aching joints."

"Half of the day was gone so after lunch they would cross the lake and work their way back to the river that would take them back to camp.

"The only thing that broke the silence was the sound of water as it dripped off the end of the paddle between strokes. They were so close to shore that it was barely deep enough to stay afloat. Hugh was studying the shoreline more than he should have been, and he neglected to see the submerged log that lay directly in their path. By the time he looked down into the water and saw it, it was too late to even holler."

"The canoe struck the log with enough force to capsize it and it would have if the canoe had not become stranded on top of the log itself. Worse than that, the jagged end of a broken branch had torn a three inch hole in the bottom of the canoe. Water gushed in, and quickly covered the bottom of the canoe."

"Between the sound of the canoe hitting the log and Hugh poorly-timed shout of, "Look out," after it was all over, more noise was made in a few seconds than had been made all day."

"But amid all of the confusion that was going on came the reward that they were after."

"Half way between the shoreline and the dense spruce thicket, a bull rose up from it's bed, oblivious to what had caused all the commotion. Hugh and the guide spotted it at the same time"

"The guide whispered, "It's a good one." "Take it."

"Hugh eased back the hammer, took careful aim just behind the right front shoulder, and let fly."

"Hugh said the bull shook like a leaf in the wind when it was hit but it somehow still managed to cover fifty yards before it went over."

"Hugh's hunt was over. Now the work began."

"In a normal situation, the guide would take care of the cutting and quartering but this situation was far from normal."

"The jagged tear in the canoe had to be mended before they could even consider heading back to camp, so Hugh carried out the butchering while the guide took care of the canoe."

"Hugh hauled pieces of the moose over to the canoe while the guide secured the load with ropes for the trip back to camp. Three hours had passed by before they were loaded and ready to head back to camp."

"The guide said, "There's no time to eat now. We'll be pushing dark by the time we get back as it is."

"Hugh nodded in agreement. He certainly didn't feel like spending the night out in the middle of the woods either, so with paddles in hand they headed back in the direction they'd come from."

"With the added weight of a moose in the canoe, it took much longer than either of them anticipated as it turned pitch black a half an hour before they reached the mouth of the river."

"Both of the men were nearly exhausted by the time they reached the river where they had to battle the current in order to make their way upstream to their camp."

"By then it was so dark that they had to use their paddles to feel their way upstream to avoid hitting a rock or another log again. Twice the guide, who was now paddling in the front, struck a solid object with the end of his paddle but managed to keep the canoe from striking it.

"Hugh felt the canoe rock each time this happened but was not upset by it either time. He had complete confidence in his guide by that time."

"They had just rounded the bend and were in the home

stretch when suddenly the back of the canoe where Hugh was seated was lifted several inches out of the water and then dropped back in just as quickly. The canoe rocked violently back and forth and water rushed in over the side until it steadied itself again. Both men shouted, "What on Earth was that?"

"The answer was heard as whatever it was stepped out of the water a few feet away from them. They could hear water dripping off the creature as it made it's way to shore."

"The guide stammered as he said, "It was that big cow again!" "We were right over the top of her back when she decided to surface. She'd a made a real mess out of the two of us if she'd a tipped this thing over, I'll guarantee you that"

"What do you say we paddle as hard as we can and get to camp. I've had about enough for one night."

"Hugh didn't argue a bit. He'd had all the moose hunting he needed for one day."

"Our moose camp- located on the banks of the river."

"Hugh kept a wary eye out as his guide paddled into Kaitchie Lake."

214

"The sight of a moose wading the river sent one's heart to pounding."

"At night, moose would seek safety from the wolves on one of the many islands on the lake."

"Startled from it's bed by a noisy canoe."

"The nocturnal cow that nearly capsized the canoe."

"Packin' in for an extended hunt."

Moose in Snow

"It snowed hard the third week they were up there and by the time it stopped, the group had a week to try their hand at moose hunting in the snow."

"When the snow stopped, the guides went out to find some well used trails for the men to sit on and watch over. Moose, like most other animals, are creatures of habit and unless they are driven away or frightened badly, develop a routine or pattern that they follow, particularly during the winter when the snow gets deep and the going gets tough."

"Harry Norstad's guide set him up on a well used trail that several moose were using. They followed between their bedding area and a willow swamp where they browsed during the day."

"There was a considerable amount of activity on the trail for him to watch that began almost as soon as he sat down the first morning. A good portion of the activity involved animals that would be allowed to travel undisturbed such as snowshoe hares that traveled up and down the well-packed trail all hours of the day. Towards evening, during the last hour or so of daylight, was the time of day when the trail watching really became interesting."

"The hares felt quite at ease during the day for very few other animals were after them during the daylight hours. However, as the shadows grew long and darkness began to set in, the animals that made their living by preying on others began their work."

"The great gray owl would begin his silent flight over the trail and death in the grasp of an owl's talons was quick and silent, save the occasional scream of a snowshoe that had met it's end."

"Lynx would also make a sudden and swift appearance in the waning hours of the day. With leaping bounds they would make their rush towards a hapless hare and a single swat from one of the cat's large furry front paws spelled the end for another of the hares."

"But it was not these lesser creatures that held Harry's attention. He was after a moose. That's what kept him seated motionless for hours on end."

"As he sat and watched, he saw at least seven different cows and their calves use the trail during the day. Two immature bulls would pace up and down the trail at different times of the day, but he was not satisfied with either one of them. It was a mature bull that he had come to hunt, one that he could brag about when he returned home."

"With only two days left of his hunt, Harry had become somewhat discouraged. Despite the fact that he had seen several moose every day he was out there, he had yet to even see a bull that was shootable though his guide had assured him that there were several nice bulls in the area."

"Shortly after daybreak, two cows and their calves had passed by on their way to the swamp and about an hour later a bull he had never seen before made an appearance down the path towards the swamp. It was large enough to cause him to ease the hammer back but then he thought better of it and eased the hammer back down again. He let the bull go on by without raising his rifle."

"It was a quarter past nine when he saw a single moose appear out of the spruce and stop at the edge of the grassy swale he sat watching over. At first it stared straight ahead and it's antlers blended in with the dark background so he couldn't tell how large it was. It slowly turned it's head, and

"A spread of 60 inches plus on this big fellow."

when it rocked it's head from side to side he knew it was a keeper. Now it became a waiting game."

"The bull stood in that one spot for several minutes before it took another step forward. It paused then for another full minute before it took it's next step forward. The moose did this several times before it was confident that all was well. Finally, it put it's head down and headed on down the trail in Harry's direction."

"By that time, between the cold and the excitement, Harry was shaking uncontrollably and there was no way he could make himself stop as the moose continued coming down the trail."

"Out of pure desperation, Harry quietly gave himself a good chewing out for losing control of himself like that. For whatever reason, Harry stopped shaking."

"With the hammer back and his front sight rested behind the bull's left shoulder, he let the moose keep coming."

"For some reason the bull stopped dead in it's tracks. It turned it's head then and stared over in Harry's direction, but Harry was ready for him. The round took the bull right behind the shoulder and it shook as the heavy lead struck it. It wheeled around and tried to head back towards the spruce but Harry's bullet had done it's work. The massive bull dropped to his knees and then collapsed in the middle of the trail."

"Harry's moose hunt was over."

"Shot close to the cabin with a layer of packed snow and eight men to pull, there was no need to quarter this one."

"Moose, like deer, are creatures of habit. Sooner or later one would choose to take the trail the hunter watched."

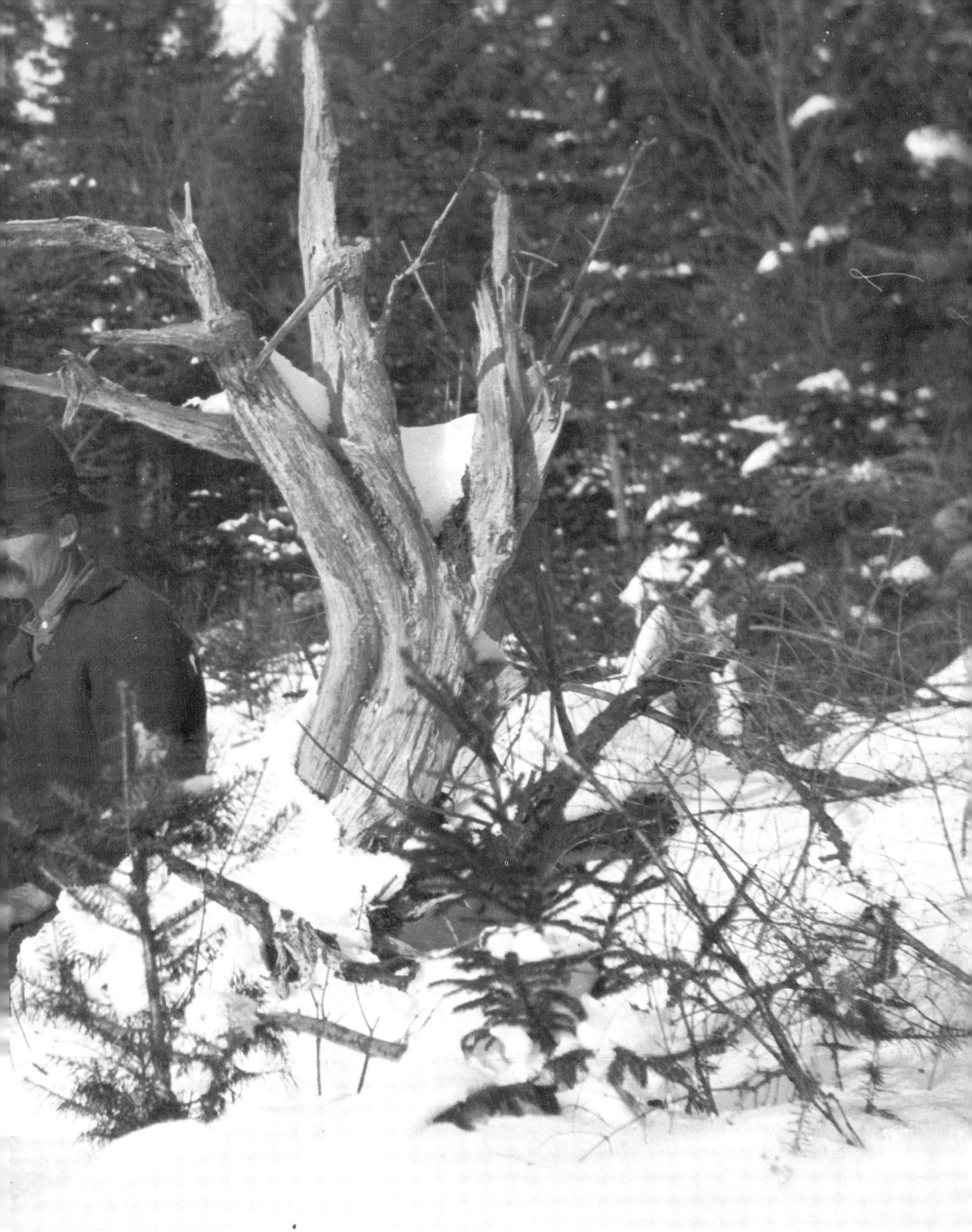

"The shot was high but still managed to take out his lungs."

"Another successful hunt at the Moose Horn Camp."

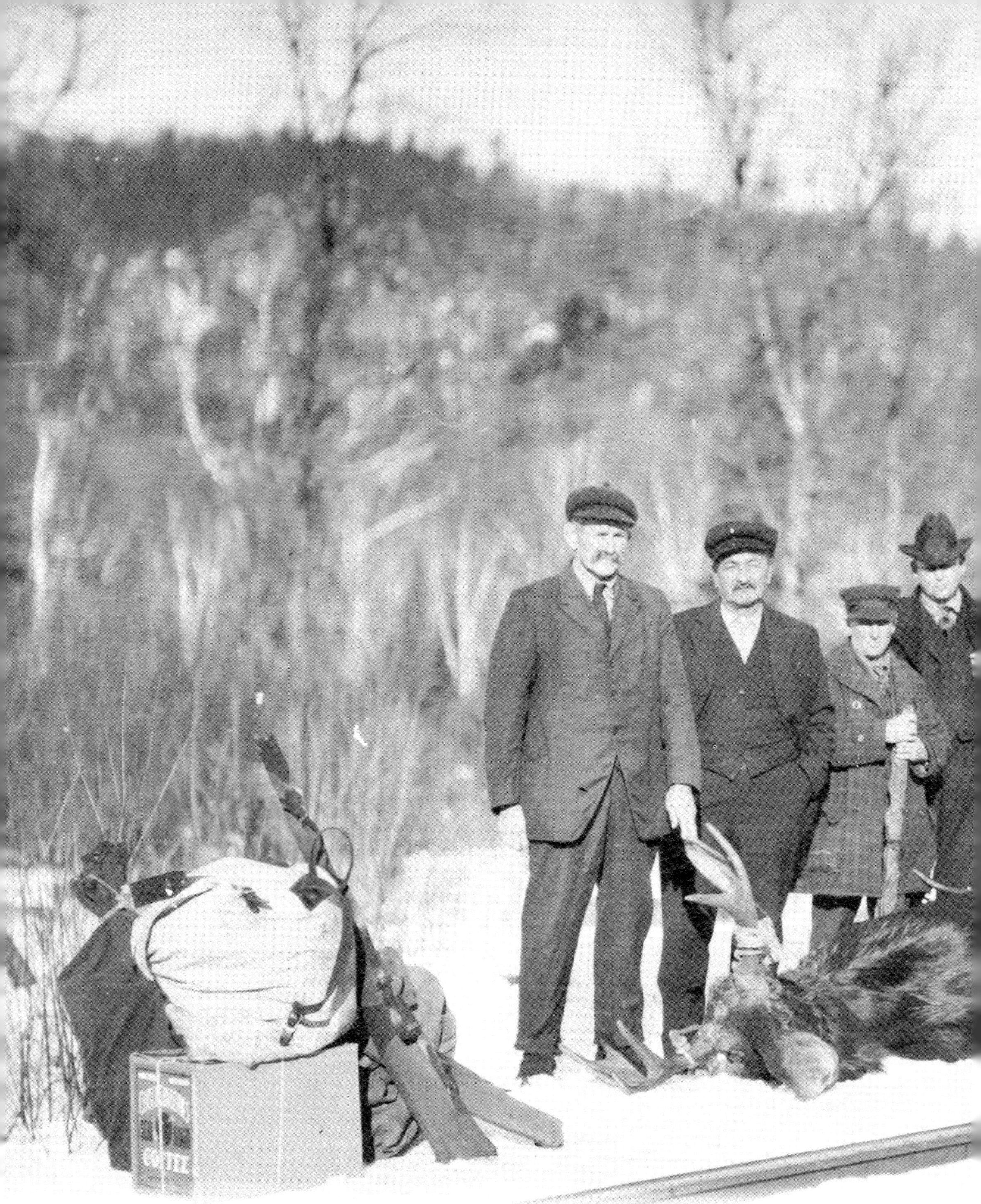
COFFEE

"All we could do was hope that the freight was on time."

"The Canadian moose hunt was your Granddad's last entry in the album Hank. He and his bunch went on several more hunts that I know of but there aren't any more photographs to be found. If there were some, I haven't the faintest idea what could of possibly happened to them."

"Charlie no doubt got the Idea after his father put articles in the album as he got older. I suppose it gave him something to page through and look at whenever he got the urge to go hunting again."

"I, myself, was never that much on hunting," Grandma continued, but Charlie found some pretty neat stories if I do say so myself."

"There was one thing your Granddad Charlie did that set him apart from many of his friends, Hank. When he retired from the bank, that man let his hair down more than anyone else I've ever known. but I think I know why."

"What do you think the reason was?" I asked.

"Charlie decided he could finally act and look the way he always felt like and wanted to. He didn't have to go around acting the part of a banker like everyone he ever met expected him to, and that included your Grandmother McCracken too. I think he enjoyed his last few years more than all the years he'd had before."

Still-Hunting The Grizzly
by Theodore Roosevelt

THEODORE ROOSEVELT -HUNTER- EXPLORER-CONSERVATIONIST.

The grizzly bear undoubtedly comes in the category of dangerous game, and is, perhaps, the only animal in the United States that can be fairly so placed but the danger of hunting the grizzly has been greatly exaggerated. The sport is certainly very much safer than it was at the beginning of this century.

The first hunters who came into contact with this great bear were men belonging to a hardy class of backwoodsmen who carried but one weapon, the long-barreled, small-bored pea-rifle. Bullets for the pea-rifle ran seventy to the pound, the amount of powder and lead being a little less than that contained in the cartridge of a thirty-two-caliber Winchester. In the Eastern States, the shots were mostly obtained at short distance and deer and black bear were the largest game. Pea-rifles were marvelously accurate for close range, and their owners were famed the world over for their skill as marksmen. Thus these rifles had proved to be plenty good for the work they had to do, but when the restless frontiersmen pressed out over the Western plains and encountered the grizzly bear, a beast of far greater bulk and more savage temper than any bear found in the Eastern woods, their small-bore rifles were utterly inadequate weapons with which to cope with him. It is small wonder that he was considered by them to be almost invulnerable and extraordinarily tenacious of life.

The grizzly proved to be a most unpleasant antagonist to a man armed only with a thirty-two-caliber rifle that carried but a single shot and was loaded at the muzzle. Any rifle used in this sport needed to carry a ball weighing from half an ounce to an ounce. With the old pea-rifles, the shot had to be in the eye or heart and accidents to the hunter were very common but the introduction of heavy breech-loading repeaters greatly lessened the danger. Grizzlies are not near as ferocious as formerly were for nowadays these great bears are undoubtedly much better aware of the death-dealing power of men. As a consequence, they are far less fierce their forefathers were. Those bears attacked the early Western travelers and explorers with no hesitation whatsoever. Constant contact with rifle-carrying hunters over a period of many generations of bear-life, has taught the grizzly by bitter experience that man is his undoubted overlord as far as fighting goes. This knowledge has now become a hereditary characteristic.

A grizzly will seldom attack a man unprovoked. One will almost always prefer to run rather than fight. However, if a man accidently stumbles on to one close up he is almost certain to be attacked for exactly the same reason that makes a rattlesnake strike at a passer-by. It is a different story. if he is wounded or thinks himself cornered. He will attack his foes with a headlong, reckless fury that renders him one of the most dangerous of wild beasts.

The ferocity of all wild animals depends largely upon the amount of resistance they are accustomed to meeting with, and the quantity of molestation to which they are subjected.

How the prowess of the grizzly compares with that of the lion or tiger would be hard to say so it would be quite unfair to start comparing them. I have never shot a charging grizzly, but owing to its tremendous bulk a man should have a thoroughly trustworthy weapon and a fairly cool head if he sets out with the intentions of slaying Old Ephraim.

I have personally known of but one instance of a grizzly turning on a hunter before being wounded. This happened to a friend of mine, a Californian ranchman, who, with two or three of his men, was following a bear that had carried off one of his sheep. They got the bear into a cleft in the mountain from which there was no escape and he suddenly charged back through the line of his pursuers. He struck down one of the horsemen, seized the arm of the man in his jaws and broke it as if it had been a pipe-stem. He was killed only after a most lively fight during which by repeated charges he had driven every one of his assailants off the field.

Two instances have come to my personal knowledge where a man has been killed by a grizzly. One was that of a hunter at the foot of the Big Horn mountains who had chased a large bear and finally wounded him. The animal turned at once and came straight at the man, whose second shot missed. The bear then closed and passed on, after striking only a single blow. That one blow, given with all the power of its thick immensely muscular fore-arm armed with nails as strong as so many hooked steel spikes, tore out the man's collar-bone and snapped through three or four ribs. He never recovered from the shock, and died that night.

The other instance occurred to a neighbor of mine who had a small ranch on the Little Missouri. He was on a prospecting trip with two other men near the headwaters of the Little Missouri in the Black Hills country when they came to a point of land thrust out into the river that was densely covered with brush and fallen timber.

Two of the party walked round by the edge of the stream but the third, a powerful German fellow, followed a well-beaten game trail leading through the bushy point. When they were some forty yards apart the two men heard an agonized shout from the German, and at the same time the loud coughing growl, or roar, of a bear. They turned just in time to see their companion struck a terrible blow on the head by a grizzly which must have been roused from its lair by his almost stepping on it. He was so close to it that he had no time to fire his rifle but merely held it up over his head as a guard. Of course it was struck down, the claws of the great brute at the same time shattering his skull like an egg-shell. The man staggered on some ten feet before he fell; but when he did fall he never spoke or moved again. The two others killed the bear after a short, brisk struggle, as he was in the midst of a most determined charge.

In 1872, near Fort Wingate, New Mexico, two soldiers of a cavalry regiment came to their death at the claws of a grizzly bear. They were mail-carriers, and one day did not come in at the appointed time. The next day a relief party was sent out to look for them, and after some search found the bodies of both, as well as that of one of the horses. One of the men still showed signs of life and he came to his senses long enough before he died to tell the story.

Upon seeing a grizzly they had pursued it on horseback with their Spencer rifles at the ready. As they drew close to it, one of them fired a round into its side upon which it turned with marvelous quickness and struck down the horse while at the same time inflicting a ghastly wound on the rider. The other man dismounted, intent on rescuing his companion. The bear then left the latter and attacked the other. Although hit by the bullet, it charged home and threw the man down, and then lay on him and deliberately bit him to death. His groans and cries were frightening to hear and after he was dead, it walked off into the bushes without again offering to molest the already mortally wounded victim of its first assault.

Grizzlies can be hunted with dogs which of course are not expected to seize him but simply to find and bay him, and distract his attention by barking and nipping. On occasion, a bear can be caught in the open and killed with the aid of horses but nine times out of ten the only way to get one is to put on moccasins and still-hunt it in its own haunts shooting it at close quarters. Its tracks are followed until it is found in its bed wherein it lies during the day or in a given locality in which it is known to exist. Otherwise a bait can be left out and watched until the bear is caught when he has come to pay the bait a visit.

During last summer we found it necessary to leave my ranch on the Little Missouri, and take quite a long trip through the cattle country of south-eastern Montana and northern Wyoming to the foot of the Big Horn Mountains. We took a fortnight's hunt through them after elk and bear.

None of us had ever been within two hundred miles of the Big Horn range before; so that our hunting trip had the added zest or being also an exploring expedition. Each of us rode one pony, and the packs were carried on four others. We did not burden ourselves with excessive baggage taking the canvas wagon-sheet instead of a tent along. Our bedding, plenty of spare cartridges, some flour, bacon, coffee, sugar, and salt, and a few very primitive cooking utensils, completed the outfit.

We went into the Big Horns with the pack-train by following an old Indian trail for two days' journey before pitching camp in what we intended to be our hunting grounds, No one who has not tried it can understand the work and worry that it is to drive a pack-train over rough ground and through timber. None of us very skillful at packing, and the loads were all the time slipping.

We spent several days at the first camping-place, killing half a dozen elk, but none with very fine heads. All of these were gotten by still-hunting, Merrifield and I following up their trails, either together or separately. Throughout this trip I used a buckskin hunting-suit, a fur cap, and moccasins. Not only was this dress very lasting, but it was also very inconspicuous in the woods (always an important point for a hunter to attend to); and in it I could walk almost noiselessly, the moccasins making no sound whatever, and the buckskin reducing the rustling of branches and twigs as I passed through them to a minimum. Both of us carried Winchester rifles. Mine was a 45-75, half-magazine, stocked and sighted to suit myself.

It was still early September with the weather cool and pleasant. The nights were frosty and every two or three days there was a flurry of light snow which rendered the labor of tracking much more easy. The peaks of the mountains were snow-capped almost all the time during our stay.

Our fare was excellent, consisting of elk venison, mountain grouse, and small trout, the last caught in one of the beautiful little lakes that lay almost up by the timber-line. It was a treat to sit at night before the roaring and crackling pine logs and as the old teamster had so quaintly put it, "we had at last come to a land where the wood grew on trees."

There were plenty of black-tail deer in the woods, and we came across a number of bands of cow and calf elk, or of young bulls; but after several days' hunting, we were still without any sign of grizzly, which was the game we were especially anxious to kill. Neither Merrifield or I had ever seen a wild grizzly bear alive let alone hunt one.

One day we separated. I took up the trail of a large bull elk, and though after a while I lost the track, in the end I ran across the animal itself, and after a short stalk got a shot at the noble-looking old fellow. It was a grand bull, with massive neck and twelve-tined antlers; and he made a most beautiful picture, standing out on a crag that jutted over the sheer cliff wall, the tall pine-trees behind him and the deep cañon at his feet, while in the background rose the snow-covered granite peaks. As I got up on my knees to fire he half-faced towards me, about eighty yards off, and the ball went in behind the shoulder. He broke away into the forest, but stopped before he had gone twenty rods, and did not need the second bullet to which he fell.

I reached camp early in the afternoon and waited for Merrifield to make his appearance. At last he came in sight, galloping at speed down an open glade, and waving his hat, evidently having had good luck. When he reined in his small, wiry cow-pony, we saw that he had packed behind his saddle the fine, glossy pelt of a black bear.

Better still, he announced that he had been off about ten miles to a perfect tangle of ravines and valleys where bear sign was very thick; and not of black bear either, but grizzly. He had run across the black bear purely by accident while riding up a valley in which there was a patch of dead timber grown up with berry bushes. He had noticed a black object which he first took to be a stump but as he drew near to it, the object suddenly took to its heels. It was a young bear, in its second year, and had probably never before seen a man, which accounted for the ease for which it was treed and taken.

Merrifield's tale made me decide to shift camp at once, and go over to the spot where the bear-tracks were so plentiful which was not more than a couple of miles from where I had slain the big elk. Next morning we were off, and by noon pitched camp by a clear brook, in a valley with steep, wooded sides, but with good feed for the horses in the open bottom. We rigged the canvas wagon-sheet into a small tent, sheltered by the trees from the wind, and piled great pine logs nearly where we wished to place the fire; for a night-camp in the sharp fall weather is cold and dreary unless there is a roaring blaze of flame in front of the tent.

That afternoon we again went out, and I shot another fine bull elk. I came home alone towards nightfall, walking through a reach of burnt forest, where there was nothing but charred tree-trunks and black mold. When nearly through it I came across the huge, half-human footprints of a great grizzly, which must have passed by within a few minutes. It gave me rather an eerie feeling in the silent, desolate woods, to see for the first time the unmistakable proofs that I was in the home of the mighty lord of the wilderness. I followed the tracks in the fading twilight until it became too dark to see them any longer, and then shouldered my rifle and walked back to camp.

That night we almost had a visit from one of the animals we were after. Several times before we had heard the calling of bull elks at night, a sound than which there is nothing more musical in nature. This night however, when we were in bed and the fire was smoldering, we were roused by a ruder noise,—a kind of grunting or roaring whine answered by the frightened snorts of the ponies. It was a bear, which had evidently not seen the fire, and had probably been attracted by the smell of the horses. After it made out what we were, it stayed around for but a short while, again uttering its peculiar roaring grunt, and went off. We had seized our rifles and run out into the woods, but in the darkness could see nothing. Later on we realized how lucky it was for us that we did not stumble across the bear. He could have made short work of us when we were at such a disadvantage.

The next day we went off on a long tramp through the woods and along the sides of the canyons. There were plenty of berry bushes growing in clusters, and all around these there were fresh tracks of bear. However, the grizzly is also a flesh-eater, and has a great liking for carrion.

Upon visiting the place where Merrifield had killed the

black bear, we found that the grizzlies had been there before us, and had utterly devoured the carcass with cannibal relish. Hardly a scrap was left, and we turned our steps toward where lay the second bull elk I had killed. It was quite late in the afternoon when we reached the place. A grizzly had evidently been at the carcass during the preceding night, for his great foot-prints were in the ground all around it, and the carcass itself was gnawed and torn, and partially covered with earth and leaves; for the grizzly has a curious habit of burying all of his prey that he does not at the moment need. A great many ravens had been feeding on the body, and they wheeled about over the tree-tops above us, uttering their barking croaks.

The forest was composed mainly of what are called ridge-pole lines, which grow close together, and do not branch out until the stems are thirty or forty feet from the ground. Beneath these trees we walked over a carpet of pine-needles, upon which our moccasin feet made no sound. The woods seemed vast and lonely, its silence broken only by the strange noises that are always heard in the great forests which seem to mark the sad and everlasting unrest of the wilderness.

We climbed up along the trunk of a dead tree which had toppled over at an angle and lodged itself half-way in its fall against a neighboring tree. When we were above the ground far enough to prevent the bear's smelling us, we sat still to wait for his approach until in the gathering gloom, we could no longer see the sights of our rifles and could but dimly make out the carcass of the great elk. It was useless to wait longer, and we clambered down and stole out to the edge of the woods.

The forest here covered one side of a steep, almost cañon-like ravine, whose other side was bare except of rock and sage-brush. Once out from under the trees, there was still plenty of light. Although the sun had set, we crossed over some fifty yards to the opposite hillside and crouched down under a bush to see if perchance some animal might not also leave the cover. We waited quietly in the growing dusk until the pine-trees in our front blended into one dark, frowning mass but saw or heard nothing save the wild creatures of the forest that had begun to stir abroad. The owls hooted dismally from the tops of the tall trees, and two or three times a harsh, wailing cry, probably the voice of some lynx or wolverine arose from the depths of the woods.

At last, as we were rising to leave, we heard the sound of the breaking of a dead stick from the spot where we knew the carcass lay. It was a sharp, sudden noise, perfectly distinct from the natural creaking and snapping of the branches,—just such a sound as would be made by the tread of some heavy creature. "Old Ephraim" had come back to the carcass. A minute afterward, listening with strained ears, we heard him brush by some dry twigs. It was entirely too dark to go in after him; but we made up our minds that on the morrow he should be ours.

Early the next morning we were over at the elk carcass and as we expected, found that the bear had eaten his fill of it during the night. His tracks showed him to be an immense fellow and were so fresh that we doubted if he had left long before we arrived. We made up our minds to follow him up and find his lair. The bears that lived on these mountains had evidently been little disturbed as the Indians and most of the white hunters who dare hunt this region are rather chary of meddling with "Old Ephraim," a name used by the mountain men whenever they referred to the grizzly. Therefore, the bears have very little fear of being harmed so we reasoned that it was far from unlikely that the bed of the one who had fed on the elk would be far away.

My companion was a skillful tracker, and we took up the trail at once. For some distance it led over the soft, yielding carpet of moss and pine-needles, and the foot-prints were quite easily made out, although we could follow them slowly for we had to of course keep a sharp lookout ahead and around us for the bear as we walked noiselessly on in the somber half-light that prevailed under the great pine-trees. The thick, interlacing branches of the pines allow few beams of light to stray through, no matter how bright the sun may be outside.

We made no sound ourselves, and every little sudden noise sent a thrill through me as I peered about with each sense on the alert. Two or three of the ravens which we had scared from the carcass flew overhead, croaking hoarsely; and the pine-tops moaned and sighed in the slight breeze-for pine-trees seem to be ever in motion, no matter how light the wind.

After going a few hundred yards, the tracks turned off on a well-beaten path made by the elk which made the beast's footprints stand out perfectly plain in the dust. He had lumbered along up the path until near the middle of the hillside where the ground broke away and there were hollows and boulders. Here there had been a wind-fall, and the dead trees lay among the living, piled across one another in all directions while between and around them sprouted up a thick growth of young spruces and other evergreens.

The trail turned off into the tangled thicket, within which it was almost certain we would find our quarry. We could still follow the tracks, by the slight scrapes of the claws on the bark, or by the bent and broken twigs; and we advanced with noiseless caution, slowly climbing over the dead tree-trunks and upturned stumps, and not letting a branch rustle or catch on our clothes. In the middle of the thicket, we crossed what was almost a breastwork of fallen logs and Merrifield, who was leading, passed by the upright stem of a great pine. As soon as he was by it he sank suddenly on one knee, turning half round, his face fairly aflame with excitement.

I strode slowly past him, with my rifle at the ready. There, not ten steps off, was the great bear, slowly rising from his bed among the young spruces. He had heard us, but apparently could not discern exactly where or what we were. He reared up on his haunches, turned sideways toward us and as soon as he saw us and dropped down again on all fours, the shaggy hair on his neck and shoulders seeming to bristle as he turned to face us.

He sank down on his fore feet, his head bent slightly down. As he did, I raised the rifle and when I saw the top of the white bead fairly between his small, glittering, evil eyes, I pulled trigger. He rose halfway up and then the huge beast fell over on his side as he went into his death-throes. The ball had entered his brain striking it as squarely between the eyes as if the distance had been measured by a carpenter's rule.

The whole thing was over in twenty seconds from the time I caught sight of the game. Indeed, it was over so quickly that the grizzly did not have time to show fight at all or come a step towards us. He was the first I had ever seen and I felt not a little proud as I stood over the great brindled bulk which lay stretched out at length in the cool shade of the evergreens.

He was a monstrous fellow, much larger than any I had seen since alive or brought in dead by other hunters. As near as we could estimate, he must have weighed nearly twelve hundred pounds and though this is not as large as some of his kind are said to grow in California, it is yet a very unusual size for a bear. He was a good deal heavier than any of our horses; and it was with the greatest difficulty that we were able to skin him. He must have been very old, his teeth and claws being all worn down and blunted; but nevertheless he had been living in plenty, for he was as fat as a prize hog, the layers on his back being a finger's length in thickness. He was still in his summer coat, his hair being short, and in color a curious brindled brown while all the bears we shot afterwards had the long thick winter fur, cinnamon or yellowish brown.

I was very proud over my first bear; but Merrifield's chief feeling seemed to be disappointment that the animal had not had time to show fight. He was rather a reckless fellow, and very confident in his own skill with the rifle; and he really did not seem to have any more fear of the grizzlies than if they had been so many jack-rabbits. I did not at all share his feeling, having a hearty respect for my foes' prowess, and in following and attacking them always took all possible care to get the chances on my side. Merrifield was sincerely sorry that we never had to stand a regular charge; we killed our five grizzlies with seven bullets, and, except in the case of the she and cub spoken of farther on, each was shot about as quickly as it got sight of us.

The last one we got was an old male, which was feeding on an elk carcass. We crept up to within about sixty feet, and, as Merrifield had not yet killed a grizzly purely with his own gun, and I had killed three so I told him to take the shot. He at once whispered gleefully, "I'll break his leg, and we'll see what he'll do!" Having no ambition to be a participator in the antics of a three-legged bear, I hastily interposed a most emphatic veto; and with a rather injured air he fired, the bullet going through the neck just back of the head. The bear fell to the shot, and could not get up from the ground, dying in a few minutes; but before he did he seized his left wrist in his teeth and bit clean through it, completely separating the bones of the paw and arm. Although a smaller bear than the big one I first shot, he would probably have proved a much more ugly foe, for he was less unwieldy, and had much longer and sharper teeth and claws. I think that if my companion had merely broken the beast's leg he would have had his curiosity as to its probable conduct more than gratified.

A day or two after the death of the big bear, we went out one afternoon on horseback, intending merely to ride down to see a great cañon lying some six miles west of our camp; we went more to look at the scenery than for any other reason, neither of us ever stirred out of camp without his rifle. We went down to where the mouth of the cañon opened out, and rode our horses to the end of a great jutting promontory of rock and out into the cold clear air. There, we looked far over the broad valley of the Big Horn as it lay at our very feet, walled in on the other side by the distant chain of the Rocky Mountains.

We turned our horses and rode back along the edge of another cañon-like valley, a place like many others in whose inaccessible wildness and ruggedness a bear would find a safe retreat. There was plenty of elk sign about, and we saw several black-tail deer which were very common on the mountains. We had not hunted blacktails at all as we were in no need of meat but this particular afternoon when we came across a buck with a remarkably fine set of antlers, I shot it. We stopped to cut off and skin out the horns, throwing the reins over the heads of the horses and leaving them to graze by themselves.

The body of the buck lay near the crest of one side of a deep valley or ravine which headed up on the plateau a mile to our left. Except for scattered trees and bushes the valley was bare; but there was heavy timber along the crests of the hills on its opposite side. It took some time to fix the head properly, and we were just finishing when Merrifield sprang to his feet and exclaimed, "Look at the bears!" pointing down into the valley below us. Sure enough, there were two bears (which afterwards proved to be an old she and a nearly full-grown cub) traveling up the bottom of the valley, much too far off for us to shoot. Grasping our rifles and throwing off our hats, we started off as hard as we could run diagonally down the hillside, so as to cut them off.

It was some little time before they saw us, when they made off at a lumbering gallop up the valley. It would seem impossible to run into two grizzlies in the open, but they were going up hill and we down, and moreover the old one kept stopping. The cub would forge ahead and could probably have escaped us but then it would run back to her. The upshot was that we got ahead of them, when they turned and went straight up one hillside as we ran straight down the other behind them. By this time I was pretty nearly done in, for running along the steep ground through the sage-brush was most exhausting work; and Merrifield kept gaining on me and was well in front. Just as he disappeared over a bank, almost at the bottom of the valley, I tripped over a bush and fell full length. When I got up I knew I could never make up the ground I had lost, and besides could hardly run any longer. Merrifield was out of sight below, and the bears were laboring up the steep hillside directly opposite, about three hundred yards off. I sat down and began to shoot over Merrifield's head, aiming at the big bear. She was going very steadily and in a straight line, and each bullet sent up a puff of dust where it struck the dry soil, so that I could keep correcting my aim; and the fourth ball crashed into the old bear's flank. She lurched heavily forward, but recovered herself and reached the timber, while Merrifield, who had put on a spurt, was not far behind.

I toiled up the hill at a sort of trot, fairly gasping and sobbing for breath; but before I got to the top I heard a couple of shots and a shout. The old bear had turned as soon as she was in the timber, and come towards Merrifield; but he gave her the death-wound by firing into her chest, and then shot at the young one, knocking it over. When I came up he was just walking towards the latter to finish it with the revolver, but it suddenly jumped up as lively as ever and made off at a great pace-for it was nearly full-grown.

It was impossible to fire where the tree-trunks were so thick, but there was a small opening across which it would have to pass. Collecting all my energies, I made a last run, got into position, and covered the opening with my rifle. The instant the bear appeared I fired, and it turned a dozen somersaults downhill, rolling over and over. The ball had struck it near the tail and had ranged forward through the hollow of the body. Each of us had thus given the fatal wound to the bear into which the other had fired the first bullet.

The run, though short, had been very sharp, and over such awful country that we were completely fagged out, and could hardly speak for lack of breath. The sun had already set, and it was too late to skin the animals; so we merely dressed them, caught the ponies-with some trouble, for they were frightened at the smell of the bear's blood on our hands-and rode home through the darkening woods. Next day we brought the teamster and two of the steadiest pack-horses to the carcasses, and took the skins into camp.

We were very loath to leave our hunting grounds, but time was pressing, and we had already many more trophies than we could carry. One cool morning then, when the branches of the evergreens were laden with the feathery snow that had fallen overnight, we struck camp and started out of the mountains, each of us taking his own bedding behind his saddle. The pack-ponies were loaded down with bear skins, elk and deer antlers, and the hides and furs of other game. In single file we moved through the woods and across the cañons to the edge of the great table-land, and then slowly down the steep slope to its foot, where we found our canvas-topped wagon.

The next day saw us setting out on our long journey homewards, across the three hundred weary miles of treeless and barren-looking plains country, on our way back home.

THE DEATH OF OLD EPHRAIM.

Credit - A.B. Frost

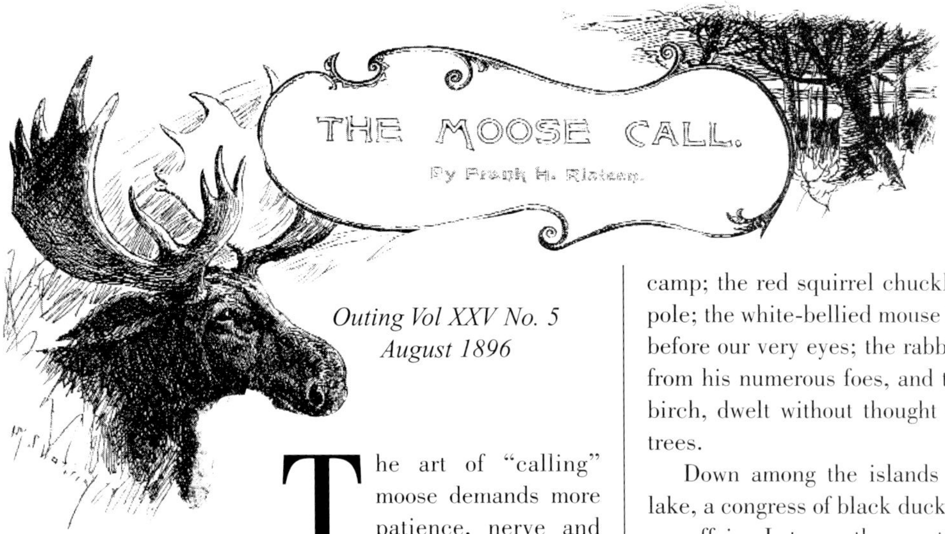

THE MOOSE CALL.

By Frank H. Risteen.

The art of "calling" moose demands more patience, nerve and skill, than any other branch of woodcraft. The animal is forever on the alert, he displays a positive genius for turning up in the wrong place at the wrong time and his powers of scent and hearing are almost incredible. It is an open question whether he is ever wholly deceived by the spurious call even when the caller is an adept.

Like other members of the deer family, however, he possesses a curiosity that often seems to paralyze his caution. This is especially the case in the rutting season, when he is very much disposed, if he has not yet mated, to look into the origin of any unusual sound.

A moose that is mated will not come to the horn if he is any distance away. He is a Mormon by nature, but he has a realizing sense of the force of the saying that a bird in the hand is worth two in the bush. A young bull moose will exhibit the greatest caution in coming to the horn, for he is well aware that a bigger moose than himself may be in charge of the harem, who will feel called upon, the moment he shows his homely nose, to shovel him into the lake.

Most of the calling done by Indian guides is a monumental farce. It would never fool the moose at any other than the mating season when he has not the full possession of his faculties. Then it is that the king of the forest, like many a human king, is tricked and decoyed to his doom by the voice of the siren. He obeys against his judgment the summons of the phantom maid from whose bower few bull moose e'er return.

Our camp was located on Little Sou'-West Miramichi Lake, one of the wildest of the many beautiful sheets of water to be found in that wonderful land of fen and forest, lake and river, the Province of New Brunswick. To the east lay Martin's Bluff, reposing like a giant, over whose recumbent form Dame Nature had thrown the gorgeous crazy quilt of autumn. To the west, clad to their summits in somber dress of spruce and fir, rose the mountains that form the great divide between the waters of the Miramichi and those of the Tobique.

The Canada jay, or "Whisky Jack," boarded with us at the camp; the red squirrel chuckled and chattered on the ridge-pole; the white-bellied mouse lugged off our beans one by one before our very eyes; the rabbit sought safety in the dooryard from his numerous foes, and the partridge, spruce as well as birch, dwelt without thought of fear among the surrounding trees.

Down among the islands that decked the bosom of the lake, a congress of black duck was in daily session discussing our affairs. Later on the senatorial loons lined up-six or eight of them-abreast of the camp and resumed the debate upon the orders of the day. At sundown the muskrats could be seen steaming out of their little docks at the head of the lake and leaving long, shining wakes behind them.

"A LONG, LOUD QUAVERING, WAILING BLAST."

Just around the turn below the cove a big mountain stream poured into the lake where the trout played and chased each other in the twilight, and sometimes broke the glassy surface for many yards around in a seeming spasm of fun and frolic. Regular whoppers some of them were, too, flapping the beam at four and five pounds.

Away down at the outlet of the lake was a bran new beaver house and dam, whose cunning builders were now yarding in a goodly store of their favorite food against the coming winter.

All these attractions, however, were only incidental—merely the side-show that pointed to the presence of the main circus and menagerie. Other sights and sounds were to be noted in this wonderful woodland region compared with which I have named were of trifling interest. For instance, there were holes, or indentations, all around the margin of the lake that looked like the print of a water-pail in the soft, spongy bog. The guide said these were the fresh tracks of caribou which were traveling to and from the barrens. There were other tracks fully as large, and with a more aristocratic, tapering toe, which sank much deeper in the yielding soil. The guide said these were made by a big bull moose, the king of North American game animals.

THE RESPONSE

We were fortunate, Fred and myself, in being able to secure for this trip a well-known guide, who is wise above all his fellows in the way of the woods, who is genial and patient whether it rains or shines, and who, as a caller of moose, has no superior in Canada.

All of the Indian callers since the world began have insisted on calling only after sundown. No doubt the moose is rather more likely to come to the horn then than earlier in the day, but this waiting and watching by night is cold and wearisome, and as the shadows deepen, the problem of planting your bullet in the right place at the right time becomes more and more dubious of solution. Henry calls only in the hours of daylight, when the game may be clearly seen.

The wind had almost died away at three o'clock, when Henry-who had been for an hour or so daubing with copious coats of pitch the yawning seams of the old Micmac canoe-said he thought we had better go up to the head of the lake and "try a little call."

That canoe was in itself a monument to Henry's matchless energy and power of resource. It was a huge, unwieldy craft, that must have weighed in its palmy days at least one hundred and sixty pounds, which Henry and another guide, to humor the whim of a New York sportsman, had some years before carried on their shoulders thirty miles through the trackless wilderness, swamping a road as they went. It must have cost the New York man five times the sum for which Henry would have built a far better canoe right at the lake. This was nearly as bad as the case of the Englishman who insisted on having his bath-tub carried through. The bath-tub is still at the lake, and so is the Micmac canoe, and there they will both remain till the crack of doom.

We pushed our way silently through the circles of water-lilies, and noisily through the sedgy shallows, and landed at the head of the lake. We went a short way into the green woods and sat down upon the prostrate trunk of an ancient pine which the loggers had felled a quarter of a century ago. The guide walked up to a white birch tree ad proceeded to fabricate his horn.

With three strokes of a knife he removed a broad sheet of bark. This he peeled as thin as possible, removed a wart or two from the yellow inner surface, trimmed the sheet in the general shape of a triangle, and then rolled it in the form of a cone. The horn thus made was about eighteen inches long, one inch in diameter at the small end, and about five inches at the big end. Shoving his hand down into the black mold at his feet, Henry yanked up a long spruce root or tendril. This he peeled with his knife upon his knee, split it from end to end, and bound it around the horn. Then, after carefully squaring off the outer end, the guide stood up, placed the implement to his lips and gave the call of the cow moose.

It is not within the compass of language to describe that call! The first short note was a high-pitched, flute-like whine or whimper that subsided into a kind of sob two full octaves further down the musical scale. The second note, which followed at once, was a long, loud, quavering, wailing blast, that filled the wide lake valley from shore to shore with a flood of melody, and then rolled like a tidal wave up the mountain side.

The silence that ensued was positively startling. Fred and I sat there like statues, our rifles motionless across our knees,

our spirits carried away from the visible world by that wild, unearthly music, every nerve within us vibrating with the excitement of expectation. Oh! there was no mistake about it! We knew instinctively that no one but a master in the art could render such a call as that. We felt perfectly sure that no bull moose on earth could resist the soulfulness of that appeal. Had the mountain before us suddenly assumed the shape of a moose and, with all the trees on its head for horns, charged down upon us we should not have been very much surprised. I looked at Fred and Fred at me. All we said was: "Heavens!" It was enough. Silence is the tribute mediocrity pays to genius.

The guide stood quietly at his post, listening with all his might, his gray eyes roaming over the lakeside barren and peering into the somber shadows of the mountain. Once his weather-stained face kindled with animation as he thought he heard the answering call. It is strange what tricks the imagination plays upon the judgment of even the most experienced in such a time of waiting. The booming buzz of the passing swamp-fly, the tremulous tinkling of the distant brook, the sob and sigh of the dying wind among the pines, the myriad murmurs of the mighty forest-yea, the very beating of our hearts seemed like an answer to the summons.

All the joys and all the sorrows of life, all memory of the outer world and its problems, vanished before the concentrated realism of that black barrier of firs that fronted the barren and seemed to guard from us the secrets of the wilderness. What innumerable troops of animals, unknown, unnamed, unseen by human eye, must have passed along that narrow thoroughfare since first the barrier was raised? What monster might even now be lurking there, perhaps in a moment to be squeezed forth into the outer light from that sponge-like mass of mystery?

After a silence of about fifteen minutes, which seemed to us an age, the guide raised the horn again on high, and again that weird, wailing cry rose and fell, eddied and echoed, among the wooded hills and hollows. We waited wistfully, but there was no response.

Then the guide shinned up a tree, from which his call would reach a greater distance, and where sounds would be audible that could not be heard on the ground. The only result was that we heard, at a distance of perhaps half a mile, the mournful call of a cow moose. It was wonderfully like the call that Henry gave, but we could see he was disappointed. He knew he had no show in a competition with the genuine article. He soon slid down from his cold and cramped position in the tree-top, and remarked:

"Well, I guess we'd better git to camp. Better luck next time."

But luck was no better the next time, nor the next, nor the next. Henry called long and loud and faithfully at all the likely places. His throat became sore with the continuous strain, and sometimes when he wished to lay himself out and do his level best, he would break into a fit of coughing, which, of course, did not improve his chances. There was even a tone of anger apparent in his calling as the sunny October days passed by, for he began to think that the whole moose family was in league against him. It really looked like it.

One evening when we reached the lake after a wet and toilsome march over the mountain, we found that a large moose had visited the "Ark" as it lay stranded on the shore, and tossed the paddles around with evident contempt. "It all belongs to hunting," was Henry's only comment.

Another evening when we returned, hungry and weary to the camp, the cook revealed himself in a state of great excitement. A big bull moose had come poking around the camp in our absence, and stood watching him as he was cleaning a mess of trout. When the moose began to shake his horns Jack rushed into the camp and made a frantic effort to find a ball cartridge for the shot-gun. By the time he found it the moose had vanished.

"I do cal'late he was the most awfullest big moose with the most tre-men-jus head of horns I ever did see!" was the comforting assurance we received from Jack. We were also somewhat consoled by the firm conviction that Jack could not, if he had had a Gatling, have hit a flock of wild barns.

There came a day at last which has a right to be remembered. We had shot two very fine caribou, and Henry trapped a bear, but still the aching void for moose remained.

It was a beautiful, still, frosty morning, the sun shining purple through the mists, and the lake lying spread before us like a burnished sheet of bronze, as we boarded the ark and paddled to the western shore through the lily-pads and rushes. Fred had no end of confidence in his 45-85 repeater, and we had no end of confidence in Fred, so I left my trusty old weapon at the camp to protect Jack from the moose, and elected to do my share of the shooting with the kodak. We climbed the spur of the mountain again, but this time our course trended more to the northward, where there was a small lake about three miles away which Henry said offered a favorable site for calling up a moose, if there was any bachelor moose still hanging around.

We had quite a tussle with the deadfalls, and then with a dense thicket of alders before we reached the scene of operations. Out in the middle of the lake a big white-breasted loon greeted us with its gruesome laughter as we pushed through the alders, then dove with a startled "How," and we never saw him again.

The footing was firmer and the view more open on the dry barren that bordered the northern side of the lake than on the other, so it was here that Henry decided to take his stand. The sun was out in full force now, but not a ripple of air was stirring and a few ghost-like wreaths of vapor still clung to the surface of the water.

The guide gave the moose call with all his usual artistic variations, and then-Well, a great many things happened just then in such a rush that they seemed to be falling over each other for fear they wouldn't happen at all!

There was a low, deep, muffled sound, which might have risen from the ground at our feet, but which, on the whole, seemed to emerge from the thick belt of barren firs that lined the opposite shore of the lake; then a quick succession of basso-profundo grunts, followed by a terrific crashing of horns against the trunks and limbs of trees! Henry's face was transfigured with excitement. He dashed down the bank, while Fred and I hustled after him with rifle and kodak in order to connect with the bull moose express. We got there in time to board the train! The cow-catcher and headlights loomed up, pushing their way through the alders across the lake about one hundred yards away. It was the king of the valley and no mistake. His ears were thrown forward, his horns shone like a crown of glory in the pallid October sun, and every hair on his big black mane stood up as straight as the sentinel firs from which he had emerged.

"Give it to him!" shouted Henry, and Fred fired. The bullet struck the moose near the right shoulder, for as he turned and charged through the hard hacks we could see that his right fore-leg was powerless. Still, he was making regular schedule time, and though Fred kept heaving chunks of sudden death across the pond at a lively rate, it really seemed, when the moose circled round and disappeared in the woods as though this wasn't our own moose after all.

Then another rush of facts set in which I hadn't time to gather up. I have a faint reminiscence of three people beating all previous records in trying to get round the head of that lake-of three people, severally and collectively, making hasty and irrelevant remarks that were still more hastily forgotten-of Henry tearing through the scrub in one direction and Fred and I in another, and then I saw a huge, black animal, with his hair turned the wrong way, sick unto death but kingly still in his majestic mien, facing us not twenty feet away! I think each of us regretted for one brief fleeting moment, that the other man had not lived a better life. A crash from the rifle-a vision of Henry, hatless and happy, bounding over the brush, and then came the war-dance and the shouting.

The noble animal measured nearly seven feet in height at the shoulder; the horns were just four feet from tip to tip.

Fred had every reason to be delighted for he had ventilated the moose three times while he was on the wing. The writer was pleased because the object of the trip was attained. Henry was glad because the record of his success as a caller of moose was still unbroken. But the happiest man of all was Jack Best, the cook, for when he came and gazed upon the placid profile of the dead, he said this was the "very identical moose" that had chased him into the camp!

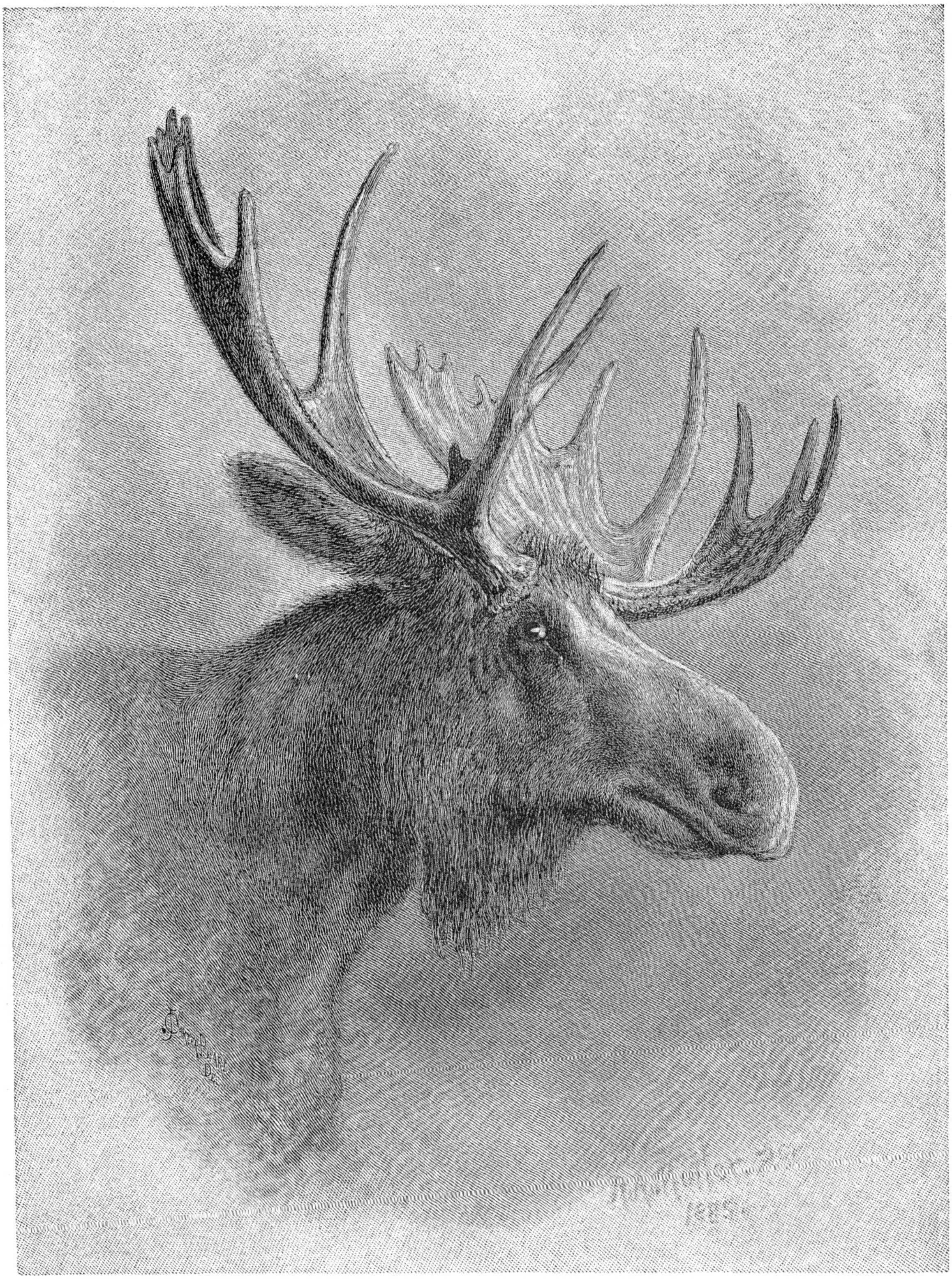

The Story of Henry McCracken
1855 - 1901

"Mother and I camping in a brush shelter."

"Tenting on a hardwood floor. It's warmer, cleaner, and a whole lot drier."

"Shore lunch fixed on a lumber camp stove."

"Family reunion: fishing trout and picnicking."

"We had a mess of fish left over even after we ate."

"There was a deep hole to fish as we fixed shore lunch."

"This was your Dad's part of the album Hank so you'll recognize a good many of the photographs in here, especially the ones that have to do with deer hunting. That's mainly what the two of you got to do together. They'll always be the best memories you'll ever have except maybe for the ones you'll share with your own kids."

"As I said, you're probably going to recognize many of these, but there's going to be a lot of them that you've never seen before because they happened long before you were even born."

"I don't know if you're aware of it, but your Dad was one darned good trout fisherman in his day. He was born and raised up in Michigan and if there's one thing that state can brag about, it's the trout fishing they have up there. Your Dad and his bunch of friends up there spent hours taking float trips down the rivers and they caught some mighty nice trout in the process."

"Fishing was something that both your Mother and your Dad enjoyed doing together. They get out and go fishing together about every chance they had, and a picnic basket usually went with them too.

"Camping outdoors made for some good family time."

"The women chose to sleep in the covered wagon while the men toughed it out in the tents."

"When we camped, the kids ran, the women gossiped, and the men fished away at their hearts content."

238

"We found a stranger in our midst."

"There were times when the women would even sneak off for a little fishing time of their own."

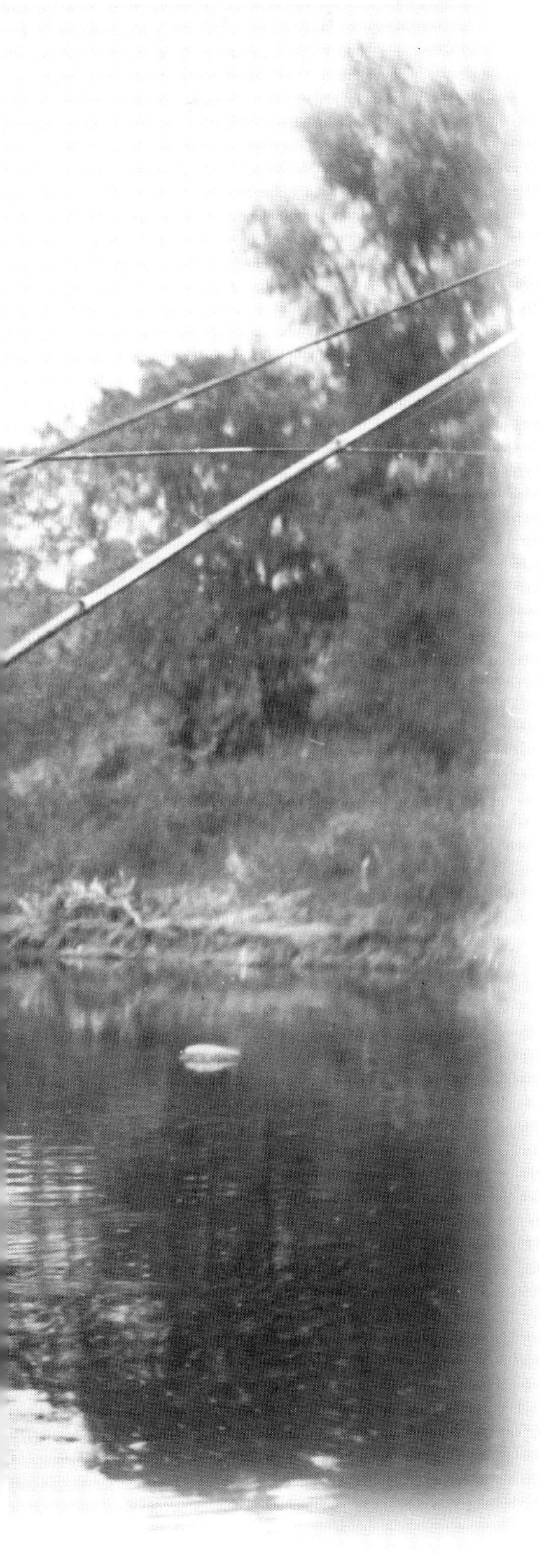
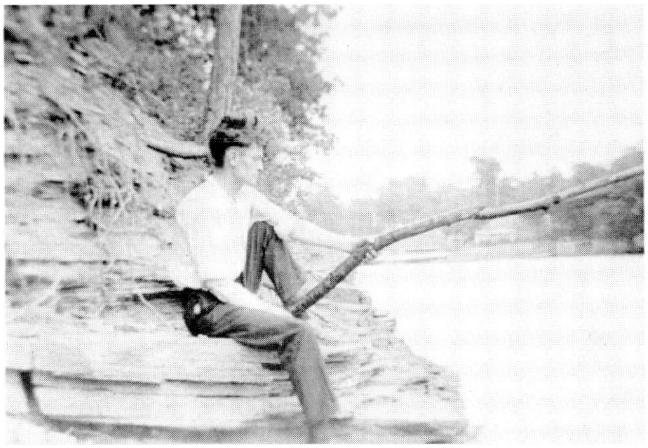
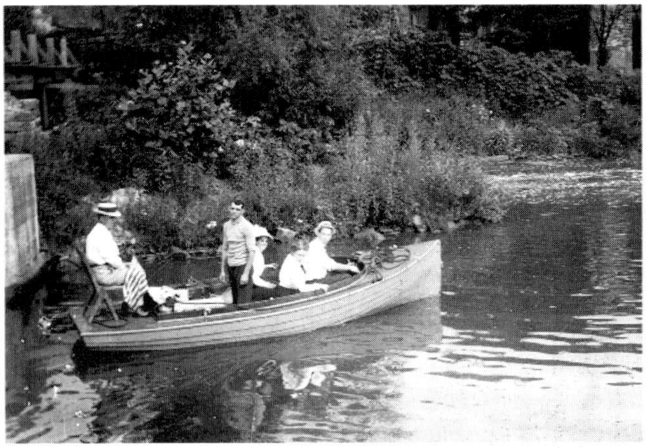
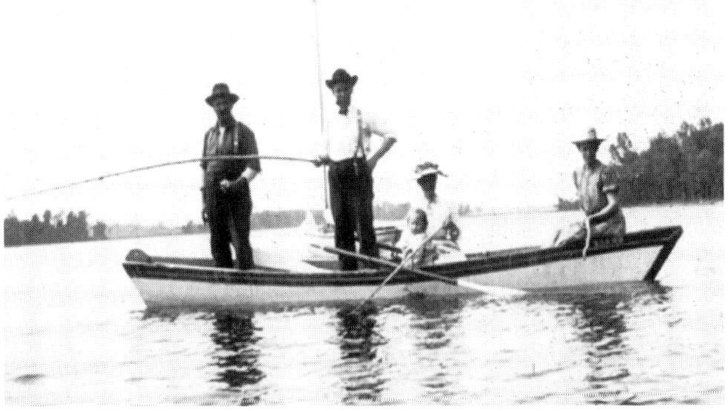
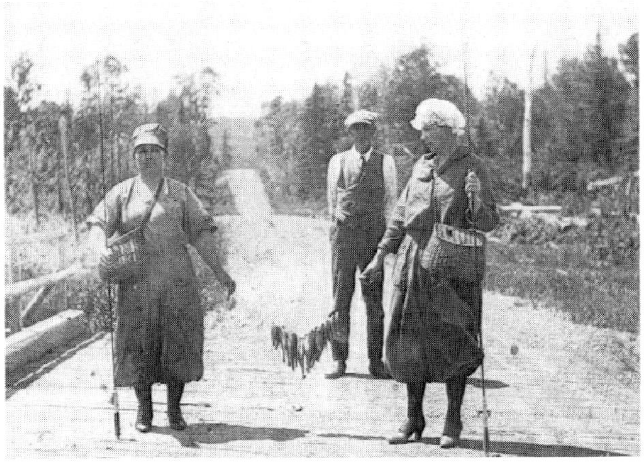

"Your Dad never missed a single deer season when he was living up there in Michigan. Deer hunting was such a ritual as far as he was concerned that he wouldn't have missed it if he'd been laying in his death bed and groping for his last breath. It meant that much to him."

"Every year, your Dad and his deer hunting friends would take off for two weeks and spend the entire time hunting for bucks in the some of the most backwoods places you could ever imagine. They'd tote their tent and nearly all of their belongings back into the woods and no matter how bad the weather was or how few deer they shot that year, they'd come back bragging about what a great time they'd had in camp."

"The way they looked and the way they smelled when they came home made a woman wonder what on Earth the big attraction was up North. It wasn't until the womenfolk started hunting deer that they found out what it was really all about."

Pitched Tents

"Several of the men that deer hunted went to the woods with as little as they could get by with. They'd pitch the simplest tent they could find and then they'd rough it out there in the woods for the next two weeks."

"Nothing at all elaborate. Camp was a place to eat and sleep."

"Cooking and eating quarters were kept separate from the sleeping area."

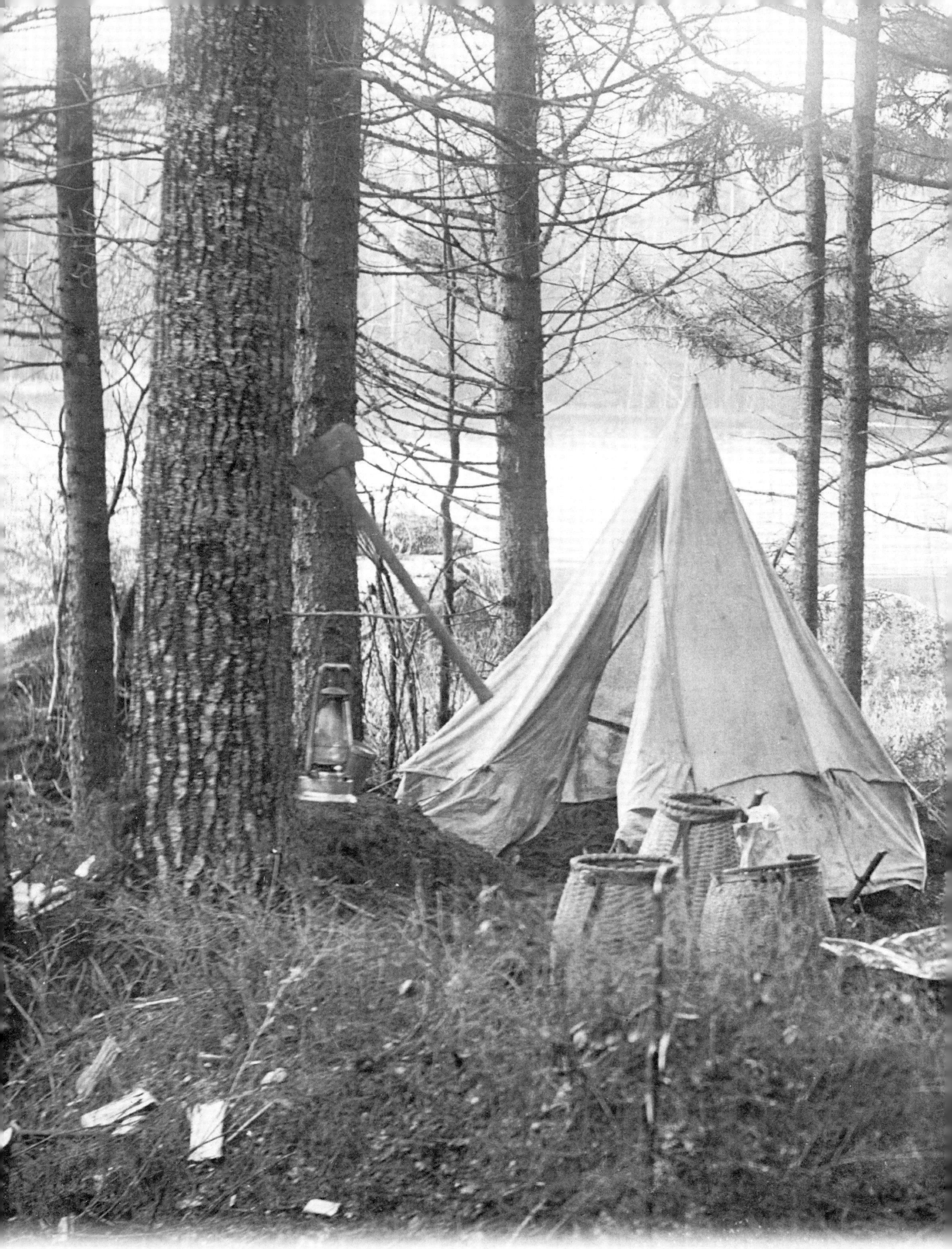

"This was a time when the entire camp could be packed in on a hunter's back."

Low Wall Tents

"Your Dad and his friends couldn't get by quite that easy. There was quite a number of them that hunted together so they used what they called a low-wall tent to hunt out of. A low-wall was bigger and heavier to get back into the woods than those tepee-type tents, but they were also a whole lot more comfortable for the men to stay in. A group that size would have been really cramped staying in a tent any smaller than that for two solid weeks."

"They usually set up one tent for the cook, to eat in and to get out of the weather if it got nasty, and a sleeping tent. They always hauled straw up with them to make a mattress of straw to sleep on. Even if they slept on the ground up in deer camp, some of those men no doubt slept better up there than they ever would have if they'd stayed at home."

"This crew meant business whatever they did and wherever they went."

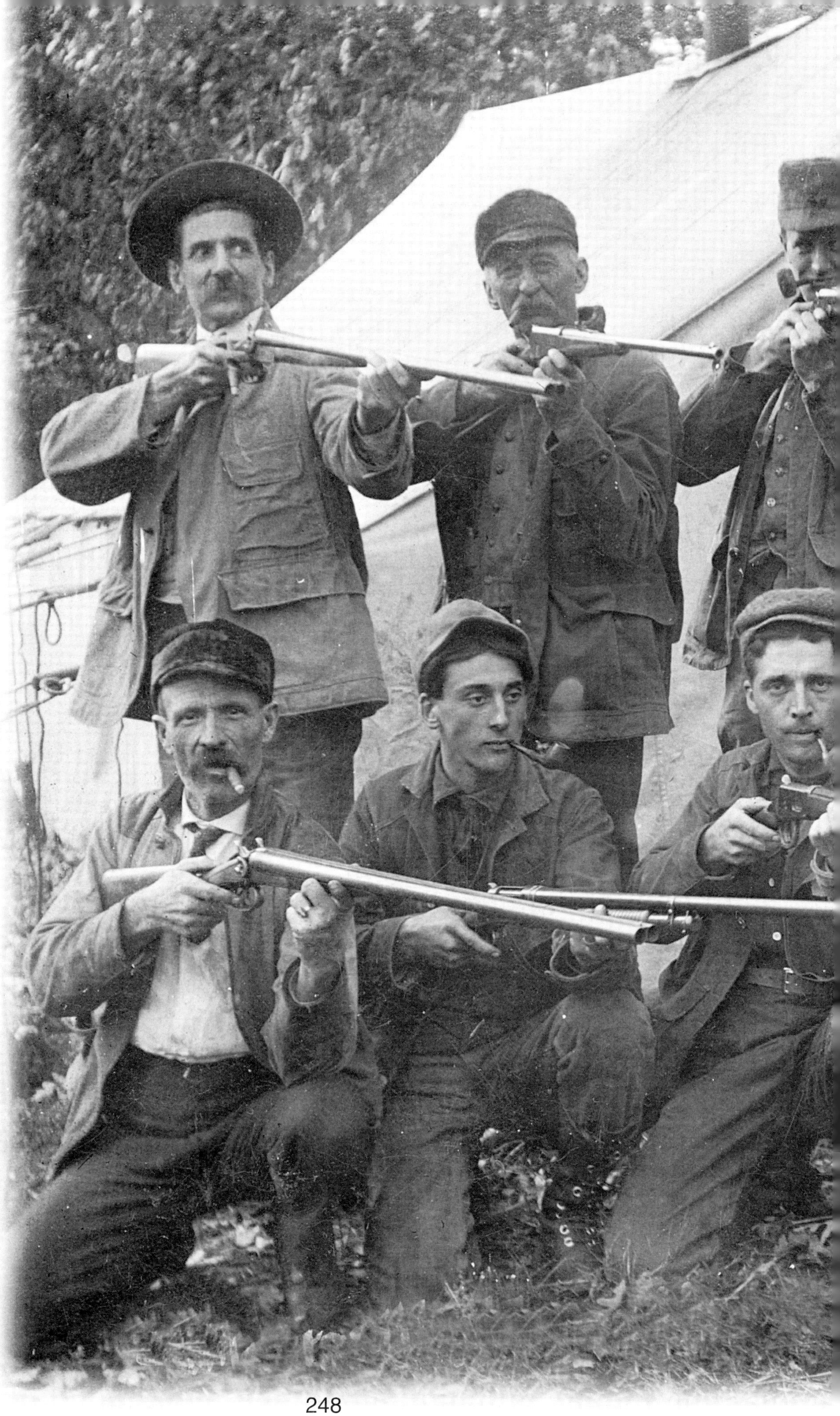

"Loaded for bear, deer, rabbits, and anything in between."

High Wall Tents

"To keep the cook in a good mood, his tag got filled first. Otherwise he'd stir up a regular hornet's nest."

"Your Dad had moved down to Wisconsin before his bunch up in Michigan got some really big ideas about tenting and having to "rough it. At least that's what they told their wives they were doing."

"They pooled their money together and bought what was called a high-wall tent. With a high wall there was no more walking around bent over and getting stiff backs for those boys. Those days were gone."

"By the time they got done outfitting one of those tents, they had all the comforts of home right up there in the middle of the woods. I'm certain a few of them had it better up at camp than they had it back home."

A Camp of Canvas

"When your Dad decided to leave Michigan and move on down to Mondovi in 1885, there was a period of several years where he didn't get to go deer hunting. It wasn't that he lost his love for the hunt, it was a case of where he couldn't take the time and he didn't have the money to go deer hunting."

"Being a farmer like he was, your Dad couldn't just up and take off any time he wanted to like some of the other men in town could. Your Dad was pretty well strapped to his farm work."

"Besides the farm work keeping him close to home, there wasn't any sense for him to go out and even try and hunt for a deer around home because there weren't any. Between the market hunters and the game hogs that hunted around there, most of the game that had been around there was pretty well cleaned out by the time he moved in. It wasn't until your Dad got on his feet and could put some money aside each year so he could get himself a hired man did he even dare consider deer hunting again."

"In a way he was fortunate to have some local men ask if he wanted to join them and hunt deer with their group up near Iron River. They weren't the kind to ask just anyone to join up with their bunch. Your Dad earned that honor by being who he was."

"On the other hand, it's sort of a shame that it didn't work out for your Dad to hunt with his brother's bunch northeast of Ladysmith. I know his brother tried time and time again to get your Dad to join them up there but there was just no way he could. Connections to get up there by train weren't all that good, and for one man to travel by himself that far wasn't the wisest thing to do either."

"I know your Dad's brother, that'd be your Uncle Homer, ran the best deer camp there was up in that area. His group did exceptionally well every year they hunted up there, even in those years when other groups would come back empty. Your Uncle's gang earned themselves a pretty fair reputation as deer hunters up around Ladysmith.

"For some reason or the other, I remember more about your Uncle's setup than I remember about your Dad's camp. I guess your Dad didn't talk about his camp up near Iron River near as much as your Uncle did."

"I do know that a great deal of thought and work went into any good deer hunting camp back in those days, wherever they hunted. That was back in the days when you either remembered everything you needed or you had to do without. There was no turning around and heading back to pick up something you forgot like some folks do these days."

Grandma had no sooner than said that, and we all turned and stared at Wonzal. Two years before he made us go back to his place three times before he finally remembered everything he had to take.

"Homer and his group were three miles back in off the main road, so they relied on using a team of horses and a wagon to get all their gear hauled back to camp. They usually managed to load the wagon heavy enough to get all their gear in on one load."

"However, when it snowed getting back into camp became a different story. The horses they used up there were light breeds, and they weren't strong enough or sure-footed enough to haul a really heavy load for long distances on a trail through the woods that was covered with loose rocks."

"Homer always said a situation like that brought back memories of the days when he used to skid logs out of the woods in the dead of winter."

"The outfit he used to log for always used oxen to skid their logs, for more years than he cared to talk about. Oxen were powerful beasts and they were as sure-footed an animal as you could find outside of a mule. However, as with all good things, there were drawbacks"

"Oxen got the job done for them but they were just too slow to earn their keep. The lumber company Homer worked for soon replaced all of their oxen with huge, heavy-breed horses that were shod with ice cleats to keep up with the times.

"Homer kept his yoke of oxen long after most other folks had gotten rid of theirs. He always figured if he was in such an all-fired hurry to get something done, then he probably shouldn't be doing it anyway and that went for his deer hunting too."

"For years when it came time to head for deer camp, Homer left a day earlier than the others would. He always made it to camp with his oxen and always with time to spare."

"Homer always took a day from camp to drive into Ladysmith to buy groceries for the camp and pick up anything the crew needed. He always chuckled when he told how the men spent more money on chewing tobacco every season than was ever spent on food."

"Homer and his oxen were familiar sights on the streets of Ladysmith for a good many years. When they were gone, much of the local history left with them."

"Packing the gear into camp was no simple matter. One of the stops we made to check the load."

"Homer and his oxen used for skidding."

"Homer and his red Holstein ox."

"Hunting from a high-wall, at it's best."

Grandma had no more than turned the page of the album when Glenn exclaimed, "Wow! Those are some really old photographs, aren't they."

"That they are Glenn. They were taken at one of Henry's early deer camps up in Michigan. I have no idea where the camp was located, who the men were that he hunted with, or what year it was. I guess no one ever bothered to write such things down back then," she said. " That might be something you boys should remember when you take pictures. They're quite meaningless without names, places, and dates on them."

Grandma was right again. That was something we were all guilty of at one time or another.

One of the first things I noticed as I looked over the photographs was the lack of snow in any of the pictures, so I brought it to the rest of their attention.

"There's no snow because they didn't want any." my Grandmother replied.

"Michigan held it's deer season early in order to try and avoid having hunters get stranded up there. When Michigan gets snow, it gets snow, and sometimes they'd get caught in it anyway."

"If they were hunting up there where the heavy snows came in off of the big lake, they could get buried under fifty inches of the stuff in a day or so. If that happened, there'd be snow to buck all the way home, and they'd be lucky if they made it home."

"I heard tell that such a thing happened a few times. They weren't found until the next Spring after the snow melted."

I had my answer in a round about way.

C.J. spoke up then. "Snow or not, it looks to me like they ate well and were having a great time when they were up there."

Wonzal's wisdom started to surface again. "That's why they went up there isn't it. They were no different back then than we are today. I know for me it isn't so much getting a deer anymore as it is to spend time with my family and friends."

I couldn't just leave a sleeping dog lie, not being the way I am.

"So is this the new excuse you're going to use year after year from for not getting a deer?" I asked.

Wonzal informed me with another punch in the arm indicated that it wasn't.

"Homer and his ox on a trip to Ladysmith, Wisconsin to buy provisions."

photo by Tiffany

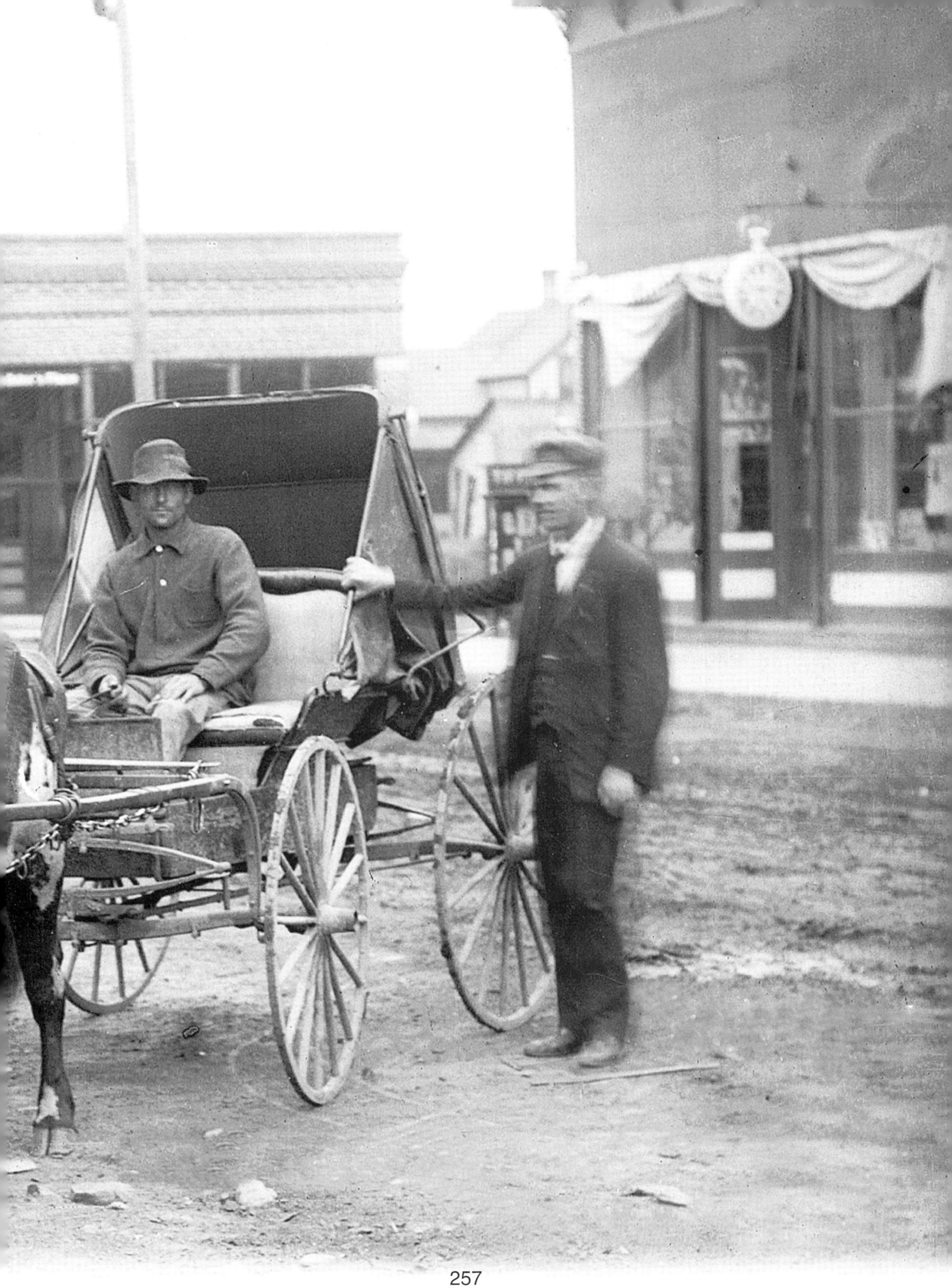

"What's going on in that picture," Wally asked." It looks like that one guy is monopolizing the conversation while the rest of the guys sit and listen to him rattle on." "It's like being up in camp with Wonzal."

It was Wally's turn to take one in the arm.

"That was part of the tradition up there in that old deer camp." Grandma said. "In the evening before they retired they'd sit around and each man would tell the rest of the men about his day. For example, he might sit and tell about what he'd seen or what he shot that day. That way each man got their turn to talk. They didn't have to fight trying to get a word in."

"The guy in this picture was telling the rest of the men in camp about the bear he crossed paths with that morning."

Wally took a step or two back to lessen the blow before he spoke up. "That's what you do Wonzal."

"We have to sit and listen to you tell that same story every year about how you shot that monstrous spike twenty some years ago."

Grandma intervened before a punch could be thrown.

Grandma continued with her story. "The men went to great lengths to be as warm and comfortable as possible while they were up there in deer camp. Some hauled straw in to pile beneath their bedding but your Uncle Homer always felt that was wasted space. He always hauled hay up for his camp to sleep on. He said it not only smelled better when he laid his head down on it, but if they ran low on hay for the livestock, he could always feed them his bedding."

Horseplay

"The skunk can stay. You can leave. The skunk smells better than you do."

"Hang on a little longer? He's beginning to tire."

"If he breaks free of the headlock, let him have it boys!"

There was one picture in particular at the end of that section that caught my attention. "What's up with the skunk in that one picture?" I asked.

"Horseplay Hank." "Nothing but pure horseplay if you ask me."

That wasn't quite the answer I expected.

"Just look at the nonsense going on in that bunch of pictures, boys. It looks to me like they had a lot of time on their hands when they were up there in deer camp. Rather than head for home like they should have after they got their deer so their womenfolk could quit doing their chores for them, they sit up there in the woods and play with their Kodaks."

Somehow, my Grandmother managed to get all of that out in one breath.

"I'm sorry," she said, "but you just touched a very tender spot with me when you said that."

There was no doubt in my mind but what I had but I had to give Wonzal credit.

If he'd have opened his mouth up like he usually did and told her what we did up at our camp when our tags were full, all Hell would have broke loose."

260

"Don't let on to my campmates that you know me or they'll run me clean out of camp."

"He had an ACE up his sleeve."

"DON'T SHOOT!" When I said "FIRE," I only meant that the shack was burning.

"I knew this was going to happen the minute I rode into camp!"

"I do know from the photographs that your Dad brought down with him and from the ones his old hunting crew sent down to him after he moved, that they didn't carry on with their horseplay every day of the season."

"Those boys had to have been out there pounding the brush pretty hard in order to wind up with the number of deer they took every season. Your Dad's old gang did extremely well compared to many groups that hunted up there."

Wally had to add a comment. "We'd have a pretty nice pole of bucks up at our camp too if Wonzal learned how to carry his end of the stick."

No punch that time. Wonzal knew he deserved that one.

"You can see here that those boys didn't waste much of their time even when they weren't out hunting. They were out catching pickerel to throw in the frying pan."

"Hang on to him Newt, he's raring!"

Grandma turned the next page and said, "I see your Dad must have taken a liking to this engraving by A. B. Frost that he put in here."

"Nearly every issue of HARPERS WEEKLY had an engraving or two done by either A.F. Tait, A.B. Frost, Hy Watson, or Fredric Remington. Seeing this one reminds me of something."

"As you boys know, folks have been hunting deer since the beginning of time. For countless centuries now, deer have not only provided food for man but nowadays the challenge they offer is unlike any other animal of the forest."

"Folks that don't hunt have always been fascinated by deer, not for the food or the challenge, but instead for the beauty a deer has to offer. That's what attracts those folks the most ."

"Deer even fascinated the caveman. He went through a great deal of effort to scratch drawings of the deer he hunted on the walls of his cave."

Over the years, other folks have been so fascinated by deer that a few of them devoted most of their life trying to illustrate the deer for others such as ourselves to enjoy."

A.B. Frost and Frederic Remington were among the best there ever was at doing this sort of thing, but there's also been a great many others besides them whose work is remembered even today," Grandma added.

"To draw or to paint, that's something that I've always wished I would have done Hank, but I've just never taken the time to find out what I could do. Deep inside I've always felt that the Good Lord may have given me the ability, but at my age I guess I'll never know."

I bent down and gave my Grandmother a kiss on the top of her head and said, "It's never too late to start Grandma."

"In fact, wasn't it just an hour or so ago that you were telling us something about folks having their dreams and their goals?"

My Grandmother looked up at me just as a tiny tear ran down the side of her weathered cheek but despite the tear, the smile on her face lit up the entire room.

"Perhaps you're right, Hank." "Perhaps you're right."

"There's something I've wondered about since that day I started deer hunting Grandma. Every year when we're up at camp, we worry about what we can do to keep our deer from spoiling on us before we get them home."

"I'm sorry," I said. "Before I continue, I need to correct myself,"

"I said the word "we" by accident. "WE" would be everyone in camp. I didn't mean to say that."

"What I meant to say was everyone but Wonzal worries about their deer spoiling, because Wonzal never gets a deer he needs to worry about."

Seven out of seven of us in attendance got a good laugh out of that one. That was one more than I expected.

"We're pretty darned lucky these days," I said. "We can run into town and buy a block of ice and then pack our deer full of chipped ice to keep them cool if we need to. A few years back, that wouldn't have even been an option ."

"Forty or fifty years ago what did hunters do to keep meat from going bad when they had no ice or refrigeration? I've never been able to figure out," I said.

"Well Hank, I'm quite certain a good many deer weren't fit to eat when they got them back home. If the deer hadn't spoiled in two or three weeks time, it had probably aged so much that it fell apart when they went to cook it."

"That might explain why the men enjoyed fresh fried venison up in camp so much. They thought it was the best tasting stuff they'd ever eaten while everyone back home complained about how strong and foul tasting it was."

265

"A mixed bag in the cut-offs of northern Wisconsin."

"Time for the butchering to begin."

"I know one thing that your Dad's bunch used to do was to gut their deer out as quick as they could. One thing they didn't do was to split their deer wide open from the chin to the end of the tail like some I've seen you boys do, for Pete's Sake."

"I can't believe some of the butcher jobs I've seen you Hun Yaks perform when you've brought your deer home. I swear a pack of wolves would be totally embarrassed by the mess you make out of your deer."

She paused for a moment, turned to Wonzal and then said, "I apologize Wonzal. I wasn't talking about you. I've never seen a deer you ever shot and gutted."

That was all we needed for another good laugh.

"Remember that picture back in your Granddad's section that showed how his bunch used to gut deer? They only made a small cut on the deer's belly when they went to gut one out. The cut was just big enough for them to reach in and pull the innards out. That not only kept the birds away from the meat but it kept the hindquarters and ribs from drying out."

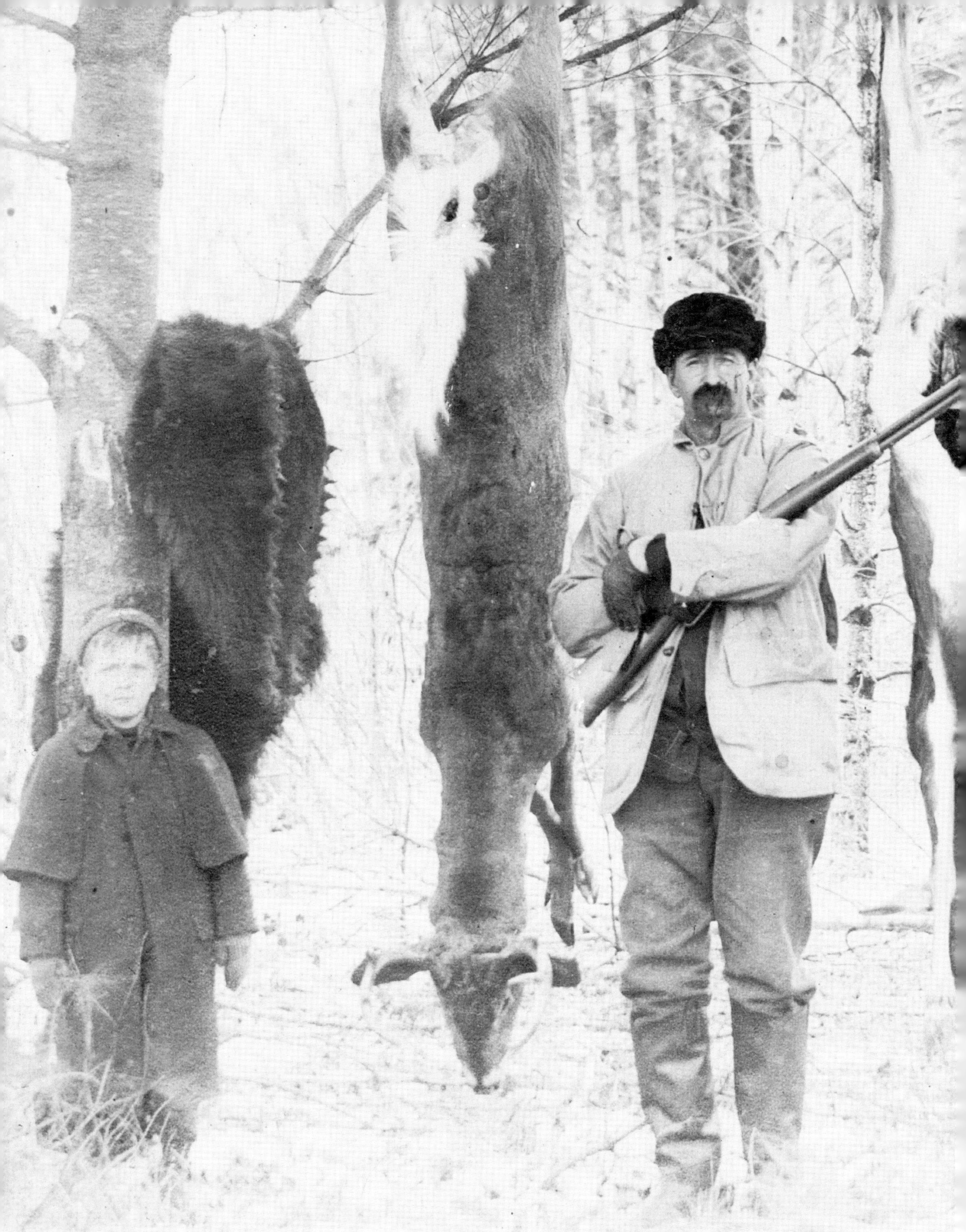

"A boy's first year in deer camp, and what a thrill it was."

"Horns were extremely hard to come by this year."

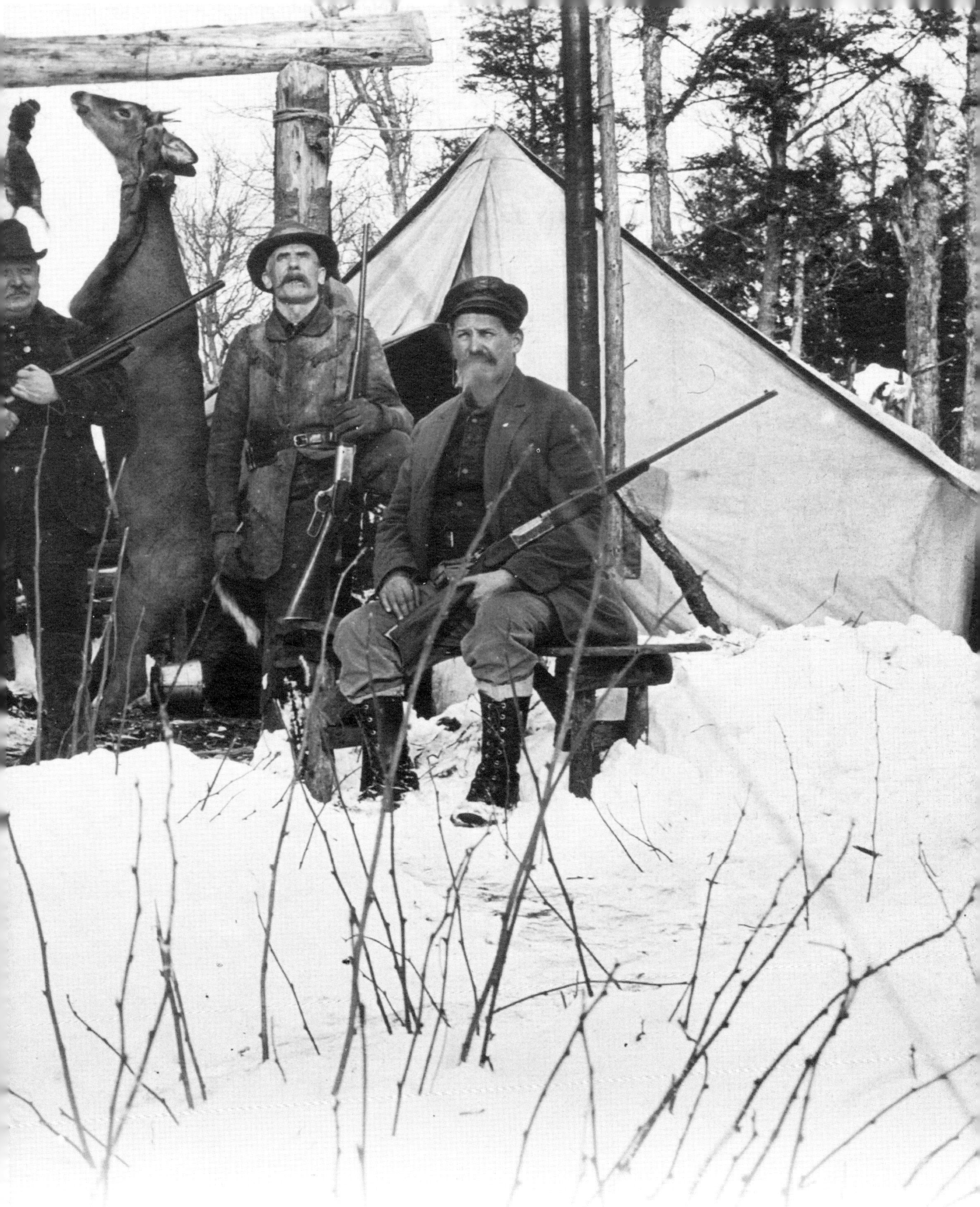

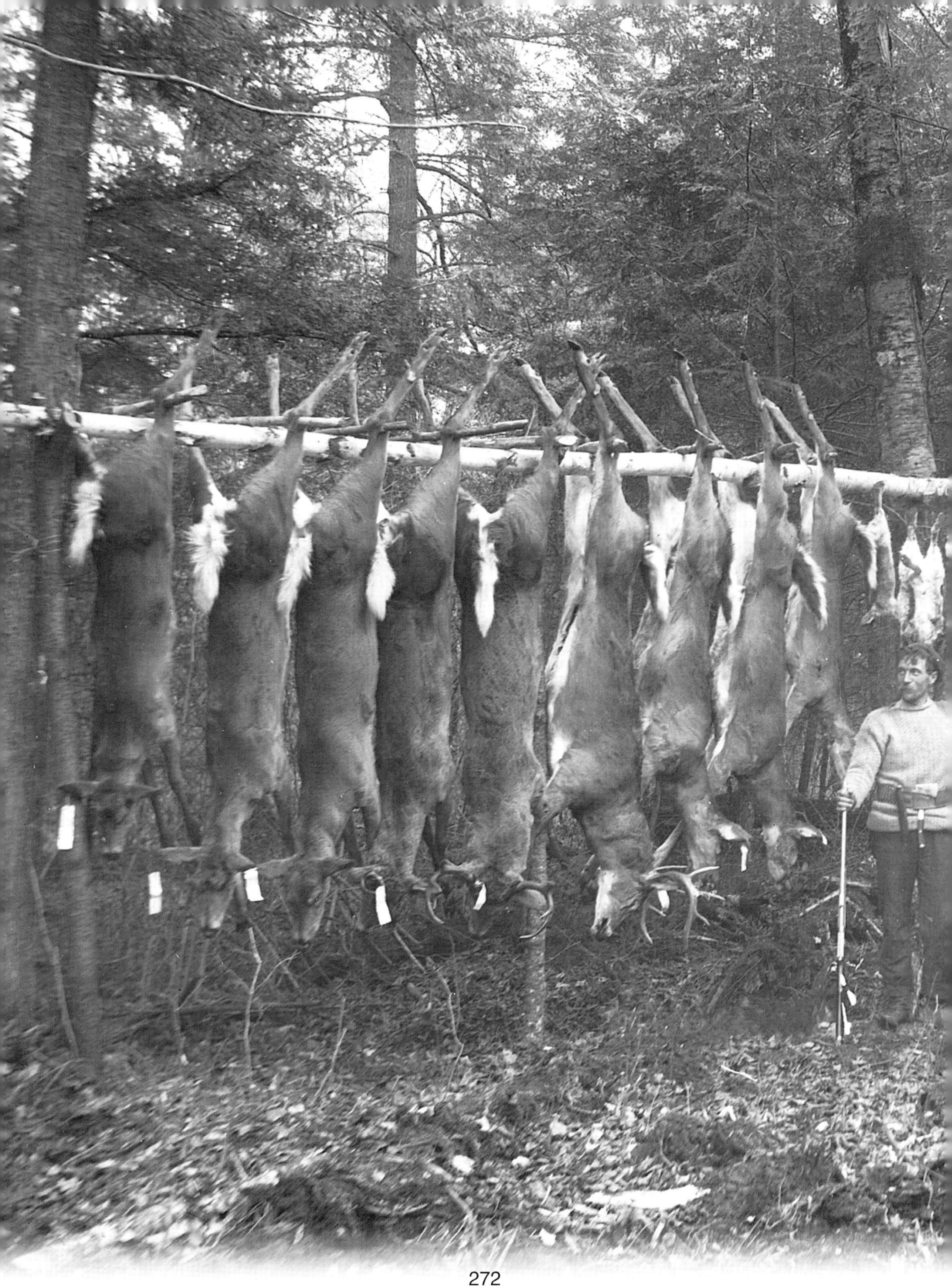

"Bagging a snowshoe rabbit at this Ladysmith camp meant good luck. The proof is as plain as day."

photo by Tiffany

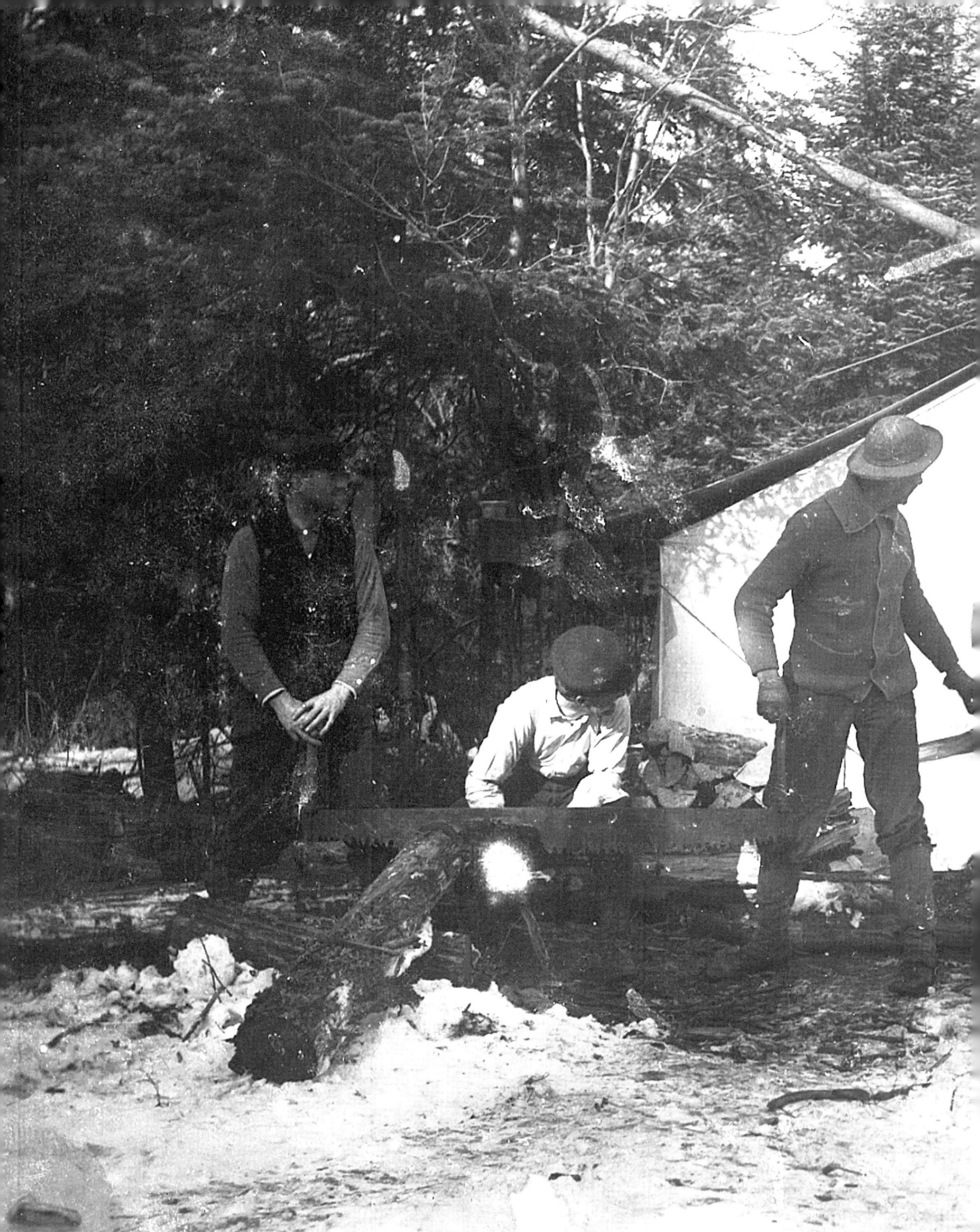

"Rabbit, Partridge, and Venison."
"What else are we having for supper?"

"As soon as they finished gutting, they hung their deer up as quick as they could so it'd cool down right away. They didn't leave it laying around on the ground for the entire day like some hunters do now days."

"And they were also very particular where they hung their deer. They'd look for the darkest, shadiest place they could find so the sun couldn't get to them and beat down on them all day long."

"They'd go far as to find a big tree and they'd hang their deer on the North side of it so it'd stay in it's shadow all day long."

"What they always hoped for of course was that the temperature would drop below freezing during the night and freeze their deer solid. Once it was frozen they were all but guaranteed that it'd be fit for their wife and kids to eat when they got it home."

"But no matter what they did to try and keep their venison from spoiling, it required a great deal of work."

"Unfortunately, when they finally got their deer home, they often found that they'd fought a losing battle."

"Some groups made certain that they had cheesecloth with them in case it got really warm out. That way they had something to wrap their deer in to keep the blowflies away."

"Several camps used to butcher their deer right up there in camp. They'd cut a deer up and pack the meat in crocks and salt it down to keep it from spoiling or they'd have pits dug in the ground or into a side hill and they'd put their crocks in the pits to keep the meat cool.."

"If a camp was really fortunate and had an icy cold spring nearby, they'd submerge a crock of meat in the spring hole to keep it cool."

"As a last resort, a few groups built a small smoking and drying tent. They'd cut their venison into strips and make jerky out of it."

Hunting Camps of Logs and Boards

Beamer have been in shock the entire time because all he did was listen and stare at the pictures without saying a word. He finally broke the silence with a question.

"Most of the hunting camps we've seen so far have all pictured tents in them. Tents certainly weren't the only thing they hunted out of up in Michigan and over by Ladysmith were they?"

"My no," Grandma replied. "The boys up there stayed in about anything they could find or build that provided a shelter of some sort over their heads."

"They didn't care if every mouse in the woods had moved into their camp or every porky pine there ever was had taken up residence underneath their camp while they'd been away for a year, the men still considered the place to be their deer camp."

"When it came to their deer camp, the men went by the old saying: "Only the strong survive.""

"They'd wade into the place and every varmint that had moved in while they were gone was either killed or driven completely out of the country. They'd sweep the place up and fix whatever the critters had chewed apart and then the crew of them would move back in again."

"The same old battle was waged year after year for as many years as the group continued to use the place as their camp."

Wally then spoke up. "It seems funny to me that it didn't make the men sick being around all that filth and vermin and sleeping with piles of red squirrel poop like they did back then."

"Oh, I'm certain it caused a few of the men to get a touchy stomach once in a great while. Overall though, I think men back then were a whole different breed than men are today."

"Most men back then were used to hard times, and things such as that didn't bother them near as bad as they'd bother a man today. Nothing at all against you boys, but I think men back then were a whole lot tougher than men are today."

Based on what we'd seen and heard so far that day, we certainly weren't in any position to argue with her.

Once Logging Camps... Now Hunting Camps

"Many of the first hunting shacks were old logging camps that had been abandoned several years before when the trees ran out. When the new growth took over and covered the area with tender browse and dense cover for the deer, the hunters moved in and took over the old logging camps."

"Most of the old camps had held up fairly well against the weather unless the tar paper on the roof had been taken when the camp moved or by homesteaders that would strip the camp of everything worthwhile. If that had happened, then the men had some major repairs to do before they could move in for the first time."

Camps of Log

"After the choice old logging camps had been taken over, many hunting groups that had seen how well log structures worked for hunting camps built their own camps out of logs."

"The supply of building material was nearby, it was free, and with a good crew working together, a hunting camp could be constructed in a relatively short time."

Horizontal Logs & Boards

"Groups often built the main structure of their camp out of logs and then, if a sawmill was nearby and the crew could afford it, they'd use rough-cut boards to finish the roof and gable ends."

"A former farmhouse and out buildings."

Vertical Logs & Boards

"An elaborate camp in the woods."

"In some areas of the country, loggers had taken all of the big, tall, mature trees and all that remained were stunted, disfigured old growth trees or short new growth trees with very small diameters. Small short logs like that made a conventional log cabin built of horizontal logs out of the question."

"However, with a little ingenuity, even logs such as these could be put to use. These smaller logs just needed to be placed vertically instead of horizontally as they normally would have been and the end product was the same."

"There was an distinct advantage using logs smaller sized logs. They were short enough and light enough that they could easily be handled. One man could lay up the walls of a cabin without any help."

The Slabwood Camp

"Beggers can't be choosers. This cabin was built of slabwood scrounged from a nearby mill."

The Boardwall Camp

"Eventually the price of lumber dropped enough due to a number of local sawmills competing for the same market so that log construction was phased out and replaced by construction using lumber and boards."

"When someone needed a camp that would last them for just a year or two, they just left the boards exposed to the elements and let nature run it's course."

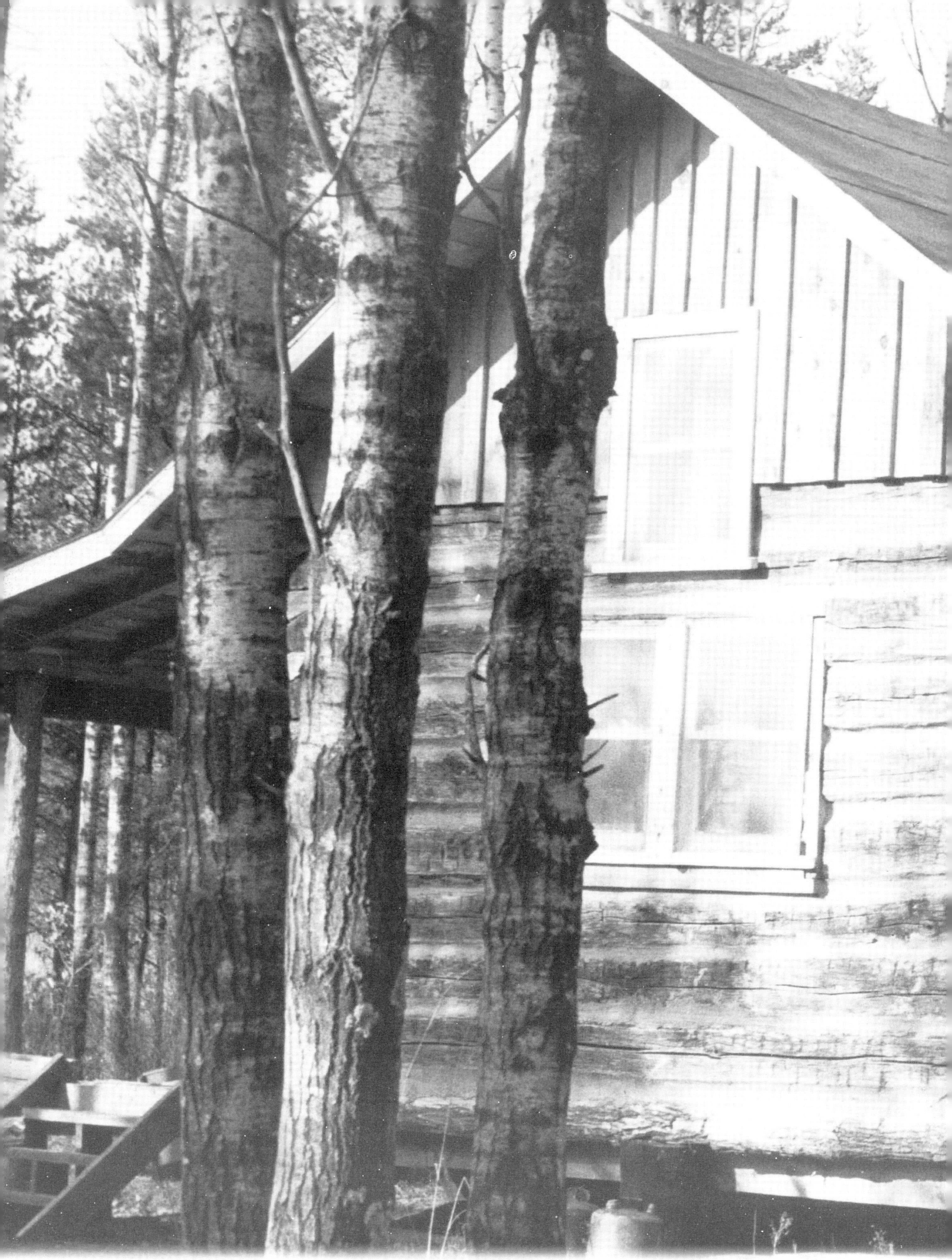

"The Pearly Swamp Camp"
Burnett County, Wisconsin.
The hand-hewned white oak
logs were once the walls of an
old farmhouse.

Camps of Log & Bark

"In some parts of the country, they used everything natural when they built their camp that they could find, even including material for the roof. Rather than boards on the roof or cover the roof with tarpaper, they used bark off of elm or basswood trees to cover the roof. If a portion of the roof was lost due to wind or heavy snow, replacement material was always near at hand."

Not Your Ordinary Deer Camp

"It has always seemed to me that no matter what might be considered normal, there's always someone around that thrives on the abnormal."

"Look at this last photo of a hunting shack for example. It's beyond me why anyone would go to all the work of building a round hunting shack."

"If you ask me, the guy must have been a little tetched in the head. He wasn't rowing around the lake with both oars in the water, if you know what I mean."

"One day I asked Hank's Granddad if he knew why any- one would want to build a round hunting camp like that."

"His answer to me was, "Probably for the same reason some farmers built round barns. They don't want a corner for the hired man to go in."

"By the time he got done saying that, he was laughing so hard that he couldn't tell me what he meant. To this very day, I still don't know what he meant."

By that time, Grandma had all of us in stitches. We excused ourselves from the table and stepped outside for a much needed break.

Tar Paper Shacks

"If they wanted their board shack to serve them for several years, then they went through the work and expense of covering the boards with lath and tarpaper. A cabin covered with tarpaper often outlasted the very foundation it was built on."

"Where the bears and the porcupines play."

"Headed out for an afternoon hunt."

"Taking time out for a little breather."

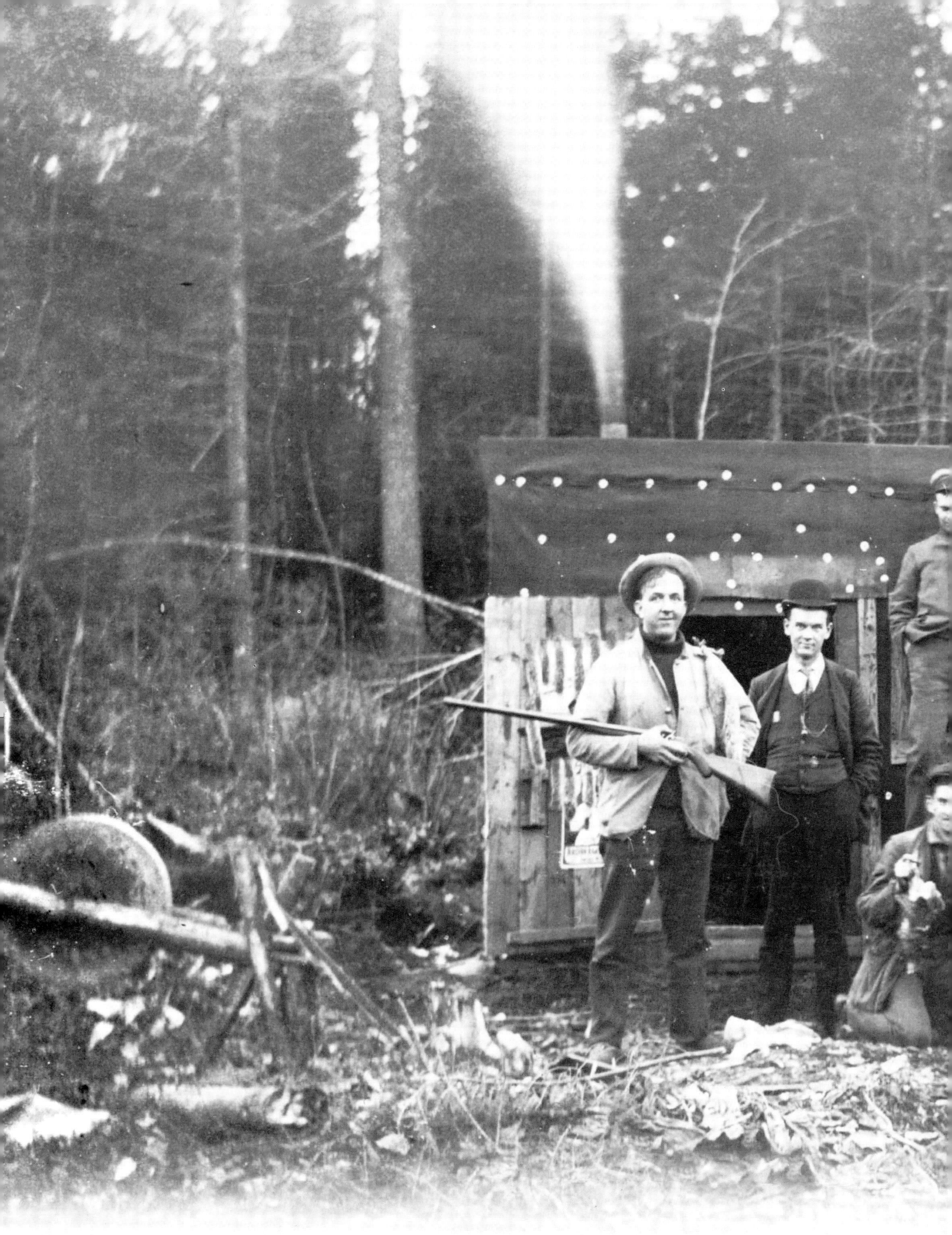

"Waiting for the rest of the gang to arrive."

"I always got a big charge out of your Dad and his hunting companions when they left home to head up to camp. The womenfolk would always pack a huge lunch basket for them to eat at noon, but they never made it until lunch time before they had it gone."

"Sometimes they weren't ten miles from home before they'd have to pull over to the side of the road and start eating. Then they'd sit down and devour the entire lunch."

"By the time they got to where they were going to camp for the night they'd be practically starving."

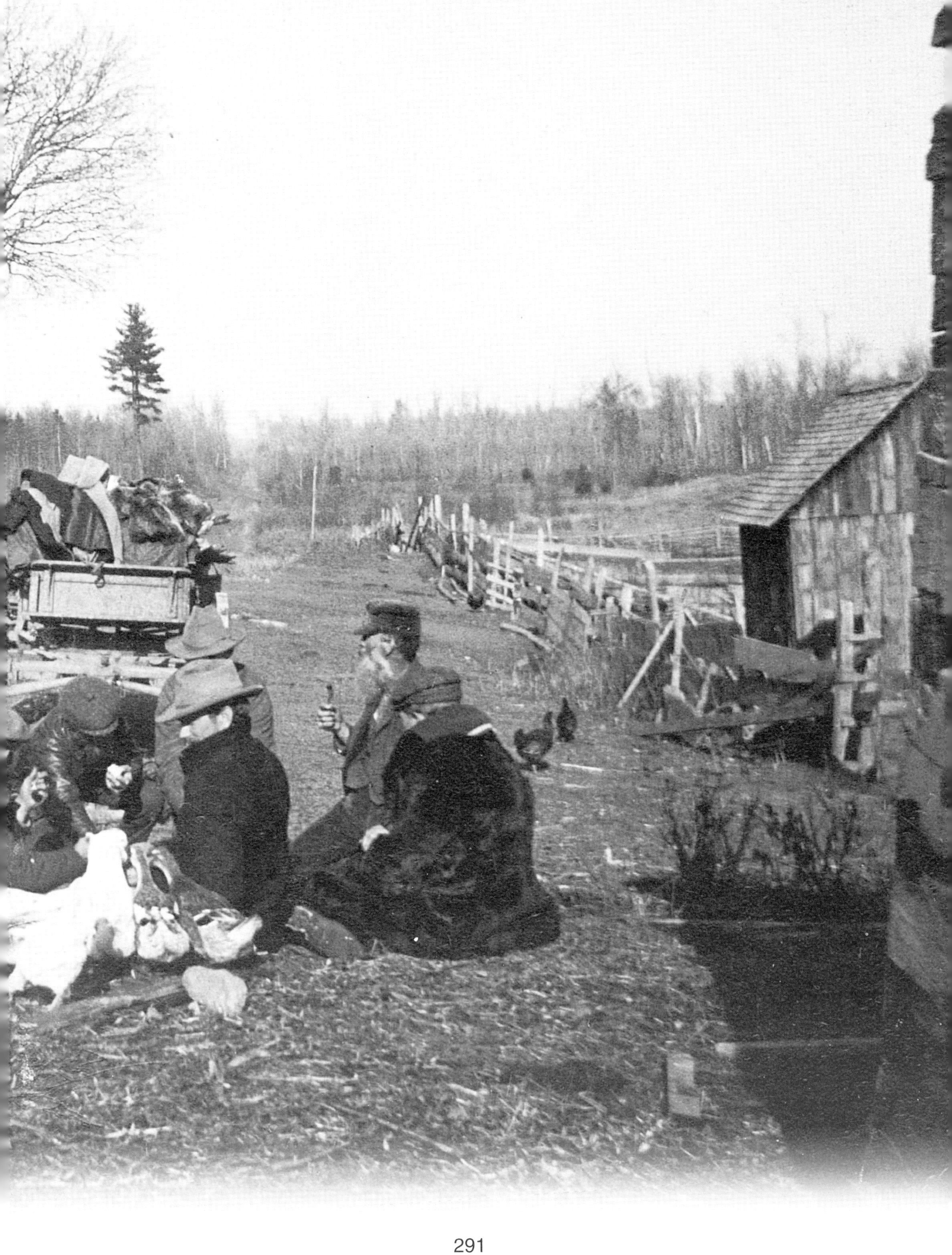

"Opening up the spring hole for coffee water."

"The first thing to do was to rid the place of varmits."

"They made it up to camp towards the end of the second day if the roads were good. If not, it meant a second night of camping out for them."

"Once they were in camp they wasted no time until everything was in order. No snow made the job much easier. Snow usually meant twice the work getting the camp ready. Only when everything was done did they pause to relax."

"In anticipation of opening morning."

"The deacon's seat sat empty when there was room to stretch out on the bunk."

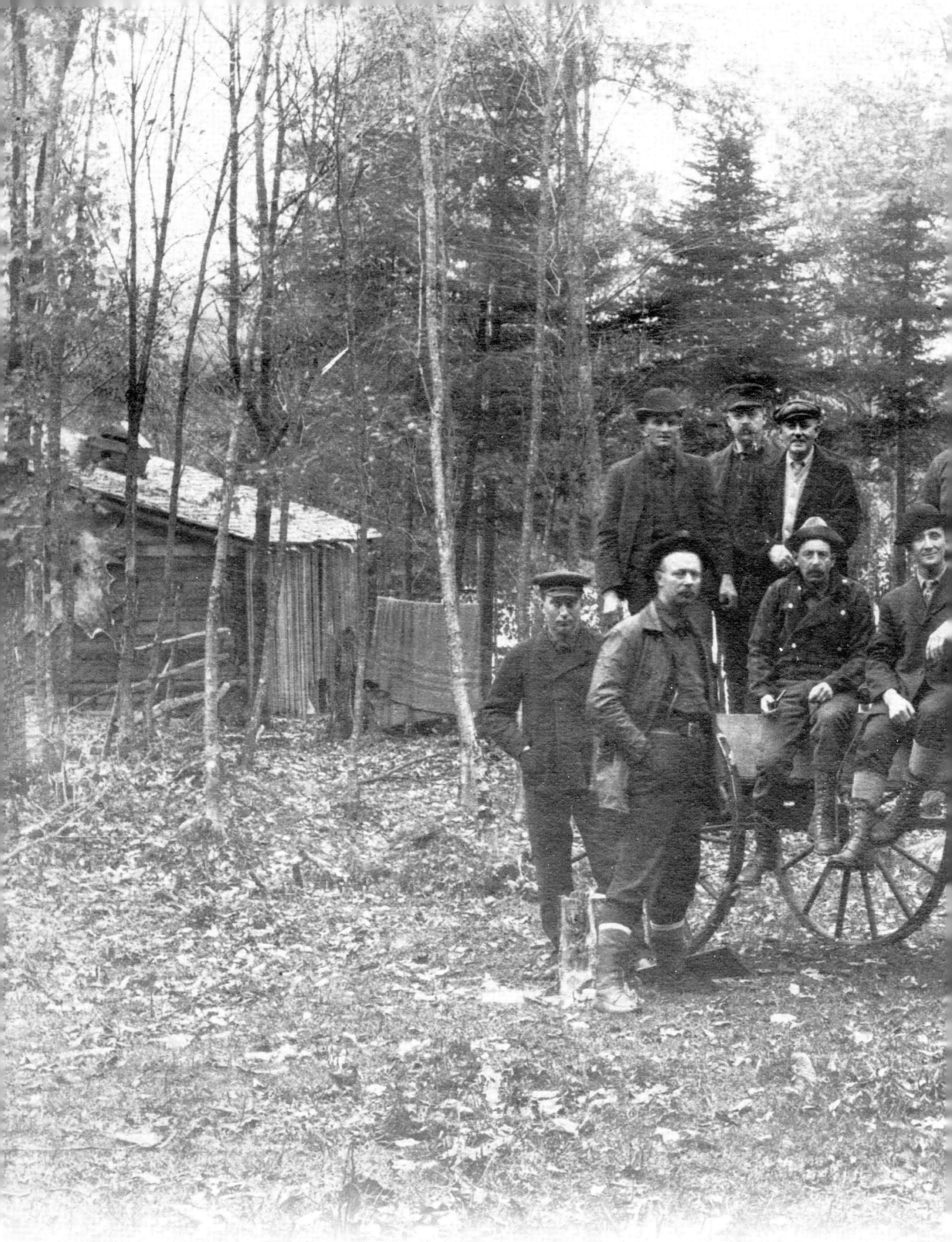

"With the camp ready to go, it was time to pay the neighboring camps a visit."

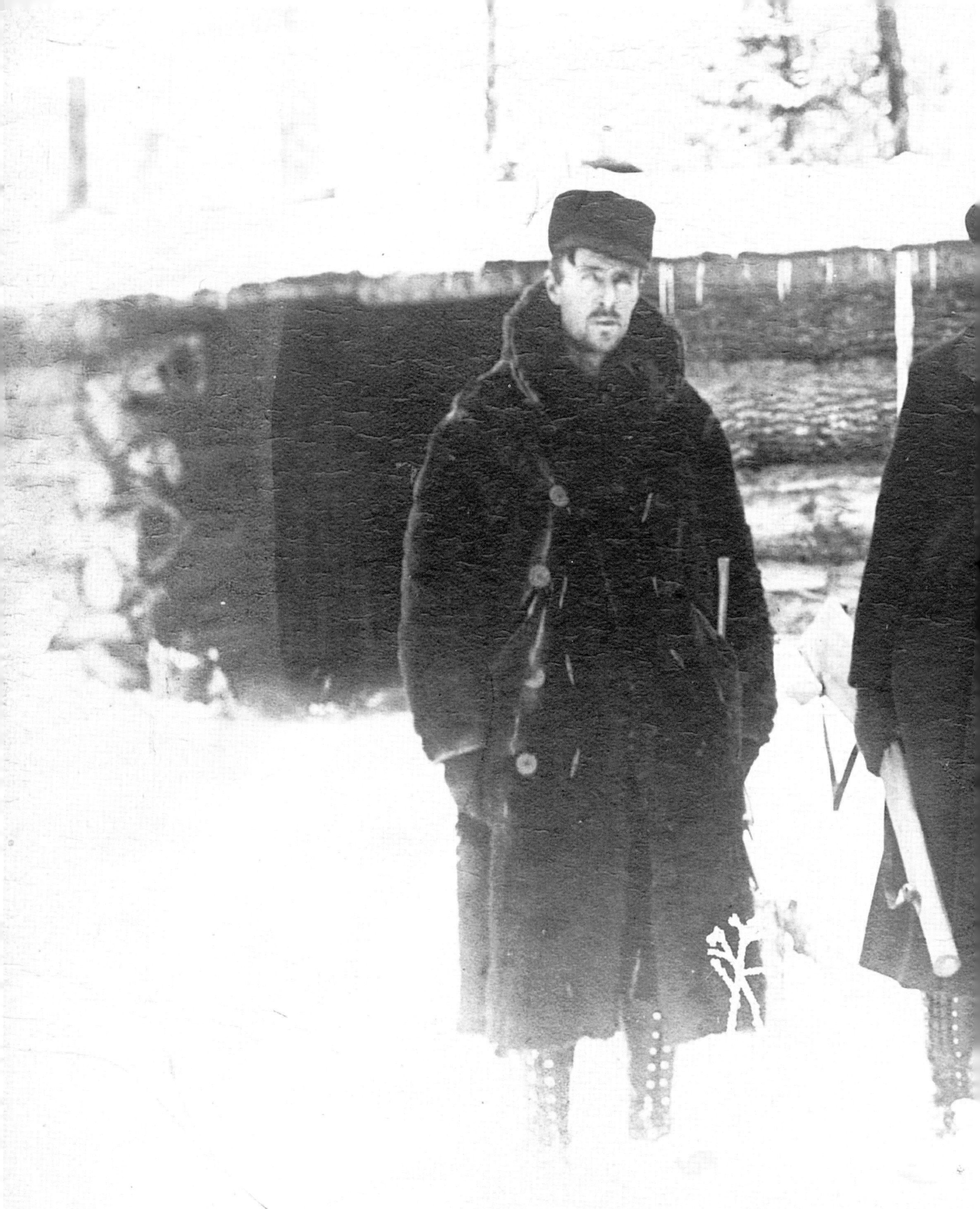

"Me thinks we've got us some trackin' snow boys."

"From here on out, there will be no more dog and pony shows without some tasty tidbits."

On the Hunt

"It's a real shame that your Dad didn't have any photographs of himself or any of the members of his group taken when they were actually out hunting to put in this album, Hank."

"I guess maybe taking pictures wasn't a big thing to do in their camp like it was in some camps." Grandma added.

"At least there's a few pictures of your Uncle Homer sent your Dad of him and his crew hunting over near Ladysmith that your Dad put in the album here."

"Homer and his bunch used three different ways to hunt when they were up there."

"Your Uncle and a couple of others in his gang used to sneak hunt. Homer loved to sneak hunt and he'd pussy-foot through the woods all day long looking for bucks."

"I'm sure there were a great many bucks that would have sought safety in an insane asylum over that way if he hadn't of shot them before they could get there. I heard tell he drove more than one buck nuts the way he could sneak up on them."

"A few of the men did nothing but take stands and watch deer trails all season long. Homer said he could never hunt that way because he couldn't sit much longer that an hour or so before he got the urge to see what was over the next hill."

"Those that could sit it out all day long did real well, I guess. They knew sooner or later that a deer had to use the trail, and they felt the need to be there when it happened."

"Two of the men in Homer's camp relied on fresh snow in order to enjoy their deer season. They just relished the idea of a fresh tracking snow and of taking off in it right at dawn until they cut a fresh track. Then they'd jump the track and stay on it all day long just to see what made it and where it would take them."

"Every evening, just before they'd laid in the night log, they'd open the door of the cabin and stare out into the darkness. Then they'd say, "If I'm not mistaken, I believe there's a few flakes of snow in the air tonight," whether there was not. It just seemed to help lift their spirits."

"Then, as they turned around and closed the door behind them they'd say, "We just might have enough snow for tracking by morning."

"I myself tend to believe that the little prayer they said each night before they drifted off to sleep may have helped a great deal more than all the wishing that they did."

"Homer admirers one that didn't get away."

"Homer would traipse through about every type of cover imaginable from blackberry thickets to oak ridges.

He loved to track bucks through the cutovers but when conditions were just right, there was nothing better than jumping a buck out of its bed down in the middle of a spruce swamp."

"I nailed him right where I should have."

Lost on the Hunt

Grandma paused for a moment before she turned the next page and said to us, "I do tend to believe that your Uncle Homer may have been one of the few men that I've ever known that would have survived a deer season like that bunch did up in Michigan lived through back in 1899."

"What makes you think that?" I asked.

"Well," she said, "back in the late teens he came back from camp one year telling how he got himself lost up there in that forsaken country somewhere northeast of Ladysmith. Wherever he was when he got lost must have been a huge tract of land as there wasn't a solitary road through the area at that time. As a matter of fact, roads hadn't even been thought of back then."

"At any rate, he told me how one particular morning that season had every ingredient that a deer hunter like himself could dream of. The temperature was mild, there was an inch or two of fresh snow covering the ground, and there was a number of huge bucks running around that needed to be shot."

"Homer said he left camp just before daybreak that morning and headed off in a northeasterly direction to hunt a slashed off area that he'd run across the year before. The year before the area had been completely trampled by deer that were feeding on the new growth and his hope was that it hadn't grown up enough in a year's time to change everything."

"The slash was nearly two miles away, so he put his head down and put some distance between himself and the cabin by the time the sun was fully above the horizon."

"It wasn't until he reached the slash and reached for his compass to check his directions that he realized he didn't have it with him. He'd left it hanging from the bunk post where he'd hung it the night before when he'd changed shirts."

"As Homer was somewhat familiar with his surroundings and he'd been without a compass before, he thought nothing of it. The sun was out to give him directions, so he checked his bearings and started pussy-footing through the slash."

"He had wandered around for nearly four hours and by eleven o'clock he was ready to take a breather. He sat down on a stump to rest for a few minutes when it suddenly dawned on him. He had been so intent on being quiet, avoiding sticks, and looking for deer on all sides of him that he was completely unaware that the sun was no longer out. In fact, a gray mass of clouds had moved in and a light trace of snow hung in the air."

"Homer had been walking for some over four hours and he realized that in less than five hours, it would start to get dark. Even if he turned around right then and headed back to camp, if he got his directions mixed up at all on the way back, he'd be pushing dark by the time he got to camp."

"Homer looked around a few minutes in an effort to figure out where he was, but he didn't see a thing that looked at all familiar to him from. He figured the best thing he could do was to retrace his own tracks rather than risk getting lost out there in the middle of nowhere. He turned around and faced the direction he'd just come from, picked out the top of a huge old white pine tree about a mile away, and headed off in it's direction."

"Fifteen minutes had gone by, and Homer had covered perhaps a third of the way to the pine tree. The air had become filled with a million snowflakes that swirled around Homer's face, landing and freezing on his eyelids, and blocking his view of the tree top he was trying to reach."

"By then the snow was coming down hard enough that he could watch as his tracks drifted over. In a matter of minutes, he found himself having to study the ground ahead in order to see the shallow dimples left by his old boot prints."

"In minutes he was enveloped by such darkness that he had difficulty seeing just a few feet ahead. At first he thought perhaps the day was coming to an end, but then he realized it was snowing so hard that it completely blocked out what daylight there was."

"Homer continued to struggle ahead, but the snow was piling up so fast that it became difficult for him to even walk. About the time he realized that it was fruitless to try and reach the pine tree, he took one more step and tripped over something soft lying just beneath the snow. He pitched forward into the snow and laid there until he caught his breath again."

"When he tried to stand, the branch of a nearby spruce tree knocked the hat from his head and a huge pile of snow fell down the back of his neck and melted, sending tiny rivulets of icy water down the middle of his back"

"He gasped as a chill raced through his body and he started to shake, partially from the cold but mainly from the exhaustion that overtook him."

"Homer had spent a night or two in the woods before and he resigned himself to the fact that the smartest thing he could possibly was to hunker down beneath that spruce and ride out the storm. When it was over, he could dig himself out and start over fresh again."

"Homer crawled under the spruce as far as he could until he was right next to the trunk. Then he dug and scraped the snow away until there was nothing but moss and spruce needles for him to lay on. He then packed the snow around him, said a prayer that he might see his family again, and fell into the most exhausted sleep he'd ever had."

"When Homer awoke, he no longer heard the blizzard winds that he had fallen asleep listening to the night before. In fact, there was an almost eerie silence around him."

"He lifted the spruce branches off and kicked away at the rim of packed snow that surrounded him until he could finally see the light of day."

"Homer crawled out from under his shelter and then stood for a moment to admire the surroundings. Everything around him was covered beneath a layer of fresh, white, glistening snow. He figured that somewhere between fifteen and twenty inches had been dumped on him since it started."

"Homer brushed the snow off his rifle, blew the snow from the sights, and started to walk away. He managed to take five steps before he tripped over the same thing that got him before, and he pitched headlong into the deep snow again."

"Homer told me it didn't bother him the first time it happened but the second time, it really set him off. A combination of frustration and curiosity found him kicking the snow away from what ever it was. He wanted to see what it was that had managed to get him covered in snow two days in a row."

"His first kick uncovered what appeared to be the tip of a deer's antler, and the more snow he kicked away the more deer antler he saw. By the time he was done, he had not only one set of deer horns lying at his feet, but two!"

"Why in the world would there be two sets of deer horns laying together like that out in the middle of the woods ?" I asked.

My Grandmother gave me the same icy stare that I'd gotten from her earlier in the day.

"Perhaps if you'll let me finish the story Hank, then we'll all know." she said.

It was my fault. I should have learned years before to never interrupt my Grandmother in the middle of one of her stories.

"When Homer was done kicking the snow away, there they were, two dandy bucks that had been fighting and got their horns all locked up." "The poor devils had exhausted themselves so bad that they died of starvation and exposure out there."

Wally then broke the silence with, "Let that be a lesson to you Wonzal." "There ain't a woman in the world that's worth fighting over."

"How would you know?" Wonzal replied. "You've never had a woman stop long enough to even take a second look at your ugly face, Wally."

That time it was Wonzal that caught the punch.

"You two can knock it off right now. I can finish the story without either of you two Hun yaks," Grandma said.

I don't think she was kidding either.

Grandma started again. "Homer felt bad for the two bucks but at the same time it sure made him feel lucky. If he'd have fallen on those horns either time he tripped, he would have been impaled on those sharp points. Then there would have been a dead man laying on top of the whole works."

"Wouldn't that have been something for someone to come across," Wonzal added.

"Homer got himself all straightened around again and was about ready to strike out again when he heard what sounded like a shrill whistle, way off in the distance."

"At first he thought it was some sort of a shrill bird whistle, but then when he heard it again he knew it wasn't any bird he'd ever run across before."

"Homer figured he had nothing to lose, so he headed off in the direction of the whistle."

"Homer was smart enough to know better than to put his head down and go as he made his way through the deep snow. He didn't consider himself a spring chicken any more and there wasn't any sense in wearing himself out when he didn't even know what the sound was that he was headed for."

"Besides that, he was still hunting. He felt if he kept his eyes open, he had a good chance of catching a buck that was still in it's bed that time of the day."

"Homer stopped every so often and listened for the sound of the whistle again. He heard it several times more but each time when the whistle sounded like it was getting closer to him, the next time it sounded further away than it was before. He was somewhat bewildered by it to say the least. "

"With nothing better to do and no where else to go, Homer decided the best thing he could do was to keep moving in the direction of the mysterious whistle that was somewhere up ahead."

"Homer glanced down at his watch and then looked at it a second time to make certain it was the time he thought it said."

"It was seven o'clock when he started out that morning and when he looked at his watch, it was half past eleven.

Homer knew if he didn't figure out where he was in the next hour or so, he'd be spending another cold, hungry night out in the woods."

"He was debating what he should when that same whistle that he'd been trying to track down let loose with another of it's shrill sounds.

"Homer nearly jumped out of his skin as a chill raced up and down his spine. The only good thing about the whistle was, it sounded just a short distance away.

That time he did put his head down and he lit out in the direction of the sound."

"He thought he and whatever it was that made the sound would cross paths in less than a mile but forty-five minutes later, not a thing did he see."

"To add to his disappointment, the next time he did hear the whistle, it was a considerable distance away. Homer had almost reached the point of turning around, when he heard what sounded like voices, just a short distance away."

"Rather than head towards the source of the sound again only to be disappointed, Homer let out with a holler, the loudest one he could muster."

"He called out, "HALLOO," paused for a few seconds and tried once more, "HALLOO," "HALLOO.""

Much to Homer's relief, there came a response ."
"HALLOO YOURSELF."
"I'M OVER HERE."

"Homer said that he took off as tight as he could towards the direction of the voice. He didn't want to take a chance of having the sound to disappear on him again."

"Less than a hundred yards away, Homer climbed over a deep snow bank and found himself standing smack dab in the middle of a skidding trail."

"He turned and looked to his right, and there stood the source of the voice. Homer gave a big wave to the man and then headed up the trail to meet the guy."

"As Homer walked towards the man, he recognized the guy as a road monkey. He had met a good many of them over the years when he was logging. The guy's job was to keep the trail clear of horse droppings so that they wouldn't freeze and cause a horse to stumble over them. It was also his responsibility to see that the iced trail didn't get to slippery and fast for the horses pulling a sleigh load of logs."

I hesitated at first, knowing the embarrassment I would face if I were to interrupt my Grandmother again. However, there comes a time in every man's life when things that need saying must be said. This was one of those special moments.

"Listen up fellas," I said. "I don't feel qualified to make a monumental decision like this by myself so I have to ask for your opinion."

"What do think? Do we call Wonzal "THE STINK BEAR," from now on, or do we call him, "THE ROAD MONKEY?"

The decision was unanimous. From that day forward, Wonzal, would for ever would be known around our camp as, "THE STINK BEAR."

I got two other things besides a good laugh when I pulled that one. I received another of those stern looks from my Grandmother and, a very subdued smile from her.

"As I was trying to say, Homer had walked almost up to the road monkey but before he could shake hands and introduce himself the guy said, "get yourself up that snow bank as quick as you can." " If you slip under the sleigh of logs that's coming down the trail, I'll have me another mess to clean up and get off the road before it freezes."

"Homer said he scrambled up the snow bank as tight as he could and got himself out of the way."

"After the load passed by the monkey said, "What in the blazes are you doing up in this country? You're twenty miles away from anywhere when you're standing there."

"Homer told the guy how he'd got mixed up while he was hunting and then tried to describe where his deer camp was to the guy."

"The only response he got from the guy was to watch him lift his hat off, scratch his head and say, "I ain't the faintest notion where you came from."

"You're best hope," the monkey said, " will be to ask the cookee who's bringing the noon lunch out to the men if he knows what you're talkin' about."

"If he doesn't know anything, you can ride back to camp with him and ask the barn boss if he recognizes the place you're talkin' about."

"Otherwise you'll have to wait around until tomorrow when the walking boss comes to pay the camp a visit. He'd know for sure where the place is that you're talkin' about."

"The cookee should be here with the dingle in a few minutes. You're welcome to eat out here with us or you can ride back to camp with the cookee and eat your dinner at the cook shanty."

"Homer said that when the dingle arrived and he saw the kind of appetites that those lumberjacks had, he knew better than to take a plateful of food away from them. He chose to ride back to the camp with the cookee instead. Besides, Homer thought he might be able to get a few answers out of the cookee as to where all the deer hung out in that area, but the two of them didn't exchange a a single word on the entire ride back to camp."

Grandma said, "When I asked Homer why the cookee didn't want to talk to him Homer said, "Oh, he wanted to talk all right." "In fact he talked to me all the way back to camp."

The problem was, I couldn't understand one word he said. I 'd never dealt with a Fin Lander before. All I ever learned as a kid in a logging camp was how to swear in Norwegian."

"As soon as they pulled into camp, three men who had been standing over by one of the sheds hoofed it over to the dingle as fast as they could to see who the new visitor was."

"Homer introduced himself to the three of them, and they in turn introduced themselves to Homer as swampers with the logging crew."

"Homer was curious why the three were in camp instead of out working with the rest of the crew," so he went ahead and asked them."

"Evidently from what the swampers told him, one of the sawyers had dropped a tree on top of them a couple of weeks before. According to them, they were in pretty rough shape when they were brought in. They'd been in camp ever since trying to get themselves mended well enough so they could go back to work again."

The sawyers then escorted Homer over to the cook shanty to introduce him to the camp foreman.

"As they opened the door of the cook shanty, Homer was met by a rush of warm air that carried with it the sweet smells of bread and pastry unlike any Homer had ever smelled before."

"Towards the back of the cook shanty, Homer could see the foreman, his wife, their two children, and a pair helpers visiting among themselves. As soon as they looked up and saw Homer, the room became as quite as a funeral parlor."

"However, as soon as Homer walked up and introduced himself to the group, he found himself seated at the table with knife and fork in hand and a pile of food set in front of him that he doubted he'd ever put away."

"As far as the cook and the foreman were concerned, Homer was a guest, and guests at a lumber camp were treated like royalty . The only thing that was asked of the guest by the camp was that the guest share all the latest news and gossip that they could dole out between fork fulls".

"According to Homer, he had absolutely no trouble keeping the entire group entertained for over an hour while he ate."

"Fortunately for Homer, the foreman had worked the area for ten years and he was familiar with every woods that had been logged off and every tract that hadn't. When Homer started to describe the area he had been hunting to the foreman, he recognized the place in moments time."

"I know the place you're talking about," he said. "We logged in there four years ago. It's about twenty-two miles away from here as the crow flies. You must have about worn your boots out getting here."

"My legs are a little tuckered from buckin' the snow," Homer told him. "Other than that I'm fine. My only question is, how can I get back?"

"You timed your getting lost just right," the foreman said. "If you'd have gotten yourself lost two days later, you'd have been in for either a very long hike or a month long sit. That would have been your only choices."

"As it is, the walking boss is due in to camp tomorrow. He's coming up from the railhead located down your way and I think you can catch a ride back with him later on tomorrow. He can drop you off almost at your doorstep."

"Until then, if you want to rest up in the bunkhouse," the foreman said, "you're more than welcome to."

"You can dry your wet duds off in there and catch a nap or two before the crew comes in for supper."

"Homer got up from the table and started to leave but instead he turned to the foreman and said, "I do have one more question to ask you."

"What in the Blue Blazes was that shrill sounding whistle I kept hearing yesterday when I was back there in the woods?"

"Oh that?" the foreman said. "That was our steam hauler going back and forth on the skidding trail hauling sleigh loads of logs out of the woods for us."

"I thought you told me you were a lumberjack a few years back. You've never run across a steam hauler before?"

"No sir, I never have," Homer told the foreman. "The outfit I worked for couldn't afford to own one of the things. If they could have, I'd probably still be logging for them today. Instead, when they couldn't compete with the companies that used steam haulers, they went belly-up."

"Homer said that by that time, between the big meal he'd eaten and the long walk he'd taken, he had all he could do just to keep his eyelids open. He excused himself from the group and headed over towards the bunkhouse to catch a few winks."

"He had no more than stepped out of the door of the cook shanty when he started thinking about how strange it was that they still referred to a camp supervisor as the "walking boss"

"It still dwelled on his mind, even when he reached the bunkhouse and laid his head down on the musty smelling feather tick pillow."

"Many years before," he thought, "camp supervisors did walk from one logging camp to another, but those days were long past. These days the only walking they do is between the railroad coach and their sleigh or buggy. It wasn't make any sense at all to him."

"Homer's eyes grew heavy and begin to close. As they did he said to himself, "What do I care what they call the guy, just as long as "the walking boss" gives me a ride back to my deer camp." Then he drifted off to sleep."

"Despite several attempts by the foreman and the barn boss to wake him that evening, Homer was so exhausted that he slept right through supper. Not only did he miss supper, but he slept through the Saturday night fiddle music, the raucous singing to dozens of ribald logging songs, and the dancing of a graceful crew of lumberjacks. He even slept so late Sunday morning that he barely made breakfast."

"Homer was the last man fed that morning and the cookees were all but done swamping the floor and cleaning up the place by the time he opened the door of the cook shanty and headed back over to the bunkhouse."

"Homer told me that he was just a few yards away from the bunkhouse, walking down the icy path with his head down watching ahead so he didn't slip and fall, when he just happened to look up."

"Homer was started by the sudden appearance of two

lumberjacks standing just off the path directly in front of him. They greeted him as he walked towards them and he nodded and said "Good Morning" to the two of them as he passed by."

"He had already walked past the two of them when a voice from above called out to him, "Hunter Man, do you greet Frenchy too?"

"Homer said he wheeled around and looked right, left, and behind him, but there wasn't another soul in sight."

"Then the voice called out again, "Hey Hunter Man, Frenchy is up here!"

"Homer thought he'd either lost it all together or he was delirious until one of men grinned at him and pointed his finger towards the sky."

"Homer said he looked up and sure enough, there stood the source of the mystery voice."

"On top of the shoulders of the two men stood the smallest lumberjack that Homer had ever seen. He looked like a lumberjack, he was dressed like a lumberjack, and he acted like a lumberjack. The only thing was, this lumberjack was barely four feet tall."

"Once Homer gathered his composure he said, "Well hello up there Frenchy," "I'm sorry, I didn't see you hiding in the clouds up there like that."

"Frenchy laughed and quickly replied, "Hey Hunter Man, Frenchy has a big bear. Do you want to see ?"

"You bet I do Frenchy, I'll take a look at your bear," Homer said. "You say it's a pretty good sized bear, huh?"

"Frenchy replied, "Frenchy shows you his big bear."

"With that, the little guy then jumped down off the shoulders of the two full-sized lumberjacks and shook hands with Homer."

"Follow Frenchy, Hunter Man," and the two headed off in the direction of the cook shanty with Frenchy in the lead and Homer trailing close behind."

"Frenchy headed towards the back of the cook shanty and as they approached the corner of the building, Frenchy held his finger up by his lips and whispered, "Quiet Hunter Man. Scare Frenchy's bear."

"They eased around the corner of the building and sure enough, there stood a bear. Not a big bear mind you, but nevertheless, it was a bear."

"Homer said he didn't know if he should laugh out loud when he saw the bear or if he should go along with the joke. However, when he saw how attached Frenchy was to his "big bear," he knew it wasn't a joke, and he knew enough not to laugh either."

"Where'd you get your big bear anyway Frenchy," Homer asked."

"Two, three months ago," Frenchy said, "Frenchy chains logs and falls in hole with bear. Bear will kill Frenchy."

"How is it you're still around then, Frenchy?" Homer asked.

"Sawyer Man with axe hits the bear. Now Frenchy lives."

"How was it that you ended up with this bear then Frenchy?" Homer asked."

Frenchy hears little bear. Little bear is now Frenchy's bear."

"What will you do with your "bear" when it gets to be a really big bear, Frenchy?" Homer asked."

"When big, Frenchy let his bear go."

"Homer said he could tell that the thought of letting his bear go really bothered Frenchy, so Frenchy quickly changed the subject."

"Hunter Man hunts deer?" he asked."

"Yeh I do. Homer told him. That's why I come up here every year Frenchy. I love to hunt deer."

"Frenchy then asked your Uncle Homer, "Does Hunter Man like big deers with big horns? Frenchy knows where they are."

"Homer told me he was all ears when Frenchy said that."

"Frenchy then went on to tell Homer about an area his crew had logged off two years before. It was a big piece that bordered the river only a few miles southeast of where Homer's camp was."

"Frenchy described the complete layout of the land to Homer. He told Homer where the big cedar swamps were that the really big bucks headed for whenever they were pushed, and he told Homer where the slashes were where deer went to feed early in the morning and again in the evening."

"By the time he was done, Frenchy had described the area so well to Homer that he felt totally familiar with it despite the fact that he'd never been there before."

"Frenchy the said, "Frenchy asks one thing of the "Hunter Man."

"Sure thing," Homer said. "What is it?"

"When Hunter Man shoots a really big deer, he will always think of Frenchy."

"Don't you ever worry yourself about that Frenchy. I always will."

"With that said, the two shook hands and parted company."

"Early the next morning, Homer and the walking boss left the logging camp and headed on down the trail towards Homer's deer camp."

"Homer and the walking boss managed to carry on a

lively conversation for the better part of an hour without letup but then came a lull in the conversation."

"As they rode along, Homer's mind wandered off to what Frenchy had said him about the, " big bucks" that were in the area southeast of his deer camp."

"Were the bucks that Frenchy spoke of actually big, or did they just appear to be "really big" to Frenchy like his pet bear did?"

"Homer figured that the only way he'd ever know for sure was to go in there and see what he came out with, but he'd have to wait until next year before he'd have time to go in there and hunt. Only then would he find out what he was dealing with."

"Frenchy with two of his lumberjack friends."

306

"A load like this was not at all forgiving if it ran over someone."

*"A Steam Hauler!
The Source of the
Mysterious Sound."*

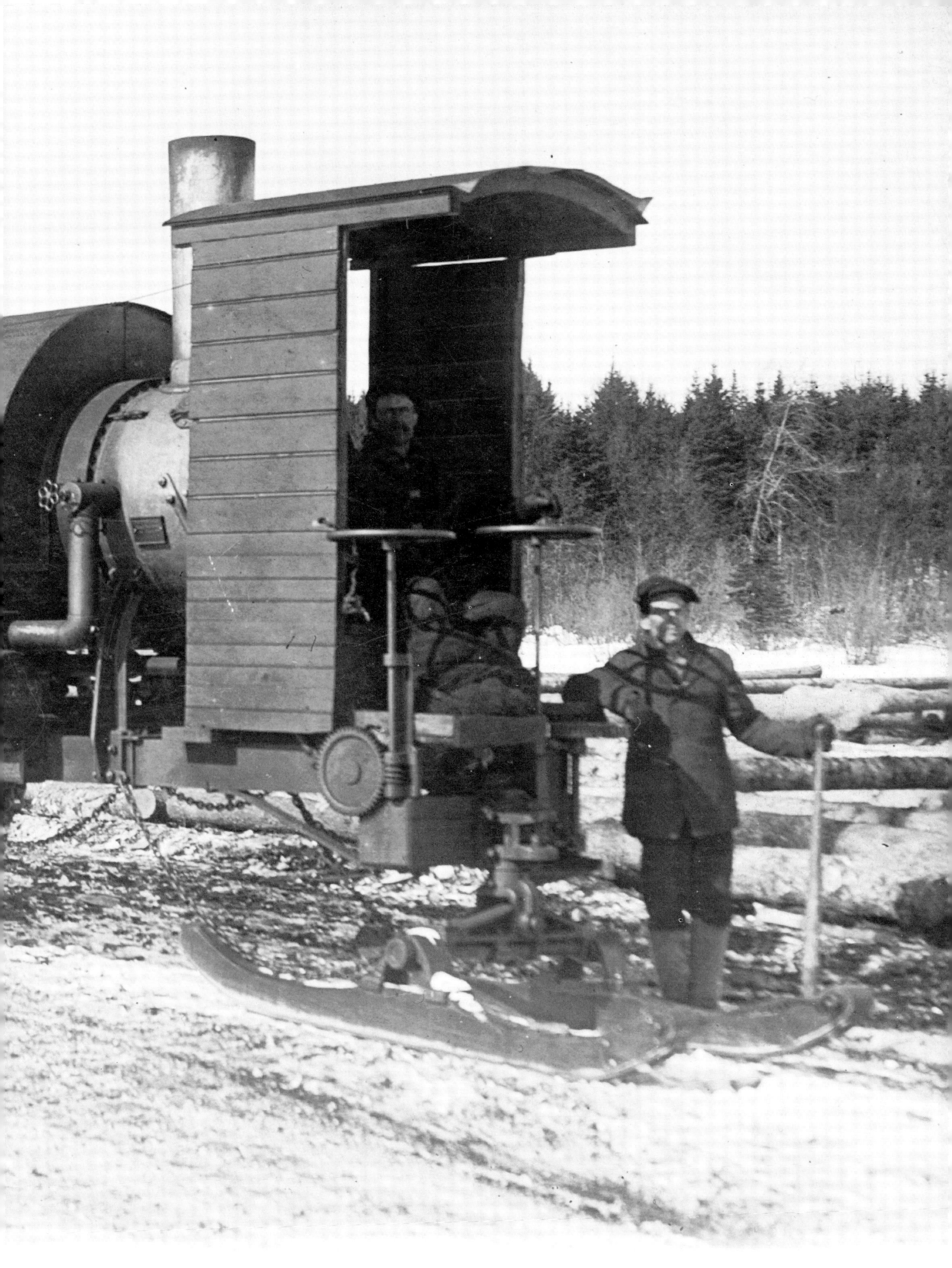

"The camp foreman, his wife and kids, and two kitchen helpers."

Tiffany Photo - Great Lakes Forestry Museum - Rice Lake, WI

"Between your Dad's old deer hunting crew up in Michigan, your Uncle Homer's hunting gang over by Ladysmith, and the bunch your Dad hunted with up by Iron River, your Dad somehow managed to accumulate a pretty fair number of photographs. They should give you a pretty good idea of the kind of success they had over the years."

"You're going to see some really nice bucks in some of these pictures but you're also see a large number of does hanging off the poles."

"You have to remember one thing when you look over these photographs. Those men didn't go hunting just for the sport of it like some do today. They no doubt enjoyed the camaraderie every bit as much as you boys do, but most of them also felt the need to justify the money they spent each year by bringing back meat to feed to their families."

Grandma said, "I know for certain that several of the photographs were taken by a photographer named Tiffany. He worked out of Ladysmith and took a good number of the photographs that you'll see in Uncle Homer's section."

"Tiffany not only took portrait photographs in his studio, but he'd ride right out where the action was so he could record what was taking place when it was taking place. I've seen some the photographs that he took of the big log jam on the Flambeau and of a number of logging camps that worked around the city of Ladysmith."

"Just imagine how much we would have missed if Tiffany hadn't gone out and taken pictures like he did. We'd have no idea what it was like or what had taken place back then without folks like him."

Grandma said, "Did you ever know that your Dad was a bit of a poet, Hank? He not only wrote poetry, but he had a sense of humor that would often show up in the poems he wrote."

I didn't want to admit it, but I couldn't remember a time that Dad had ever said anything that rhymed, let alone write anything that rhymed. I did know my Dad had a sense of humor however. I had bore the brunt for a good many of his good-natured practical jokes over the years.

"Henry always liked to tell your Granddad Jennings and I the story about the cook they had in camp one time up at Iron River."

"This cook used to fix some of the best tasting food around but he seemed to delight in creating some of the strangest concoctions imaginable. The men never knew for certain what they were eating."

"It got to the point where the men were constantly asking him what he was going to fix for the next meal and it irritated him to no end."

"One night he said he was going to fix a very special stew for the crew and when he served it, they waded into it with forks and spoons a flying. A fight nearly erupted over who was going to get the last bowl of it. It was so delicious that the men took their bread and wiped the pot clean."

"When supper was over, they all sat around the table with their toothpicks in hand and begged the cook to tell them the secret ingredients he used in the stew. They wanted their wives to fix the same thing for them when they got back home."

"The cook went ahead and told them, and as it turned out, it was the last meal that he ever fixed in camp. In fact, he was never asked to comeback again."

"What in the world did he put in the stew that turned the whole bunch against him like that?" Wally asked.

"Perhaps Hank would like to read his Dad's poem about the meal to the rest of you. It pretty much sums up what happened."

I'd taken a drink of water right before Grandma handed me the piece of paper with the poem written on it.

I slowly unfolded the paper and before I could swallow, I blew my entire mouthful of water out my nose and all over Wonzal.

The poem I read went like this:

> You've always used steak,
>   in the stews that you make
> But this time
>   you must have used fowl.
> The cook then replied,
>   "Something different I tried
> That weren't fox on your fork,
>   it was owl."

Glenn got a severe case of the dry heaves and C.J. and Wally both threw a hand over their mouth as quick as they could.

Wonzal was on the verge of swooning as he said, "Good Lord Hank." "Please, I begging you. Don't ever pull anything like that on us up at deer camp, or anywhere else for that matter. I'd never eat again."

I just grinned at them, shrugged my shoulders,. They had to suffer a few seconds.

At just the right moment I said, "Don't worry about it Wonzal. The only meat I'd use in a stew is weasel."

My campmates and their cast iron stomachs made a beeline for the door.

"One tasty critter."

"An abandoned lumber camp before these boys moved in."

"The result of a hard day's work."

"One of the few that preferred a Marlin."

"Making good use of Nature's own Buckpole."

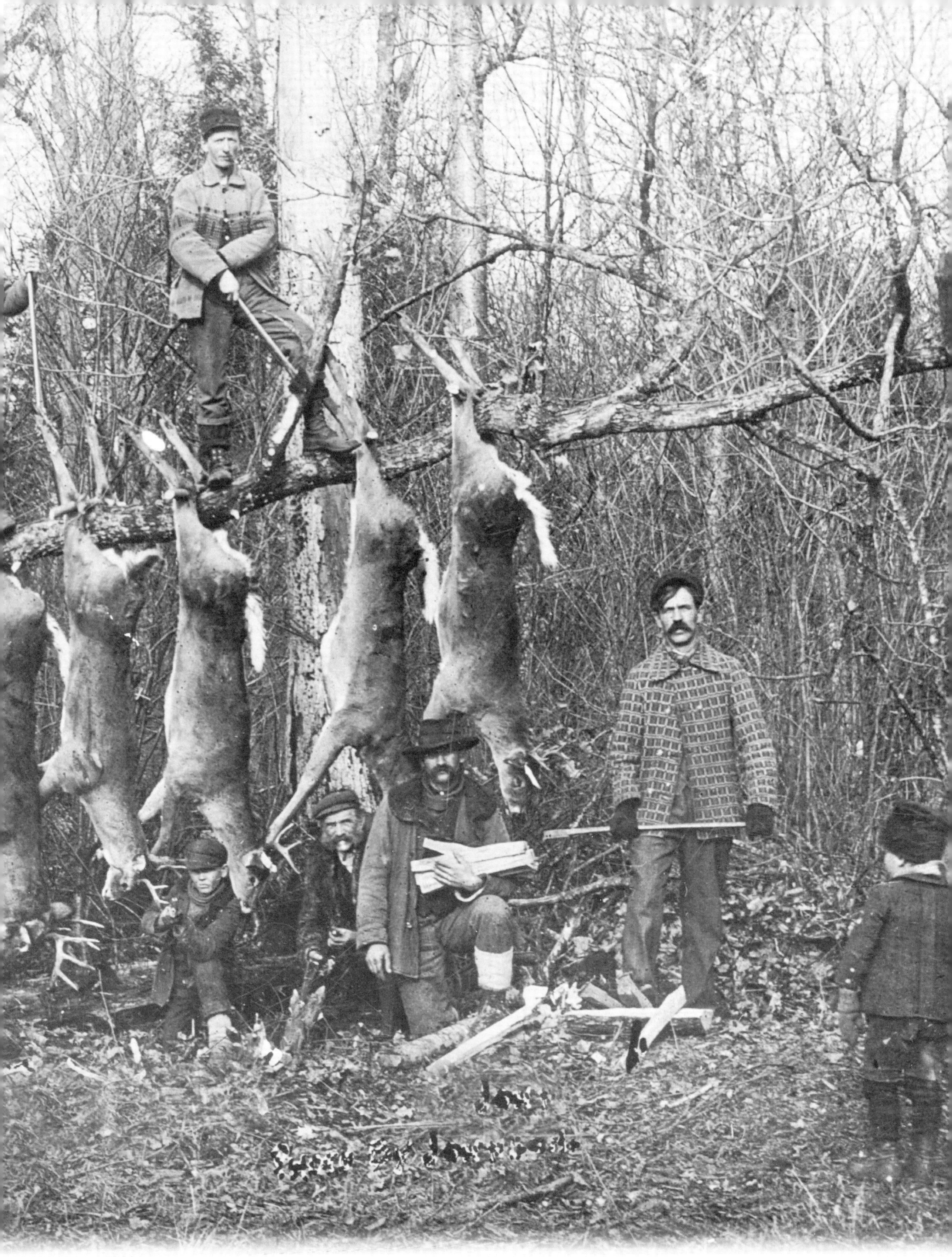

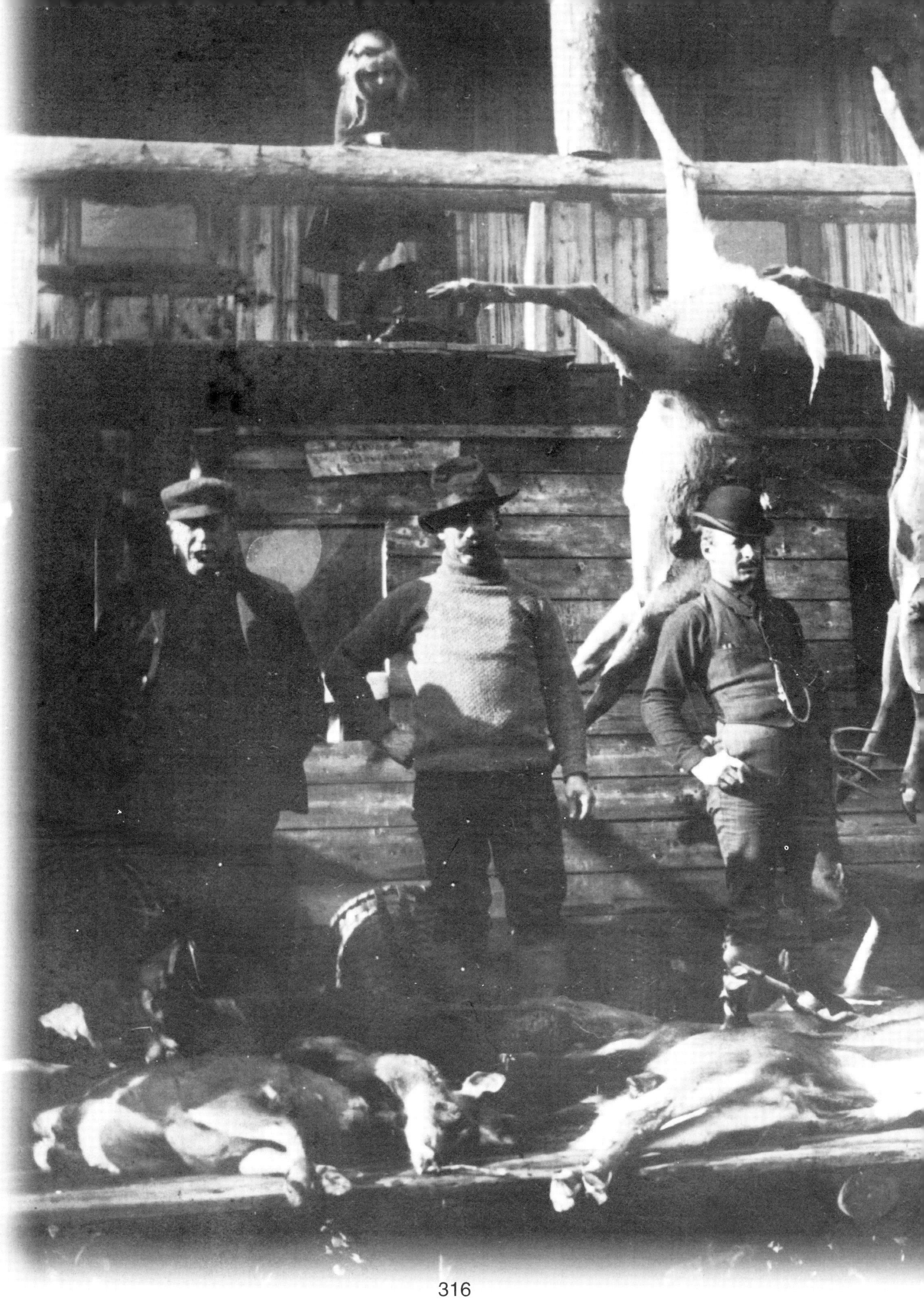

They won't be going home empty-handed!

"A group that no deer in it's right mind wanted to tangle with."

* * * * * * *

"You know first hand what's like to take a train up to go deer hunting Hank, so these next few photographs will be reminders to you of the trips you took up to your camp outside of Gunderson with your Dad."

"Of course your Dad was an old hand when it came to taking a train up to camp. He and the group of locals he hunted with rode the train many times whenever they went up to hunt at Iron River."

"He and his bunch certainly weren't the only deer hunters to take advantage of what the railroads had to offer. Because the railroad was often the only way for deer hunters to get into some of the more remote areas of the state in order to hunt, hundreds upon hundreds of deer hunters rode the train up to camp every year to go deer hunting."

"The railroads had a good thing going and they knew it. The new growth of popples that shot up after the loggers moved out literally covered the entire area. With all the new browse and cover they provided, the deer population simply exploded. The railroad companies saw to it that their advertisements made sure to mention the fact about the large number of deer that could be found in the woods to the North."

"The railroads made it as convenient for the deer hunters as they possibly could. They provided a coach for the hunters to ride in on their way up for which they charged a fee of course and they had a number of flatcars for the hunters to load their gear on for which they charged an additional fee."

"The railroad was also willing to drop hunters off wherever they chose. Generally it would be at a depot or at a siding somewhere along the way."

"If the hunters were dropped off at a depot, they could either stay in one of the local hotels which were often owned by the railroad, or they would be picked up at the depot by a hired teamster who would take them back into their hunting area. The same teamster was also hired to take the crew and all of their gear back out of the woods at the close of the season."

"Many hunters chose the option of being left off at a siding somewhere out in the middle of the woods where they could get off and set up a camp to hunt out of."

"The long ride out to the siding at season's end."

"Waiting to be picked up when the freight stopped by."

"Then, when season came to a close and it came time for the hunters to return home again, the railroad would pick the hunters and all of their gear up at a predetermined time. Then the hunters, their gear, and all of their game would be taken to the nearest depot where other hunters and their deer were waiting by the dozens to be picked up."

"The railroad provided a string of empty flatcars on which all of the deer, tents, and camping gear were loaded, for a fee."

"As you can see by these next few pictures, deer hunting and railroading made for big business for several years before roads were built and the automobile drove into the picture."

"Thousands of deer were taken as a result of using the railroads."

"Once they arrived back home, it was time for the kids to compare bucks."

"It takes some folks a little while to develop a taste for venison."

"For some strange reason or the other, both Hank's Dad Henry and his Uncle Homer seemed to be fascinated by black bears since the day they started hunting."

"There was no lack of bear sightings in either the Upper Peninsula of Michigan where Henry first started hunting or in the area around Ladysmith where Homer spent his time. Generally if it wasn't Henry or Homer who'd run across a bear or two during the season, it'd be at least one member of their group who would come back to camp describing the bear or bears that he'd run into that day."

"The men would usually pass up the opportunity to shoot a bear unless it was big enough to brag about or it chose to confront them rather than turn and run away. In most instances when they were forced to shoot one, it would be either an old boar guarding it's territory or a sow with cubs. Both would sooner turn and challenge a hunter instead of hightailing it out of the country where they'd be safe."

"There were several reasons why no one in their groups chose to take a bear even when they were faced with the opportunity:"

"Getting a bear out of the woods always required help unless of course it was a small bear which they wouldn't shoot anyway, and to ask a member of the group to leave his hunt to pull out a bear didn't go over any too well."

"A bear was always in it's prime in the late fall so it carried with it layer upon layer of fat that would turn rancid if it remained on the meat too long, and would end up spoiling the meat."

"No one in either of their camps were that crazy about eating bear meat anyway and certainly not when there was a frying pan full of fresh venison and onions staring them in the face."

"If they did decide to shoot a bear and took it home, the sight of it would scare the living daylights out of their kids and they'd end up with nightmares for the next two weeks."

"However, the deciding factor when a hunter had a bear in his sights and was about to pull the trigger was the thought of the tongue-lashing their wife would give them if they dragged one of the things home. That no doubt saved the life of more bears than you could ever possibly imagine."

"Despite all of the obstacles they had to face, a good many of the men still went ahead and shot a bear or two during their lifetime. I know of at least three that Hank's Dad brought back and Homer took at least that many over the years up there at Ladysmith."

"Homer with one of his bears."

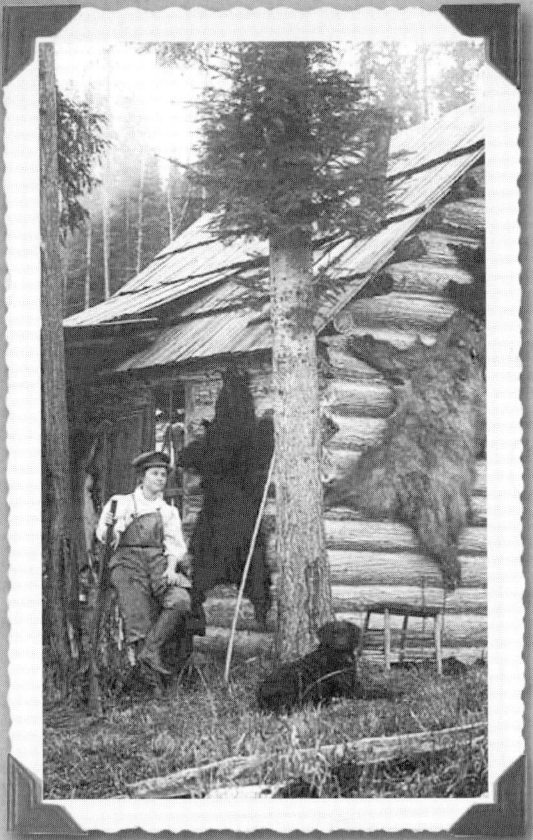

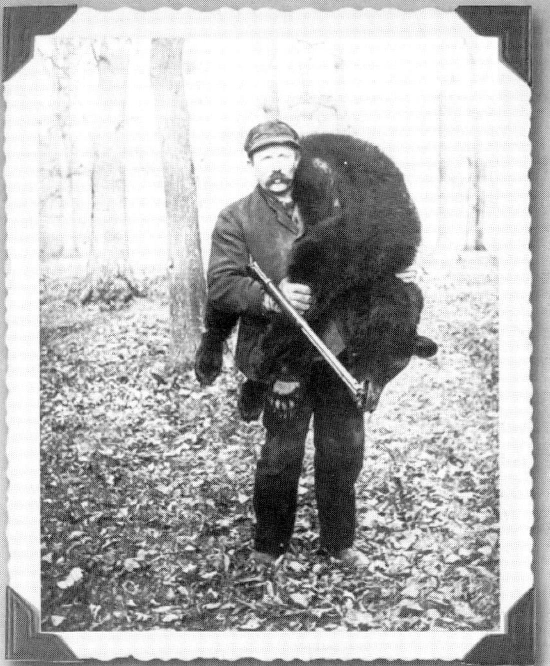

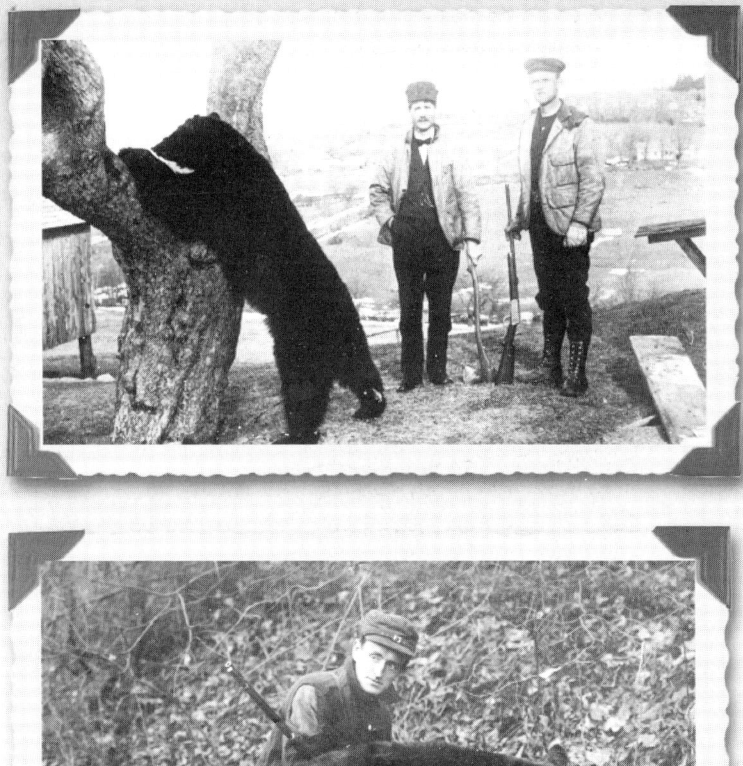

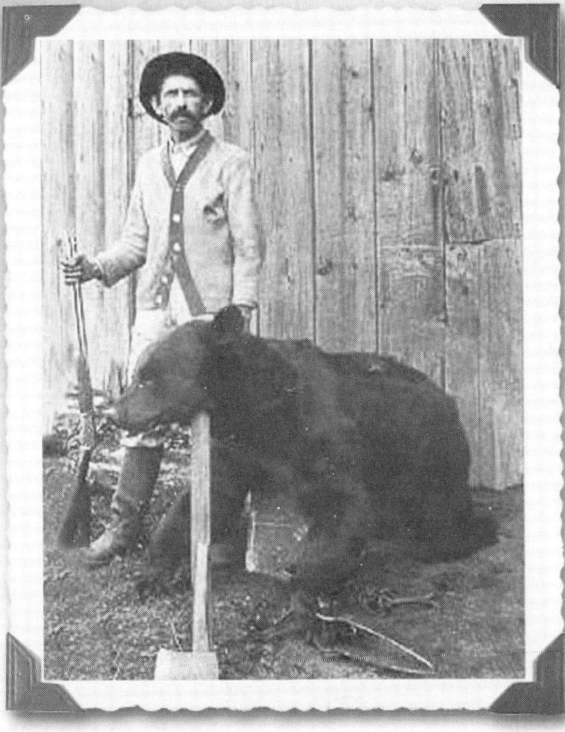

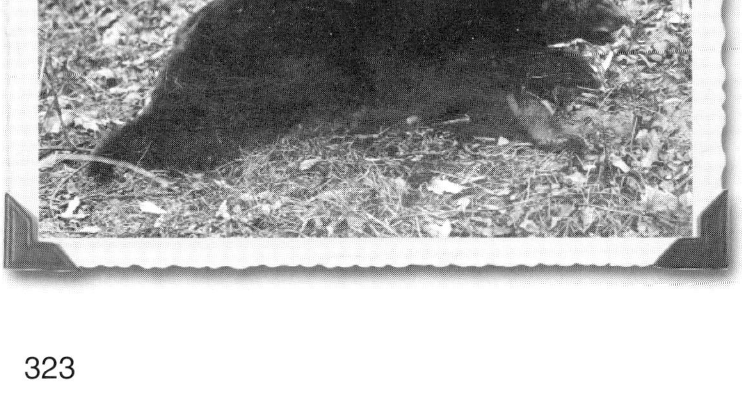

"It took a good bruin to outwit a bunch like this."

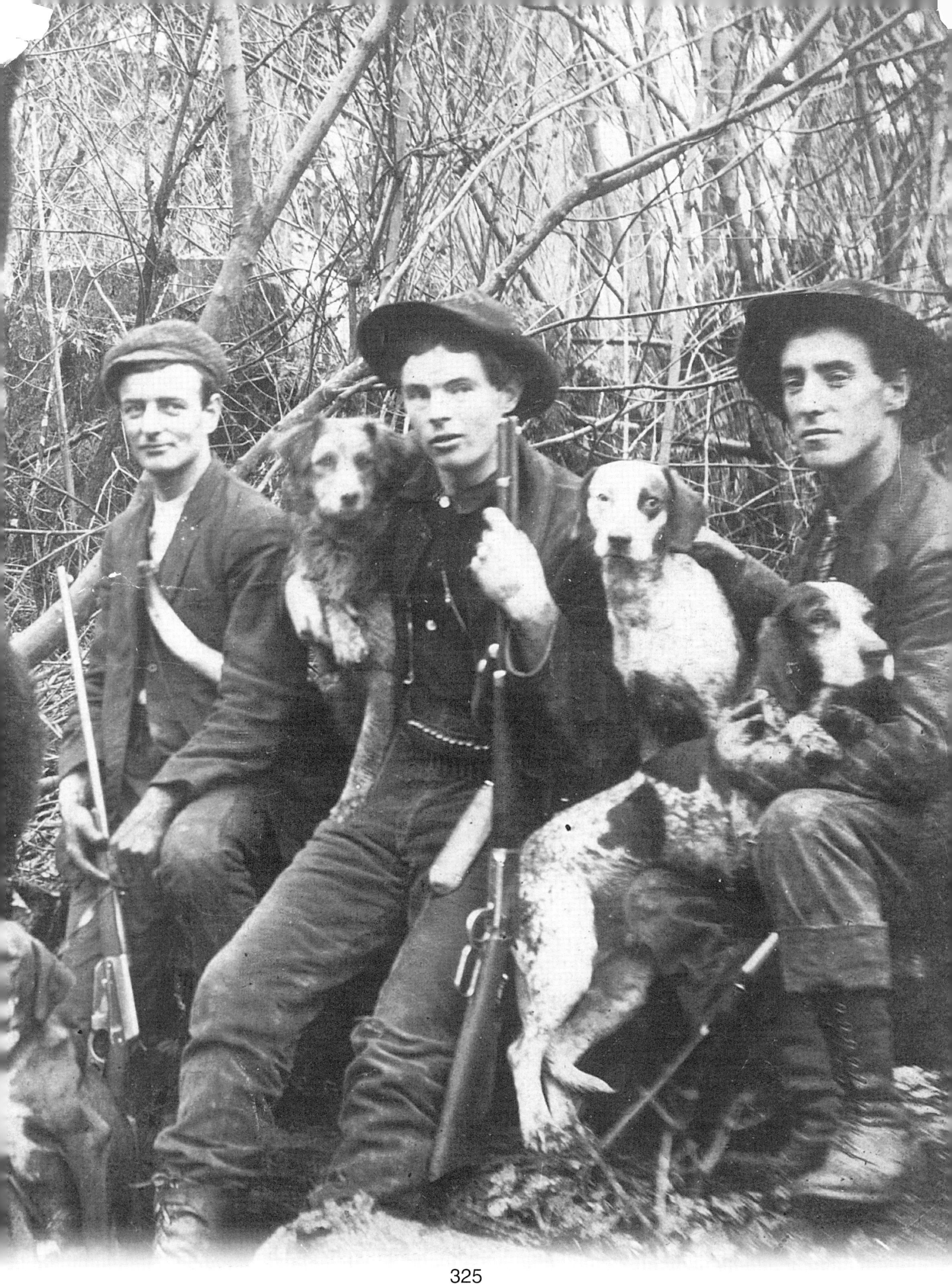

The Black Bear

Currier & Ives

"Henry always got a big kick out of these bear pictures that he put here in the album. He had some old stereo view cards he'd collected over the years and one day he up and cut the pictures apart and put them in here."

"By the way Hank, you'll find out in a minute or so you weren't the only one victimized by your Dad's practical jokes."

"Years ago it cost a great deal of money and took a considerable amount of time for Homer and his family to visit Henry and his family down at Mondovi."

"They finally managed to save enough money one year to go down to Mondovi and spend the Fourth of July with Henry's family. It was a break that everyone needed and they were having a wonderful time down there.

Homer's kids took to their Uncle Henry so well that they followed him around like puppy dogs everywhere he'd go and everyone got along just great."

"Then one day after dinner, Henry sat down in his rocking chair with this album and Homer's two small children and was showing it to them."

"When they got to the part with the bear pictures, Henry talked in a real low voice as he described what was going on in each picture to the kids. Then, right at the end of the story, Henry let loose with a really loud roar that scared the living daylights out of the kids."

"It sent the two little tykes running and screaming as

tight as they could go to their mother."

"Henry thought it was funnier than a three legged goat and he laughed until he had tears in his eyes. He however, was the only one that laughed."

"Neither Homer's wife nor Henry's wife thought he was any where near as funny as he thought he was."

"Things were a little tense for a time to say the least, but they cooled off by the time Homer and his family headed back home."

"It wasn't over for Henry however. He took a severe tongue-lashing from his wife for pulling a stunt like. It was such a chewing that the next time Homer and his family came to pay a visit, Henry had completely changed his ways."

"The next time, when he finally managed to talk the kids into setting down with him again in the rocking chair, he talked in a very low tone the entire time. Instead of scaring the daylights out of them when he came to the bear pictures, he told the kids a story about "Mr. Furry Bear" and told them how "Mr. Furry Bear" wouldn't hurt a flea. Henry never growled once the entire time."

"The next time they got together, Homer's wife was the one who did the growling. Henry's story of "Mr. Furry Bear" had come back to haunt him."

"Homer's wife Wilma had never been to his deer hunting camp near Ladysmith before so when the entire family had a chance to go down in October just when the leaves were at their peak, she jumped at the opportunity."

"For Homer, it would be the first time since he'd started hunting down there that he would get to camp before deer season started. He'd have a chance to do some scouting ahead of time and to get the camp cleaned up before the entire group moved in."

"Homer, Wilma, and their two kids had spent two very relaxing and uneventful days in camp. It was everything that they'd hoped for."

"It was the last day of their stay, and the family had just finished their breakfast of smoked ham, fried bacon, and eggs. The kids had been sent outside to play while Homer and Wilma did the dishes and got things packed for the return trip home. Then their oldest daughter walked through the door."

"Where's your little sister?" Wilma asked.

"She's outside," the little one answered, "with Mr. Furry Bear."

"It took a few seconds before what the little girl said sunk in."

"She's WHAT?" Wilma screamed.

"Erleen is playing outside with Mr. Furry Bear." That was the answer Wilma didn't want to hear."

"Wilma stepped over to the window, peered out through the dusty old pane and said, "Oh Good Lord Homer, she isn't kidding.""

"What the two parents saw that day would be enough to stop anyone's heart. There stood their littlest daughter, a sucker in one hand, and petting a 600 pound bear with the other."

"Homer slowly worked his way over to the doorway and whispered to his little girl, "Give Mr. Furry Bear your lollipop, honey and come here." The little girl turned and said, "What'd you say Daddy?"

"I said, give Mr. Furry Bear the Lollipop and come here."

"The little one turned and started for the cabin door, sucker still in hand with Mr. Furry Bear following close behind. Three feet in front of the door way the little girl stopped and turned towards the huge bear, barely inches away from her then and said, "Here you are Mr. Furry Bear," and she tossed the sucker on the porch."

"The bear picked it up, turned towards the woods, and lumbered off into the brush."

"That fall when Homer's gang pulled into camp, there was a note nailed to the front door of the cabin that read:

THE FOLLOWING ARE NO LONGER
ALLOWED IN THIS CAMP
NO BACON
NO SMOKED HAM
NO SALT PORK
NO LOLLIPOPS

NOTICE: *There is $25.00*
in the pantry cupboard
for the man who gets
MR. *Furry* BEAR
signed
WILMA McCRACKEN

My Grandmother then closed the cover of the album and as she did she said, "Well boys, that's the last photo Henry ever put in the album. That's the end of it," she said as she yawned and stretched her aching back.

"It's been a fun day for me, but it's a good thing it came to an end when it did," she said. "I'm all tuckered out."

"What time is it anyway?" Glenn asked. "I feel like I've been standing here for hours."

"It's no wonder, you have been" I said. "It's almost half past five. We've been at this for nearly five hours!"

Wally and Glenn both said at the same time, "I gotta get for home. My kid probably did the chores and it'll take me two hours to undo what he messed up on." With that, the two of them hit for the door.

Before everyone disappeared I hollered, "We'll meet over to my palace tomorrow at one o'clock. I've got an idea or two that needs discussing, right quick."

With that said, I thanked my Grandmother for all she'd done for us that day. I gave her a big kiss on the cheek, said my good-byes, and I headed out the door.

As I walked towards home that evening, I knew I had learned one thing for certain that day. I'd be adding a few chapters of my own to that old album.

I doubt very much that my Grandmother had any idea what that old hunting album may have started.

Comes to a Close

The closing of the McCracken Family Album brought to an end the hunting, fishing, and trapping adventures of the eldest McCracken's. However, the very existence of the album has inspired Hank McCracken and his crew of sidekicks to create a few new hunting adventures to record in their own hunting album.

A Palace in the Popples Part II finds Hank and his crew doing their best to follow in the footsteps of Silas, Charles, and Henry McCracken. Their adventures take them into the mountains of the West, the spruce-covered regions of Canada, and the Flambeau and Chippewa River areas of Northern Wisconsin.

The group's desire to one day have a place to call their own becomes a reality in PART II. They eventually end up owning a section of land to hunt on and building a "PALACE IN THE POPPLES" in which to stay.

Designed & Printed at:
Rice Lake Printery
2100 Pioneer Avenue
Rice Lake, Wisconsin 54868
Phone (715) 234-8701

Layout & Design by Wayne Simon